Groundrush

Greg Barron

Groundrush

Random House  New York

I am grateful to the Phillips Exeter Academy and to the Syracuse
Writing Program for their generous support during the writing of
this book. For their considerable help, I would like to express my
gratitude to Jerre Mangione; John McGrath; the late Donald Dike;
the late George P. Elliott; Michael Bromka; Elias Kulukundis; and
my editor, Gary Fisketjon.

All rights reserved under International and Pan-American Copyright Conventions.
Published in the United States by Random House, Inc., New York, and simultaneously in Canada by Random House of Canada Limited, Toronto.

Library of Congress Cataloging in Publication Data
Barron, Greg, 1952–
   Groundrush.
   I. Title.
PS3552.A73696G7 813'.54 81–48277
ISBN 0–394–52214–1   AACR2

Manufactured in the United States of America
98765432
First Edition

For Debra Steffani

groundrush (skydiving term): "The earth a gigantic painting beneath you, beautiful and serene, dreamlike, and you just hanging there in space, taking it in—then the sudden groundrush, the panic, too late the tug on the rip and, finally, the realization that it is all over."

Contents

THE RAWLINGS RATTLERS

1968   10–0
1969   10–0
1970   9–1
1971   10–0
1972   10–0

1973

September 14	Butte	H
September 21	Billings East	H
September 28	Bozeman	H
October 5	Missoula	A
October 12	Charles M. Russell	
	(Great Falls)	A
October 19	Great Falls	A
October 26	Anaconda	H
November 2	No game scheduled	
November 9	Billings West	A
November 16	Helena	H
November 23	No game scheduled	
November 28	Kalispell	A

It was all over after tomorrow. Beowolf's gaze rose to the stadium's castle crown of blunt stone teeth and up the flagpole, which stood against the sky like a pointless lance; in the frigid gray dusk the pennant whipped in the wind. Winter was coming on.

For a moment all was silent. To Beowolf, alone on the school bus, it seemed as if the earth had stopped spinning. Thunder then gathered and broke through the crowd outside as Coach Moon, clipboard in hand, ascended a makeshift stage to address the rally. Jeannie handed Moon the microphone. His players stood beneath him, facing the crowd and the unlit bonfire. Proud, hunched into the wind, hands thrust in pockets, they were anxious to get on the bus where it was warm, yet didn't want to miss this parting moment of glory. Beowolf ran his hand along the steel handhold of the seat in front of him. The bus was old and olive-green, an Air Force reject. He rubbed his hands together. Nobody on the team wore gloves. Everybody wore hats. Hats were a rule because a body's hair would be wet after practice. Moon's words burst from his mouth in steady spurts, dissolving in the open air. He was talking about Kalispell, about tomorrow night's game. All week he'd been telling them that this was something they'd remember for the rest of their lives. Beowolf did not doubt it.

Through the windows out the other side of the bus, Beowolf gazed over the Great Plains flowing serenely from the east, amber waves of stubble, to the point twenty-six miles away where the prairie collided with the Rockies. The foothills glistened with fresh snow. The harvest long over, the prairie awaited that first snowfall which would hide its reaped fertility beneath a pure, frozen white veil. Sitting stolidly among these fields was the high school, as weatherbeaten and stoic as the Montana highways that crisscrossed the state like hardened arteries.

The night before, lying in bed, high on weed and low on Jesus, Beowolf listened to a faraway hound barking in the wind, barking incessant short bass *ruffs* punctuated by single, prolonged, wolfish yowls that made all the sense in the world and conjured up death with a capital D. Every few minutes a car would whoosh past, drowning out the hound for a moment: Beowolf's ears would prick up as the car sped away, listening for the bark that would refill the vast vacuum outside.

The land forced loneliness on you as naturally as it forced self-reliance. At night, when Beowolf ran that straight stretch of asphalt darkness between his home and the slaughterhouse, when his body was on automatic pilot, when it was quieter than a hole in the ground and he was lost in thought, or dreaming, say, of a picture-perfect punt return, a feeling that something was following directly behind would sometimes sneak up on him and pounce into consciousness. The back of his neck would tingle as he darted forward and shot a backward glance that would expose as the mere padding of his own footsteps the phantom that had been tracking him. The land would rip the bones from your back if you let it. If you let it, the land would leave you as mutilated as a rattlesnake on a summer highway.

Moon, towering impassively above the crowd, spoke in his ever-constant monotone. "Like holy fuckin Moses," Beowolf said aloud. He'd taken to talking to himself lately. Lying in bed last night, listening to the barking as thoughts of Jeannie twisted through his mind like a thumbscrew, he announced: "The shit has hit the fan." To cap everything else off, his brother, who had just arrived home from Missoula, had caught him smoking a joint. In the South Pacific it was the beginning of the monsoon season; for Beowolf it was the season for shitstorms. "Go away," Jeannie had told him last night. "Go away" was taking its time sinking in.

Though Moon was not often generous with praise, he was at present commending Frankie Dimitruk. If you knew nothing else living in Rawlings, Montana, you knew that Frankie was a shoo-in for All-State quarterback. That he was only a sophomore was cause for a communal wet dream.

MD, the team captain, once pissed down Frankie's leg in the showers, and while Frankie was laying a cuss on MD fit to peel the hide off a Gila monster, Moon entered, hesitating in the doorway; the only person who didn't seem to notice him was Frankie. Witnessing the growing petrification in his teammates, Dimitruk honestly believed—becoming increasingly profane as his conviction gathered force—that it was he who had aroused in them the fear of God. Moon cleared his throat and Frankie, stark naked, turned timorously about-face. His Adam's apple bobbed once or twice. He grabbed a towel. Everybody was chuckling nervously and glancing at corners. Moon finally cracked one of those rare smiles, which intimated that God does indeed protect drunken Indians and stupid Polskeys. "Someone flush your jock again, Frankie?" he said, and the locker room busted a gut.

They hazed you and made you sing when you were a sophomore, which was the worst thing about being a sophomore—unless you were a piss-ant to boot, and then the worst thing was Bull Run. Singing, you'd stand naked on the training table and bellow it out to a cacophony of derision. If you didn't sing loud and proud enough, they'd drench you from behind with a garbage can full of freezing water. They pelted you with dirt and tape balls anyway— though they never pelted Gray. Gray had been different. Nobody had dared to touch Gray. And now Gray was back in town, playing in a band and working at the record shop, and people had begun to refer to him not by his last name but by his first, Peter, which nobody other than Beowolf and Jeannie had even seemed to know before he left town a year ago in September. The sportscasters hadn't even used it when they announced the starting lineups. His sophomore year, when Beowolf was a freshman, they called him the "Gray Ghost." But it never caught on, so they dropped it. The next season, the football program described him as "a Houdini in football pads." The season after that, last season, he was gone, gone from Rawlings for a full year and out of football forever, so nobody had to worry about what to call him anymore.

While Gray was gone, Beowolf had thought about him with a grim obsessiveness otherwise reserved for the contemplation of dead relatives. On occasions when he might have discussed Gray with someone other than Jeannie, an anxiety would paw at his throat, his voice would miscatch, and his mind would stutter over what he'd meant to say. Confused and inarticulate, he'd sometimes tell himself it was irrelevant; feeling as if he'd just missed the game bus, he would say nothing at all. But now Gray was back, and Beowolf's whole life trembled, as fragile as an ill-fastened looking-glass in an earthquake. Beowolf wished Gray were gone forever.

Nobody had liked Gray before, other than Beowolf and Jeannie. He'd been one hellacious ballplayer, though, nobody could deny that. He'd swing out of the backfield, glide over the middle on a short pass pattern—hovering as much as running, sensing through the airways how the enemy would converge—and snare the pass on his fingertips, give a juke with his hips, cutting, skipping, starting and stopping, dodging linebackers; then, shifting gears, he was gone, gliding upfield to elude more agile foes. "I smell smoke!" some gleeful soul in the stands would cry after the play was over. "Smoke!"

The bonfire had burst into leaping yellow, gasoline-fed flames the moment Moon handed the microphone back to Jeannie. The crowd was going apeshit, chanting along with the cheerleaders. Jeannie followed Moon down into the throng, where she ardently joined the other cheerleaders bounding around the bonfire, their breathpuffs as robust and voluptuous as refrigerated prom orchids. On the final note their war song swelled as a helmeted effigy was uplifted, then consummated by a unisonant shout of triumph as the figure was cast onto the pyre.

Beowolf stared at the burning straw and rags. The effigy's number was off-center. It had been 9, Beowolf's number, until he insisted that Jeannie change it to 19. It hadn't been fair, her giving the thing his number. The flames bit and spat, enveloping the Kalispell dummy.

Wavy climbed the steps of the bus and deposited his skeletal frame in the driver's seat. He looked older than Methuselah, whom he was forever jabbering about. "Man!" he exclaimed aloud. "That Helen the Bod gets me hot under the armpits!"

Beowolf couldn't help snickering. The cheerleaders burst into another routine; Helen's tits threatened to topple her over as she kicked and spun.

"What? Ho!" Wavy cried with a start, staring now down the aisle. "Youngblood! You skeerd the daylights outta me. Why you sittin in here when the party's all out there?"

"Same's you, I imagine. Too cold."

"Cold's right." Wavy shivered. "Cold nuff to make a polar bear hunt cover. I'm too old for this."

"How'd you like the weed last night?"

"Good herbs, youngblood. I never been known to look down my nose at good herbs. But you be careful, youngblood. You be crackin skulls tomorrow night. No time to be gettin shanghaied."

"No more," Beowolf lied. "I'm giving it up."

"Well, no need going overboard."

Beowolf grunted and laid a hand on his pants pocket, which contained three slim joints. Then he pressed his fingertips against his groin to test the tenderness. He had pulled the muscle five weeks earlier, in the homecoming game against Anaconda, and still it was tight and remotely sore, painful when he ran hard and likely to buckle when he stood after sitting for any length of time.

Outside, the cheer ended. Beowolf spied Jeannie. Sometimes during games he would catch her poised on the sideline watching a play develop, and in the instant before emotion sprang into motion, she would be leaning slightly forward, arms tense at her sides: her face wide-eyed, expectant and beautiful, just like a little girl's on Christmas morning, just like right now as she watched the fire consume her handiwork.

The night before, as she stitched a face onto the effigy, Beowolf told her his dream. He was sitting above her on the sofa in her den while she sat cross-legged on the floor, working her needle in and out, staring intently into the effigy's face. The tip of her tongue peeked out from between her lips.

"You're not even listening," he said after a while.

She glanced up, blue eyes peering into his face, mouth slightly open. "Yes," she replied. "I am." She bent back over the straw man and coolly recited his nighttime saga. "You missed the game bus, you didn't know why—or why they left without you. You got to the game at halftime and got bawled out by Peckinpah and had to play in your sneakers because you forgot your cleats. You got beat deep for a touchdown because you kept slipping. And we lost. To the Denver Broncos."

"You only know because I've told you before."

"Then why tell me again?" she asked without looking up.

"Because I had it again."

"I'm not your analyst."

Beowolf sighed. "Don't you care that I have these dreams? They mean something, you know."

"Yes. They mean you're afraid of missing the bus, you're afraid of forgetting your cleats, and you're afraid of getting beat deep." Jeannie looked up and shrugged her shoulders, offering him her sweet-and-sour smile. "You're afraid of everything."

"Come here."

"What for?"

"Comeere, just comeere."

Jeannie rose from the floor and plopped herself down next to Beowolf on the sofa. Drawing her knees up to her chin, she wrapped her arms around her legs. From the living room came the sound of the TV test pattern: Eric, Jeannie's dad, had fallen asleep. Beowolf kissed her.

"You've been blowing weed, haven't you?"

Beowolf grinned, he knew, a jackass smile.

"I knew you had." She tried not to smile back at him. "If Moon knew what you're really like, your ass would be grass—as you would say."

"If my ass was grass, I'd smoke it."

Jeannie laid her cheek on her knees and regarded him skeptically. "You won't smoke for the game, will you?"

"Where'd you get the idea I'd do that?"

"Gray used to smoke for games."

"I'm not Gray."

"I never know what you're going to do."

"Well, you can bet I won't get high for a game." Mildly chastened, Beowolf presented her with a contrite smile, laying his hand on her bare foot. Her arms hesitantly released hold of her updrawn legs, which spread apart and crossed, Indian-style. "Weed mellows me out too much. I gotta be"—baring his teeth and bulging his eyes —"mo*bile,* a*gile* and hos*tile* for a game." He rolled his eyes and keeled over.

"You goofus," she said, forgetting herself and laughing as he laid his head in her lap.

"You're getting to sound just like Jason."

"Jason catch you smoking?"

"Yep."

"Oh, brother."

"Ya know," Beowolf said, looking up at her, "I'll never figure out how he used to do it."

"Do what?"

"Get high for games."

"*Jason?*"

"Gray."

Abruptly casting off that guarded affection which had lately characterized their mutual disposition, he pressed his face against her stomach and wholeheartedly embraced her, realizing even as he did it what a mistake he'd made. He rose to his knees and kissed her lips. But it was no good. Her body began to tremble. He held her in his arms. "I can't," she cried. "I can't do it anymore. I can't."

"Can't what?"

As she buried her face into his shoulder a violent spasm passed through her body, emerging as a single audible sob.

"I'm sorry," Beowolf said, squeezing her tighter. "It'll be all right."

Her body convulsed with renewed anguish. "No, no." She shook her head. "It won't be. It never will be. I can't, I can't do it."

"Do what?" Beowolf asked again. "Do what?"

"*Any of it.*" Momentarily her face rose from his shoulder, her eyes piercing him, her mouth sucking in air. "When I come back from Kalispell, when everything's over—" Her voice broke into a moan as her face contorted once again in pain. She began to pound her fists on Beowolf's shoulders. "I can't see you anymore. I can't."

The force of her fists was not great, yet Beowolf grabbed each of them and held them tight. "Is it Gray?"

"*Go, you!*" Jeannie wailed, her arms struggling abjectly for freedom. "*Go away, go away!*" And at that moment the door to the den opened and Eric stuck his head in.

The gasoline had all burned off, leaving the bonfire smoking from too much green wood. Jeannie leapt before the pile of sticks and rubbish, rousing and conjuring the crowd. As she danced, her chestnut hair played upon her shoulders in a luxuriant, flowing slow-motion. For years Beowolf had watched her. For years, when running at night, he had stopped before her house—the house where he would one day spend so many hours—to peer at the windows, islands of light, their bright mystery enclosed by draperies shutting out the night, shutting him out. Now, after three and a half years of high school, her hair still danced, playing more gently, more innocently than her legs, which leapt in frantic, practiced steps beneath her red skirt.

Porkbutt Pete, the trainer, climbed the steps of the bus and dumped his body into one of the front seats. He sat there wheezing. Some of the sophomores began filing in, slapping Wavy five and marching past Beowolf down the aisle. Peckinpah appeared, glanced sharply down the aisle, then parked himself next to Porkbutt. Everybody was boarding now. Granville Skaggs, the middle linebacker, slid into his customary spot across from Beowolf. "Get a load of this bus," he said. "Looks like it's seen action in the war." Doe Konichek removed his overcoat and tossed it onto the rack overhead. Even in a sport coat and tie, Doe looked like a bit player from *Hee Haw*. Lombago sauntered past to the ass-end of the bus, which was reserved for sophomores.

Hap entered. His red-and-white duffel bag slung over his shoulder, he squeezed down the crowded aisle. When he reached Beowolf, he swung the bag to the floor and kicked it under the seat. "Cold," he said, sitting down. Beowolf smiled. Hap: the apostle of the obvious, his oldest friend. They always sat together on the bus. Hap rubbed his hands briskly together as if to kindle them. "How ya feel, man?"

"Awright."

"Man! I can't believe how cold it is out there! And it'll be colder tomorrow night. Frostbite City! Wow! Lookit that!" Hap nodded out the window. "They must be freezing their nipples off."

As they prompted the crowd through megaphones, the cheer-leaders capered, dipped and sprang into the air, their bare legs flashing white against the smoking bonfire backdrop.

"They're warm enough." At a football game a body might be cold on arrival. He might be freezing. But once the game's begun, the temperature becomes as irrelevant as the setting, which is the same for both teams. The game's the thing.

Snare drums struck up a slow, martial beat, ominous in the scattered light. Beowolf worked a tooth under the corner of a fingernail, and after several tries managed to rip off a sliver from the top of the nail. A tiny gash of blood appeared where the nail tore a thread of skin from the finger. He swore and chewed the nail. Jeannie's hair cascaded gently over her shoulders.

After tomorrow his career would be over. He couldn't help but feel that somewhere along the way something terribly important had escaped him. He was not the same as when he'd begun, not by a long shot. In the beginning he'd known what he wanted. His brother had been captain and quarterback; enveloping Rattler Stadium on Friday nights, the autumn sky was wide and spangled with distant stars, the perfect backdrop for the glow of stadium lights. But this was all past. His head was in a spin. He thought too much and didn't think straight, thinking instead in inarticulate spasms—he couldn't even consider them deep thoughts, thoughts that might have provided some compensation had he considered himself a thinker, which he did not. He never got anywhere, never decided anything. The only thoughts he seemed capable of concentrating on were, in fact, thoughts he preferred to forget. A person needs to touch, to hold something, fight for it and keep it, hold it always close to himself. He didn't know.

"I wish we could get out of here." He yanked at the knot in his tie and undid it. "Hate this fuckin noose."

"Fuckin-ay," Hap replied.

The ceiling lights flashed on. Moon appeared at the head of the bus.

"Who's missing?"

Beowolf glanced at the seat across the aisle.

"Bigfoot," Granville called out.

At that moment Bigfoot lumbered up the steps. "Sorry I'm late, Coach." He tried to squeeze past, but Moon wouldn't yield. Moon was big as a bear, bigger even than Bigfoot. "I had to pitch a loaf, Coach."

Everybody cracked up except Moon. Moon didn't get it. "Okay, let's roll," he said to Wavy. Frowning, he sat down in the front seat with Donnie, the head manager.

Wavy honked twice and doused the lights, and the bus lurched forward with a grunt and a sneeze. The fight song pierced the heavy dusk as the bus, swarmed by the crowd, pulled away from the curb.

"What say, Wolfman?" Bigfoot slid into the seat with Granville.

"Hey, man, how ya feelin?"

Bigfoot farted. "Not bad."

"C'mon!" Hap yelled. "You're gonna melt my glasses, ya fuckin grunt." In Hap's vernacular, all linemen were grunts. But Bigfoot was *especially* a grunt. He epitomized grunthood.

Bigfoot farted again, this time with malicious intent. Granville moaned. Reputedly, Bigfoot could pass gas at will.

"I thought you just got done pitchin a loaf," Beowolf said.

"Pitchin a loaf nothin," Bigfoot answered. "I got the Hershey squirts."

"You best cork yourself then," Hap smirked. "Otherwise you be catchin a pantsful of shrapnel."

Beowolf laughed, then glanced back toward the school for a final look. The students were bundled, brimming with a vitality that occasionally sprang wildly to the surface. Girls always looked prettier with red noses and rosy cheeks behind a steady stream of mist. Beyond the crowd was the ailing bonfire and Jeannie. She stood with her arms at her side, watching as the bus eased away. Then she waved: the way a child waves, or the way an adult might wave to a child, bending her fingers. And as she turned, as she began running toward the warmth of the school building, Beowolf was overcome by a flash impression that this was the close of a real-life movie, any single frame of which he wanted only to freeze in time. He wanted time stopped. If they couldn't go backward, neither would they have to go forward, and he could live with the still-life poignancy of this moment, fixed in his memory like a poster tacked to the bedroom wall.

"She runs like a girl," Hap said.

"Yeah." Beowolf turned away from her. "She throws like a girl, too."

Beyond the bonfire was the overbearing presence of the school: square, brown-bricked. Connecting it to the new gym was a glass passageway, above which the football stadium's parapet could be seen gnawing at the sky, and above the parapet, alone against the dusk, the red pennant frantically waved. On the banner were a coiled rattlesnake and the slogan DON'T TREAD ON ME. But from so far off in the twilight, and with the wind so fierce, the rattlesnake and the slogan were indistinguishable from their red background.

The bus jerked onto the highway, and the spectators fell to the wayside. Bigfoot had closed his eyes. Hap was thumbing through December's *Playboy*. As the bus churned noisily toward the mountains, Beowolf saw that there was only *now*, with no hiding from its moment. A body could run and run, run until his heart burst, but it was no good, he could never escape. There were nuclear warheads across the Missouri River, but that wasn't the trouble. Tomorrow was his final game. But that wasn't it either. More than anything else it was the girl who had stood waving only moments before. Their intertwined lives would never be the same, for better or for worse, after Thanksgiving.

Jeannie's wave, that particular wave, belonged to him.

Through the twilight the school bus sped. MARLBORO COUNTRY flashed past on a billboard: a Bunyan-sized cowboy on a white stallion sat lighting his cancer-stick with an orange campfire ember. On the watertower, superimposed on the other graffiti, huge red letters proclaimed JESUS SAVES. ROACHES was postfixed underneath in black. The bus turned onto River Road and rumbled past Wheelan's Feedlot and the slaughterhouse. On the opposite bank of the river LeMay Air Force Base was lit up like the planet's biggest used-car lot. The bus slowed down and turned onto 254. The bridge rattled, the river below was black as pitch. Winter coming on sure as hell.

For miles there was nothing but cropped wheat and an occasional farmhouse. Propping his knees into the back of the seat in front of him, Beowolf tried to make himself comfortable. He squeezed his duffel bag between his head and the window, and tried to doze.

The Kalispell game was always climactic. Football fever infected Rawlings late in August with the advent of Summer Practice. Intensifying with each victory, it waned only after Thanksgiving. A loss to Kalispell spelled disaster—which was what happened in Jason's final game. With the prize for victory a third consecutive State Championship, Rawlings had been upset. Beowolf hauled ass the two hundred and twenty-six miles home with his father, as if sheer distance could ease their frustrations. "Next year," his father muttered. "Next year." Beowolf, a freshman that season, fought back his tears, fearful of what his father might think. It was the only game his brother ever lost. "Next year," his father repeated, trying to appear at least faintly philosophical. With abrupt intensity, he turned, mad sparks lighting his eyes. "We're gonna rip their fuckin heads off next year, huh?" Beowolf bowed his head and nodded, feeling too insignificant for words. His father passed up his customary Thanksgiving bender down at the Bum Steer, drinking at home instead. And as it turned out, for him there was no next year. When the State Championship returned to Rawlings the following Thanksgiving, he was dead, killed in a skydive.

When Beowolf envisioned Jason's high school days, the emblematic image was of Jason scrambling for open territory. Jason wore white Pumas and had the quickest set of wheels west of the Mississippi. Dropping back into the pocket to pass, he would take off scrambling at the slightest provocation. He'd duck a lineman and reverse direction, slam on the brakes—stutter-step, searching downfield for a receiver—then he'd cut back and fire a bullet on the dead run. He would trot up to the huddle that was forming as if nothing resembling magic had occurred. After the game he smelled of Atomic Balm.

The Kalispell game haunted Jason's conscience. The frustration of having been upset on Thanksgiving was compounded by the loss of the State Championship to Missoula, whose record of nine wins and one loss Rawlings not only matched but seemingly surpassed, for Rawlings had beaten Missoula. Before the season had begun, however, the league directors decreed, despite denunciations from the Rawlings camp, that in order to repeat as State Champion, the championship team had to win outright, and that in the event of a tie in the standings, the championship—symbolized by the enormous gold-plated trophy that was now riding in the front of the bus —would be awarded to the school that had not won the championship the previous year. The "repeat rule" made no sense and was regarded by Rawlings partisans with utter disdain. The league directors, appointed by the various school boards, *wanted to give everybody a chance to win.* They wanted, they claimed, *to perpetuate the remarkable balance of the league.* Yet the rule seemed solely calculated to handicap the burgeoning Rawlings football dynasty. "Everybody's beautiful," crowed Beowolf's grandfather. "Let's everybody go play frisbee!"

But even if Rawlings had been awarded its fair share of the State Championship Jason's senior year, it still would have been no good. A good season for Rawlings was when they went undefeated and untied; a bad season, when they didn't.

"The worst thing about losing," Jason nowadays would explain, "is that you get used to it." Life had changed drastically for him after high school. As a safety at the University of Montana, he had played in only seven winning games in three years. Each loss killed him a little more, and each losing season blended into a broad pattern that culminated during the just-completed U of M season in a highly publicized football scandal.

The temperature inside the bus was uncomfortably warm, over-compensating for the cold outside. Beowolf opened his window several inches to allow the cold to fight back.

"Hey man," Hap said, "I'm freezing my ass off!"

Beowolf closed the window, then his eyes. Minutes passed. The heat was oppressive. Usually, riding the bus to overnight road games, he would oscillate between sleeping and waking, rarely achieving either, yet comfortably suspended behind closed eyelids in a state of drowsy thoughts and half-dreams where reality dissolved with the low hum of the school-bus engine into the realm of infinite possibilities. But tonight he couldn't relax.

"Hot damn!" Hap cried. "Hotter than a half-fucked fox in a forest fire!"

Beowolf's eyes popped open. Jerking himself up, he forced the window wide open for the frozen rush of air to chill his face.

"C'mon. Come *on!*" Hap threw Beowolf an elbow. "Colder than snakeshit."

When his eyes began to water, Beowolf lowered the window to a crack. His face had tightened around his skull.

"Hey, Wavy!" Hap shouted up the aisle. Across the aisle, Big-foot jerked awake. "What's the story on this bus? Turn down the heat."

"Can't!" Wavy hollered back, scanning his rear-view mirror for the invisible voice. "Dang thing's busted! All's ya got is hot or cold."

"Hey, fishbait," Bigfoot snarled at Hap. "Shut the fuck up. There's people trying to fuckin sleep."

"Why don't your grandfather pick a decent bus?" Hap muttered.

"Why don't I rearrange your face?" Bigfoot reached past Gran-ville and shoved their window wide open. His hand struggled into his pocket for a carbohydrate supplement, which he eventually popped into his mouth.

"Can you imagine Pap driving this junk heap?" Beowolf asked Hap.

"This junk heap *reminds* me of Pap."

"He would've at least shagged some ass to get the heater fixed.

Hell, he gave up drinkin Thursday nights just to have a clear head for Fridays."

Hap snorted. "Never knew Pap to have a clear head."

Pap was Beowolf's grandfather. He had driven the game bus for four and a half years, until midway through last season, when Moon fired him and hired Wavy. On Pap's first trip, to Butte for the opening game of the 1968 season, Jason, a sophomore, led Rawlings in a stunning upset of the defending State Champion Rustlers. During the trip home, Moon, having successfully debuted as the Rawlings head coach, displayed an elation that nobody suspected would become so rare when, as the bus barreled down the highway, he clapped Pap on the shoulder and appointed him official driver to all the away games. Feeling knighted perhaps, basking in the glow of Moon's magnanimity, Pap spat against his closed side window a blast of tobacco juice that peppered Peckinpah and Porkbutt in the seat directly behind him. Gasping at his mistake, he promptly swallowed his whole damn chaw and gagged on it for a solid minute, nearly colliding head-on with a cattle truck —an event that would have marked the quickest rise and fall ever of a Montana football powerhouse. But Pap kept an even keel through the rest of that incredible season, and during subsequent seasons was known to boast that "they'd sooner leave minus jockstraps than leave without me." And he was right. The Rawlings Rattlers had lost only one game while Pap was in the driver's seat.

Beowolf opened the window a bit wider and slouched back down in the seat. The chilling air churned about his head.

"I'm freezing my ass off, *will ya?*"

Beowolf closed the window slightly and shut his eyes again. Pap was dead. So was Beowolf's father. His mother died in childbirth, and he was raised by his grandmother, who died when he was eight. She sang "Twinkle, Twinkle" a lot and never referred to piss as *piss,* but always as *tinkle.* When Pap would charge into the house announcing, as he bounded for the bathroom, that he had to take a piss, Beowolf's grandmother would shush him, saying, "You have to *tinkle,*" and Pap would gruffly reply: "Yeah, I gotta do that too, but first I gotta piss."

Beowolf's thoughts had seeped through to bedrock. He shifted his position, fixing momentarily on his father during that ill-starred Kalispell game, jumping up and down like a barrel bouncing downhill: "Hey Ref! Ref! If ya had one more eye ya'd be a cyclops! Hey Ref!" Pap hadn't blamed the refs. "Excuses are like assholes," he told Jason. "Ever'body's got one, and they all stink." But his adage was wasted on Jason, who didn't blame the refs either. He blamed himself. "If I'd called a different play," he'd said last night, chewing minute steak, "things would've been different."

"You weren't calling the plays," Beowolf mentioned. "Moon was."

"Still, I didn't like the idea of throwing on third and one. We never throw on third and one."

"Moon figured we'd pull a fast one."

"We pulled a fast one awright." Jason stuffed his mouth with baked potato.

"Sometimes you get all the bad bounces," Beowolf said, at which Jason only sneered.

"Like with us this year against Anaconda," Beowolf added.

"You make your own luck."

"Maybe." Beowolf believed very much in luck, mostly the bad kind.

"If I'd been smart, I would've checked that play off."

"Moon would've marched right onto the field and kicked your ass in front of ten thousand people."

"We wouldn't have lost the game."

"You didn't know that then," Beowolf said. "Otherwise you would have checked the play off and taken the ass-kicking. It's simple as that. You can't second-guess yourself, man. Nobody's perfect. *God* completes only seventy percent of his passes."

Jason grunted.

"Probably the only dumb call Moon ever made."

"It should've worked! They were playing us so damn tight, expecting the run. Shit!"

"They were guessing. They were lucky."

"Fuck luck," Jason blustered. "Reynolds was a damn good safety. Gave a hundred and ten percent all the time." He crammed a piece of minute steak into his mouth. "He was the best."

"Too bad Reynolds didn't go to U of M. You'd be playing side by side."

"No we wouldn't," Jason snapped. "If Reynolds went to U of M, I wouldn't have been switched from quarterback."

Beowolf laughed. "After you went to Missoula, Pap used to go around saying to all the parents of the guys who went with you: *See! Ya spend all that money goin out to see the Grizzlies play football—all the way to Missoula, yup!—and ya don't even git a quarter back!* Get it?"

"Yeah, I get it."

"Most people he had to explain it to."

Jason shook his head.

"He wouldn't have missed a Rawlings game to save his neck. That's what he'd try to convince those parents of—to stay home and watch some real kick-ass football."

"Pass the potatoes," Jason said.

Beowolf grabbed a baked potato, leaned back in his chair, and arched a spiral across the table. Jason squeezed hard, and the potato popped open, steaming.

"You sure are a shitty cook. I'm surprised y'ever got as big as you did." Jason slapped a glob of margarine onto the potato. "This meat's so tough ya gotta sharpen your knife to cut the gravy." He swooped the minute steak up in his hands and ripped into it like a bulldog into a rabbit. He tore it in half, chewing on the piece that protruded from his mouth. Then he ripped that in half too.

"You think you'll miss football?" Beowolf asked.

"I still *got* another season," Jason said petulantly, champing away at his meat. "Might even be a good season considering what I found out before I came home. Actually, it's probably a good thing Reynolds never went to U of M. You could start next year at free safety, ya know. We could play a season side by side. Jason Bailey and his kid brother. They'd eat it up out there."

Beowolf wasn't much interested in Jason Bailey and his kid brother. "They might not even recruit me."

"Yes they will. I know they will."

They ate in silence for a while, to the tune of a Golden Oldie from the radio on the counter. When the "blast from the past" was over, Dandy Dan Douchette, the D.J., gave plugs in the same breath to a rock concert in Great Falls and the football game in Kalispell, before slipping into his familiar spiel concerning the virtues of Complexion G-2. He had the soul of a zit-cream commercial. He was from Los Angeles.

"Dandy Dan Douchebag," Beowolf muttered.

Jason laughed. Then, abruptly: "You guys, your cocks are on the chopping block. Ya gotta do it Thanksgiving."

"We will."

"How were the scouting reports?"

"Good as ever," Beowolf replied. "Superscout says Earthquake Allen's playing at over two-twenty. He's been killing people. We're keying on him."

"Who is?"

"I am."

"*You?*" Jason shouted. "You're a free fuckin safety for chrissakes!"

"They don't figure to throw much. We got it all figured."

"Don't get burned, man."

"I won't."

"Play it smart."

"Plan to."

Jason leaned back in his chair, chewing. "Ole Superscout, he's fuckin amazing. Did I ever tell you about the time in Bozeman, my junior year, when they shook him out of a tree? I only know about it"—he swallowed hard—"because I play with some guys from Bozeman, and they told me. Said they exposed his film and busted him over the head with his camera. It all made sense too, because we had a tough time with Bozeman that year."

"I wonder what happened to him *this* year in Anaconda," Beowolf said bitterly.

"Have you seen him yet this year?"

"No."

"Well, you'll see him in Kalispell."

"No shit."

"How's practice been?" Jason asked.

"Good. Everybody's crackin heads."

"Your groin awright?"

"Awright to play."

"Groin's a bad thing to hurt," Jason reflected. "Only way it heals is you stay off it."

"Has all the time in the world to heal after Thanksgiving."

"Whattaya mean? Ain'tcha playin basketball?"

"Basketball's a joke."

"You're quitting?" Jason asked incredulously.

"Already quit."

"Why?"

Beowolf stared at his plate. "Give my groin a break."

When he was on the freshman team, Beowolf had regarded the varsity players through star-struck eyes. Living monuments, polished blocks of granite. After home games, he waited for Jason in the locker-room doorway. Jason's friends called him "Boy Bailey" and let him in on wisecracks as they filed to and from the showers, good-natured banter flowing unceasingly from their lips. In the showers they would sing off-key as the windows above the lockers steamed over and the bittersweet pungency of Atomic Balm emanated like pure oxygen through the room. A body could get high on Atomic Balm.

> Keep the ball rollin,
> Keep the ball rollin,
> That's the name of the game, babe . . .

They sang like drunks, sometimes forming a crude dance line. They were always singing, even during practice. If somebody made a particularly dramatic run or catch, somebody not involved in the play would inevitably bellow:

> *Hollllly*wood!
> dadadadadadada
> *Hollllly*wood!

Jason, though, was a howler. After games he'd howl like a wolf the entire time he was in the locker room. And emerging from this steam dream into the clear moonlight, he would yank his Green Bay Packers woolen cap over his gleaming hair and bay at the moon a few more times just for good measure. Appearing as fresh as winter's first snowball, he would pat Beowolf on the back of the head and ask how he'd liked the game, as if the game had been played especially for him. The reply always revolved around a nucleus of superlatives.

Beowolf had wanted, more than anything else in the world, to be like his brother.

3

Every hero is a dog six days a week, but even if a body's family lived on Hill 19 like Bigfoot's family and couldn't buy a raffle ticket on a dead skunk's ass, he could still have that seventh day if he wanted it badly enough, and that seventh day could be the redemption of all the others. For Beowolf the cycle was winding down. Yesterday, as dusk gathered over the field, he plodded around the track trying to stretch himself out without aggravating his groin. It was the final practice in pads. Peckinpah stood forty yards beyond the string of grunts, holding a football in the air. "Linemen! Hands on knees!" he called out. "On the third hut!" The grunts fell forward into three-point stances. With his whistle between his lips, he barked out the side of his mouth, "Hut one! Hut two!"—then, as Beowolf expected, he dropped the ball, causing two or three grunts to jump off the mark, falling for it, and earning for themselves a sprint after practice through the Tunnel of Love.

Moon was leaning on the hood of his car, Porkbutt at his side, as Beowolf jogged past. Moon asked, "Howzit feel?" and Beowolf answered, "Awright, Coach." Then Beowolf was beyond them on the straightaway, listening to the crunch of cinders beneath his cleats. The grunts finally ran the sprint.

"Backs! Hands on knees!" Peckinpah shouted. "On the drop of the ball!"

At the tail end of the straightaway Beowolf had his back to the proceedings, but he could imagine the backs straining to see the football through the dusk, knowing they had to explode off the mark. Peckinpah started in on the "huts" and the whistle. Then there was silence. As Beowolf went into the turn he heard their stampede, and knew nobody had jumped. It was no secret that backs were smarter than grunts.

When Beowolf arrived at the opposite turn, the grunts were assembled in three-point stances along the goal line. Bigfoot was wheezing at the end of the line. He'd had a cold all week, but that wasn't it—he just naturally sounded more dead than he was. "It's a good day to die," Beowolf said to him as he passed.

"Fuck you, goldbrick," Bigfoot answered; the whistle blew, Bigfoot jumped forward a step and hopped quickly back.

"That's one for Bigfoot!" Peckinpah shouted gleefully.

Moon smiled. So did Porkbutt. As Beowolf jogged past, he noticed that even when he smiled, Porkbutt retained on his face the rancorous expression of a person who'd just eaten shit.

On opening day of Summer Practice, standing there like the Pillsbury Doughboy, Porkbutt would declare, "You are what you eat," then lecture the team on the importance of a good diet. "And eat roughage, boys," he would say in conclusion. "Eat roughage." Hap called it "diarrhea of the jawbone"—the exact same shit he'd regurgitated the summer before.

On the straightaway, Beowolf could make out Bigfoot standing on the forty-yard line, staring at him, as the backs ran their sprint. His hand was against his chest with the middle finger erect. Beowolf laughed. Between sprints Bigfoot would sometimes say, to nobody in particular, "It's a good day to die," which was a line that the old Indian chief kept saying to Dustin Hoffman in *Little Big Man*. Then he would choke on a breathless laugh and sprint back down the field. It *was* a good line, because dying was exactly how a body felt running wind sprints at the end of practice.

Beowolf hadn't run sprints in over a month. Luckily he'd been hurt at the right point in the season; the week after Anaconda there was no game, so he could sit out practice for a whole week and rest his groin. Last season, his ribs had been so badly bruised that he sat out not only a week of practice but the game on Friday as well. Watching from the sidelines made a body feel like an outsider. The good-natured ragging about his malingering or the real concern that someone occasionally expressed could never quite bridge the gulf between him in street clothes and his teammates in full gear. Beowolf knew that he didn't belong in street clothes. Watching from the sidelines, he did not belong at all. He felt guilty. Even so, sitting out that week of practice after Anaconda had been a relief. He'd also missed occasional practices over the next two weeks, when his groin hurt too much to run on. His conscience he assuaged with the knowledge that his convalescence was necessary and that even though he missed practices and was regularly excused, when he did practice, from hit-its and wind sprints for fear that he might aggravate the muscle, he hadn't missed any games. And he'd played goddamn hurt. Everybody knew he was playing hurt. Still it was godawful strange to be alone, jogging around the track while everybody else was on the field busting hump. It made him feel like a ghost.

Beowolf never felt quite right without the gratifying tinge of soreness in his muscles that resulted from hit-its and wind sprints. Hit-its followed calisthenics at the beginning of practice and were enough in themselves to make a body want to pack up and hop the first bus out of town. They were the most exquisite form of torture Beowolf had ever known: running in place, falling to his chest at MD's command to *Hit it,* springing back to his feet with a shout, running in place again. Last week—Monday, Tuesday and Wednesday—they had done forty hit-its each day. Thursday, Friday and Sunday they had done forty-five. Today they did "fifty for victory," which they always did for the last hard practice before a game. Immediately afterward, "fifty for victory" made a body feel as if he owned his arms and shoulders not because he could command them to do anything, but only because they ached so bad they couldn't possibly belong to anybody else. Later, during practice, they were tight and sore, strong and good.

Beowolf felt battered rather than sore, and he didn't feel tight at all anymore. Yet he'd learned to compensate for what he had lost. He was a veteran. He had learned to use his head. When he couldn't practice, he'd watch game films in Moon's office of the team they would play next. Superscout's reports, which were mimeographed and handed out each Sunday, he studied as never before, and when he practiced he concentrated on reacting to the keys that tipped plays off. Every play, he'd come to believe, was tipped off by something, and the better prepared a person was mentally, the more readily he could react to the keys. Sometimes a play was given away before the ball was even snapped—like against Billings West when their quarterback, barking signals on the line of scrimmage, tended to bob his head like Joe Namath whenever he was going to pass. Against Billings West, Beowolf picked off his fourth and fifth interceptions—honyos—of the season. It was his best game ever; he'd been named "Beast of the Week," and against Helena, the next week, he returned a punt for a touchdown and picked off his sixth interception, thus becoming the seventh player on the team to make Headhunter.

For every touchdown, touchdown pass, hundred-yard game, sacking of the quarterback, fumble recovery, interception, or otherwise outstanding play, a decaled capital letter was ceremoniously affixed, on the following Monday, to the front of that player's helmet. If a player was good enough, HEADHUNTER would eventually be spelled out. Jason had made it three times, which was a record he shared with MD. MD managed it this season in the sixth game, which was astounding considering that he was a safety. Bigfoot made it in the fifth game. Hap only got as far as HEADHUN —a letter for each of his touchdown receptions. At the end of the season, at the awards banquet, each Headhunter was presented with an official Blackfoot tomahawk, along with an emblem for his jacket. Then, forever, whenever a fellow Headhunter asked—already knowing, of course—if you were one of the elite, you could lay open your palm so he could slap it, and you'd say: "Bet your fuckin life I am."

Other teams had different insignias on their helmets: stars, buffaloes, American flags, black dots or tomahawks. Kalispell had skulls and crossbones. *Everybody* on Billings East had CHAHUNDA on the back of his helmet. Nobody from Rawlings could figure out what the hell CHAHUNDA signified, but Doe Konichek sure thought that Chahunda fella was good. *Doe* was short for *Dodo.*

Beowolf believed that everything he'd gained from football was well earned. A body was what he was willing to suffer, and nobody suffered more than the Rawlings Rattlers. Football began in May with a month of Spring Practice. Then, for two and a half months of summer, there was Captain's Practice every night. Then there was Summer Practice through the dog days of August, when the team worked out twice a day in the heat and dust, wheezing for breath through parched throats, *dying,* often until somebody quit the team.

Practices during the season were long and meticulously organized. Drills and plays were repeated endlessly. Peckinpah would rant and rave, his arms thrashing the air, telling them how lousy they were, while Moon was mostly cool, almost never raising his voice. On those rare occasions when he got in on Peckinpah's act, however, he would rage like Jehovah, firing his clipboard to the ground or using it to bat somebody's helmet. The players' shoulders would slip a notch or two in a way they never did as a result of Peckinpah's fury. When Moon calmed himself, he'd say something short and sweet, balancing his words between his teeth before biting them off into everybody's ears. "We should . . . be able . . . to tell . . . our opponent . . . where we are going to run a play," he might say, "and then . . . run it there anyway." The team would nod, solemnly believing, repenting for whatever had brought on this clipped manner of speech. The practice would perk up. It had to. A body either cut it for Moon on the practice field or packed up his gear and hit the road. On the practice field were no hiding places. You couldn't bullshit Moon. Moon saw everything.

"Goddammit, Konichek!"

Beowolf, on the far straightaway, had to turn to see Peckinpah. The football was still bouncing. Up ahead, Porkbutt was sporting his shit-eating grin.

"Ya miss the bus by three seconds, Konichek, ya miss the goddamn bus!" Konichek had jumped the gun again. He was a grunt. "I'll have you out here all night if I have to, Konichek, but you're gonna get it right! *Ball, Konichek!*"

Beowolf was into the turn now; he could see, without having to look over his shoulder, Konichek pouncing on the loose football.

"You're like a ten-watt light bulb, Konichek. *Not too bright.*"

Coach Rose had joined Moon and Porkbutt—freshman practice was over. Porkbutt was busting a gut, doubled over the hood of Moon's station wagon.

"Howzit feel?" Coach Rose asked as Beowolf jogged by.

"Fine, Coach."

Peckinpah, he was a major-league shithead. Yet the team couldn't do without him, as anybody who ever played for Rawlings knew. Moon organized, Peckinpah cracked the whip. At the end of each season speculation arose as to whether or not Peckinpah would be around for the next one. People kept figuring that he'd move on to one of the head-coaching jobs he'd been offered. Hell, Moon wasn't but forty.

But Peckinpah hung around season after season to do Moon's dirty work. He was a dapper buzzard with a dark, sinister tan, even in winter, and straight, neatly trimmed black hair. He was horse-faced, with a nose you could hide a small dog in. "Can park a fire engine in *that* garage," Hap said—Hap no prizewinner himself in the looks department. Peckinpah's facial features hardly shook his conviction, however, that he was God's gift to women. It was common knowledge at the high school, even among students, that Mademoiselle Bukowski, the French teacher, creamed in her coffee every time he was within sniffing distance. She was no prize stock —uglier even than he was—but it wasn't difficult to imagine Peckinpah cashing in.

It was also common knowledge that Peckinpah enjoyed an occasional cocktail now and again. He led the team in DWI's and was the main reason none of the Rattlers frequented the Great Falls bars during the season. Bumping into Peckinpah meant a summary suspension from the team. If a body wanted to get drunk during the season, he either went to the Big Sky Drive-In or he cruised around in a car. And it was only since October first—when Rollo Bastione, the sheriff, was shot—that a body could cruise in comfort, because Rollo would just as soon lock them in the slammer as sneeze. Everybody knew Rollo was the way he was—such a royal dipshit—only because he'd been too much of a spaz in high school to make the team. A number of parents had even said as much.

Peckinpah was jogging the length of the field. Backs and grunts alike stood along the goal line. For many of them it was their last wind sprint as Rattlers. *A hundred yards and a cloud of dust.* Beowolf shook his head. He was finished. He turned off the track and hustled over to the goal line. Peckinpah stood at the opposite end of the field.

"On the whistle!" Peckinpah shouted.

Beowolf assumed a three-point stance.

"Ready! Set!"

The whistle sounded and the wave of bodies surged forward. Beowolf ran easy, and as the wake of the wave pulled away from him—two, three, four, five yards—he was overcome by the sad beauty of the staggered line of numbered backs in the twilight, each individual body seemingly separated by greater and greater distances of space. It was a sight that could turn a body to stone.

Beowolf waited at the gate for Bigfoot to run his Tunnel of Love. The others filed past pulling off their helmets, their cleats raising a steady clatter on the sidewalk leading to the locker room. A handful of cross-country runners came wheezing around the stadium, cutting through the mob. Cross-country was a quiet sport, not like football—nothing but the pat of footsteps, heavy breathing and the silent beating of a single heart. "They're freezing their pricks off," Bobby McCall said. One of them collided with Geek Larson and bit the dust. "Dumbass," Geek sneered. The boy staggered to his feet and took off without looking back.

"Can y'imagine," Hap asked, "doing *that* all season?"

"Yeah," Beowolf replied. "I can imagine."

"What're you waiting for?"

"Bigfoot."

"Shit, I'm going in." Hap picked at a ripe pimple.

Sprinting through the iron skelton that ran beneath the end-zone bleachers, the average player had to crouch to avoid cracking his head. Bigfoot, nearer seven feet than six, had to resort to all fours, lumbering through the shaft like a lost, angry bear. He jogged to the gate after he emerged from the far end, deserting Konichek. Konichek should have owned stock in the Tunnel of Love.

"You peckerhead," Bigfoot said to Beowolf.

"Don't blame me, sport."

Bigfoot walked bowlegged because of his crotch rot. "Sonofabitchin tunnels." Grabbing the cage of his helmet, he yanked the helmet off with one hand—a method that made Beowolf cringe. He'd tried it once himself, damn near ripping his ears off along with the helmet.

For Summer Practice, Bigfoot always shaved his head down to the scalp, permitting, as the season progressed, only a cruel arrowhead of hair to grow down the middle. Though it wasn't the haircut expected, it was understood by the coaches, in all its glorious ugliness, to be at least as fervid a profession of dedication as the traditional zip. By season's end, he always looked like the last of the Mohicans; and though he scarcely needed this embellishment to stand out from the crowd, the Mohican cut would remain his hairstyle until the following summer, when he would again shave completely for Summer Practice.

Bigfoot's face was round as a basketball, with huge fiery nostrils that belonged on a bull. It was riveted to his body by a sinewy stub of neck that grew like a volcano out of his shoulders. He had a barrel chest, shot-put biceps and timber legs. And as if his blend of Negro and Indian blood wasn't enough of a reminder to Rawlings of the persistent existence of other races, he would act, speak and *look* like an African gorilla: swinging from a horizontal lockerroom waterpipe by a single woolly meathook, grunting, baring his teeth and grabbing at the chest hairs of passers-by like King Kong snatching at airplanes. "Odds or evens!" he would cry, seizing somebody's hair. He'd give the tuft a hearty yank and proceed to count each sprout.

"That sonofabitch," Bigfoot said. "Just once I'd like to grab that damn whistle and strangle him with it."

"Ain't a new idea. Just never been done."

"God, I'd like to." Bigfoot sneezed. "Fuckin cold out."

The locker room was warm with the steamy salt stench of naked bodies and Atomic Balm. Beowolf undressed and showered. Everybody was subdued except for MD, who was stalking sophomores for "odds or evens." One of the sophomores, Guy Lombago, hadn't had many chest hairs at the start of the season and had only a handful now. MD had been swearing all season long that Lombago would be bald by Thanksgiving. The sophomore slunk around the locker room like a high-strung cat, removing his T-shirt only at the last moment before dashing in and out of the shower. He was free of the locker room in nothing flat.

"Where's Lombago?" MD eventually asked.

"Gone," somebody told him.

"That smelly bastard!" MD slammed his locker door. "He never even took a shower."

"Took a North Dakota shower."

All the sophomores were gone. Everybody was leaving. Bigfoot swung his duffel bag over his shoulder and yanked his stocking cap down over his forehead. "Adios, Wolf." He headed for the door, walking as if he had a load in his drawers. Through the doorway his gargantuan body disappeared into the night, leaving a draft to whisk up the aisle. "Close that fuckin door!" somebody yelled. Beowolf pulled his jersey on over his head.

Beowolf was always the last to leave the locker room. He tucked his jersey into his pants, buttoned his pants, zipped his fly and fastened his belt. He pulled his socks on and stepped into his loafers. He sat back down on the bench and pushed his locker door gently shut. He clicked the shackle of his lock back down into the casement and spun the dial three full revolutions, leaving the ninth notch at the top for luck. Still he sat. There was a draft each time somebody left. He studied his hands, studied the lock. He picked up his helmet and looked at it. He would take it home with him tonight. He wouldn't need it tomorrow and he liked to sit it on his dresser so he'd have something to look at while lying on his bed —something other than Steve McQueen on a motorcycle and the "Yea, Though I Walk Through the Valley of the Shadow of Death" poster that Jeannie had given him. Tomorrow the team would get out of school early for a light practice in sweats. Then everybody would go home for something to eat and to collect whatever overnight things they needed. Then they'd return to school for the rally and the bus trip. Beowolf swung a leg over the bench, straddling it. On the far wall it said: GIVE 110% AT ALL TIMES.

When everybody was gone, Beowolf rose from the bench. The steam had condensed into droplets on the windows above the lockers. He pulled his woolen cap down over his ears, shrugged on his overcoat and buttoned it up. He carried his helmet by the face bars as he headed slowly for the door. At the bulletin board he stopped and gazed at the newspaper photograph of Earthquake Allen, KALISPELL WORKHORSE. Earthquake was big, black and grizzly—two hundred twenty pounds—with a scar running north like tiny railroad ties from his eyebrow to his scalp. He was Kalispell's answer to Bigfoot. Earthquake was shorter than Bigfoot, though, and he was a running back, musclebound, built more like a boxing glove.

Next to Earthquake was a photograph of MD. The opening line of the accompanying newspaper column read: "Yes, Virginia, there is an MD—and the initials don't stand for Medical Doctor." Halfway down the column, Beowolf's eyes fixed upon an underlined passage. *"When I was a kid," he remarks thoughtfully, "I learned to ride a bike just so I could ride it into things—like trees."* MD, the columnist maintained, "marched to the beat of a different drummer."

Tacked to the top of the bulletin board was Bigfoot's "Tarzan jock." Two weeks earlier during practice, Bigfoot's jock snapped underneath, leaving him to "go commando." At the end of practice, when the whole team was being run through a series of Tunnel of Loves, Bigfoot managed, hidden in the dusk beneath the bleachers, to duck aside and strip off his pants; he emerged on the subsequent run-through wearing nothing between his jersey and his high-cut Johnny Unitas cleats but a flap—like a shrunken Indian loincloth hanging ineptly over his bait—which was probably how he'd caught the cold he now couldn't shake, running around in November with no pants on, not even a healthy jock.

Beowolf was sweating beneath his overcoat. He switched off the lights and was walking toward his car when Peckinpah, bundled up like Admiral Peary, drove past on his motorcycle. Peckinpah was crazy. The motorcycle turned and doubled back. Beowolf opened the car door and tossed his helmet onto the floor.

"How's the leg feel?" Peckinpah shouted over his engine. Peckinpah never called a groin a groin, he always called it a leg. The motorcycle was idling fast because of the cold.

"Feels awright."

"You been taking the whirlpools?"

Beowolf nodded. What the hell did he think?

"We're counting on you, ya know."

Beowolf nodded again. He glanced into Peckinpah's eyes, then beyond to nothing in particular. Peckinpah seemed to expect a thank-you.

"This is your last game."

"Yeah."

"Well. Let's make it a good one."

"Yep."

For a moment it seemed as if Peckinpah would zoom off. Instead, he stared into Beowolf's eyes. Beowolf glanced away again. Peckinpah said, "Ya know, the way I see it, football is like life. Ya gotta hang in there tough. Ya can't quit. Ya know what I mean?"

"Yeah."

"Well . . ."

It was as long a conversation as Beowolf had ever had with Peckinpah. He didn't know what to say.

"So, what're ya doing next year?"

Beowolf shrugged. "Going to college, I guess."

"That's a good idea." Peckinpah was staring at him—staring too hard. "You could be good, ya know."

Beowolf glanced over Peckinpah's engine, not saying anything.

"Well . . . Get some shut-eye."

"Sure."

When Peckinpah finally roared off, Beowolf shook his head and snorted uneasily. Encasing Peckinpah's head had been a football helmet, minus the face bars, with HEADHUNTER spelled across the front.

4

He could be good. Coach Rose, the freshman coach who manned the headphones in the pressbox during varsity games, had said so too. "You've got a good head for this game." But ever since the Anaconda game, Beowolf found himself wondering, day after day, why he was even playing. What was the good? Why was he punishing himself? Football had never been his life the way he'd wanted it to be, the way he had once fancied Jason's life was; that life, he knew now, existed only in the naive imagination of a younger brother and in the deluded memory of Jason himself, who, without thinking, *never* thinking, still believed he had lost in a football game whatever it was that was good in life. The game wasn't worth it anymore. It was like beating your head against a rock.

The bus was west of the Continental Divide by now. It was pitch black outside. During the summer Beowolf had driven through these mountains often, breezing along with Jeannie on the back of his motorcycle, heading for her family's cabin, north of Kalispell in the redundant town of Falls Falls. But the mountains were never as awesome then as during the winter in the dark. By autumn, Jeannie had grown reluctant to ride the motorcycle. Too many close calls. Beowolf had become slightly paranoid himself. The bike had become for him something like his favorite old climbing tree in the gorge below the dam, which he would climb all the way to the top when he was a kid, hanging on up there for dear life while the wind whipped him around, but which he regarded nowadays with a chilled shiver. Fear had gradually superseded the pleasure of the ride, tipping the balance of the thrill toward terror. Jeannie was right last night when she'd said he was afraid of everything. Of course he was afraid! With the exception of Jason, everyone in his family was dead. Why shouldn't he be afraid? A body never knew what might happen next. Beowolf worried about nuclear war and cancer; he worried about breaking his neck on the football field or on his motorcycle; he worried about Jeannie and about growing old. He was afraid of heights. More than anything, he feared paralysis.

He knew he would regret being out of football. It was not something he could lie to himself about. In a way, he loved being a Rattler. He loved playing the game. The game was like this: You scored or you didn't score. You did your job or you didn't do your job and were replaced. You knew the rules and you knew yourself, and you added to the rules everything that made you distinctly *you* and you got the bottom line, which was: You were a winner or you were a loser. There was a well-ordered simplicity to the game, a cleanliness, even. You could be exhausted, wheezing under the mud- and sweat-caked bodies smothering you, and even as that moan rose from your gut you knew you belonged, you had chosen this life and had endured the endless hours of pain to be a part of it, to be a part of this game and this exact sort of moment, for you made in the game only what you paid for in practice—which was as reasonable a proposition as Beowolf had ever been offered.

High school in Rawlings was wedded to football, and Beowolf had always fought desperately to be on the inside pissing out rather than the other way around. When you were a Rattler, thousands of people watched you. You ate, talked, dressed and acted like a Rattler. It was like being in the army; insiders were army and the rest were civilian. Everybody was one or the other and there was no in-between—which perhaps was why Gray had never fit in.

Beowolf stared out the window into the darkness. Even Gray must have regretted leaving football. He'd been the best natural runner Rawlings ever had. Moon had said so himself and Moon never even liked him, even though Gray had been sent to Rawlings by his father for the express purpose of playing football for Moon. Beowolf watched and cheered from the sideline during his sophomore season as Gray slashed through the line like a singed cat, every muscle in his body jerking him in a different direction: he'd fake out tacklers, bounce or slip away with a sort of frenetic repugnance at having even been touched, hating to be touched, he'd cut sharply for the sideline, then glide upfield toward that wide open patch of end zone, swinging the ball too freely on his arm—"It's not a loaf of bread!" Peckinpah would nag during practice, "Tuck it in!"—he'd break stride in his graceful flight only to slip a final tackle: braking and dipping untouched behind the would-be tackler, sailing home free. Afterward, he'd make a body laugh, perched on the backrest of the bench as high as a kite, wearing his illegal grin, having made it look so easy. Everybody thought he had the world by the shorthairs. But he didn't have the world by the shorthairs. As good as he was, football was also a torment to him, for even as he basked in the glory shone on him, he paradoxically professed a hatred of the game, confident perhaps that no one would suggest he leave it.

After home games, Gray would sit on the bench in front of his locker, dripping wet from the shower, a towel draped laterally over his head, nursing bittersweet melodies from his harmonica until the locker room emptied. In the parking lot, Jeannie sat alone in her father's car, waiting for him, and Beowolf would offer her a restrained wave. Climbing into his car—the car his father had left him when he died—and pulling out of the parking lot, Beowolf watched her in the rear-view mirror, still sitting there, as alone as could be. This vision of her waiting would stew in his own emptiness as he drove home to the house he shared now only with Pap, mingling with the growing distaste he felt for Gray, whose head, folks were beginning to remark, had "grown too big for his shoulders."

That Gray got psyched for every game by blowing a joint was common knowledge, and during his first varsity season Beowolf believed the coaches were simply ignoring this fact. They didn't give a damn, he supposed, so long as Gray kept running the way he did. But by the start of his second varsity season, after Bull Run, after Gray was gone, Beowolf was positive the coaches had never known anything about it. "That Gray boy," Peckinpah said, "he looked like he'd been strained through a condom."

Because Gray did not look like a football player, the coaches had pinned the number 1 on him to make him appear taller; and they padded his weight in the football program more than they padded everybody else's. Appearance mattered—which was why, for instance, they made everybody get crew cuts for Summer Practice. "To be a man," Moon declared, "you should look like a man." Players who were fat or slow did not exist. Players who were short or skinny were always suspect. And when Gray—a senior, the team captain and a two-time All-State running back—reported to Summer Practice with shoulder-length hair, the coaches didn't buy it. Had they ever known what a pothead he was, they surely would have busted his ass faster than a body could exhale and holler howdy. Moon was straighter than God.

In everything, Gray ran against the grain. When, for instance, as a sophomore he was ordered by Jason to sing, he'd drawn his guitar from his locker and, with the boundless enthusiasm of a piss-ant who was finally getting his big chance, hopped onto the training table and belted out a medley of Broadway show tunes: *Oklahoma! Hello, Dolly! Hair!* Nobody knew what to do, so they didn't do anything, just hurried up and dressed. He didn't stop singing until the locker room was clear. Beowolf was only a freshman, and didn't see the performance, but at the supper table Jason told about it, laughing and vowing never again to make Gray sing. Long afterward, when he became friends with Gray, what Beowolf found so amusing about the story was that Gray despised Broadway show tunes.

After Gray's junior season ended with Beowolf still riding the pines, watching him run wild over Kalispell, Gray swept out whatever corner of his psyche it was that enabled him to so effortlessly excel at running with a football, and while everybody else played basketball or wrestled, he played music. Beowolf never said so, of course, but after they became friends and he began hanging around the bars in Rawlings and Great Falls listening to Gray pick his way through the night, singing and playing the harmonica, he realized that if not for the renown Gray had earned in football nobody would have wanted to hear him play at all. He wasn't at home on stage; but then, he didn't seem to be at home anywhere except on the football field during a game. With his red hair and freckles lit up by the spotlight, he looked like a kid, slightly awkward and unsure of himself, as if it were only by some tremendous force of will that he was able to mount the stage at all. His audiences never seemed to care that his voice wasn't strong or that his guitar missed or stumbled over notes. They were out for a good time, to drink and watch the best halfback in the state.

Jeannie was in love with Gray back then. But Gray was too strange for words. He didn't love Jeannie—or at least didn't act it. Sometimes they went to movies together, but mostly Jeannie just trailed after him. In the barrooms she would sit alone at the table nearest the stage, and as Beowolf watched her grow captivated by Gray's rhapsody, the old sorrow would fill him to bursting. He would never sit with her. Not then anyway. He'd scarcely spoken to her.

What Jeannie saw in Gray was apparent to Beowolf, if to no one else. Sometimes, playing the harmonica, Gray would surrender himself to an intensity remote from the audience, private and hot and painful, deep beneath the surface of sweat and the simple sound of blue notes, and while his hands and mouth worked over the instrument his face would redden, his eyes shut tight, oblivious of the audience the way he never was while playing guitar. Unconsciously, irrepressibly, he would turn himself inside out to reveal a soul remarkably isolated and indomitable, untouchable yet begging for a caress.

Jeannie made herself so available to Gray that the situation eventually arched the eyebrows of every red-blooded, meat-eating male in town. Gray didn't even seem to desire her: her in that cute cotton sweater, dancing and gyrating and shaking her pom-poms. Gray was aloof from his own teammates, never had much to say, and ate fruit and cheese and sunflower seeds—which was probably why he never managed to beef up like everybody else. He had what was called hypoglycemia. The doctors claimed that he had too little sugar in his blood. Many people, however, had come to suspect just the opposite.

His father, who owned Gray Chevrolet in Helena, had given him a Corvette after his first varsity season ended with Rawlings reclaiming the State Championship, a car nobody ever saw him drive. It sat parked in knee-high grass behind his aunt and uncle's garage —it was parked there still, rusting now and dirty. Rawlings Sports had given him a pair of white cleats that he never wore. But the most incriminating evidence against him was, of course, Jeannie, who had tried to make a gift of herself.

She was cool and overt in her infatuation. Closely observed by everybody, she commanded a proud and natural composure that approached but never slipped into arrogance; nor had her face ever suggested that blanket empty-headedness common to adolescent good looks. Flushed with a yearning for life that focused for some reason on Gray, she sustained her nobility even as the object of her desire eluded her grasp. Nuances of perfection unveiled themselves to Beowolf in the form of a glance or a smirk or in the disappointment she sometimes exuded like a circumspect judgment of the whole world, which would drive people crazy wanting to know her. "He's fucking her, isn't he?" Hap would ask Beowolf with a suffering, slightly maniacal look in his eyes. "Is he banging her or what?" MD once asked him. "Who am I?" Beowolf irritably replied. "Her gynecologist?"

Gray was strange all right. "*Queer* more like it," Peckinpah claimed the day Gray left the team and left town, left Jeannie crying in full view in the gym lobby, cursing Peckinpah for what he'd done, glass from the school trophy case shattered all over the floor. Gray never had the world by the shorthairs. When he wasn't carrying a football, he was a confusion of exposed nerves. He couldn't relax. Exactly what was wrong he seemed altogether unwilling or unable to articulate. "Was Gray a homo?" Beowolf once asked Jeannie, after it was safe to ask her about Gray—long after he had departed. "You oughta know," she answered, "if anybody does."

Except for Jeannie, and Beowolf later, Gray cut himself off completely. He wouldn't talk about Helena, his hometown; he seemed, in fact, to have been born a freshman in high school. Instead of conversing, he made simple declarative statements. When Beowolf once mentioned that his father used to drive to all the games too, when Jason was playing, Gray replied, "I hate my father." That was all. He wouldn't talk about him, and Beowolf could remember once when he wouldn't talk *to* him either. After the Helena game he left his father standing there open-mouthed with the poor guy's cronies clustered all around. His father quit coming to the games after that. Beowolf felt sorry for the guy and he felt sorry for Gray too, walking off the field and out of the man's life. He felt sorry for them both because the father didn't look like such a bad sort; like everybody else, he just wanted something to be proud of. What Gray did to his father was crazy, especially because Gray, more than anyone Beowolf had ever known, was sensitive to things—to the feelings of the piss-ant, for example. Gray never hazed anybody or gave anybody any trouble. Except the coaches. He detested Peckinpah, sneeringly referring to wind sprints as "Simon Sez," because Peckinpah, in the twilight at the end of practice, instead of simply conditioning them would try to trick them with his whistle, his football or his signals, trying to trick them into jumping offsides so he could run somebody through the Tunnel of Love afterward. It made no goddamn sense, and during Beowolf's first Summer Practice, Gray actually said something about it. Near the end of a particularly rough workout, everybody was dying and Peckinpah was deep into his Simon Sez routine: blowing the whistle, dropping the ball, shouting signals and lambasting Konichek. Gray finally shouted, "Let's can the crap!" and it seemed to Beowolf that the earth jerked momentarily off its axis and ceased spinning through space.

Peckinpah had a look that could stunt your growth, and this was the look he shot at Gray. And during that prolonged moment when the planet hung motionless, there could be no mistaking his absolute hatred of Gray. He glanced then at Moon, who had been leaning against his station wagon on the sideline watching them run, but was now gazing into the sky as if a blizzard might be coming on or maybe just a flock of Canadian honkers. Peckinpah said, "On the third hut," and the earth seemed to right itself, and Simon Sez continued. Gray didn't say anything again that day, or *ever* for that matter, because after practice he was summoned to the coach's locker room, where Moon told him that he was a valuable member of the team but hardly unexpendable, and that if he ever again pulled anything resembling what he'd done during wind sprints, his ass would be out in the cold. "And do you know what he was doing the whole time he was telling me this?" Gray, awestruck, wondered aloud. "He was sitting on the throne, taking a dump!"

Beowolf knew he thought about Gray too much. He'd thought about him too much when he was gone and, for a completely different reason, thought about him too much now that he'd returned. Gray had come back to town three months ago, no one knew why. He got a job at the record shop and moved back in with his aunt and uncle, peacefully this time around. His hair was long but neat, and the fact that no one other than Jeannie had heard from him suggested that he'd probably ceased fighting the world, perhaps lowered his expectations. At night he still played in the bars, and Jeannie claimed that he'd gotten a lot better. And last night she'd said *Go away.*

Beowolf slammed the window shut and swore, feeling suddenly helpless and angry. What was she talking about? *Go away.* Only the day before, she'd wanted him to marry her. She'd practically begged him. He knew she loved him, loved him alone.

"What's wrong?" Hap asked.

"Nothin."

"Groin?"

"It's this fuckin bus."

Beowolf stared into the blackness. West of the Great Divide the sky was clear. The stars were out. Montana was like two completely different countries sometimes. Mountains or flatlands, extreme highs or extreme lows: the schizophrenic state.

Hap closed his eyes.

"Hey," Beowolf said. "Jason's home."

"Oh yeah?" Hap's eyes opened.

"Yeah, he's coming up to see the game."

"Why didn't he just go up from Missoula?"

"He wanted to talk to me."

"What about?"

"Whattaya think?"

"How the hell should I know?"

"The game tomorrow, whattaya think?"

"He drove all the way from Missoula for that?" Hap was incredulous. "Man, he's cracked."

"He also wanted to talk to your dad. Your dad offered him a job for after he graduates."

"Really?"

"Yeah."

Hap's dad dealt insurance for State Farm. But Jason wasn't gonna deal insurance. After his senior season, he planned to join the coaching staff at U of M. "We could play together," he'd said last night, "and then I'll be your coach. I'll coach the defensive backs. Won't *that* be a kick in the ass!"

"So what's he say about the scandal and everything?" Hap asked. "Is he off the hook?"

"Well, *he* didn't do *anything*," Beowolf answered indignantly. "What was happening was just that guys were getting paid for jobs that didn't exist. Jason was supposed to inspect fire extinguishers, but nobody cared if he did it or not; they paid him anyway. Everybody had a job like that, and it was Shannon who set the whole thing up. He's not just fired now either, like the other coaches. He's going on trial, because it was state funds."

"You couldn't pay me to go to U of M," Hap commented smugly.

"No, *I* couldn't."

"What's that mean?"

"Nothin. You'll find out."

Hap opened up his *Playboy*. He flipped a page, scowling. Then he flipped another. Then he flipped an annoyed glance at Beowolf. "What the hell you talkin about?"

"Nothin, just nothin. Really."

Beowolf closed his eyes, feigning sleep, and thought again of Gray. After Gray had lit out for Kalispell, Beowolf didn't hear from him, nor had he expected to. Since returning, Gray made no effort to speak to him. That he thought Beowolf was a coward shouldn't have mattered.

Beowolf thought too much, was all. This was what he had figured out. A body could cease living with all the damn thinking he'd been doing. His life was mired in thinking and thinking, grasping at the straws of a lost football dream. Football could be his life no longer. It did not matter, did not work. A body striving for the ideals plastered in slogans on locker-room walls paid for the attempt in real pain, and even for a team as good as the Rattlers the dream of greatness could never quite be reconciled with reality. All-State running backs wound up selling you a car or an insurance policy, carpeting your house, putting a washer in your toilet, or running off to Kalispell the way Gray had done without even playing his senior year. The seasons all ended. Things became dull and horrible. Time passed. And as the years would slip from memory's grip, the significance of names and events would blur and fragment into answers to trivia questions asked in barrooms, where there was little else to talk about. This was the residue. Everything else was lost completely. Beowolf could not quit thinking and he could not quit having shitty-weird dreams or quit feeling the anxiety of the whole universe bearing down on him the way it did five weeks earlier, when Anaconda came to town—the way it was bound to do again. Concerning Gray, it did no good to tell himself that events were not his fault, that the Bull Run which was Gray's downfall had been, like most everything else, beyond his control. He could not deny the feeling that, having budded at the close of the event in question, had since blossomed into the full realization that he was a Judas. At best, a stupid, unwitting Judas.

Time and events had gone haywire. And it wasn't just that he'd become a pothead either. Madness glimmered beneath the surface of everything. The whole fucking world was out of kilter. In Canada, a thirteen-year-old had died of what scientists claimed was old age: his hair turned gray and started falling out—that whole routine. Flying saucers were being sighted all over the place, and meanwhile the world was running out of gas. And cattle mutilations! Someone was getting kicks out of castrating cattle and leaving them to die. The President was a crook. The polar icecaps were ready to flip over. The country was going metric!

The homecoming game against Anaconda was the killer. Rawlings had played the game in the shadow of Nixon's Minuteman missiles in a Condition Three Alert less than three miles away. They played the whole damn game precisely where X marks the spot when the nukes start flying—not that that was any excuse for blowing the game. The damage done, nobody could forget the Anaconda game. Not the team. Not the town. Not Jason. And not him. Maybe it would be like Jason's Kalispell game. Maybe they'd never be able to swallow it—*God!* It was godawful hard to believe we'd sent men to the moon.

Beowolf craved a good howl.

Ahhhh-woooooooo! Ow Ow Ahhhh-woooooooo!

He wanted to bay at the moon, or sit around the locker room with the others, playing spades or picking over somebody's carcass. He wanted to go out to a movie with Jeannie. He wanted to sleep with her for the first time again. He wanted everything else to just go away.

What would he do tomorrow? Write Dear Abby? What would Jeannie do? It was funny in a way. He envisioned himself as a headless chicken: life running out not linearly but in senseless circles. He ran and ran, mile after mile in a circular route on the God-forsaken highway, never getting anywhere, never even getting out of Rawlings—someday, dammit, he would just keep running, keep running straight when he came to the slaughterhouse instead of turning up Hill 19, keep running straight over the bridge and straight out of Rawlings forever, just running and not thinking about it. Running straight into the night like in the end of a movie or something, running straight into the mountains because all there was to be was a marathon man padding along, one step in front of the other, enduring the pain and breathlessness for nothing but the endurance itself, running in a void, running straight into the ground. There was no victory for the marathon man.

Beowolf didn't feel like a kid. When he was a kid he was a kid, and when he went to bed at night he knew he'd wake up in the morning still a kid. His days slipped effortlessly through a continuum of a hopeful future already present, then passed into inconsequence to make room for what was next. Now he was a fucked-up adolescent. Except for his fair share of zits—which Hap had, by some cosmic injustice, wound up with—he had all the adolescent fuck-up's symptoms. He needed a new frontier, that was it, and the moon just didn't cut the mustard. *One small step.* He needed to break out of Rawlings on his motorcycle, high-jumping the borderline barbwire like Steve McQueen, because he was enwombed in this damn bitch of a town, the bottom man in a suffocating pile-up, the aimless runner of a long, pointless circle.

Tomorrow was for circling, for closing his most stupendous circle. The thought of flying off on a tangent afterward was terrifying.

5

It was a four-mile course and all there was to do was sweat and think. From his home, Beowolf would head toward the river out Route 254, pausing on that solitary stretch to the slaughterhouse only when he came to Jeannie's house: down the gravel drive from the highway, silhouetted lonesome and dark against the night sky, hazes of soft yellow light glowing randomly within. Sometimes he would also stop at the slaughterhouse, if it didn't smell too bad, and bat the breeze with Wavy, who lived out back. Beyond the slaughterhouse he would run the dirt road along the river up Hill 19— where ditchweed shot up in the spring, and gave you a headache if you smoked it—and turning back onto pavement at Wheelan's Feedlot he'd wind through Lewis and Clark Park, watching over the river for flying saucers, which Jeannie's dad had seen twice; he'd cut through the cemetery where practically his whole damn family was buried, emerging as a silent banshee onto River Road, heading toward the dam. But he'd never run as far as the dam, swinging instead onto Central Ave, where a huge buckshot TRES- PASSERS WILL BE PROSECUTED sign boasted that River Road had become the Anaconda Company's private drive; and he'd run Cen- tral Ave into and through town, running almost as far out of town as the high school before veering off the highway to run the dirt tractor path through the wheat, past isolated farmhouses and barns to where the tractor path ended, finally running past the farmhouse where Helen the Bod lived, running brokenfield through her fa- ther's wheat back to Route 254, full circle home.

He ran last night despite the cold and despite having been through practice that day and having blown a joint after supper. He had been considering going for an orbit anyway—he needed air —but it was Jason who iced the idea.

Accustomed as he was to having the run of the house, Beowolf had neglected to take Jason's presence into account when he went to his bedroom after supper to light up. Sitting against the wall on his unmade bed, silently getting high, he was considering what

Jason had said about his going to U of M when Jason barged in, exclaiming, "What the hell you doin?" The scene wasn't quite real. It had happened in a previous lifetime or something. Beowolf shuddered and smiled, true to his déjà vu. It *had* happened before: five weeks earlier, when Jason sped all the way home from Missoula after hearing about the Anaconda game.

"I'm trying to relax," Beowolf nonchalantly replied.

"Gimme that shit!"

Beowolf slapped his hand away. *"C'mon."*

"What're you trying to do?"

"I'm trying to get high in peace. Haven'tcha ever seen the stuff before?"

"Yeah, I've seen the stuff before! And I've even smoked it. But not before a football game!" Jason lowered his voice. "You're gonna blow that game."

"The game isn't for two days yet, and all I'm gonna blow is this joint." Beowolf couldn't contain a second smile. "Cool your hoofs, will ya?"

"When did you become such a smartass?"

"When did *you* become such a *tight*ass? Jesus."

Jason shook his head disdainfully. "You should see yourself," he sneered. "Look at this place."

"Can we forget it?" Beowolf asked. "I'm sorry you caught me smokin. Okay? Look." Beowolf snuffed out the joint in an empty Campbell's soup can. "I'm going runnin. Wanna come out and run?"

"Sheeee-it." The door slammed behind Jason, leaving Beowolf to wonder if, had it come to dukes, he could have handled his brother. He never had fought him. On the wall was a caveman holding a spiked club. *Yea, Though I Walk Through the Valley of the Shadow of Death, I Shall Fear No Evil. For I Am the Meanest Sonofabitch in the Valley.*

Beowolf winced, *Fuck!* He laid his head back on the pillow and stared at the ceiling. "He ain't my fuckin father," he said aloud. He rolled over and inhaled deeply, craving that bittersweet redolence of lovemaking which he could sometimes detect. The bed, the room, he smelled weed. That was all. His sheets were dirty. They hadn't been washed since Jeannie took care of it the afternoon following the Anaconda game, the afternoon Jason had stormed home. Slamming the door, Jason had burst into the house like the world was on fire. Jeannie, who was cooking breakfast, gasped and fumbled an egg that splattered across Beowolf's bare foot. Jason demanded, "What happened?" Seeing Jason that way, so damn desperate, Beowolf—hungover, his mouth tasting as if he'd suppered with coyotes—could not contain that smile which hit everyone below the belt. Confused by the smile, apologetic, Beowolf began recounting the catastrophe while Jeannie wiped up the mess on the floor. The hemispheres of Beowolf's brain twisted in wild, contrary directions—he was abruptly resentful at having to explain, always *explaining* nowadays, staring at Jason still standing there by the refrigerator not wild anymore but somber behind half-mast eyelids, as if somebody in the family had died. Beowolf was afraid he might puke again.

He wished his thoughts hadn't carried him so far. He tried once more to pick up the faint scent of lovemaking. Above the door, across the ceiling like a lifeline on the palm of a hand, a crack ran to the crumbling plaster in the near corner. Beowolf had moved his bed several months earlier to avoid the fallout. He stared at the crack, then at the wallpaper roses. The room had been his grandmother's and still bore her wallpaper of faded roses. He glanced at his helmet resting on the dresser beside the autographed Butte game ball that Moon had given him when, in seventh grade, he was recovering from a rattlesnake bite—and at just that moment when his sensibilities became so keen and futile that he rolled over to bury his face in the pillow, the flitting emanation of lovemaking rose from his bed like a last gasped breath. He glanced across at Steve McQueen on the wall. "Come out and run," he said aloud to hear his own voice. "Maybe we'll spot a saucer." *The Great Escape.* He glanced at his guitar standing in the corner, flaked with plaster. He hadn't played guitar since Gray left—almost fifteen months ago.

He rose from the bed and stripped naked. He stepped in front of the dresser mirror to have a look at himself. He was losing weight, living on TV dinners, Wheaties, garbage burritos and pound cake. If it weren't for the fact that he ate so frequently at Jeannie's, he'd probably have died by now of malnutrition. His eyes were bloodshot and he hadn't even finished the joint. He needed a good night's sleep. On his forehead he wore a tiny pale scar—the mark of Cain, he called it—that he'd acquired bashing his head on a rock, leaping free of that damn rattlesnake. He locked his bedroom door and put his helmet on. Moving closer to his reflection, he studied the HEADHUNTER. Half of the two middle letters had been chipped away. Much of the helmet's red paint was smudged pink. When he was a freshman—he hadn't known anything when he was a freshman—he thought the streaks of pink paint on a helmet were indicative of fierce collisions on the football field. There was evidence on his helmet of Butte gold and Bozeman blue. There was some white, too, from Missoula or Anaconda, he didn't know which. Some paint smears actually did result from hits; but mainly they were collected during Wednesday afternoon psyche sessions, when the team beat their helmets against the locker doors.

Beowolf reached under the face bars and pulled the cap off his tooth. This was how he looked during a game. Mean, lean and hungry. His original tooth had darkened and died after being knocked loose when he was a freshman. The dentist did root-canal work and tried to bleach it at first, but the discoloration showed through anyway. Ultimately, he had to file the tooth down and fit it with a removable cap. Beowolf removed the helmet. Without the helmet on, with his uncapped tooth, he looked like the village idiot. He fitted the cap back into place.

After Thanksgiving he would grow his hair down to his navel and not give a damn what anybody said or thought.

He stepped carefully into his jock. "We call those things *marblebags,*" Jeannie told him once. He pulled a T-shirt over his head and sat down on the bed. He flexed his legs, rubbing his hands over the ridges of muscle. He examined the two cross-shaped scars on his calf where Bigfoot had made incisions with his fishing knife over the fang wounds so that he could suck out the venom. Against the grain his fingers grazed the stubble of his ankles—his legs were shaved up to his calves. He rubbed one of the brown blotches of accumulated Tuf-Skin, which Porkbutt sprayed on prior to each taping, until the oversized freckle peeled off like a layer of dead skin. His ankles looked diseased. He examined his big toes. By mid-season these toenails always fell off. They would turn black first, gradually come undone from the skin, and finally just rip off along with a sock. His toes were black where the toenails had been. He touched his groin. It felt okay. He pulled his sweatpants on and tied them at the waist.

He ran through all seasons, through all crises, through all

moods. Running stretched his legs, which had a tendency to cramp up on him, and it helped him to fall asleep. He was, by nature, not a very good sleeper. He liked his legs. He liked them very much. They were the best part of his body. With the exception, of course, of the kielbasa in between them.

Beowolf finished lacing up his sneakers, slipped into his hooded sweatshirt and took two joints from his top dresser drawer. He glanced out the window. Two months earlier Jeannie had helped him tack up see-through plastic over the windows of the house to keep out the draft. During the day, the plastic dirtied the sunshine and blurred the view, which wasn't much to begin with: highway and wheat fields out front and wheat fields out back. At night, the outside was tinted even darker than it actually was, making it seem weird, out of this world, as if the house had fallen into an aquarium twenty thousand fathoms deep.

"The house is going to hell," Jason had said at supper.

"Yeah," Beowolf replied. "I'm gonna paint it next summer." He had no intention of painting it next summer or ever.

The cold air jumped him the moment he opened the back door. He jerked the hood over his head and tied it in place beneath his chin, and as he began jogging down the driveway, loosening up, he found himself quite unaccountably happy, this night, to be out of the house running. The wind cut into his eyes, prying at crusty tears. He clutched the two joints inside the sweatshirt's front pouch, padding along, inhaling the chill and feeling very much alive. The night was clear and frosted by tiny stars, the highway brightly illuminated by a full moon with a yellow halo around it. Venus was low on the horizon, shining brighter than the other, more distant stars, which somehow seemed more permanent and real. There was a halo around Venus, too. Bad weather coming on. But it might not affect the game at all, Kalispell being west of the Divide.

His groin felt tight, so he eased along, not pushing it at all, just easing along. His legs needed the work. They hadn't been getting it in practice, so they needed it now. He was beginning to warm up, still feeling fine and mellow with his face so frozen it hurt to smile. In the distance was the light from Jeannie's house.

"You're crazy to be running in this cold," she said. "Especially with your—your *thing.*"

"My what?"

"Come in, come in. It's freezing."

"What's freezing?"

Beowolf was enveloped in the warm kitchen smell. Their kitchen always smelled of stuffed Sunday, like this was where he belonged, like home. Ever since Pap died last Good Friday, Jeannie's house had truly become for him as much of a home as his own house. On more than one occasion he'd spent the night on the couch in the den when going home would have been too lonely. Everything here was relaxed and comfortable with Jeannie cooking and sitting close beside him, Eric offering him a cold can of beer and talking football. Beowolf felt adopted. Upstairs was Jeannie's mother's haunt. She was a timid hypocondriac who seldom appeared. Sometimes it seemed to Beowolf that Jeannie was more of a wife to Eric than her mother was.

Beowolf heard the TV in the living room. *"My what?"* he asked again.

Jeannie glanced over her shoulder toward the living room, then prodded him backward beside the refrigerator, where she kissed him. "Your injury. Your thing." Beowolf felt her hand slip coolly beneath his jock; her moods had become so unpre*dict*able. She kissed him again and said, "Your thing."

"I told you, that's not my groin. Last time I pulled *that*"—he glanced down her arm—"was before I knew you."

Jeannie laughed as she removed her hand. Beowolf was left staring into her cool blue eyes, then she turned away.

"Do you want a cup of hot chocolate?"

"No. I gotta run. But I'll be back later, okay?" He kissed her and left.

Back on the highway whatever brief happiness had gripped Beowolf earlier lost its hold completely. The wind was strong enough to throw him off balance several times, nearly tripping him up. He watched the sky for flying saucers. Eric had seen them hovering over the Missouri River within spitting distance of the Air Force base. Eric believed that the saucers were related to the recent outbreak of cattle mutilations, that extraterrestrials were studying earthly anatomy, paying particular attention, for obvious reasons, to reproductive organs—which all sounded to Beowolf like something out of *Monsterland Movie,* which Eric faithfully watched on TV every Saturday night. The cattle mutilations were hardly a local phenomenon. For years now they had occurred not only throughout the western United States, but apparently throughout the world. Even in Russia. Until they began happening in Cascade County, however, nobody from Rawlings could have given a shit.

Turning off the highway, Beowolf saw in the distance the smoke streaming from the stovepipe above Wavy's shack. The wind had swept away the stench, so it was possible to chew the cud with Wavy for as long as he cared to. At the door of the shack he hesitated, running in place. He hadn't stopped by since the Anaconda game. His fingers passed over the joints. He knocked on the door.

"C'mon in, youngblood," Wavy cried. "Hurry up! No Eskimo well-digger's ass ever held a candle to this." Wavy glanced up at the moon. His teeth clicked several times together, either because of the cold or simply because his mind was working. "Moondog too." He pushed the door shut and shivered. "Ya seen the moondog?"

Beowolf nodded.

"Badass weather comin. Siddown, youngblood, siddown. Where ya been holin yourself up? Bigfoot says ya turned hermit, says ya won't go out or nothin since ya got hurt gainst Anaconda." Wavy returned to his stool by the stove, where he'd been reading his Bible by lamplight. His Bible was the kind a little kid might have, with color pictures and halos over the good guys.

Beowolf shrugged. "I'm out right now."

"Well, shit, youngblood. Ain'tcha got more sense than to be out on a howlin night like this?"

A body couldn't win. "I was itchy," Beowolf told him. "And I wanted to bring you something. It's a present." Beowolf opened his fist to expose the skinny treasures.

"Whoooo-babe!" Wavy cried. "Do your duty, youngblood." When he swung the stove door open, Wavy's sleepy turtle-eyes flickered in the glow of the fire. His teeth clattered. Beowolf licked a joint and held it to the heat. He inhaled deeply and handed it to Wavy.

"Whoooo-boy, you is a piece-ah work, youngblood! You is a piece-ah work!" The reefer tip lit up bright orange against Wavy's brown face as he sucked in and clenched his teeth. "*Yessss,*" he exhaled. "You is a piece-ah work."

Taking another drag, Beowolf felt the weed already having its sport, rushing like a ghost downstairs, upstairs and all through the attic that was his head. He passed the joint to Wavy and took off his sweatshirt. Wavy's chest expanded, drawing in the good herbs.

"Man, you got a good set of bagpipes for someone within sniffin distance of ninety."

Wavy exhaled. "Yeah, I din wear em out the way you're doin, runnin all the time. Why you run so dang much, youngblood? You awways runnin."

"Fuck slow, run fast. Always sit near the door."

Wavy slapped his knee and laughed so hard it looked like his teeth might fall out. Sometimes they did.

"That's what Jason says," Beowolf informed him. He took the joint from Wavy and inhaled, a warm cloud of faintness gathering in his head. He stared at the joint and thought of Helen the Bod's milk-chocolate-colored nipples: like toadstools with the heads clipped off, standing at attention in the moonlight. A true dream girl, Jason maintained, would be five eight, 38–24–38, blond, blue eyes, gorgeous alabaster tits, and a soft, tight pussy. She would spread her legs for you, and when you were done she'd turn into an ice-cold six-pack.

"Naw," Beowolf said. "I dunno why I run. I must fuckin like it or I wouldn't do it. Sometimes I just glide along, not thinking, not even knowing how good I feel." He sucked on the joint and stared at Wavy, now battling a grave sensation twisting tight in his cerebrum. Stoned again. STONED AGAIN was what it said on the T-shirt that Jeannie had given him at the beginning of the season. Thereafter, the PROPERTY OF RAWLINGS RATTLERS T-shirt that he'd worn for three seasons under his shoulder pads for games was used during practice only, so that he could wear STONED AGAIN, inside-out, in its place. Beowolf exhaled. "To tell the truth, I'd rather be in town playing eightball with Bigfoot." He stared at Wavy. His body went rigid. The hairspring of tranquillity abruptly snapped. He stared at Wavy.

Sometimes when he was stoned, Beowolf would come apart at the seams and his soul would kick free of his inner fuzziness to focus on him from some remote, unobstructed distance a glaring hot scrutiny, as if he were nothing but a puny biology specimen—nothing more nor less than that Russian Pavlovski's dog—and his soul, this estranged sensibility observing him so critically, would threaten to abandon him forever, to evaporate into thin air, leaving him panic-stricken and alone, a mechanism incapable of making up its own mind.

"Whatzamatter, youngblood? Look like ya seen a ghost." Wavy laughed and glanced at Beowolf's hand. "Don't bogart that joint, youngblood."

Beowolf flicked the ash and rubbed it into the floorboards with the toe of his sneaker. He passed Wavy the joint, seeking to regain his lost equilibrium.

Wavy's shack was so small that, without much effort and from any location inside, you could spit on any wall. It was eerie in the lamplight—like Wolf DeViscera's torture chamber on *Monster-land Movie*. JFK, Martin Luther King, Jesus H. Christ and RFK all stared vacantly out from the gloom. Crucifixes were strategically situated on the walls, making it impossible, if a body had his headlights on, to avoid having one within immediate sight.

"One thing you don't have to worry about, Wave, is vampires."

Wavy exhaled. "I don't wanna hear bout no monsters," he said.

Wavy believed that everybody was haunted. He, for instance, was haunted by Pap, as were several other people. Wavy believed that Pap's ghost had more than a little to do with Rollo getting gunned down in October. "The dead can't hurtcha," he'd said at the time, "but they sure can make ya hurt yourself."

Beowolf took a hit off the joint and passed it back.

There are three things a man should do in his lifetime. At least that's what Pap always said. Kill a man, have a son and write a book. By the time he was twelve, Beowolf knew it was all a lot of phone-bone. But when he was younger his eyes would widen, listening, and he'd whisper: "Did you kill a man, Pap?"

Pap would answer, "Yup." He'd grunt and spit and say, "Killed a man awright. Fact, I killed several men. Here, lemme show ya." Pap sprang off his rocker and plunged through the front doorway like Bronco Nagurski, whom he was always telling about. Beowolf waited on the porch.

Pap returned with his double-barrel twelve-gauge. "See them notches on the stock?"

Beowolf nodded.

"Well, whattaya think they're doing there? Hitchin a ride?" Pap spat an amber stream over the porch railing—a poof of dust burst like gunsmoke from the earth.

That was the first Beowolf could remember of the notches. But the scene recurred innumerable times after that, the only variation being the occasional substitution of a Bowie knife, a horsewhip or a pistol as the prop. Then, the summer before last, Rollo confiscated all of Pap's weapons after Pap went gunning for a Hollywood director who, in the course of shooting his western in Rawlings—Rawlings, he claimed, was "the last great western American town" —also shot thirteen wild mustangs that had been accidently stampeded by a helicopter into a barbwire fence. The notches began appearing in less congruous places—the kitchen table, for example. "Ya kill somebody today, Pap?" Beowolf asked, arriving home from practice one day. "Knock him over the head with this table?" Pap didn't answer, just sat there stewing in his own juice. He would sit for hours at that table or down in his Bum Steer corner, staring into space with, Beowolf knew now, murder in his heart.

"Wuddja kill em for?" Beowolf would ask when he was young.

"*Why?* Why, cause they treaded on me, boy! Yup. Wuddja spect? There's two things ya don't do in this world: ya don't argue with a locomotive and ya don't tread on Bad News. I pulled their picket-pins, boy, put em to bed with a pick 'n shovel—with a prairie dog for a mailman! Ha! Yup! So's I'm the one doin the treadin now!" Pap slapped his own ass with both hands and ripped off a rebel battle cry—"*EEEeeee-Haaaaaah!*"—then he commenced howling.

"Wow!"

"An I'll tell ya somethin else, boy. Before *I* kick—an I'm gonna kick like a hog-wild mule so help me God!—Goddammit! *I ain't gonna kick period! How-Woooooo!*" Beowolf cowered as Pap, on the warpath, danced madly around the porch. "I'll write that damn book too!" Pap finally proclaimed. "Yup. Whatcha call my mem-wires. *How-Woooooo!* Gonna call it *The Book of Bad News. How-Wooooooooooooo!*"

Sitting on the front porch a couple of years later, Beowolf asked skeptically, "Y'ever go to jail, Pap?"

"No jail could hold me, boy!"

"But did y'ever get arrested?"

"For what?"

"For *murder.*"

"Hells bells, boy! Course not! I got medals for killin them skunks. They were lowdowns, boy, ever last one of em: rustlers, an robber barons, an murderin, thievin, ass-scratchin skunks, an weren't-worth-a-good-goddamns, boy. Yup. They give me medals for killin them skunks." Pap sprang off his rocker and Bronco Nagurskied through the front door to retrieve his medals.

Wavy exhaled a thick cloud of smoke, which tinted the lamplight like dust captured in a moonbeam. "Whatzamatter, young-blood? Your eyes're narrower than two piss-holes in snow. Whatchew lookin at?"

Shaken from his reverie, Beowolf snorted. He took the joint from Wavy. "Thinkin bout Pap killin that guy."

"Killed'm awright, killed'm dead. Saw it with my own two eyes, youngblood. They was drunk, youngblood, mean drunk—the scabs, I mean, not Pap—though Pap *might've* been drunk too for all I could tell—it's a safe enough bet—though he had a prizefight next day . . ." Wavy mused. "Never stopped'm before . . . Drunk or no drunk, to do what he did, from so far off—fact is, it's a dang sight more markable if he *was* drunk—that shot he took.

"I was bound and gagged, youngblood, when he caught up to em —on the riverbank right out there." Wavy jerked his head toward the river. "Yep. I was ready for a dip into the Great Beyond."

"Legget?" Beowolf asked. "The guy's name?"

"You got it, youngblood. He was a devil."

Wavy took the joint from Beowolf and, as he inhaled, gave Beowolf a penetrating glance, reminiscent of the one he'd displayed last spring when he first informed Beowolf that Pap actually did once kill a man—one of the Anaconda Mining Company's scabs who torched Pap's saloon.

"You wait till now to tell me this?" Beowolf had screamed. "I wanted to know! You wait till after he's dead?"

"That's *exactly* what I was waitin for, youngblood!" Wavy exclaimed. "Doncha see? He was on trial for murder."

"He was acquitted."

"That don't mean who done it or who didn. I got eyes. I—"

"It was half a century ago!" Beowolf cried. "They can't put you on trial again. That's double indemnity or somethin."

"I dunno nothin bout double demnity. All I know is the hang-man."

"And I thought he was such a bullshitter saying he killed a man."

"Oh, youngblood, he *was* a bullshitter," Wavy assured him, complicating matters further. "He couldn *remember* killin the man. Very next day he got his clock cleaned by Leland Tyrone in a boxin match. Why, Pap had more wind than a fatass buffalo goin uphill."

But Beowolf had not wanted to hear any more. Slamming the door of the shack, he'd left Wavy absolutely flabbergasted.

"What diff'rence does it make?" Wavy had called after him. "What diff'rence does it make?"

None, now he was dead.

Wavy exhaled and handed Beowolf the joint. "Legget was a devil, youngblood. They burned the Ringside cause the union held meetings there. Then they headed out here to burn the barn— purely for spite, the barn bein where the dogfights were held." Wavy's eyes, points of light in the perpetual twilight of his home, studied Beowolf toking up. His choppers clattered, bone on bone. "Legget was snick'rin, youngblood," he continued. "He had me all tied up and he give me a shove, snick'rin *'Jest like a nigger to go swimmin with his hands tied behind his back.'* That's what he said. And jest then"—Wavy took the joint from Beowolf but didn't pause to toke up—"jest then I catch a glimpse of his snick'rin Lucifer's face ripped clean off with buckshot, as if God Awmighty himself wiped it with a thunderbolt."

Wavy sucked on the joint, the tip instantly alive, fierce orange in the darkness.

"And it was Pap?" Beowolf asked.

"It was Pap awright. An don't go thinkin he did it cause he gave a dang bout the union. He didn know a Wobbly from a sidewinder. He blew Legget's lamp out and sent the rest of them skunks scur-ryin cause Anaconda, jest cause they owned the whole blessed state, thought they could tread on him. Anaconda thought they could tread on Bad News."

"Pap killed a man."

"An saved the life of one," Wavy mentioned, snuffing out the joint.

"Keep it," Beowolf said, indicating the roach, which Wavy pocketed. "Wanna smoke this other number?"

"Do a buffalo dump on the prairie?"

Beowolf opened the stove door and lit the joint. He passed it to Wavy.

"It was cold, youngblood," Wavy eventually continued. *"Real* cold. But don't go thinkin he dove into that river to fish me out cause he gave a dang bout a poor nigger's life. Till the day he died, if ever I set foot in the Bum Steer, he'd come up to me and say, *'Disappear, nigger.'* He didn like havin me around. Not cause I reminded him of somethin he wanted to forget—he'd long since forgotten it, thanks to Leland Tyrone. He jest didn like niggers. But I'd grant'm that. He saved my life.

"He saved my life I dunno why—maybe he was drunk. I think he prob'ly was. Or maybe he jest awways wanted to save a body's life, even if it was jest a nigger's. Maybe it was the same as how he awways wanted an excuse to kill somebody, *even himself* if he had to. Jest on principle."

6

Everybody always said that Pap would drink himself to death, and on Good Friday he abruptly fulfilled their prophecy by downing a shot of rattlesnake venom.

He'd been released from the drunk tank into Beowolf's custody only a few hours earlier, his face as raw as uncooked tenderloin, his front teeth missing. "Pap, you're a mess," Beowolf told him. "You can't even walk straight." The way he sprattled along, heading for the Bum Steer, made walking look like a lost art.

Pap didn't answer, just kept truckin along with fire in his eyes, raising a steady cloud of dust.

"Skip it this year, Pap, your mouth is all cut up. It ain't gonna work this year. Christ, will ya get the shit outta your ears and listen?"

But once Pap was set on doing something, the only way to stop him was to hogtie him or beat the shit out of him the way Rollo had done the night before.

"Don't your mouth hurt?" This was the wrong approach. "Shit, I'll pick up a bottle for you, anything you want, and you can soak your mouth at home. Don't go tonight—listen to me, man! *Just not tonight!*"

Beowolf couldn't understand it. He wanted to punch someone, he wanted to kill; his thoughts twisted and jerked. Rollo had refused to keep Pap locked up another night.

"He assaulted an officer," Beowolf had insisted. "You can get sent upriver for that."

"I was off duty," Rollo replied, glancing up from his paperwork.

"Then how did he wind up down here?" Beowolf persisted. "You arrested him."

"Citizen's arrest," Rollo grunted. "Your grandfather's a menace, kid."

"You were as drunk as him, you were fighting. He wasn't fighting with himself. Why didn't you citizen-arrest yourself? You clubbed him with a nightstick! Why don't *I* arrest *you* if you can arrest him like that?"

Rollo smiled, sweet and sour as yellow snow. "If you'd been there to arrest me, kid, I'd have arrested you. You're underage."

"I'm underage, yeah!" Beowolf railed. "And you're *fat!* So what? Why didn't anyone else arrest you? Dale says you couldn't have hit the ground with that sheriff's hat of yours given three tries. That's what everyone's saying about it. And you were swinging a goddamn nightstick!"

Rollo had turned scarlet. "Get out of here, kid."

"You cocksucker."

"What?"

Rollo started up from his desk. He grabbed the nightstick off the wall. "What did you say, Bailey?" He spat the name out the way a person spits out a mosquito. "How would *you* like to get locked up for the night?"

Beowolf didn't answer. It wouldn't do to be jailed with Pap on the loose. Not today. "You shouldn't do this," he said quietly.

Rollo marched up to him. "Get that old geezer out of my office," he commanded, even though Pap had already staggered out into the waning sunlight. "And you get out, too."

Greasing his bearings on rattlesnake venom was Pap's rite of spring: a Promethean gesture harmonized with nature's escape from Old Man Winter's full nelson. Buoyed by a spit and a snort and a belch and a fart, and to the metaphoric accompaniment of the sun sinking slowly in the western sky, he would raise the snakebite to eye level, pondering for a moment the unholy dram. Then he would silently toast the spectators, and with a flick of his baby finger and a flourish of his bony wrist, he would wet his ever-lovin whistle with gusto, to the mass amazement of the denizens of the Bum Steer Saloon.

Pap's stunt was the traditional kickoff of the Easter Weekend Rattlesnake Festival. Whether or not the dog- and cock-fights would be held this year, however, was a subject of much debate. Ranting wildly the previous night, Rollo had pledged to uphold the law by busting anybody involved in the fights, or betting, for that matter, on unlicensed horse races or anything else—he'd bust the whole damn town if he had to—which was why Pap finally busted *him.* Across the head with a beer bottle.

What redeeming social value Rollo had Beowolf did not know. Rollo had always been overzealous in his duties, overimpressed with his own authority, overfed by his wife; but having primarily contented himself, as Eric's deputy, with the persecution of adolescents, he had not been generally recognized, until he was elected sheriff, as the overbearing blowhard that he was. When Rollo was still a deputy, Eric once defended him to Beowolf. "Sure he's a sonofabitch," Eric conceded. "But I need somebody like Rollo, somebody easy to hate. If you can control him, you can put a sonofabitch to good use." But Eric had obviously failed to control him. It was incredible to Beowolf that the town had turned Eric out of office in favor of such an asshole.

Pap sat at his corner table nursing an Olympia and firing periodically into his spittoon while Miss Snake-Charmer slowly snake-danced across the Bum Steer's mahogany bar: hypnotizing, tantalizing, slowly shedding her skin. "Make my snake dance!" somebody yowled.

"Don't give it to him," Beowolf implored Dale. *"Please."*

Dale was a sawed-off contemporary of Pap's who looked like a mucus-slobbered bullfrog retched by a sick rattlesnake, reconsumed, reretched, reconsumed and finally reretched with a vengeance. "Got in a knock-down drag-out fight last night with a man name Jack," he would tell you. "Yeah, Jack Daniels." In 1930 he'd bought the charred remains of the Ringside and reconstructed it in Pap's image, in Pap's *aura* rather: adorning it with pictures of Pap, moose and buffalo heads, shotguns (ON SALE), assorted Indian weaponry and various rusted animal traps.

"He's gonna kill himself if he drinks that stuff," Beowolf insisted. "Look at his mouth. Look at him, *will you?"*

Pap squinted at Miss Snake-Charmer. He hadn't even washed his face from the night before. It was swollen and scraped and caked with blood. With his middle teeth broken, his fangs hung like stalactites from his upper gums.

"I mean, look at him, man!"

"If he wants it, he's gonna get it," Dale adamantly replied.

"It's gonna kill him."

"Man wants to die, that's his business. If he wants it, he's gonna get it."

Beowolf pushed his way through the crowd gaping at Miss Snake-Charmer, pushed his way through to Pap's corner. "Pap," he said. "Come on, let's go home." Pap ignored him. Beowolf laid a hand on his shoulder and the man exploded. *"Will you leave me be?"* His eyes burned deep into Beowolf's.

"Ya know somethin?" Beowolf said. "You ain't got a lick a sense." He walked away to lean against the pinball machine.

> Don't lose your cool
> If this pinball machine tilts.
> If you had five balls,
> You'd come unbalanced too.

Taped to the upper corner of the scoreboard, the sign was brown from tobacco juice. Pap spat on it every once in a while for a change of target. He hated the machine; only way to beat it was to pull the goddamn plug. Periodically, Dale would scrub up the dried rivulets that ran south over the machine's go-go girls. "Fuck it then," Beowolf said to himself. He fished a dime out of his pocket and shoved it into the slot.

When the bare-bummed sidewinder on the bar finally succumbed to that customary panic of hers, which mounted in exact proportion to her display of untanned flesh, she streaked through the clutches of the saloon's inmates and through the swinging doors until next year—same time, same station. Having crescendoed, the hubbub fluttered about the barroom like a claustrophobic bat, finally disappearing altogether among the shadowed rafters. "Okay," Dale called out from behind the bar, "step right up!" Everybody gravitated toward the bar for a free shot of home-brewed giant-killer. Miss Snake-Charmer, admittedly, was a tough act to follow. Beowolf tilted and the lights went out. No balls left.

Above the bar revolved a clock in the shape of a beer keg, its Olympia label prominent in the front window as well, along with the arterial message forever whispering past the gas pumps and across the highway, whispering through the twilight to the wheat fields: *It's the water.*

What's the water? Beowolf wanted to know. The stuff of life? He had read that the human body was 85 percent water, leaving a 15 percent margin of mystery. Pap's body was 85 percent Olympia and Bum Steer panther-piss. The mystery was how he'd lived so long.

Once upon a time Pap built the Ringside Saloon. He'd been Bad News Bailey in those days, a bronc-buster and prizefighter. Spanning the Bum Steer barroom were amber-tinted boxing photos and promotion posters. Dale had treated them with chemicals to retard their aging and had framed them in handsome shellacked bark. From the front window of the saloon, along the side wall and across the rear wall, the pictures traced Pap's rise into prominence on the Montana boxing circuit, from a twelve-round KO in his first bout in 1919, through a long string of victories during the twenties, to his finest moment as a boxer: towering over the prone body of Leland Tyrone, the "Kalispell Cyclone." That first fight with Tyrone established him as the best fighter in Montana. Some claimed it nearly won him a shot at Jack Dempsey.

The mournful rhythm of a twangy country dirge began to throb from the jukebox, and with everybody jammed against the bar, Pap was alone in his corner sipping Olympia. Beowolf considered claiming a seat and trying once again to talk him out of it. But he knew it was futile. "Man wants to die," he said to himself, "that's his business." He didn't really believe that Pap would die. He crossed the barroom to the nether side of the shithouse door, where, alongside the purple neon fly-screen that electrocuted insects with a sharp hiss, the picture of Pap's rematch with Leland Tyrone hung. Tyrone was issuing a sharp right uppercut, the tail end of a whirlwind combination: Pap's head was snapped northeastward, his eyes bugged westward. There were still some old-timers who would claim to their dying breaths that Tyrone slipped something into his glove between the twelfth and thirteenth rounds—something like a horseshoe for good luck. Beowolf examined Tyrone's glove closely, as if, this time, he'd notice the faintly protruding outline of a blunt object. It was, as always, a waste of time. Others maintained that it was only because his saloon had been razed the night before and because he faced a murder rap that Pap lost the fight. But Beowolf never knew Pap to make excuses. If Pap believed that Tyrone had put something in his glove, he never remembered to complain about it; and if Pap had a good deal on his mind before the fight, he had nothing on his mind after the fight, because Tyrone's haymaker wiped his blackboard clean. The fight, needless to say, was lost; the purse of three grand was lost; and a good portion of Pap's sense was on the lam.

"Five bucks!" someone from the bar called out.

Pap nodded his head, acknowledging the bet.

Others, having downed their shot, began turning back to Pap, laying wagers on the Grim Reaper. There were, however, no true doubters. Seeing was believing, and it had all been seen many times before. The bets served merely as a collection plate for Pap.

The chairs around Pap's table were reclaimed as the crowd pressed into the back corner, penning Pap in. The plug was pulled on the jukebox. Gradually the bar grew silent.

Pap hemmed and hawed and farted and drank, hemmed and hawed and spat and stank, and finally, revved up, snorted like a bull moose and began milking the death-defying holiday for all its bloody worth. It never ceased to amaze Beowolf that in spite of Pap's tangleweed brain, to his Good Friday congregation, he was an enthralling jawsmith. Having preached his bone-rattling tales of death in the Old West for two score of Good Fridays, his yarns had, in some sentimental niche in the collective imagination of the town, incrustated like a radiant patina on a fine old saddle, providing that same timeless quilt-and-fireplace reassurance that the wives and kids acquired back home watching *The Wizard of Oz* while baking cakes and brownies for the big Easter bake-off. "He puts his money where his mouth is," was how Dalc explained it. "Which tends to make a body *wax* whatchacall *eloquent.*"

As Pap began telling about Meriwether Lewis and the Northwest Passage, Beowolf sauntered up to the bar and swiped himself a bottle of Oly. He leaned against the bar and gazed across the back wall. In the middle of Pap's boxing career there was a central photograph. It was larger than the boxing shots, larger than life itself by virtue of its subject: Pap standing toe to toe with a grizzle bear. It was slightly blurred—snapped on the run, the old-timers claimed. Bullshit quite possibly, but the picture and the legend behind it had nonetheless gnawed deeply into Beowolf's conception of things. The bear was pawing its eye because that's where Pap spat: he'd said, *I'm gonna find me a grizzle bear and spit in its eye* and that's what he'd done and the photograph was hanging there to prove it, prove that Pap spat point-blank in the eye of a grizzle bear.

Pap had sunk into a lonely sort of reverie, narrating the visions flickering through his brain. "The Sioux, the Cheyenne, the Dakotas, the Tetons," he was saying, "the Crow, the Blackfoot"—with an incantatory cadence summoning visions of the long-lost tribes that had lived off the buffalo. Beowolf returned his attention to the grizzle bear. He sipped his beer. He felt better now about Pap drinking his poison. It seemed that with all these people watching, nothing bad could happen. Pap's voice flared up. "Injuns!" he cried. He war-whooped and leapt to his feet flapping his arms wildly and dying a thousand deaths as he re-enacted how Custer celebrated the nation's centennial with Crazy Horse and Sitting Bull. Fatigued by this display, his tone sank to a somber key. Collapsing back into his chair, he began telling about Chief Joseph and the attempted exodus into Canada of the Nez Percé Indians —"the harmless-est redskins that ever walked the earth. Knew one myself. Used to wonder where was all the wild meat. He was a drunk, lived up Hill 19. I used to tell'm, *dead.*"

By the time Pap got on the subject of the Anaconda Mining Company, he had worked himself up into another lather. "And they strangled anybody that got in their way!" he roared, strangling himself until he gagged. "They strangled everybody!" He released his grip and continued: "They shanghaied farmers from the Dakotas and Minnesota and Indiana and Chicago into coming out here. Go west, they said. Go west! They told em it was like a garden of paradise. Garden of paradise, *my ass!*" he sneered. "More like a desert," he snapped. "And after they tricked all these folks into coming out here, after the crop failures and famines and all the labor trouble working for Anaconda—them, them *Commies!*— these Montana folk hankered to give Horse Greeley a good swift kick in the chops." The saloon busted up laughing. "And—and— and," Pap stuttered, his needle stuck, waiting for quiet. "And give," he finally got out, "the Anaconda Company somethin worse!" Pap's arm shot up in a *fungoo* gesture and the crowd roared its approval.

"Hey, ace," somebody said to Beowolf. Beowolf turned around. It was Bigfoot. "Gimme a hit of that beer." Beowolf handed him the beer. "He's beat up bad."

"I tried to talk him out of it."

"He's gonna kill himself."

"Naw."

"One of these days he will," Bigfoot said. "One thing ya gotta give him though. The man's got hairs." He hustled his balls, giving Beowolf a meaningful look.

"Hell," Beowolf said. "For all we know that stuff might not be rattlesnake venom at all. Who's gonna taste it and find out? Dale,

he's just an Old West jocksniffer. How do we know he milked a
rattler and not just a fifth of gin?"

Pap was talking about Moon now. "And this buffalo-assed bird,
an eagle, come along and shits right on his head. But," he added
after a moment of silence, *"he was wearin the hat!"* The crowd
chuckled as Pap launched into his spiel on good luck and bad luck.

"I don't see why Pap gets off so much on the subject of Moon,"
Bigfoot said. "I mean, they ain't much alike."

"No, they ain't," Beowolf agreed. "But *he* don't know it." Beowolf shifted uneasily. "Besides, he's not so high on Moon anymore
—ever since that Bull Run with Gray last summer." Beowolf
jerked his head, abruptly disconcerted. "I don't know what goes
on in his head. He called driving the bus his *duty* last season—until
Moon canned him. He's crazy. I think he just likes to tell that story
about the bird and Moon's hat. I don't think he believes anymore
that Moon's gonna save the world."

"You see a snake is a snake and a rattler is a rattler," Pap was
explaining. After Moon there was nothing he could ever think of
to say, so he'd fill the thought-gap with extemporaneous ravings
until Dale brought him his hemlock and a cold Olympia chaser.
"And a rattler, goddamn, a rattler'll kick ass from here to hell and
Kalispell, yup. Duck's on the pond, that's for sure. And a dog's a
man's best friend. *Miiiid-niiiight!"* he yowled. A shiver raked like
a paw down Beowolf's spine. Midnight was Pap's old fighting dog.
"Miiiid-niiiight!" The crowd began to shuffle and chuckle rest-
lessly. They made way for Dale. Beowolf's ears were pricked for
another yowl. But it never came. Dale laid the tray down before
Pap.

"I'm getting a better look," Bigfoot said. He pushed his way into
the crowd, guzzling Beowolf's beer. Beowolf stared at the backs
of the people, watched Bigfoot get swallowed up except for his head
—Mohican cut—and shoulders, which rose well above the crowd
as he worked his way slowly toward Pap's corner. Beowolf imagined Bigfoot grabbing the shot of venom and flinging it to the floor,
or perhaps even swallowing it himself. But he knew it wasn't gonna
happen. "Man wants to die," Beowolf said to himself, "he's got the
right to die." He didn't think Pap would die. Not in a million years.

Pap rose. Beowolf could see the white crown of his head. He
glanced around the barroom: in a handful of seconds he followed

Pap's rise and fall as a boxer, he watched him spit in the eye of a grizzle bear. Pap's head dipped suddenly back and Beowolf knew it was over. "He ain't swallered it yet!" some idiot cried out. "Look! He ain't swallered it!" The man was shushed.

An hour later, Pap turned red, white and blue, and keeled over. He died with his boots on.

7

In the dark, Hap was gazing at his *Playboy.* Bigfoot was sleeping like a baby. Beowolf studied his hands. There was the game to think of, he should be thinking of the game. He had bitten his fingernails down too far.

Until this season, Hap and Beowolf had been close companions. For three years they had competed against each other for a single starting position on the team without any lessening of their friendship. In retrospect, this struck Beowolf as extraordinary. Competition among the Rattlers was keen, and despite the team's ostensible camaraderie, rivals tended naturally to steer clear of each other off the field.

Beowolf won the split-end position their junior year; and while Hap resumed his position on the bench, Beowolf proved to be a capable performer. At the beginning of the present season, when Beowolf found himself reluctantly transferred to the defensive team, where a safety was needed, Hap inherited the split-end position, establishing himself immediately, to the surprise of everybody, as one of the premier pass receivers in the state. During the first half of the season he seemed destined to win All-State honors.

Surfacing simultaneously with Hap's talents, however, was Beowolf's perception that what he alone had earned, Hap had been given. As a safety, Beowolf was overshadowed by MD. Had he remained at split end, where he had played all of his life—and with Frankie Dimitruk now at quarterback—he would have been a shoo-in for All-State. He was better than Hap and everybody on the team knew it! That he had been cheated in the juggle of personnel was obvious. Yet he knew Hap wasn't to blame.

Beowolf could recognize his own pettiness for what it was and he could assure himself, as he had been assured by Coach Rose, that switching positions was a personal sacrifice that, in the long run, had strengthened the team. But what he knew could not override what he felt, and he felt that Hap possessed something that truly belonged to him. So at the precise moment they each succeeded, finally, in becoming a starter on the best team in Montana, a coolness settled between them, then an absolute frigidity, which only a warm rush of sympathy after the Anaconda game could thaw. And it was not Beowolf's resentment alone that led to their disaffection.

When she was in junior high school, Helen the Bod would walk home from school with Beowolf. Her name wasn't Helen the Bod in those days, just plain Helen. She had brown hair, complacent brown eyes, a blank face with a creamy complexion and a space between her front teeth. She was bigger than any of the other girls. She was bigger than Beowolf. And by virtue of being built so much like a grunt, she managed to put Beowolf very much at ease.

She was in love with Beowolf's knuckles in those days. Whenever they were scraped and swollen and caked with blood from playing Knuckles in the Boys' Room, she would beg him, walking home, for a closer look, and she would make him stop and stand still so that she could ogle them. "Do they hurt?" Beowolf would give her a look, *whattayathink,* and proceed to tell her *of course* they hurt, but that it was all part of the game. The only way to win is to force the other guy to quit, and the only way to do *that* is by knowing—even while the guy is rapping your knuckles with the deck of cards however many times he's entitled to—that every dog has his day and he who laughs last laughs best, because that guy would sure get what was coming to him when it was his turn to get *his* knuckles rapped. Helen was so in love with his knuckles that she would invite him over to her house to play Monopoly, just to steal a peek. Beowolf didn't like Monopoly much and he didn't much care for girls, but he enjoyed having his knuckles fussed over in front of Helen's brothers, who were all thumbs when it came to Knuckles.

In high school, while everybody else was growing up, Helen was growing *out,* until ultimately she sported the most prominent melons in town; and during that protracted period when Beowolf was languishing in his love for Jeannie, Hap was doggedly stealing his way under Helen the Bod's blouse, under her double-D bra, into her heart, and ultimately—incredibly!—striking paydirt in her pants.

For years Beowolf had desired nothing but to be loved by Jeannie. Everything he did seemed, in retrospect, to have been solely directed toward this end, though he certainly hadn't wished for things to happen as they had to Gray. After storming off the practice field that last time, Gray had flung his fist through the glass of the school trophy case, and when school, then police, authorities went looking for him, they found that he had not only skipped school, but had skipped town as well. His name was affixed to a select list of former Rattlers, THE QUITTER'S HONOR ROLL, which MD referred to as the Hall of Shame. People joked he hadn't belonged at Rawlings High School in the first place—his parents alive and well, living in Helena and all.

"Are you all right?" Beowolf would ask Jeannie when he saw her in the halls at school. After all, he had been Gray's only real friend. Before long he was taking her to the movies, and afterward they would drive to Buffalo Wallow to watch the river and talk about Gray. The weeks, the months and the football season passed, along with her period of obligatory mourning. For Christmas she gave him a book about himself, *Beowulf,* which he never read; and dancing at the New Year's Ball she exuded a freshness that seemed a season ahead of its time. Beowolf felt new himself. He'd had a good season and the world had opened its arms. Winter passed almost unnoticed, overshadowed by an affection that warmed and deepened as springtime faintly hovered in the air. Then Pap died.

For Beowolf, Pap's death had assumed an even greater significance than the death of his father. He couldn't explain why. But after Wavy informed him about Pap's having killed Legget, Beowolf realized that the heightened impact of Pap's death was not simply due to his own guilt at not having hauled his ass out of the Bum Steer. There was more to it than this.

As the days passed, Beowolf seemed to effortlessly gravitate into the center of Jeannie's gentle orbit. She cooked his meals and cleaned his house. "I love you," she finally told him. And as abruptly as this recent agony had gripped him, a joy he'd never before experienced swelled within him. He had nothing more to lose, everything to gain—nothing to lose but his virginity, which he lost soon enough at the cabin in Falls Falls.

Through May and June, through the summer, they made love as frequently as they pleased at Beowolf's house. Jason was in Missoula, where an alumnus had given him a job. Emerging from the locker room after Captain's Practice, Beowolf would feel strong and good, cool with his hair wet from the shower, and evening settling in. Jeannie would be waiting for him outside the door, and he'd embrace her so hard her back sometimes cracked; she'd gasp and cry out and laugh, flushed with color. There was nothing to say, only to do, to do. They would drive to his house. He wanted her always, to nestle in her hair, to never need to say anything but always have her around him in delicate, ecstatic counterpoise, their lives constantly surging together.

Summer Practice began and Jason came home one weekend. "You guys work harder than us," he observed to Beowolf after watching a practice session. "We got the whole weekend off." That night Jason went out on the town. By his own account the next morning, he happened into Helen the Bod down at Burgermaster's. "She ain't nothin to write home about, unless, of course, you grew up on a dairy farm." Jason cracked up at his own joke and for the briefest instant Beowolf despised him. "What a pair of udders!" Jason bellowed. "Size of milk pails!

"Cow's gotta get milked," he continued, a grin plastered over his face. "Field's gotta get plowed." And while Jason recounted how he'd hustled her off to the Big Sky Drive-In, where, during *The Texas Chainsaw Massacre,* he "threw a fuck into her," Helen the Bod metamorphosed as mixed pangs of revulsion and pity bit into Beowolf like something alive. She metamorphosed from that ignored detail of his past, *Helen,* the flat idea corresponding to the girl who had once taken such a shine to his knuckles, into a plump, wholly palpable object of appetite, as tempting and trifling as a ripe red apple. It was as if, because of Jason, Beowolf's sensibilities abruptly shed some final delicate vestige of innocence just as a newborn animal's eyes finally blaze through their milky haze to see the world for the first time as it really is. It dawned on him that she had, for years now, been eminently available to him.

"You still seeing that girl, Jeannie Todd?" Jason asked him.

"Yeah, why?"

"Been in her pants?"

Uncomfortably, Beowolf smiled.

"Well, have you or haven't you?"

Beowolf nodded.

"You bastard," Jason remarked in wonder. "My little fuckin brother. Well, you best say your good-bys unless you're planning to get shackled to her."

"I love her," Beowolf said hesitantly.

"*Love?* Love somebody when you're old, when you're thirty and no one else wants you. Love *anybody* now! Women are like buses, man. You miss one now, but there'll be another one by in an hour."

Summer Practice, the first in which Beowolf hadn't been forced to endure the agony of Bull Run, ended Labor Day weekend. Brimming with the hope and expectation of a magnificent season, Beowolf and Jeannie decided to seize this final opportunity to spend a weekend in Falls Falls; on Sundays during the season, Beowolf would have to stay in Rawlings for game films. Leaving the locker room after the final workout, Beowolf slapped Hap five in celebration of the fact that they were both now starters. Caught up in this wave of good feeling, he spontaneously invited Hap and Helen to come along to the cabin with them. "It'll be fun," he assured Jeannie as they waited in front of Helen's house. Jeannie gave him a puzzling, disconcerting look.

Lying on the sleeping bags before the fire that night, with Hap and Helen finally tucked away in the bedroom, Jeannie whispered: "I wish we hadn't brought them."

"I know," Beowolf answered. He held her against his body, rubbed her smooth ass. They had spent the evening drinking Oly and sipping Wild Turkey, playing hearts as partners against Hap and Helen, Hap growing progressively drunk and obnoxious as Helen kept trying, without success, to shoot the fuckin moon. Hap finally fastened his killer smile on her and said, "Your brain's as fuzzy as your cunt."

Helen sat stupefied. It was Jeannie who slapped him. "You always get so damn nasty when you're drunk. Why do you drink at all?"

Hap rubbed his cheek, looked bleary-eyed from Jeannie to Beowolf to Helen and back to Jeannie. He struggled to his feet, offered a ludicrously dignified "Good night" and stumbled into the bedroom, closing the door behind him.

"Poetry in motion," Beowolf muttered. He glanced at Helen. Hap could be such a prick.

Jeannie jumped to her feet. "Get out here!"

"Let him sleep alone," Helen softly protested. She smiled uncertainly at Beowolf, then said perhaps the funniest thing she'd ever said in her life. "You don't need a partner if you've got a good hand."

Beowolf keeled over onto his side, aware even as he did so that he was being keenly observed, not necessarily with affection. Jeannie was glaring down at him.

"Let me talk to him." He clambered to his feet and marched into the bedroom.

"Cut it out, will ya?"

"She's so fuckin stupid," Hap complained. He was staring out the window into the dark.

"Take her to bed, she's not so dumb. You pick at her."

"She's *dumb,* and you know it. She's got this big fuckin cavity in her head."

"*Ya can't fuck her brain*—that's what you're always saying."

"Fucking's got nothing to do with it."

Mildly disgusted, Beowolf studied Hap for a moment. He shrugged. "Well, she can't sleep out there with us."

Hap didn't reply.

"Jesus, Hap, break up with her then. You don't even *like* her."

Hap crossed his arms, shook his head. Beowolf could see now that he was really drunk, and ashamed.

"I'll send her in."

With Helen out of the way, Beowolf fed another log to the fire and laid his head in Jeannie's lap.

"Poor Helen," Jeannie said, gently stroking his temple and cheek. "They don't even *like* each other." Beowolf wrestled her down onto the sleeping bags, forcing her onto her back. She fought back laughing, trying to shove him off.

"Well," Beowolf replied as he pinned her, kissing her. "They're getting in some healthy fucking anyway."

Jeannie's body went limp. "Hooray," she said.

The season began. The Rattlers beat Butte and Billings East. The leaves on the trees along the riverbank began changing color. The harvest was over. Jeannie would rise early and walk to Beowolf's house almost every morning before cheerleading practice, sometimes when it was still half night. She would tiptoe into his bedroom, quietly undress and slip into bed beside him. Gently enticed from his dreams by the soft embrace of her full naked body, Beowolf would open his eyes to find her face gazing back at him. The week of the Bozeman game there was a brief spell of Indian summer, and Rawlings recorded their third straight shutout, extending their winning streak to twenty-three games. On Sunday morning, walking home from school after watching the game film, Beowolf spied Helen lounging in the hammock behind her father's barn, puffing on a cigarette.

Hap didn't like her, that was for sure. Even before becoming a minor celebrity over the first three weeks of the season, playing a position that didn't even belong to him, it was apparent that he did not like her. Now, with five touchdowns under his belt, he hardly acknowledged her existence, except when he was horny. "I'm horny," he announced periodically. "Need somebody to blow my horn."

Beowolf approached her quietly from behind. "You smoke too much."

She gasped. "You scared the hell out of me." She took a slow drag off the cigarette. Then she smiled. "How are you?"

"Awright. How're you doing?"

"I'm okay." She gazed at him as at an animal that might have wandered into her yard—a horse or a steer perhaps—not knowing quite what to expect. "So, how were the films?" she asked, drawing on her cigarette.

"Okay, okay."

"It was a good game." She smiled at him again, rocking languidly in the hammock. "You looked awful good."

"Thanks." Beowolf trained a wry smile on his face. "*You* look awful good." He jammed his hands in his pockets.

Her breasts shook for a moment as she laughed, then once again they began to heave rhythmically beneath her blouse, shifting against the lilting of the hammock. Her jeans clung as snugly as a Band-Aid to her thighs and hips.

"Is that all you ever smoke?" He gestured at the cigarette.

"What do you mean?"

"Y'ever blow weed?"

"No." She sounded defensive.

"Y'ever want to?"

"Do *you* smoke it?" she asked.

"Sure."

"Why? What does it do for you?"

"Gets you high, you feel good."

"It's bad for you."

"No more than that cancer-stick," Beowolf replied.

"I've never smoked it."

"Y'ever want to?"

"I'd try it, I imagine."

"When?"

"Anytime, I imagine."

"When?"

"Right now, if we can go someplace."

"How bout tonight?"

Helen swayed back and forth in the hammock. "You want me to come over?"

"Let's go out to the river," Beowolf suggested. "We'll go out to Buffalo Wallow. Nobody'll be there tonight."

"It'll be cold tonight."

"Won't be too cold. I'll bring blankets."

"What time?" Helen asked.

"How bout seven? I'll stop by."

Walking home, Beowolf felt exceedingly worldly and fluent, on the brink of something. He could not sit still in the house. From room to room he wandered, touching things, looking at things, gazing for a long while at a photograph of his mother. There was nothing to do alone in the house. He wandered outside onto the front porch. It was warm for so late in September. Impulsively, he marched down the steps and down the highway to Jeannie's house for lunch.

That evening, Helen proved to be true to Beowolf's image of her. Gazing over the river as they anxiously smoked the joint, scarcely speaking, Beowolf sensed that by simply touching her, when that inevitable moment arrived, he would set into natural motion that chain of impulses he so coveted. He glanced at her when they finished the joint.

"How did you like it?" he asked.

"I don't feel anything."

"The first time is hard."

Awkwardly, she smiled. Beowolf avoided her gaze by glancing at the river, a wave of anticipation shivering over him. Then he laid his hand on her thigh.

Afterward, as Beowolf rested on top of her, barely in a sweat while she clung shifting beneath him, his cock shriveled up, slinking away from her. Ultimately, she sighed. "Don't feel bad. You

did no worse than Hap . . . I figured you'd want to know that."
He *didn't* feel bad. "I don't wanna hear about Hap." He didn't feel
particularly *good* either. What he felt was a strange mingling of
pleasure abruptly chilled. He drew the blanket around them and
slid off to lie against her side. He wanted to go home.

With Jeannie it had not been like this.

Beowolf gazed for a moment through the darkness at the *Playboy* in Hap's lap; a cream-skinned beauty, laid open, gazed back.
Hap flipped the page. Outside the bus, the lights of Missoula were
rushing past, and it seemed to Beowolf suddenly that there must
be a mystery behind each one. People live two contrary lives. There
was the surface existence, the life a person reveals to the rest of the
world; but there was a deep, secret life also, a life that the world
never sees.

"Do you," Beowolf had asked Jeannie in the middle of the night,
that first time at the cabin, "ever think much of Gray?" Her back
was turned. Was she awake?

Her voice seemed to materialize out of thin air. "Yes."

Beowolf rolled her over, holding her against him. "Why didn't
you . . . you two ever?"

Jeannie looked into his eyes, patted back his hair, which had
grown long over the winter. "You'll have to cut your hair for
Spring Practice," she said.

"Why?"

"They'll make you, just like last year. You don't want to do Bull
Run again."

"Why didn't you?"

Jeannie sighed. "We almost did." She smiled at him tolerantly.
"You wouldn't get it."

"Am I stupid? Don't gimme that." Beowolf propped himself up
on his arm. He flicked her hair back from her face. "You loved him.
I know you loved him."

"He didn't love me," she answered.

"Why didn't he?"

"How should I know?" She shifted onto her back to look at the
ceiling. After a while she said, "He couldn't."

"Why couldn't he?"

"He couldn't because . . . he couldn't because he wasn't like
everybody else. You wouldn't know."

"Whattaya mean, I wouldn't know? I was his best friend."

"Don't interrogate me. You wouldn't know this."

"Know *what?*"

"He couldn't love *anybody,* that's all." She stared at the ceiling. "It wasn't just me. He couldn't love anybody."

"Did you sleep with him *ever?*"

"I told you, no." She turned to look at him. "Don't you believe me?"

"I just thought . . . I don't care. I just want to know."

Jeannie began to laugh. "Oh, you bullshitter!" She turned her back on him, still laughing. Beowolf laid his hand on her shoulder, but she wouldn't roll over. She stopped laughing and abruptly sat up, facing him, her breasts so firm and lovely. She reached over to gently hold his head in her hands, staring into his face, straightening it the way a person straightens a crooked painting. With mock severity she said, "No, I didn't sleep with Gray. Look at your sleeping bag." She threw back the quilt.

Beowolf did not want to look. "Why?" He looked. The fire was low, it was too dark to see. "What is it?"

"Blood."

"Blood? Is it okay? Are you all right?"

"Virgins bleed."

"Virgins bleed?"

"Yes. Virgins bleed."

8

During a practice the week of the Anaconda game, Beowolf and Hap got into a fight after they collided chasing an errant pass. Peckinpah ran them through the Tunnel of Love after practice until Hap couldn't continue, stopping in the middle of the tunnel. Beowolf stopped right behind him, hanging onto a girder for support. From the bleachers above them, Moon shouted "Let's go!" and they shuffled the rest of the way through. Moon made them shake hands—"Save it for Anaconda," he told them—and jog it in to the locker room.

In bed the next morning, Jeannie asked, "What's going on between you two?" She was lying on her side, her back to him.

"Nothing," Beowolf answered. "We had a fight."

"Why?"

"*What is this?*" he cried. "The third degree? We ran into each other."

"He keeps calling me up," she mentioned softly, still not looking at him.

"What about?"

"He talks, he's upset—I don't know what about. Last night he asked me out."

"That asshole."

"What's going on between you two? I don't need this right now."

"Why? What's the matter?"

"Nothing's the matter. I want to know what's going on."

"Nothing's going on."

"Why won't you tell me?" She wouldn't look at him. "You won't tell me something."

"It's all right," Beowolf told her. He reached over and squeezed her shoulder.

"No. It's not all right."

"What's wrong?" he asked.

Her body quivered.

"Jesus, don't cry," he said.

Jeannie rolled over and looked him in the face. "I'm not adjusting well."

"Adjusting well to what?"

"To life."

"*Life?* What are you talking about? What *life?*"

"Life, period. I'm afraid."

"Jesus."

Beowolf lay back, looking at the crack in the ceiling. "I'm insecure."

"*About what?*" Beowolf muttered, his eyes still fixed on the crack in the ceiling.

"Life. About life."

He looked at her. Her body was trembling. He hated this sort of shit more than anything. "Sorry," he said after a while. "Sorry I yelled." He reached out and rubbed her shoulder. "I'm sorry." He kissed her neck, then lay back again to look at the ceiling. "I've had a bad week or something. I don't feel right."

"I don't feel right either."

"You're *not happy?*" he asked sarcastically.

"I feel sick. I don't want to fight. I got sick yesterday."

"When?"

"After I left here. On my way to practice."

Beowolf was silent. "Sorry," he finally said.

"Why do you keep apologizing? *Why?*"

"I'm not apologizing."

"You just did."

"*I'm sorry you were sick!*" he cried innocently. "That's all."

"It wasn't your fault."

"Well, I'm sorry I apologized then! Jesus!" He threw his arm out angrily and rolled onto his side to face the faded roses on the wall.

"Go ahead, roll over."

"You did it."

"I didn't *roll over,* I was already over."

"A technicality."

"Do you love me?" she asked pointedly.

"Yes."

"Do you want me to be happy?"

"*Happy?*" he cried. He shot up into a sitting position and looked at her. "You act like happiness is a natural right."

"Yes!" she replied, sitting up as well.

"That's *pursuit* of happiness, not happiness . . ."

"You're not pursuing. You've stopped."

"It's life, liberty, and the pursuit . . ."

"You don't even try."

"Pursuit of . . ."

"Shut up."

"Pursuit of happiness."

"Shut up! Just quit it."

She threw back the covers and swung her legs over the side of the bed. And just as Beowolf reached out for her, she sprang away from him with her hand clamped over her mouth, running naked for the bathroom.

Beowolf had offered Rollo fifty bucks to keep his fat trap shut. When she saw the headlights coming, Helen had darted into the bushes. Beowolf was struggling into his pants when he was captured by the patrol car's spotlight. Over the car's loudspeaker Rollo's voice commanded him to "Hold it right there!" The spotlight passed over the bushes and into the water, then fixed on Beowolf once again.

Rollo got out of the car.

"Who you down here with, Bailey?"

"Nobody," Beowolf answered. "I doin somethin against the law? Swimming?"

"You ain't swimming," Rollo sneered. He nudged Helen's panties with his toe. "You a trans-scxyule, Bailey?" Rollo picked up Helen's bra, sniffed at it, and said, "Jesus, this ain't Jeannie Todd's." He began collecting Helen's clothes. "Go ahead," he said. "You ain't doin nothin illegal. Get dressed, go home."

"What're you gonna do with them?" Beowolf pointed to the clothes in Rollo's arms.

"I don't know. This—" Rollo held up the bra, trying to be funny. "I may send this to 'Ripley's Believe It or Not.' The rest . . . I'll find someone interested in the rest."

"Don't do that."

"Tell her to come out," Rollo ordered.

Beowolf picked up the army blanket and headed toward the bushes.

"Tell her!" Rollo abruptly raged.

Beowolf ducked into the bushes and wrapped Helen in the blanket.

"When I tell you to do something—God*dam*mit!—do it!"

"I'll give you fifty bucks, Rollo," Beowolf said, emerging from the bushes with Helen cringing at his side.

Rollo showed his teeth.

"That a bribe, Bailey?"

"Yes."

"Well, you best make it a good one then." He turned to Helen. "You got your tittie caught in a wringer, girl."

"I ain't got much money."

"Fifty bucks and her." Rollo nodded at Helen.

"I'll give you fifty bucks," Beowolf said again.

"I said, fifty bucks *and her.*"

"Rollo," Beowolf seethed. "Rollo, I'll give you fifty bucks and your fuckin life—*I'll kill you,* Rollo. You give me half a chance *and I'll kill you!*" And Beowolf meant it and, trembling with rage and hatred, perhaps would have done it right then if Rollo hadn't shrunk back, groping for his pistol. Rollo knew that Beowolf meant it; he knew then that Beowolf was Pap's fuckin grandson and that Beowolf already owed him one.

"Fifty dollars then," Rollo said agreeably, gripping the pistol.

But Beowolf had never given him the fifty. He never got the chance. Three days later, when he learned that Rollo had parked a .38 slug in his own fat ass, Beowolf almost believed in God again. Rollo had been making noise down at the Bum Steer about cracking down on the moonshine trade when, inexplicably, the pistol in his shoulder holster discharged. The bullet tore into the wallet in his back pocket, blew a hole through Abe Lincoln's head, richocheted off a Cascade County sheriff badge, and burrowed into his gluteus maximus. Writhing in the sawdust, Rollo had nobody to blame but himself. He was laughed out of town by sundown the next day, unheard of since. But before he left, he'd thought to tell Hap.

Beowolf never fucked Helen again. He didn't even want to see her. Why, he wondered, had he bothered with her in the first place? "There's *something* . . . there's something about you," he finally told her, angry and perplexed. "Just stop loving everybody. You've got this idea in your head, you think everybody's so—*I'm* so nice.

Well, I ain't! I shouldn't have done it and I'm sorry. Look what's happened!"

"What's happened?"

"Hap wants to kill me."

"Hap has no right . . ."

"Well that's good to hear!" Beowolf exclaimed. "That he has no right to kill me. Do you know he's started calling Jeannie?"

"He has no right to feel bad," she asserted.

"People feel bad whether they have the right or not. Just quit loving everybody. You're too nice. You're not doing yourself any favors . . ."

"I don't know who you're talking about," Helen quietly insisted. "Besides Hap."

"*Jason!*" Beowolf spat out at her. "Jason for one. How could you—*with Jason?*"

A look of fierce defiance snapped onto her face, an expression that Beowolf had never seen there. "I never did any such thing with Jason!"

Beowolf was stunned.

"Why?" she demanded. "Who said I did?"

The worst thing about Helen the Bod was that she did not matter. In the end, it didn't even matter that Rollo discovered them that night; or that Beowolf threatened to kill him; or that Rollo, out of pure malice, told Hap. Helen didn't serve as an explanation for the way things stood with Jeannie. Jeannie had forgiven him when he found, after the Anaconda game, that he could keep it to himself no longer. He'd been afraid that she would stop coming to his house; but she started coming more than ever, every morning and sometimes in the evening too, quietly, passively, never mentioning Helen, even though they spent two hours a day cheerleading together. After a time Beowolf realized that Jeannie didn't care about "the thing with Helen." It was he who cared about it. Jeannie had made it seem like nothing. And it *was* nothing—nothing compared with the thing that Jeannie, in the wake of his confession, finally found the courage to tell him.

Beowolf opened the window a crack. The night ripped past the bus. Winter coming on, sure as hell. In Rawlings, winter would last forever. Beowolf's thoughts kept slipping backward. This bus trip, this game, it was like the end of his life. He felt like a man condemned to witness his own life in a mish-mash of time sequences unreeling before his eyes: judged and judging, on the lookout for evidence of redeeming social value, reviewing his past as if history might truly hold lessons to be learned and a person wasn't innately a Chicken fuckin Little with a lopped-off head.

He should be thinking of the game, he told himself, of Earthquake Allen.

He nudged Hap.

"Ya know, I always hated Kalispell. I hate em worse than Anaconda, ya know?"

"They both eat shit."

Anaconda was not Hap's favorite topic of conversation. Had it not been for the Anaconda game, Rawlings would be playing tomorrow night for the State Championship.

The day of the Anaconda game had been anxious—not because of any concern over the Miners, who entered the game as decisive underdogs, but because of events outside of Rawlings and having nothing to do with football. An international crisis had bulled its way, as so rarely happened, into the consciousness of Rawlings, Montana.

The Sunday before the Anaconda game a big stink had been made in the papers because the President had fired some lawyer the night before. The papers were calling it the "Saturday Night Massacre," which sounded to the people of Rawlings as though it wouldn't be long before they made a movie of it—and not a very good movie at that, because the only *massacre* was the firing of this smartass, Archibald Cox, who would probably be played by Glenn Ford because weren't they just dead ringers for each other? It was a trough full of horseshit, was what it was.

In Rawlings, it was business as usual—until Friday morning, when the town awoke to the news that, just across the river, nuclear missiles were as erect as hard-ons at daybreak. Ostensibly, it all had something to do with another war in the Middle East. But the papers were screaming bloody murder. The President was off his rocker; he was distracting attention from his own problems. Who knew what to believe? The world had gone to hell in a handbasket, was all anybody knew.

After the game, at the Big Sky Drive-In, Beowolf got drunk with Hap, who burped in technicolor on the hood of some guy's car, and the guy wanted to bust him in the nose—only not really, because Hap went berserk, screaming at the guy to get his fucking ass outta the car and bust him one then. But the guy locked his doors instead, and he and his girl friend watched the pancake congeal on the hood of the car until the movie ended. The missiles were still up. Beowolf had a sleep and a dream: a falling dream, a groundrush dream, screaming as the earth lunged up at him. Jeannie, who'd shown up in the middle of the night, shook him awake and he puked in the bathroom and couldn't fall back asleep. He was hungover the next day when Jason rushed in and caused him to smile that horrible smile. And still the missiles were up.

The missiles went back underground Saturday night while Beowolf was at Jeannie's house in the den. That was when he told her about the night at Buffalo Wallow with Helen. That was when Jeannie told him, "Well, just guess what?"

"You said you were taking pills," Beowolf insisted.

"I was taking the goddamn pills."

The night streamed by.

Beowolf imagined her touch, her substance, and a wave of remorse swept through him. He pictured evening on the lake, the splashes of fish snagging night insects, the boat, the cabin, the fire inside. Jeannie with a full belly was sometimes a luscious image, lovely as May at the lake, inspiring in Beowolf that instinctive protectiveness that, had he let himself go—had he been capable of shucking those doubts and deliberations that burdened him—would have compelled him contentedly to her side. Yet the power of this instinct, this animal love, he seemed capable of sustaining only at odd moments: during evanescent daydreams or during lovemaking. Afterward, he would feel as he did watching her brush her hair in the early morning. She would wear one of his football jerseys after taking a shower: a quarter-moon of her ass would peek out as she tilted her head first to one side, then to the other, giving each half of her head seventy-five brushstrokes. When she finally removed the football jersey, her belly never showed signs of life. She would dress quickly and leave him lying there in bed, trying to fall back asleep for another hour. His soul, it would seem, had left him. He was as hard and hollow as the chrysalis of a butterfly.

Last night she'd told him that she couldn't see him after she returned from Kalispell. It had arisen out of nowhere—out of a goddamn hug he'd given her around the waist! She'd become so touchy lately! Eric entering the room quickly ended everything. Beowolf went home. In the morning Jeannie did not come. Beowolf lay in bed waiting for her, watching the clock and growing angry. At school he avoided her. Now everything was left hanging. It was ridiculous! After Kalispell, the whole problem would be gone. The season would be over and they'd have time again to do as they pleased.

It was all Gray's doing. Gray had been hanging around her while Beowolf was at practice. It was no secret. Jeannie had told him. "We talk," she said. He should have told her in the first place, when Gray first returned, that he didn't want her to see him.

There was the game to think of, but he couldn't concentrate. He'd studied Kalispell for two weeks now, yet didn't feel psyched for the game at all. He always felt self-conscious at the Wednesday psyche session before practice. It was the same every week. MD would give his usual spiel on "putting out," on giving 110 percent. Somebody would finally shout something like, "Let's lay these fuckers out!" and MD would begin bashing the trash can with his broken baseball bat, then everybody would assault their locker doors with their helmets. The chaotic pounding would settle into a powerful rhythm after a while, continuing for a length of time proportionate to the amount of respect they had for their Friday-night opponent. Finally MD would erupt from a teeth-gnashing trance to bellow "BEAT KALISPELL!" or whomever they were playing that week, whereupon the chant of *"Kick Ass!"* would be added to the thunder of helmets. Beowolf would find himself pounding his locker, chanting the familiar tune, careful not to scrape off whatever hard-earned HEADHUNTER letters he possessed, waiting to break free. He didn't dare glance down the aisle. He wanted to evaporate. To be observed by somebody equally self-conscious, chanting and screaming and beating his locker with his football helmet, would make him feel like an ass.

His first psyche session, sophomore year, had been traumatic. John Tinker, a middle linebacker who had taken over as captain from Jason, had stalked up and down the aisle like a Marine drill sergeant with a wild hair up his ass. Beowolf's heart was beating to the fervid cadence of *"Kick Ass!"* while his eyes from out of their corners glimpsed Tinker bristling up and down the aisle, blood boiling to *"Kick Ass,"* pounding backs and slapping heads. It took no genius later to figure out who MD, as captain, modeled himself after.

"Are you up?" Tinker screamed.

He collared Beowolf and spun him around. "Are you up?" Beowolf fumbled, the ungodly tear ducts instantly swelling. He couldn't respond. "Are you up?" It was too late now. He'd already blown his cue, by acting as if he'd been nabbed red-handed in some unholy crime. "Are you up?" Tinker's face was scorched red, veins burning through his neck. He gave Beowolf a shove, sending him crashing backward against his locker door.

"Are you up?"

Beowolf bellowed an animal cry as he leapt past Tinker for the door and the open air, "ARE YOU UP! ARE YOU UP!" reverberating through his head as if it were hollow and down to his soles, charging breathlessly toward the practice field with the rest of the team at his heels in a pack, cleats clattering a locust swarm of noise. They were after him! They would kill him!

But they didn't kill him. They were following him. He was leading the charge!

Moon liked his players to be sky-high by Friday. He wanted them to be hungry, to play with reckless abandon. "You've got to be willing to give up the body," he would say, irrepressibly evoking for Beowolf the vision of Midnight, Pap's old fighting dog, whose jaws were still working overtime even after his insides spanned the fighting pit like party streamers. "In order to live," Moon professed, "you must die."

Hunger was something a player was expected to cultivate. The will needed exercise as well as the body, for it was the will that would carry the body where the body ordinarily refused to go. Jason always had this ability to sacrifice his body utterly. The rules of the game got drummed into a body's head until they became second nature: they were meant to be taken literally, and that was how Jason took them. The sign said WINNING ISN'T EVERYTHING, IT'S THE ONLY THING, so that's what winning became, the only thing, and Jason believed it and played like he believed it—which was why he made such a damn good captain. He got whatever he wanted simply by wanting it so badly. DESIRE. And there was quality to this way of life: living by will and stiff-arming fate. This was what the game was all about. Jason had *made* himself as good as he was.

Beowolf watched the night stream by. *Kalispell.* Where was his craving to throttle these people? He pictured the Kalispell running backs, Banzai Burns and Earthquake Allen. Earthquake was two hundred and twenty pounds, Superscout said, and it was Beowolf's job to contain him. Gazing at Earthquake's photo on the locker-room bulletin board, Hap once remarked: "Eats puppies for break-fast, hair and all." That was Earthquake. He was another Midnight. Midnight ate a puppy or two. But mostly he preferred them full-grown. "I fought him too long," was what Pap had said, digging the dog's grave. Beowolf answered, "No shit."

"When I die," Pap declared, scraping dirt into Midnight's final resting pit, "I want my hide dried out and made into a saddle, yup. Then I kin awways be between the two things I love most—a beautiful stallion and a beautiful woman." The odds were, in Beo-wolf's estimation at least, that if he were made into a saddle in Rawlings, Montana, he'd wind up between a spiritless gelding and a cowboy's fat ass. But Beowolf didn't mention it. Instead he said, "Want me to lop off your head and tack it to the Bum Steer wall? Then you can spend eternity where you really love it most, outta your head in a saloon"—a rotten thing to say, especially with Pap's dog freshly planted. But Pap just spat on the grave and flung a final shovelful of earth over Midnight. Then he sort of laughed. Darting an abstracted glance over each shoulder he giggled as if he'd been let in on some profound, maddening joke. It was a godawful crazy laugh.

Pap. Old Pap. For as long as Beowolf could remember, his face had been as craggy as a dried riverbed, the color of parchment. Pap always reckoned he'd make it to a hundred; then his odometer would kick over the hump and he'd be good as new. But once Midnight was killed, Pap went downhill fast. When Roy Rogers' horse kicked off, Roy had it stuffed and installed in a place of honor in his living room. Pap wanted to do the same thing with Midnight, but he couldn't find a taxidermist up to the task.

With his shirtsleeves Beowolf wiped the sweat from his forehead. Across the aisle, Bigfoot had switched places with Granville and now sat by the open window. He was asleep as usual, his gruff, rasping inhalations accompanying the ceaseless whistle of night streaming past. The bus had turned north at Missoula into a valley corridor between mountain ranges looming in the vast night-shadow. For miles the mountains had been converging like slow-motion jaws, now finally poised to clamp shut. Beowolf opened his window wide and craned his neck all the way out. The moon had risen full and majestic to expose the raw, interminable crown of mountains to the east. It would be a full moon tomorrow if the sky didn't cloud over, a full moon for his final game. Hap gave him a shove. Beowolf pulled his head back in and closed the window. "Felt good," he said. He cracked his knuckles, one after the other, trying to recapture a thought.

He'd died enough. Everybody had died. Even the real good ones, like Jason. Jason's career had been framed by upsets: the glorious upset of Butte and the ignominious upset by Kalispell. Hap's career was framed by sound defeats. From Spring Practice when he was a freshman to the Anaconda game this season, he had died a thousand deaths. He had never suffered the agony of Bull Run, as Beowolf had, but he'd been racked elsewhere, wriggling alone under a disdainful scrutiny.

In response to some inner rhapsody during that first Spring Practice, Hap had coated his football cleats with white housepaint, and after an endless week of ridicule and vicious collisions with agitated teammates, Peckinpah finally descended upon him like a mad dog on red meat.

"*You!*" he screamed at Beowolf. "Geddown on the ground!"

Beowolf assumed a three-point stance.

"Not like that!"

Beowolf couldn't speak.

"Like a dog, boy! Like a dog!"

Beowolf fell to all fours, believing he was the guinea pig for some new form of sacrifice.

"*You!*" Peckinpah cried. He stabbed a finger at Hap. "Co-meere!"

Hap rushed to his side.

"Put your foot up here . . . *Here!*"

A hand slapped down upon Beowolf's back, followed instantly by a football cleat.

"Have you ever seen such fine shoes as these?" Peckinpah asked the team. He was speaking in that civil tone that hereafter would always put Beowolf on guard. "I mean, check out the spats!"

Blood had flooded Beowolf's head, where it seemed to curdle, clotting his breath. He stared into the rootless blades of grass, suffocating in the scent of the new-mown field. He was afraid to turn his head or better accommodate his body to the cleats planted in the small of his back, hoping in absolute stillness to sink into the turf while this stagnant moment passed. It was nearly dusk, practice would soon be over. An intent brown beetle forged its way through the grass stalks between his colossal arms.

Peckinpah spat.

"You must think you can whup some tail, wearing shoes like these, boy." Beowolf felt Peckinpah bend down and rub the cleat. "Gotta keep these babies clean. They get dirty and they don't look so good." Peckinpah snorted and spat, the sputum landing inches from Beowolf's hand, oozing through the grass. "Yeah, you must think you can whup some tail real good awright . . . Guess then, you don't mind if we find out just *how* good you can whup it, huh? Okay!" Peckinpah's whistle screamed. "Everybody to the end zone!"

Beowolf sprang to his feet and sprinted across the field.

Moon stood under the goalpost smoking a cigarette.

"Okay! I want backs and ends lined up over there." Peckinpah pointed to the far corner of the end zone. "Everybody but Willie White Shoes . . . Linemen get outta here."

Bodies scrambled into place behind Tinker in the front corner of the end zone, piss-ants to the rear. The grunts retreated to the sideline. Scurrying in one another's way, the student managers aligned two tackling dummies, two yards apart, on the five-yard line at the hashmark.

"Okay." Peckinpah smiled ominously. "You start over here." He shoved a football into Hap's breadbasket and stalked over to where the ten-yard line met the sideline. Hap followed close at his heels in an anxious running-in-place sort of stride. "When I blow the whistle, you sprint straight out to the hashmark, then cut into the end zone between the bags. Got the picture?"

A swell of chatter arose among the older players. The whistle sounded. Tinker, who had received no instructions, raced parallel with Hap to the hashmark, then cut between and beyond the bags, where he collided with vicious impact into Hap; the ball popped loose, bouncing away.

"Geddup! Geddup!" Peckinpah screamed, beating the air with his arms. "Geddup! Geddup! Geddup!"

Hap struggled to his feet, snapping himself back into his predicament.

"Get back into position!"

Hap retrieved the ball and returned to the sideline.

Tinker trotted to the back of the line, grinning like a crocodile behind the cage of his helmet. He stood behind Beowolf, breathing hard, certainly not out of fatigue.

"You fumble that ball again," Peckinpah warned, "I'm personally gonna kick your ass off this field. You get me?"

Hap nodded.

"You get me?"

"Yes!" Hap shouted.

"I wanna see some tail-whuppin, y'understand?"

"Yes!"

"I wanna see some desire, get me?"

"Yes!"

"I wanna see some *balls!*"

From behind his mirror sunglasses Peckinpah glared at Hap like some futuristic insect from *Monsterland Movie.* Beneath his mirror-eyes his proboscis protruded, his silver tongue glimmered—then it screamed cold, shrill fury.

Two bodies, one of them Hap, sprinted, cut and collided at the predetermined point.

"Go for the end zone, boy! Run!"

Hap sprang to his feet and returned to the sideline.

After five collisions, Hap was staggering. After ten or eleven, Tinker said, to nobody in particular, what seemed obvious to everybody. "He ain't got a prayer in hell." Then he shouted, "Nail that guy! Kick his ass!"

"Geddoff your ass, you!"

Hap staggered to his feet and lumbered back into position.

"Geddoff your tail," Peckinpah warned, "or geddoff this field forever! You understand?"

Hap nodded.

"You understand?"

"Yes!"

Hap was heaving for breath, cradling the football as if it were his sole possession.

Moon had moved to his car, which was parked on the track. He was leaning on the hood, smoking. Coach Rose was observing from up in the pressbox.

The whistle screamed.

Hap was pounded to the ground.

He had been tackled fifteen times when MD finally got his shot. He was the first of the freshmen and he gave Hap as good a lick as anybody; the ball squirted loose again.

Peckinpah pounced upon Hap, grabbing him by the jersey and screaming in his face, his free arm beating the air. The freshmen managed to rouse a bit of chatter on MD's behalf.

"Ball!" Peckinpah cried. *"Ball!"*

Hap pounced on the football, clambered to his feet, and lugged the ball to the sideline.

He'd been tackled twenty-five times when it was finally Beowolf's turn. Adrenaline shot from the balls of Beowolf's feet to his head and back again, his body coiling and recoiling, up and down, up and down on the balls of his feet, his fingers fisting in and out. Hap rose and staggered back into place.

"You haven't scored once," Peckinpah sneered.

Beowolf's head was burning.

"Put a hurt on that guy, piss-ant," Tinker demanded. "Nobody else left."

The whistle blew.

Beowolf charged the hashmark, planted his foot and cut. Hap made it as far as the tackling dummies before they hit. He had run hard for Beowolf, but once they collided his body went limp. Beowolf slammed him to the ground. On the ground, Hap slapped the side of Beowolf's head as hard as he could manage, which wasn't too hard. They clambered to their feet, staring hard into each other.

"Okay! Playtime's over!" Peckinpah declared. "Line em up for wind sprints!" His whistle blew.

That night, Hap tried to restore his cleats to their original color by slopping on a bottle of bootblack. But the shoes emerged from the ordeal as broken-spirited and crusty as their owner, stiffened in a luckless shade of purple-gray. The next day, Hap wore a brand new pair of Adidas that he'd spent all morning scuffing and soiling. Before practice, he apologized to Beowolf for smacking him.

That was Hap for you. Painting his goddamn cleats white. *White fuckin cleats.* Beowolf opened his window. Everybody knew what white cleats meant—ever since Joe Namath burst in living color from some wild adolescent dream, All-American wet and gleaming. Broadway Joe, a maverick who converted scores on the field into scores off the field: scores and scores and scores of women creaming in their panties because he could throw a football. The lessons he taught were these: *If ya got it, flaunt it* and *If ya can do it, it ain't braggin.* His lessons, of course, provided little solace for the multitude. Hap neither *had it* nor could *do it,* and consequently paid for his presumptuousness.

Yet Hap struggled and squirmed and hung on. He hung on painfully season after season, for it was his fate to die and to die. Then, briefly, the agony was recompensed by a stint in the limelight. Nobody had expected it, least of all Hap. Then there was Anaconda.

Whenever Rawlings played Anaconda at Anaconda, it always seemed as if there were more bodies in the marching band than there were in the stands. Anaconda took State every year in marching bands. Their cheerleaders weren't half-bad either, though they rarely had anything to cheer about. This year, Anaconda had won only one of their first six games—one win being, not infrequently, their seasonal output. By contrast, the Rattlers, after shutting out their sixth consecutive opponent and extending their winning streak to twenty-six games, had been christened "The Zero Heroes" by *The Rawlings Trumpet.* Kalispell was expected to be their only serious obstacle in capturing their third consecutive State Championship.

When the Anaconda debacle was over, the Rattlers hurried to the locker room, where they sat entombed in silence, not moving, hardly breathing, floating through time like formaldehyde frogs, until Moon finally stormed in, Peckinpah in tow, to cuss them out as never before—Peckinpah couldn't get a cuss in edgewise—then stormed back out with Peckinpah still at his heels. Beowolf busied himself undressing, sidestepping the agony that would bushwhack him when the shock wore off. MD took over where Moon had left off. Nobody would shut him up, not even Bigfoot. Hap still sat there on the bench, all hangdog, not undressing, just taking it and taking it.

In the shower, Beowolf pressed his fingers against his groin. *Goddamn Porkbutt,* he kept thinking. *Goddamn Porkbutt.* Though Porkbutt hadn't exactly refused to tape his groin during halftime, his declarations that he would "kowtow to no pussy-shit" had led Beowolf, against his better judgment, to let the tape job slide. The groin was sore to touch. It hurt to walk. He bit into the shower water and squirted it out through the gap in his teeth. He grew calm watching the rush of dirty lather run down the drain.

Drying off, Beowolf glanced down the bench at Hap, still sitting there stock-still, dressed and dirty. Beowolf sat down naked and watched the somber procession of naked bodies, bodies beginning to dress. He scanned the mosaic of light-green tiles issuing from underfoot in a resolute exodus across the locker-room floor and halfway up the walls to where they halted, at attention, before the omnipresent commandments:

IT'S NOT THE SIZE OF THE DOG IN THE FIGHT,
BUT THE SIZE OF THE FIGHT IN THE DOG THAT COUNTS

THE DIFFERENCE BETWEEN CHUMP AND CHAMP IS U

Beowolf rose from the bench and stepped into his underwear and trousers, pulled on socks and shoes, jersey next—no deodorant, the pores are open and raw—fastening trousers, zipping up the fly, buckling the belt, pulling on the sweater—Hap still sitting there, not moving—the overcoat, the hat. He sat down again watching bodies file past and out the door, sitting, thinking, trying to ground his thoughts in something physical, something to do—abruptly reliving the fourth-quarter desperation of inconceivably losing a football game: needing the ball and needing to score, the clock accelerating with the momentum of three quarters of the game behind it and the offense still not working, not working at all, Moon bellowing; the defense, run-down and angry, losing its poise, MD finally being thrown out of the game. Motion and time surging together, spiraling faster and faster into an eclipsing blur. "Get your ass in gear! Get it together!" A time-out. Then, under pressure, the offense finally began to click: Hap and Geek each caught passes, running out of bounds to stop the clock. A second time-out was called. They were at mid-field. Moon forbade the offense bug juice, he was so disgusted with them, sending Donnie out to the huddle with a can of Ball Control stickum instead, which Hap and Rocky Bellito sprayed on their hands. The ball was in the air every play after that. Finally, Rawlings called its last time-out. One more play. Then, with the football airborne, dreamily spiraling, there was hope for an instant: dashed as the season slipped through Hap's fingers and the already protracted nightmare was consummated. Beowolf collapsed to his knees, his head slumped to the earth as he cried, cried for the life of him, cried for the body lying face down in the end zone as if he'd been shot.

Beowolf was sweating like hell under his overcoat. When everybody was gone except Hap, he rose and limped down the aisle.

"It wasn't your fault, man."

Hap didn't move, still sitting there dressed in his uniform. "I lost it in the lights."

"Yeah."

"I lost it," he said, shaking his head. "I lost it in the lights."

"Forget it," Beowolf told him. "It was our fault, too. It was my fault."

"It wasn't your fault," Hap murmured.

"Fuckin *game.* You ever gonna take a shower?"

"I dunno."

"Take a shower so I can go home, will ya?"

"You can leave. I ain't keepin ya."

"Yes, you are." Beowolf grabbed the back of his jersey. "C'mon. Let's get this off." He pulled the jersey over Hap's shoulder pads, over his head and off. "There. C'mon." Hap unfastened his shoulder pads and dropped them to the floor.

"You doing anything tonight?" Beowolf asked.

"Nothin important," Hap replied. He untied his Adidas and yanked them off. "Probably just hang myself."

"Pap left a jug of moonshine. I've been saving it."

"I ain't drinkin that embalming fluid."

"Fuck it then."

"Where d'ya wanna go?" Hap asked.

"Drive-in?"

"Yeah, awright. Anybody else going?"

"Just you and me."

Hap struggled out of his pants and girdle pads. He stood and looked at Beowolf. "I feel like—" He shook his head. "I don't know what I feel like."

"Get in the shower. I have to tell Jeannie."

Outside the locker room, Jeannie stood waiting, standing there like a vision in the darkness, arms hanging at her sides, barely breathing, waiting for him as he plunged into the open air: waiting for him as if she didn't trust herself to begin moving. He marched up to her and embraced her.

"Are you all right?" she asked.

"Pulled groin."

"Will it be okay?"

"I don't know."

The temperature had dropped, the wind had picked up. The darkness was like liquid against his face. He rubbed her back, squeezed her body and pressed her cold face against his own. The night lapped his face.

"Aren't you cold?" he asked. "It's gotten cold."

"A little." Her eyes were moist. "I'm sorry."

"Are the missiles still there, do you know?" He could think of nothing else to say.

"Yes."

The northern lights wavered across the heavens, sidewinding like snakes.

"I'm going out with Hap tonight."

"Hap?" Jeannie pulled away. "How can you go out with Hap? You aren't even speaking to him."

"I have to."

She buried her face against his shoulder. He brushed back her hair and kissed her on the forehead. "I'm sorry," he finally said. He hugged her, feeling nothing he could name. "You have the most beautiful hair."

"Where will you go?"

"The drive-in."

"Let's go to your house." She glanced up at him. "Let's just go to your house."

"I can't," he insisted. "I can't."

"You're getting drunk?"

"Yes."

"Can I go?"

"No."

"I want to get drunk," she murmured with no real enthusiasm.
"I want to get drunk, too." Her eyes were moist. She was going to
cry again. "I love you," she said. "Do you know?"

"Yes, I know."

"You don't even *like* him," she insisted.

"Yes I do."

"He's been calling me up," she complained. She hugged him as
tightly as she could. "Why's he been calling me up?"

Beowolf loosened her hold on him. He wanted to feel nothing.
"He won't call you anymore. I have to go." He turned his back and
headed in toward the locker room.

"Wait," Jeannie cried. She stamped her foot like a little girl. Her
lips parted, quivering, her face bent out of shape. "I *need* to talk
to you." She stood there, abruptly sobbing, trembling like something newborn in the midst of measureless space.

"Hey, don't cry." Beowolf hobbled back to her. "What?"

She leaned on him, crying. "I love you," she said. She looked up
at him. She wiped her eyes against his overcoat. "You see I do?"
Her head fell against his shoulder again for support. Her body
trembled. "When I was little, I always, I wanted to be in love and
have babies, when I was little—I love you, do you know?"

"When I was little, I wanted to kill Indians," Beowolf answered. "I used to pretend I was being chased through the wheat
and down into the gorge below the dam. Down there I'd shoot
rattlesnakes with my twenty-two and make believe they were redskins. I killed a lot of rattlesnakes and got bitten for it once, and
it doesn't have a damn thing to do with now. None of it." He
kissed her eyes, her lips. An anguished cry arose within him.
"What a fuckin waste!" Yet he resisted the impulse to surrender
himself wholeheartedly either to despair or to Jeannie's affection.
"He lost it in the lights."

"Who?"

"Hap. Lost the football in the lights . . . I have to go."

Jeannie straightened up, blinking, wiping her eyes. She gently
forced Beowolf away from her.

"Would you like me to come over later tonight?" she asked. "I'll come over later if you like."

"How will you get out of the house?"

"I'll sneak out. And I won't drive. I'll walk. Do you want me to do that?"

"If you want to, do it." Beowolf moved to hug her, but she backed away.

"Good-by." She darted forward and kissed him, and hurried toward her car.

"Jeannie!"

"What?"

"Be careful."

She opened the car door.

"Jeannie!"

"What?"

"What'll you tell Eric if, in the morning . . . What'll you tell him?"

"I got up early and went out to look at the missiles."

9

Hap had been born under a bad star, for it was his nature to choke, as he had in seventh grade when Beowolf was bitten by that rattlesnake. While Bigfoot administered to Beowolf, cutting his leg open and sucking out the venom, eventually hauling him out of the gorge below the dam where they'd been fishing, Hap lost his head completely, running in circles, wailing for help and nearly scaring Beowolf to death. It was Hap's nature to panic, which was why, Beowolf supposed, Midnight had been so partial to Hap's flank, and why, against Anaconda . . . Hap couldn't even catch fish! On the day Beowolf was bitten, Hap hadn't caught anything but weeds and a drowned beagle, whose tail he ripped clean off trying to pull the bloated carcass free of a cross of fallen limbs.

Reeling in a rainbow, Bigfoot sang out, "This sure beats school!"

Hap sneered and flung the dog's tail as far as he could into the river. "It stinks," he muttered as he began untangling his line.

"What's the matter with you?" Beowolf asked.

"I don't know. I throw my line out same as you. I got a fly on the end same as you."

"You got bad karma," Beowolf informed him. "That's why you can't catch fish. *Field and Stream* says so."

"What's karma?"

"It's like B.O. or somethin."

"Get out."

"I can smell it," Bigfoot said.

"That's *the dog.*"

"The fish smell it all the way down to the fly," Beowolf told him. "It's a fact. Some doctor wrote about it."

"Bullshit."

"It's true."

"How d'ya get rid of it?" Hap asked suspiciously.

"Try taking a bath once in a while, why doncha?"

"I do take baths."

"You're stuck with it, then."

Bigfoot laughed. "Bad karma! Bad karma!" He stomped around Hap, splashing water and pointing at him. "Bad karma! Bad karma!"

"You should talk about karma," Hap sneered. "Your karma you could bottle and sell to the Defense Department."

"Hey, Taps, the fish like my aroma. I got seven in the bag. I could live down here, man! Bad karma! Bad karma!"

Bigfoot had taken to calling Hap "Taps" the moment they met. "This is the kid I told y'about," Beowolf had said that morning to Bigfoot. "The kid who got us kicked out of Boy Scout camp cause he said 'Taps *who.*'" Beowolf had been canned, immediately after Hap, for staggering from cabin to cabin and tent to tent, *dying laughing,* repeating between gasps the scoutmaster's question, "Who'll blow taps?"

As it turned out, being booted out of Boy Scout camp was the best thing that happened to Beowolf that summer. He'd come home and painted the slaughterhouse with Jason, making lots of money and meeting Bigfoot. Bigfoot had appeared in the doorway of the slaughtering room one evening after his father had gone home and Jason had left for Captain's Practice. He was sucking hard on a cigarette protruding defiantly from his lips. But cigarettes hadn't stunted his growth any; he was built like a brick shithouse even then. Beowolf was rolling paint on the wall.

"Jason Bailey your brother?"

"Yeah." Beowolf glanced at the Indian, then returned his attention to the wall. "What of it?"

"Nothin of it."

Bigfoot approached, flicked ashes onto the floor. "You always paint with him?"

"First time."

Bigfoot silently watched him paint, his arms crossed in an arrogant pose.

"Ain'tcha gotta carve that pig?" Beowolf asked after a while.

"Kin wait'll mornin. He ain't goin nowhere."

"That your dad's?" Beowolf asked, gesturing toward the .22 used to kill hogs.

"Yep."

"Does he like it?"

"Like what?"

"What he does."

"What's *liking* got to do with it?" Bigfoot flicked some more ashes.

"Nothin. Just wonderin."

"The Chief likes it okay."

"That his name, *the Chief?*"

"Yeah."

"What's he chief of?"

"Chief ass-kicker of this town, for starters."

"Oh," Beowolf said. He rolled on some more paint. "You go to West?"

"Yeah."

"I go to East."

"I couldn't have guessed." Ashes flicked again. "You play football too?"

"Yeah. You?"

"I gotta work," Bigfoot replied. "But I'm gonna play in high school. The new coach visited my house."

"Moon did?"

"You know him?"

"Sure. He's over my house all the time. He's my father's best friend. They played together in high school."

"Big deal." The Indian spat. "Is he gonna be any good?"

"Sure he'll be good. He played for Vince Lombardi, ya know."

"Yeah, he told me."

"What's he doing over to your house anyway?" Beowolf asked.

"He wanted to know that I'll be playing in high school."

"You're big enough for it. You a tackle?"

"Fullback."

"Naw," Beowolf said, "you're a lineman if I ever saw one."

"What position *you* play?"

"End."

"Can ya catch?"

"Course I can catch," Beowolf indignantly replied.

"Catch this." Bigfoot lifted a leg and ripped off a fart fit to pucker a hog's butt. "See, I play end too. But mostly I play fullback."

Beowolf laughed; then, disconcerted, he dipped the roller into the paint pan and continued with his work. "We'll be on the same team then," he eventually said. "Ya tough?"

"Wanna find out?"

"Just askin."

Beowolf painted for a while in silence, wishing the Indian would go away.

"Going to the dogfight tonight?" Bigfoot asked.

"Naw."

"I didn't think so."

"I don't wanna see dogs tear each other up."

"Yes ya do."

"Whattaya mean by that?"

"I mean just what I said," Bigfoot replied. "And I mean to be sittin up in that loft tonight where no one can see me with a bottle of likker, and I'm gonna drink and smoke and watch them dogs go at it. Y'ever been drunk before?"

"Yes," Beowolf lied.

"No ya ain't."

"How d'you know?"

"No one from East drinks. You're a buncha candyasses. You don't know a boilermaker from a boiled fuckin egg."

"No, I guess I don't," Beowolf retorted. "I guess I wasn't just about raised in the Bum Steer. Ya know who Pap is?"

Bigfoot nodded.

"Well, Pap's my grandfather, bub. That's Pap's dog fightin tonight—Midnight."

Astonishment dashed the smirk off the Indian's face. "No shit?"

"Yeah."

"Pap, I know bout Pap. Wavy told me." Bigfoot's tone was tinged now with reluctant respect. "Is he really your gran'pap?"

"Yep."

"I'm gonna ask Wave," Bigfoot blustered, "and if you're jerkin my chain, you'll be buckin for a knuckle sandwich on a hard roll."

"Who's Wave?"

"He's *my* gran'pap. And he knows everybody and every*thing.* He's night watchman out back."

Beowolf stared at the Indian, then quietly said, "That ain't your gran'pap."

"Who says he ain't?"

"He's . . . colored."

"Ya got somethin gainst it?"

"You ain't colored. You're Injun."

"I'm *both*. Where the hell ya think I got this?" Bigfoot ran his hand down his scalp. "Santa Claus? . . . If Pap's really your gran'pap, what's he drink on Easter?"

"Rattlesnake poison. And he drinks it on Good Friday, not Easter."

"Is that for real or just more of Wavy's horseshit?"

"It's real."

"Hot damn! That's sumpin I gotta see."

"Ain't much to see. He drinks it like a body drinks a shot of anything: whiskey, sour mash, black jack, brave maker . . ."

"Jesus."

"Mad Dog Twenty-twenty, scamper juice . . ."

"So what's your front name, Bailey?"

"Folks call me Beowolf."

"*Baywolf!* Man, you oughta sue! Who the hell gave you a name like *Baywolf?*" Bigfoot arched a gob of spit out the doorway.

"It wasn't my dad."

"Your ma?"

"She's dead. It's a nickname."

"My name's Bigfoot."

Beowolf laughed. "And you laughed at my name? Where'd ya get a name like Bigfoot? You a monster'r sumpin?"

"My dad gave it to me," Bigfoot replied. "Got somethin gainst it?"

"I ain't got nothin against it . . . You really got a bottle for the fight?"

"Yeah."

"Bottla what?"

"Likker."

"What kinda likker?"

"*Good* likker. How the hell should I know? Ya comin or what?"

"Yeah, I'm comin."

"Well, pack up this crap then and let's go."

"It ain't for two hours yet."

"I wanna show ya somethin first."

"What?"

"Wavy. We'll spook him. He's the scaredest cat livin."

"What's he scareda?"

"Ghosts."

"Ain't no ghosts."

"Yeah?" Bigfoot said. "Live out back a slaughterhouse long enough and see if there ain't no ghosts. When Wavy gets scared his teeth fall out. Ever seen a guy so scared his teeth fall out?"

"I seen a guy's hair turned white as bone, just like *that.*" Beowolf snapped his fingers.

"Whose?"

"Pap's. When he was hit by lightnin."

"He was hit by lightnin?"

"Knocked him flat on his can."

"Say," Bigfoot mentioned irritably. "Can't you cuss?"

"Yeah, I can cuss."

"Well, I ain't hearin much."

"Didn know we was havin a contest."

"So Pap was hit by lightnin, huh?"

"Twice."

"Man, I'm gonna bust you one, I swear!" Bigfoot said. "Lightnin *never* strikes twice."

"Says who?"

"Everybody says."

"Well, Pap ain't everybody."

Bigfoot gave Beowolf the raspberries.

"Go ahead, blow it out your saddlebag," Beowolf said, "I ain't lyin. Ask anybody. His hair went white as bone, just like *that.*" He snapped his fingers. "And it was the second time, ask anybody." As an afterthought he added: "Scouts' fuckin honor."

"If you're so fed up with fishing," Beowolf said to Hap, "I can show you something if you want. I used to come down here all the time." The gorge had always been Beowolf's retreat, and within the gorge a cave—its crevice narrow and camouflaged by overgrown bushes, making it a truly secret, good place. He would squeeze inside, and if he'd shot any rattlers he would inspect their amputated rattles, which he collected in a mayonnaise jar. Sitting all balled up, he would daydream, and his imagination would irrepressibly turn to the girl who lived down the highway and went to West because the district line cut right between their houses. With her on his mind he would grow fidgety, and finally he'd have to do something. When he was done he'd rub his hand in the earthy

decay that filled the cave with its fertile smell, and he would peer
out through the bushes, curled up safe in the cave—peer out at the
forest and the river and the sunlight and the whole world standing
still waiting for him.

"What is it?" Bigfoot asked.

"A cave and a jar full of rattles."

"Rattlesnake rattles?" Hap asked.

"No, *baby* rattles," Beowolf replied sarcastically. "Come on."
Through a thicket he led the way to a deer trail.

"Any snakes round here now?" Hap asked.

With a smug snort, Bigfoot answered. "Not this time of year,
numbnuts."

"Hey, Wolf," Hap said. "Is Jason gonna play tonight?"

"Yeah. Picture'll be in the paper this afternoon."

"What's the new coach like?"

"Big and bald. He'll be in the picture, too."

"How ya think we'll do?" Bigfoot asked.

"We'll win."

"Gainst Butte?" Hap scoffed.

"Yep."

"Butte's good."

"So're we."

"Who says?"

"Jason. Says we're gonna kick ass."

"Whattaya expect him to say?"

"The truth."

"Truth is," Bigfoot said, "we ain't kicked Butte's ass since the
days of yore."

"You going?" Hap asked Beowolf.

"Yeah."

"Can I come?"

"If ya want. Pap's drivin the team bus, ya know."

"Can we go on the team bus?" Hap asked excitedly.

"Are you kidding?"

"Who gives a shit if Pap's drivin the team bus then?"

"Pap gives a shit."

"Well, I don't."

"Ya know," Bigfoot said, "I remember one year when Butte
sucked."

"We must've sucked worse," Hap remarked.

"Well, they sure don't suck this year," Beowolf said flatly. "Defending State Champions is all."

"We're never State Champions," Hap muttered. "We're like an expansion team."

"You wanna go too?" Beowolf asked Bigfoot.

Bigfoot nodded.

Nailed to a tree on the riverbank was a TRESPASSERS WILL BE PROSECUTED sign. "Forgive us our trespasses," Beowolf said, crossing himself. He turned up another deer trail leading to higher ground, where an upshoot of granite boulders buttressed the bluffs at the top of the gorge. Beowolf stopped. He stared into the bushes at the base of the boulders.

"What is it?" Hap asked.

"It's my place."

Beowolf parted the bushes to reveal the cranny between the rocks.

"What did ya do in there?" Bigfoot asked.

"Sit."

Beowolf picked up a stick and bent through the bushes. He rustled some leaves inside the crevice, checking for snakes, then tossed the stick aside. Squeezing sideways, he tried to fit through the cave's entrance. "I'm getting too damn big." Stooping lower, he plunged his leg in as deep as it would reach. Within the cave there was a sudden rustling—his calf was stabbed with pain and he screamed, smashing his forehead as he leapt on hands and knees through the bushes, seeing by their faces that they knew.

He had believed he would die. But he didn't die. RAWLINGS RATTLERS NEVER SAY DIE—RHS 1986 was what it said on the peewee football the nurse gave him the next day when she learned that it had been Beowolf's brother who had quarterbacked the Rattlers to victory over Butte. The footballs were being given to newborn males as an invitation to try out for the team when they were old enough. When Beowolf came home from the hospital on Sunday, Moon showed up to see how he was making out. "We'll be expecting the same out of you," he said, beaming as he handed Beowolf the Butte game ball. "You missed it," his dad told him. "Your brother was fantastic."

10

After upsetting Butte, "The Big Red Machine"—as they were promptly billed by *The Rawlings Trumpet*—cannonballed through its schedule with Moon at the helm laying on the steam. The hometown spirit sprang to life as the town's usual endeavors were hurtled momentarily to the wayside. The annual pilgrimage to Kalispell was inaugurated by a red-and-white streamer-lined procession of cars. "Looks like we're going to a funeral," Beowolf excitedly remarked to his father as the cars wound through the streets of Rawlings, heading for the highway. "We are," his father declared. "We *are.*" And when the smoke cleared that night over Kalispell to reveal that "The State" was indeed theirs, Rawlings burst into a euphoric revelry the likes of which had never before been witnessed. Parades and banquets and oratories. A team photograph blanketed the front page of the *Trumpet* on Thanksgiving Day, accompanied by the headline A TEAM NAMED DESIRE. Beowolf's father didn't come home from the Bum Steer for three days. And as it turned out, it was a good thing Rawlings could win the whole shebang only once a year. When they won it again the next year his father busted up the Bum Steer good and threatened, with Pap's raving complicity, to burn the saloon to the dust, the night's work earning him three days in the slammer—all of which prompted Wavy to remark, "You Bailey boys is all alike. Gloryhounds, every last one of ya. Pap. Your dad, smokejumpin like he was twenty-two. Now Jason. An *you next,* youngblood, you Baywuff. Whatchew gonna be when you grow up? A movie star?"

Ever since he was old enough to get knocked down, Beowolf had played football: first in choose-up games, then in Midget League and in junior high, where his performances always paled in the light of Jason's reputation, and finally in high school. His father, who had played alongside Moon on the famous '47 and '48 teams, had instilled in both of his sons not only the intense desire to play the game but also the desire to follow further in his footsteps by bringing home to Rawlings the State Championship. "Ya gotta want it the way we wanted it," his father would say. "It's gonna be sitting there ripe for the plucking. But nobody's gonna hand it to you. You're gonna have to grab it. Like *this.*" His father raised a clenched fist, flourishing it in Beowolf's face.

Long before he restored glory to Rawlings, Moon was a legend —less, to be sure, in the town at large, where the remote triumphs of '47 and '48 had become merely facts acknowledged, like pennants on a barroom wall, than in the Bailey household. The ranch-house in which Moon had grown up had been pointed out and remarked upon so frequently to Beowolf that he couldn't walk past it on his way to or from school without offering it some brief meditation. From Rawlings, Moon had gone on to star at Notre Dame, graduating an All-American to the Green Bay Packers. Injuries plagued him in the pros, however, and after six seasons he retired to coach high school somewhere in Wisconsin. "I'm a cowboy at heart," he told the *Trumpet* when he returned home. "I'm gonna raise cattle on my ranch and football players on my gridiron. I'm gonna raise holy hell by producing the best team this state has ever seen." On Sundays, Moon began dropping by Beowolf's house to watch the pro games on TV, and on Monday Pap would always recount how Moon could down a whole damn case of beer by halftime without even taking a time-out to bleed his lizard.

Over the years Pap developed a childlike fascination with Moon that Beowolf could not fathom. Whenever the coach was discussed, Pap would inevitably chip in his two cents, always managing the last word, the same refrain. "Could be lected mayor of this piss-ant town, yup. That is, if he had an itch to be. Trouble is, then he wouldn have time to git done what really needs gittin done, yup —coachin the Rattlers."

Moon believed in plain, old-fashioned winning. "If you're gonna play the game, you should play to win. There isn't anything else, just winners and losers." Accompanying his conviction that a body could achieve absolutely anything if he truly threw his heart into it was a sometimes astounding tendency to demean a good effort by insisting upon more than a body possessed—and frequently getting it. Folks swore he could squeeze water from a stone. If a body wasn't within a hairline of being a stretcher case, Moon could convince him that the pain he felt in his knee was really in his head, and he'd make him ashamed of himself to boot. It was a stock joke that Moon treated everybody on the team alike—*like dogs.* He was the way he was, Beowolf figured, because in his last season at Green Bay Vince Lombardi had arrived with a creed of pain and discipline, fielding teams of walking wounded that still managed to mangle the NFL.

During Beowolf's first Summer Practice there had been a guy on the team subsequently known as "Bag-of-Wind" Wynn. On the last day of drills, Wynn made the mistake of informing Moon that he had taken his aching shoulder to a family doctor, who told him not to practice for three days because he had "acute contusions of the trapezius." Moon wasn't impressed. Against doctor's orders, Wynn showed up in pads for practice that afternoon. *Acute contusions,* Beowolf thought, *of the trapezius!* At the end of practice, after Peckinpah announced a Bull Run and rattled off six names, Beowolf's included, he turned on Wynn. "Do you know what an *acute contusion* is, Wynn?" Nervous as a prairie dog at a coyote convention, Wynn stiffly shook his head. "It's a bruise," Peckinpah sneered. "Do you know what a *trapezoid* is?" Wynn just stood there, knowing what he was in for, looking sorrier than cattle shit at the packing house. "It's your shoulder, Wynn."

"But I thought—" Wynn began to protest.

"We're not interested in what you *thought,* Wynn. We're interested in you from the neck down. Now get your tail over there with the rest of them deadasses."

Moon brooked no mistakes. Beowolf had known all along that it was Hap's nature to choke, to step in shit, to drop the big one; and he'd believed, until he'd been switched to free safety at the beginning of the season, that Moon knew it, too. Had Moon been unsure of it at first, he was dead certain of it now. Hap, in the end, was a loser. The Monday after the loss to Anaconda, Peckinpah declared: "Hazard, I trust you about as far as I can spit." Then he spat into the wind. Had it not been for Hap's reputation as a good receiver and for the fact that Moon had nobody to take his place other than Guy Lombago, a bona-fide piss-ant, Hap would have been benched. After Anaconda, Moon used him almost exclusively as a decoy to draw coverage away from the other receivers. Rocky Bellito, a sophomore flanker, had emerged in the meantime as the team's best receiver. In an article entitled "The Future Is Now," the *Trumpet* predicted that Frankie Dimitruk and Rocky Bellito would provide Rawlings with an All-State passing attack for the next two years; Moon was quoted as saying that Bellito wasn't "afraid to catch the ball in a crowd." Hap, of course, *was* afraid. Hap had no hairs. He'd always hated contact, Beowolf knew, and it was only because his split-end position accommodated this aversion that he was able to play the game at all. His only other talent was kicking extra points and field goals. But Rawlings never kicked field goals. When Hap once ventured to suggest to Moon that they give it a try, Moon gave him a smug head fake. "We don't kick field goals, Hazard. We score touchdowns."

11

"What do you think would happen," Beowolf asked Hap, "if Rawlings didn't have Moon anymore?"

Hap glanced up from his *Playboy*. "If he went someplace else, you mean?"

"Yeah."

"Where else would he go?"

Beowolf shrugged.

"He'll be here forever," Hap said.

"Why do you say that?"

"They need him here. Besides, he's got everything he wants here. A ranch and everything else. Why would he leave? Where would he go?"

Beowolf stared out the window. "How do you think Peckinpah would do as head coach?"

"Peckinpah's leaving?"

"How should I know?"

Hap shrugged. "Moon's the man. Peckinpah couldn't do what Moon did."

"No," Beowolf agreed.

"His teams'd hate him too much. We never hated Moon."

"I did," Beowolf said.

The lights burst on; in the window Beowolf's reflection stared sullenly back at him. The lights went off, then blinked on again, and up the aisle Moon rose, puffing on a cigarette, the lights flashing frantically. Hap crammed his *Playboy* into his duffel bag.

"Okay, gentlemen, listen up. We'll be in Kalis—" Moon turned to Wavy and said, "Enough with the lights."

The lights kept right on flashing. Donnie, the head manager, sprang to Wavy's side and tapped him on the shoulder. The lights blinked on and stayed on.

"Okay, listen up," Moon resumed.

At that moment Bigfoot, across the aisle, let loose a snore that shook the whole bus with laughter.

"Somebody wake his butt up," Moon said.

"Don't do *that!*" MD cried, cringing theatrically in the seat behind Bigfoot.

Everybody laughed again, including Moon. Granville gave Bigfoot a nudge.

"Mornin," Bigfoot said.

"Sleeping beauty," Hap muttered.

"We'll be in Kalispell in nineteen, twenty minutes," Moon announced. "Rooms at the motel have been assigned alphabetically. Donnie has the list. Check with him when you get off the bus for your room number. Lights out at ten-thirty. Breakfast at nine-thirty. If there are any problems, I want to know about them." Moon consulted his clipboard. "Okay," he added, looking back down the aisle. "Let's just remember who we are and what we are."

Moon seated himself next to Donnie, his massive body claiming three quarters of the seat. Donnie sprang to Wavy's side again; Wavy killed the lights.

After Thanksgiving, Moon would be gone. Beowolf peered into the window. Nobody else knew.

As far as Beowolf was concerned, Pap went bonkers on the subject of Moon long before he flipped out on everything in general. Moon was the only person ever to fascinate Pap half as much as Pap fascinated himself. After his trial for murder nearly half a century earlier, Pap spent his days brooding down at the Bum Steer, punch-drunk and everyday drunk. How long this period lasted Beowolf did not know. He knew only that so powerful was the blow Pap had received from Leland Tyrone that for a time—maybe a year—he drew little more than a blank from his memory bank. Nevertheless, as he gazed at the pictures of himself that hung on the barroom walls, these fragments of his past eventually took root in his still fertile imagination. Pap's eyes sprang back to life one day as he began spinning wild yarns about himself. Ebbing and flowing between the credible and the fantastic, the drift of his tales altered with each retelling, as he elaborated and improved and reconstructed a past based on a few images forever captured by the camera lens.

Either he was the greatest bullshitter of the century or he wasn't, but there was a very real possibility that he was, and when Moon returned to Rawlings to immediately capture the State, it may have been that Pap found himself within arm's reach of something—someone—equally worthy of his sanctified bullshit. He never tired of telling Moon anecdotes, constantly embellishing them, polishing them, wholeheartedly enamored with the coach the way a small boy is with the image of a distant, untouchable hero—as if the hero were the sole and supreme embodiment of some otherwise extinct ideal. Occasionally, he would dredge up a new story and quickly make it old through constant wear and tear until Beowolf's father would tell him to clap his trap. Then the story would go underground in Pap's bombed-out basement of a memory, only to be excavated several months later, dusted off—"I almost forgot that one, yup!"—and spruced up until Beowolf's father would again have to tell him to stow it. By rotating his stock in this manner, the stories recurred in broadly predictable cycles. Beowolf never had too many of them to ponder at any one time, just the same ones over and over. It was like learning catechism. Common utterances and everyday occurrences, in Moon's case, were aggrandized into adages and feats bordering on the epic. Hardly a day passed when Beowolf wasn't reminded that Moon "could be lected mayor of this here piss-ant town, yup," or when there wasn't some supper-table discussion about Moon and the prospects for "next season." By the time he entered high school, Beowolf was in absolute awe of the man. To look Moon straight in the eye was nearly impossible; he would fix his sight on some target on his forehead or look straight past him over his shoulder.

Throughout the ordeal of his freshman season, when everyone expected from him at least a modicum of competence, if not greatness, Moon bestowed upon him a familiarity that was like a curse —a familiarity so rare among *varsity* players, let alone freshmen, that many of his teammates made him an object of cheap shots on the field and, elsewhere, of silent scorn. That winter, when Beowolf mustered enough nerve to venture into Moon's office—"Come on in!" Moon thundered good-naturedly, "I'm not gonna bite your head off!"—the coach assuaged his doubts concerning his size and speed. Beowolf had hung in there on the freshman team, that's what Coach Rose had told Moon, and that was what freshman football was all about: weeding out the ones who wouldn't hang in there, who weren't tough, who didn't really want to crack heads. He was expected to grow in size and strength just as Jason had grown. Not only would he make the varsity team next season, *if* he kept hanging in there, he would someday be a solid starter as well.

Beowolf played basketball that winter, and in the spring ran the two-mile on the track team and survived the month of Spring Practice in which Hap perilously experimented with white cleats. In the summer he suffered through Captain's Practice each evening, and as the days remaining before the onslaught of Summer Practice dwindled, he found himself not terrified, but astonished— increasingly astonished that he was not scared shitless of the imminent Summer Practice, which, he was now convinced, would reveal something miraculous. Through winter, spring and summer he had not grown appreciably faster nor bigger, yet he had grown to believe that everything he'd ever dreamed of becoming had been virtually promised to him by Moon.

There was a drought that summer, and everybody was saying how the range wouldn't support a horned toad. Crops withered and, to the west, forest fires burst out with a regularity that made a body think God was a sure-fire pyromaniac. Less than a week before Summer Practice began, Beowolf came home to learn that his father had been killed—not smokejumping, his summer occupation, but off duty, skydiving up north. They found him with a deathgrip on his rip.

"I tole'm, *sumbitch,*" Pap said, crouching forward in his rocker. "For years I tole'm. If man was meant to fly . . ." Pap spat a stream of tobacco juice over the porch railing. "Man who flies is *meant* to crash."

Eric stood in the sunlight halfway up the porch steps.

"I tole'm," Pap said again, "I tole'm only three things fall outta the sky."

Beowolf, who stood in the doorway, didn't say anything. Eric couldn't resist. "What?"

Pap spat. "Rain, birdshit and *fools.*"

Nobody laughed.

"He pulled the rip too late," Eric said.

Beowolf didn't feel anything yet. He turned to go inside, yet hesitated, leaned against, clung to, the door frame.

"Groundrush," Pap said to Eric.

"Say what?"

"Groundrush. Mesm'rized by the earth. A body don't even feel like he's fallin. Then, quick as a rattler snap, the earth rises up to swatcha like a fly." Beowolf looked at Pap, who was shaking his head, white-maned, his face wrinkled as a burnt boot; Pap spat an amber dart that raised a poof of dust in the front yard. "Son of a *bitch.*"

"I'm sorry," Eric said.

"Gravity, I used to tell'm, *gravity* is cause the earth sucks."

At the funeral Moon told him to hang in there tough, and when he returned home he went running even though he rarely ran in the daytime and had Captain's Practice to contend with later on. The sun was fierce as he padded along the highway. Jason would leave for college soon and Beowolf wondered how he and Pap would manage. *These things happen?* He padded along the sun-baked highway, chasing water mirages springing up from the steaming tar in the distance, his mind turning recurrently to the vision of the earth as his dad had described it: a gigantic painting beneath you, beautiful and serene, dreamlike, and you just hanging there in space, taking it in—then the sudden groundrush, the panic, too late the tug on the rip and, finally, the realization that it is all over. Padding along, Beowolf had a premonition of his own death: he would die young, he believed, was on a collision course with he did not know what, but the time was coming for the crash. He wouldn't break down, though. He wouldn't cry. He'd hang in there tough and not fall apart piece by piece—because a body is a per-petual-motion machine. He wouldn't give in to anything until he gave in to everything, just as his father had done and would have wanted him to do. His legs carried him along as they always had, not fast, but steady, and he thought of them now, of how they'd always carried more than their share of the load; he attuned himself to their warm, constant strength and found that he didn't feel like crying anymore. He would never cry again, he'd just pad along the highway at a pace he could live with, until the final mile when he'd run himself breathless into the ground. A run that didn't end in agony wasn't worth the running. He'd run and run, and each time die strong—Summer Practice was coming and something amazing was going to happen. He had entrusted his spirit to Moon and now something was going to happen in Summer Practice.

Something happened, all right. Bull Run. And Beowolf wound up scarcely regretting that his father was dead.

That first night with Jeannie at the cabin it had occurred to

Beowolf that he had no idea how he truly felt about his father. He had felt embarrassed when Jeannie asked him; he felt brave talking about him. But these were foregone emotions, his deeper feelings keeping their distance, estranged, forgotten, as lost as his memory of that snakebite, which, for all its intensity, he *knew* he couldn't actually remember, obscured as it was by the constant telling and retelling that ultimately was all he could actually recall.

"I'm sorry if—I didn't know if you ever wanted to talk about it," Jeannie said. "You talk about Pap all the time." Her face had lit up, radiating a fine, unspeaking intelligence. She was scrutinizing his face. "You've always been like a lost little boy."

"Thanks," Beowolf snorted. He looked away from her eyes to find above the fireplace the head of a grizzle bear, watching him. The fire was out. It was almost dawn.

"Pap spit in the eye of a grizzle bear once," Beowolf told her.

"Well, I doubt *that,*" Jeannie laughed.

"He did," Beowolf insisted. "And I can prove it. There's a photograph of it in the Bum Steer."

"How could there be a photograph?"

"His friends took it. See, there was this grizzle bear loose in the Rattlesnake Range and Pap decided he was gonna find it and spit in its eye—this was back when he was a boxer, before the Ringside burned down—"

"Do you not want to tell me about it?" Jeannie asked.

"I'm telling you about it."

"I mean about your father."

Beowolf lay back and held her warm body against his own. "I do," he said. He shook his head, staring at the ceiling. "I'm just trying to think—I'm trying to remember to tell you. Pap was crazy. He's easier to talk about. My father wasn't crazy. Except in some ways. In season—fire season—he'd work for a week, all through the Northwest, then he'd have a week off. He'd spend it skydiving or talking up his adventures down the Bum Steer. He was really hung up on the feeling of free flight—smokejumping, the chute opens automatically as soon as you jump; but skydiving, you pull a ripcord." Beowolf paused. "It's like he needed that time, that *instant,* of not knowing if he was going to float or crash."

"Why didn't it open?"

"He pulled the ripcord too late."

"Why?"

"When you're high up, everything looks real beautiful. He used to talk about it all the time. Looks so beautiful you can forget what you're about. You get sort of hypnotized—you don't even seem to be falling—like sometimes when snowflakes are rushing the windshield of your car and you find yourself watching the snowflakes instead of the road. You get kind of dreamy. Groundrush, it's called. Suddenly the ground rushes up at you and you realize you haven't pulled your rip.

"Anyway," Beowolf said finally, "that's how he died."

"You never mention him. I thought . . . I never knew. How was it for you?"

"What?"

"Him dying."

"I guess, I don't know how to say . . . it was very real when he got killed. It's like, you get used to things being normal: things that get broken get fixed or they never mattered much in the first place and other things take their place." He glanced at Jeannie. "Yeah. You don't even think about being alive most of the time. How good it is. Him dying was very real. I think I expected Moon to take his place."

"Why?"

"He was my father's best friend, I thought."

Jeannie reached across and stroked the side of his face, hugged his head.

"I think a lot about what it must be like all alone like that, knowing you're about to hit the ground. I can be doing anything —and suddenly, there I am about to crash. I have bad dreams. Groundrush dreams. I wish . . . I think of having a chance to say something to him. Just a couple minutes and I think I could tell him everything I ever wanted to tell him." Beowolf pulled his head away and looked into her eyes to gauge what impact he was having; he wasn't sure of what he was saying. He twirled some of her hair around a finger. "I liked him. He was a good guy. He liked to take us out for steaks." Beowolf shifted his body to stare once again at the ceiling. "I never felt like I showed him much."

Jeannie waited, eventually propped herself up on her arm. Her lips parted, but she didn't say anything. Then her eyes narrowed, her head jerked slightly. "I don't get what you mean," she said. "Show him what?"

Beowolf shook his head, shrugged, stared past her at the ceiling.

"What?" she asked again.

"I don't know."

Jeannie reclined along his side, resting her head on his shoulder.

"For my birthday he gave me a football."

"What birthday?"

"Every birthday." Beowolf glanced at her distractedly, then looked away. "That was my birthday present," he said softly. "I had a garage full of footballs. He gave me a football every goddamn birthday."

12

Through the cloudless blue sky the morning sun burned so fiercely that Beowolf was reminded of how as a kid with a magnifying glass he would focus the sun's heat on an anthill to make the ants dance. "Hotter'n hell with the blower on," somebody complained as the team took its warm-up lap around the practice field. Beowolf hit the earth and bounced up running in place, rising and falling endlessly, up and down, one two, *hit it,* fall, up, *ho,* up, down, rising and falling, finally on legs like painsticks, the scent of freshly mown grass steamy and nauseating—the grass so incredibly green, an island in the tawny sea of wheat and prairie scrub. *Is this me,* he wondered, *here?* His father was dead and Jason was gone, the earth spun through space, the sun rose and fell and had finally greeted Summer Practice with a hot, malicious glare.

Before practice, the team had gathered, brush-cut and beaver-faced, on the infield of the baseball diamond to hear Moon deliver what Jason referred to as the "sermon on the mound." "Summer vacation is over. Everybody on this team will be treated the same. Every position is up for grabs. Nobody has their position won. I'm not interested in what you did for me last year. Last year is dead and done with. I wanna know what you're gonna do *this* year. Football games are won with basics: blocking and tackling. And conditioning. Fatigue makes cowards of us all," he declared, repeating the adage that hung on the locker-room wall. "The game is won in the trenches. It's a lineman's game. You have good linemen, it doesn't matter who's carrying the ball. As far as I'm concerned, backs and ends are simply a necessary evil, and they better be able to block and tackle or they won't be playing for this team. You tight ends, remember, you're just linemen with eighties on your backs.

"We're gonna run to daylight. We're gonna run and run and run some more. We're gonna keep the ball on the ground, not like last year. We're gonna run it over their faces because when you put the ball in the air only three things can happen, and two of them are bad. We saw last year what happens when you put the ball in the air.

"I'm not here to mold your minds. I'm here to mold your bodies into a football machine this town can be proud of—and that's what I'm gonna do, even if it kills you. If you're wondering what I can do for you, you don't belong out here, you're not a Rawlings Rattler, and you can get the hell off this field right now so you won't waste my time later running you off. I want men on my team who want to play football. Hitters and Headhunters, grade-A choice, red-blooded meat eaters, men who attack a ballcarrier with their face, men who play with reckless abandon. And if there's anybody listening who doesn't think he can measure up, then get the hell out of here. I want football players out here. I want Rawlings Rattlers. I want men with desire, men with an ability to go the extra distance, go that extra step. A Rawlings Rattler is a man who's called upon to do more than he's capable of doing, and does it. Can you measure up to that?

"We're gonna forget last year." Sweat had darkened the armpits of Moon's jersey. It beaded at his temples and ran down his face. A blue golf hat protected his head from the sun. "Last year is dead and done and it'll damn well never happen again as long as I'm coaching here. Take all your would'ves and could'ves and should'ves and just chuck em. Cause all those excuses and a quarter'll buy you a cup of coffee and that's all, that's exactly what they're worth. Last year. Nothin.

"Excuses are something I never wanna hear. But more than that, they're something I never wanna see. I'll have football players out here, not excuses for football players. They say I treat everybody alike," Moon concluded, and having so far managed his entire speech without once altering that precise uniformity of tone and pitch that was so calm, so *controlled* as to seem inhuman, he paused to glance over all their helmeted heads. "They say I treat everybody alike. Like dogs. And they're right. You'll be treated like dogs and you'll thank me for it come Thanksgiving."

Porkbutt then gave his little spiel. "The human body is a machine . . ." He oiled his tongue for a while on the subject of keeping the body in good tune: getting good sleep and good food. "Eat roughage," no drinking or smoking or getting into trouble. Live like a clock. Take salt pills before and after practice, drink plenty of liquids, report all injuries.

When Peckinpah took over, whistle screaming like a hot rod laying rubber, the team broke into a quick lap around the field and assembled in the end zone for calisthenics, which began in a wave of brisk enthusiasm and ended with the interminable hit-its and the stink of new-mown grass.

Peckinpah's whistle sounded and the grunts jogged to the far end of the field for grass drills with Coach Rose. Peckinpah ran the backs and ends through the ropes: running straight through, legs churning up and down, stepping in every square; then through again, cutting back and forth across the ropes at forty-five-degree angles; hopping through on both feet; hopping through on one foot; hopping through on the other foot; finally running straight through again, stepping in every square. A quick sprint through the Tunnel of Love, twenty-five quick push-ups, jogging to the two-man sled, where everybody gave it his best shot, Peckinpah anchoring it down—"Hit! Hit! Hit!" he cried, his bare chest and shoulders damp with sweat. "You hit like a fairy! You're no Rattler! Hit! Hit! *Will you guys hit?* Hit!" Beneath his mirror sunglasses, his buzzard features twitched in the heat. Moon stood high up in the bleachers watching over everything. Everybody took several shots at the sled, then Peckinpah's whistle blew and they ran through a series of pass-catching drills. The sun glaring down, a morning as dry as dust in a mummy's pocket. The drills were endless: pass patterns, blocking, back to the two-man sled for one quick pop. "Hurt this baby!" Peckinpah screamed. "Hit! Make it hurt! It's gotta hurt! Hit! Hurt this baby! Hit! Hit! Hit! *Run, will you run?*" The whistle again. They jogged to the seven-man sled, hitting each dummy, spinning off and hitting the next, then starting all over again going in the opposite direction. The whistle. Running everywhere. Skeleton drills. Pass defense. Another sprint through the Tunnel of Love and twenty-five more push ups. "You're not in shape!" Peckinpah screamed. "You're fat! You're fat! You're all fat! Every stinking one of you! *Fat!*" Beowolf struggled to keep up, keep moving. Burning with fatigue, he couldn't catch his breath. His jock chafed; crotch rot tomorrow for sure. Inside his helmet he was suffocating.

Moon's whistle finally sounded, and the backs and grunts, bled dry, charged together to the middle of the field. "Waytago," some of them wearily enthused. "Waytago, waytago. Lookin good! Hey awright! Lookin good!"

Peckinpah's whistle dropped from his mouth. "You guys look *bad,*" he sneered.

"Okay, men," Moon said, having descended onto the field. "Two lines. Linemen and linebackers, backs and ends." Seniors headed the lines, then juniors, then sophomores. "We're working on tackling here, only going half-speed now. We're concentrating on form." Peckinpah shoved a football into Catfood Harris' breadbasket. "You attack with your face," Moon instructed. "Keep your weight evenly distributed on the balls of your feet. Keep your head up; you drop your head, you wind up arm-tackling. I don't want arm-tacklers. A good runner'll rip your arms off . . ."

"*And I hope he does,*" Peckinpah hissed.

"Okay, let's go!"

Peckinpah's whistle blew. Catfood angled at half-speed across the open area between the two lines while Tinker sprang from the front of the other line. Catfood was flattened, left wriggling in the grass. "Half-speed!" Coach Rose cried. "Whatzamatter with you, Tinker? You trying to kill somebody?" Tinker bustled to the end of the line. "We're working on *form,*" Moon said. "We'll have plenty of opportunities to crack heads." Catfood got up and staggered to the end of the line, behind Beowolf. "That cocksucker," he gasped, holding his ribs.

"Okay! Okay! Let's go!" Peckinpah shouted. "Let's be hungry out here!"

The morning dragged on. After tackling drills, the grunts jogged to the opposite end of the field to work with Coach Rose. Moon ascended the bleachers. Backs and ends formed a circle around Peckinpah for Bull-in-the-Ring.

"Okay, Gray. Get in here!"

Gray shot eagerly into the center of the circle.

"Okay, let's have some *real* contact now!"

Peckinpah left the inner circle to prowl slowly around the periphery. Gray assumed a crouched, linebacker stance, slowly circling, keeping a wary eye on Peckinpah.

"Jenkins!" Peckinpah cried.

Jenkins leapt forward, Gray spun, there was a resounding crack of helmets and shoulder pads as Gray hit and gave ground, eluding the tackle as Jenkins fell to his knees.

"Jenkins!" Peckinpah bellowed. "What was that supposed to be?

Use your arms, Jenkins! Hit'm and hold'm, hit'm and hold'm! Hang on to that man!"

Jenkins retreated to the perimeter.

"Casey!"

Again there was a crack of helmets and pads as Gray hit and spun off, escaping.

"Get outta there, Casey! You hit like a fag! You wanna quarterback this team, you better hit. Everybody on this team hits, everybody blocks and tackles. Got the picture?"

Casey nodded.

"Got the picture?"

"Yes!"

"Bailey!"

"Yes!" Beowolf shouted.

Peckinpah stopped dead in his tracks, turned—grimacing—and pushed through the perimeter to Beowolf. "What *the hell* are you doing?"

Beowolf couldn't speak.

"Man, you are one dummy package, Bailey." He shook his head. "Bailey!"

"What!" Beowolf hollered.

"Get him! Get him!" Peckinpah was jumping up and down, stabbing his finger at Gray. "Get him!"

Beowolf sprang into the ring; Gray charged for the first time, spearing and driving him backward, straight back to the perimeter, where he tripped over somebody's feet and fell on his ass.

"Bailey!"

Peckinpah towering over him, Beowolf scrambled to his feet.

"Bailey," Peckinpah said softly. "You're too nice, Bailey. You're too damn nice. You got a big jock to fill, but you ain't showin me much."

Bull-in-the-Ring continued. Gray was finally deposed by MD, who took his place. Beowolf took a beating from almost everybody. So did Hap. But Peckinpah chose to single Beowolf out, eventually sticking him in the ring and giving everybody a crack at him. "Eat dirt, Bailey! Eat dirt!"

Moon's whistle finally summoned everybody together, the two platoons charging to the middle of the field, where they slapped each other on the helmets and backs, trying to work up a chatter.

"Nutcracker," Moon said.

The team jogged off the field to the nutcracker pit, where the managers had aligned two tackling dummies two yards apart. Backs and ends formed one line—between the dummies was the hole they would run through—and grunts and linebackers formed another. An offensive and a defensive grunt hustled into place, falling into stances facing each other across the gap between the dummies. Gray jumped into position behind the offensive grunt. "On two," Peckinpah said, gripping the football. "Five-man line . . . Ready! Set! Hut one! Hut two!" He handed off the ball to Gray as the grunts collided: Gray hit, spun and slithered through the hole like a wet weasel.

When Beowolf's turn came, Doe Konichek was blocking for him against Tinker. Beowolf took the handoff and plowed straight into Konichek, who had been straightened up and driven back by Tinker; Tinker grabbed Beowolf and flung him to the ground. "Geddup! Geddup!" Beowolf sprang to his feet. "You let that man do that to you?" Peckinpah screamed at Konichek. "You see what that man did to your ballcarrier?"

Doe searched the ground for an answer.

"Did you see?"

"Yes!"

"Is Tinker better than you?"

"No."

"I can't hear you, Konichek! Am I hard of hearing?"

"No!"

"Is that man better than you!"

"No!"

"Bailey, you run like you got a brick in your pants. Is that man better than you?"

"No!"

"Get in there, Bailey!" Peckinpah commanded. "Show Konichek how to block. Tinker, stay in there. Konichek, you carry the ball."

Beowolf hopped into the pit opposite Tinker, whose face behind his cage was like a clenched fist. "On two . . . Five-man line . . . Ready! Set! Hut one! Hut two!" Tinker's forearm caught Beowolf under the chin, forcing him up; Tinker drove him backward into Konichek, sandwiching him in a sharp crack of pads.

"Geddup! Geddup! Is he better than you, Bailey?"

"No!"

"He just ate you up and spat you out! Get outta there, Tinker. I'll find somebody for you later." Tinker jogged to the end of the line. "Are you better than this man, Bailey?" Peckinpah pointed to No-Neck Bronski, the next grunt in line.

"Yes!" Beowolf shouted.

"Get in there, Bronski. Bailey says he's better than you. Konichek, carry the ball."

Bronski flung Beowolf aside and hit Konichek so hard that it raised a bit of chatter along the line of grunts.

"Get back in there, Bailey! I'm gonna find somebody who you're better than. Who's next?" Joe Lee, another senior grunt, hopped into a four-point stance, his feet digging into the ground, his body tensed, itching to explode. "Is he better than you?" Peckinpah asked Joe Lee.

"No way!"

Joe Lee boxed Beowolf's ears and drove him back. Konichek slammed him in the back again before being wrestled to the earth.

"Eat dirt, Bailey! Eat dirt!" Peckinpah screamed. "You're too nice, Bailey, you lead with your face! You're no Rattler! Are you a Rattler, Bailey?"

"Yes!"

"Get in there, Bailey! You're showin me nothin! *Nothin!* You're showin me how to turn the other cheek. You're showin me how to lose. You should move to Anaconda the way you block. Konichek, carry the ball. And *run,* will you!"

It was painful enough being beaten up in front of the entire team by veteran grunts fifty or sixty pounds heavier than he was. Konichek only made it worse by repeatedly plowing into him from behind.

"You're no Rattler, Bailey! You're no Rattler! You think you're a Rattler? You're no Rattler! You're like a cheap whore. Can't stay off your goddamn back!"

Moon finally ordered Beowolf out of the pit. Beowolf returned to the end of the line.

"That was bad," Hap mentioned; Beowolf's body was killing him, and he didn't need to be told.

As Summer Practice dragged on, Pap became unbearable. "Howzit shapin up? State Championship? What'd Moon say? Has he let on? Did he say anythin bout the Championship? What about you, boy? Ya gonna be playin or yankin splinters outta your ass?" Every night, the same questions.

The interrogation was disheartening. Beowolf's relationship with Moon had cooled terribly. He was hurt and afraid, and the only thing that tormented him more than football practice was the thought that he might be a quitter, like all those others who slunk away between workouts; *how could they ever show their faces again at school?* The prophesied size and speed obviously had failed to materialize, and he felt like the "deadwood" that Peckinpah was so fond of alluding to. Even Hap was listed ahead of him on the first depth chart of the season. His grandfather's inquisition only reminded him of what he wanted to forget.

"His hat!" Pap exclaimed one night over supper, giving Beowolf a start. Pap's expression turned conspiratorial. "Does he still wear . . . the hat?" His eyes bulged wide, waiting for a reply.

"His hat? What about it?" Beowolf's jaw jutted out like a battlement.

"Why doncha know, boy, bout that hat? The blue one with the red band I'm talkin bout, yup."

"What about it? He wears it every day."

"Good! Ayyyy babe, duck's on the pond." Pap spat and laid out an open palm that Beowolf hesitantly slapped. "Duck's on the pond, yup."

Stone-faced, knowing he was being set up, Beowolf asked, "What's so good about it?"

"No one's ever told ya bout it, eh? Strange, yup, stranger'n science. Well, I reckon . . ."

"Fiction."

"Eh?"

"Stranger than fiction."

"Yup, stranger'n friction, too. Reckon I'll have to tell ya bout it myself. S'prised I never told ya before . . ."

"So am I."

"Man name Morgan'r sumpin—the dude, you know, was coach for a time down to Bozeman—he give Moon that hat when Moon took the coachin job here. Yup. Morgan and him—or whatever that sumbitch's name was—were both your pa's sidekicks. Played together. The hat was for luck."

Pap spat; Beowolf waited.

"Ya mean, *that's it?* That's all there is to the hat? Why make such a big deal . . ."

"Whoa boy! Now jes cool your jaws an ease up on the reins, youngster. Don't awways be so damn trigger happy, goin off so goddamn half-cocked all the dad-blasted time." Pap spat and caught his wind. "Moon could be lected mayor of this here piss-ant town, ya know, yup. Sure's a devil in hell could. If he had a mind to, that is. It ain't no *ord'niry* hat, boy." He said *ord'niry* the way a body might say *cow pie* after just stepping in one. *"No it ain't.* Gawd Awmighty, strike me dead if it is! Let me tell ya . . . The first day he wore it, this fat-ass bird come along—musta been a eagle—an takes the biggest blasted dive-bombinest ornery crap you ever seen, right smack dab on Moon's head!" Pap spat. "But he was wearin the hat, see.

"Doncha git it, boy? He never wore no hat before then! Doncha see? It's good luck, boy. Yup. Moon's good luck too. Could git lected mayor of this piss-ant town if he had a mind to. Yup. He's good luck, boy."

"Bullshit," Beowolf said.

"No! Eagleshit, boy! Eagleshit!"

The sun rose and fell, the earth spun through space, the Rawlings juggernaut was forged in the sweltering heat of the practice field, which had become a brimming dust bowl. Hit-its were unbearable: rising from, returning to, choking on dust, dust caking their hot armored bodies. A swallow of water or a sliver of ice pilfered from the ice bucket occasioned a moment of animal bliss too soon terminated. During the second week of practice there was an epidemic of crotch rot. A body couldn't keep his goddamn jock dry from one practice session to the next; it was forever chafing him, chafing him raw. Baby powder and Vaseline became necessities. When Hap's inflamed rot persisted in oozing puss and blood, Tinker flipped him a can of Ball Control. "Works wonders in minutes." Once Hap began enameling his crotch with the glutinous aerosol, the older players hid behind locker doors or quickly withdrew into the shower room; Hap knew something was up, but he let it carry him along, chuckling in the manner of a small boy who hears but fails to understand a dirty joke. It was only when his crotch began to sting—when, wincing, he sized up his glazed pecker soldered to his scrotum—that he realized the joke was on him. As Hap tore into the shower room, everybody busted a gut laughing, catcalling and slapping Tinker on the back. Hap stood under a torrent of blistering water, scrubing himself down with soap until the hot water gave out. That night he shaved himself bald; his hair had fused into a rat's nest.

The key to making the team was to avoid Bull Run. Bull Run was the kiss of death. By the final day of practice, Beowolf and Hap had convinced themselves that there would be no Bull Run this year; the team was already lean, shedding unneeded bodies daily.

Practice that final afternoon was longer than ever, but when Moon's whistle summoned the exhausted team to the center of the field, everybody still displayed his ingrained eagerness. Beowolf was anticipating sprints: sprints, then a shower and he could go home, have supper and go to bed. But Peckinpah's tone was soft when he finally spoke, as ominous as a handshake from the undertaker. Moon had moved to the far end zone, where he stood smoking a cigarette beneath the goalposts.

"It's time we trimmed the fat off this team," Peckinpah said, his teeth immaculately white in the dying daylight. "Time we separated the bull from the steers." He paused for dramatic effect, still grinning from ear to ear. Then he began rattling off names.

Beowolf knew that his name would be among them. He was dead and he knew it and for the first time since his father was killed he felt that he might just melt in tears and die there in the dust in front of these others, all at once, melt into the dust and never come up again for air because he could not stand it anymore. He knew he was dead meat, knew he couldn't do it, any of it, and also knew he'd have to come up for air sooner or later to face the others. His name rang hollow and final from Peckinpah's lips and Beowolf looked at Moon—away from it all, far downfield—and he looked beyond Moon to where the earth and sky collided; but before he could summon a thought he was being screamed at to hustle his tail into place. Each moment snapped past like stop-action. There were six of them, paired off facing each other, ten yards apart. The rest of the team jogged to the sideline, where, catching their breath, they stood impassively.

"As you all know," Peckinpah announced, "Bull Run is a tradition here at Rawlings. We wanna find out who *really* wants to be a Rattler, we wanna see some *desire* . . ." Beowolf was thinking *Hap,* scanning the numbers opposite him; he would beat Hap at least. Hap wasn't there. "You are the Rattlers. We have a long way to go yet, but we've put in a tough Summer Practice. You are the Rattlers. You and one other. *For your viewing pleasure"*—Peckinpah grinned—"we're gonna separate the bull from the steers."

Peckinpah turned to face those paired off in the middle of the field. "When you hear the whistle, go. After you hit, rotate to the left. I wanna see some hustle outta you deadasses, that's why you're here."

Peckinpah glanced downfield at Moon. Then he wheeled and blew the whistle.

Beowolf charged into the body charging him.

"Geddup! Geddoff the goddamn ground!"

The six participants scrambled back into place, assuming the position to the left of their previous starting point.

Peckinpah's whistle sounded again.

Beowolf was thinking of *Hap,* how did goddamn Hap . . . He collided and scampered back into place.

The whistle sounded. "Eat dirt!"

After six collisions they completed one full screwturn. Flurries of cheers accompanied the crack of impact as those on the sideline reveled in the spectacle, rooting for favorites. For them, Summer Practice was over.

After two more screwturns, Jackson stumbled away, heaving, and just kept on heading west. "You're no Rattler, Jackson! You're no Rattler!" Soon after that, somebody else didn't get up off the ground, didn't get up until Peckinpah, hovering over him, hollered for him to get his goddamn tail off the field. "Another steer!" Dust was everywhere. Beowolf responded to the squeal of the whistle, ramming into anonymous bodies, hanging on for himself, trying desperately not to sink forever into the faceless dust. "Eat dirt!" Peckinpah screamed. "Swallow it up!" Blood from Beowolf's nose had run into his mouth; pain hammered along the inside of his skull. The whistle. Each cycle came faster with only four participants. Finally, somebody else staggered off, leaving only three. Wynn was among them—Wynn, who was a junior and who they said could bench two-eighty.

The whistle. He collided with Wynn, gasped for breath. Peckinpah directed Wynn and the other to lock horns. The whistle. Beowolf knew he was through after this, but finally not even caring, caring only for his next breath, which would not come; the dust was killing him, he was not a Rattler, he was nothing, he was nothing but hurt. The other staggered off, not a Rattler, leaving only him and Wynn, whose body hunched crooked, heaving, ten yards away. The whistle. Wynn staggered forward and straightened up at the last moment, absorbing in his chest what little power Beowolf had mustered. Contorted inside his helmet, Wynn's face mirrored Beowolf's own pain. Wynn couldn't go on.

"You're *nothin,* Wynn, just a big bag of wind. You're a steer. Ya know what I think, Wynn?" Wynn headed for the gates. "I think you oughta move to Anaconda and change your name to *Lose!* You hear me, Wynn! You are one big *bag of wind!*"

Beowolf pissed blood that night and was on the practice field the next afternoon, the first day of school.

13

"Why does Peckinpah hate you so much?" Gray asked, harmonica poised at his lips.

"Hate *me?*" Beowolf answered. Gray had never spoken to him before. "He doesn't hate me."

Gray snorted and began playing his harmonica again. Beowolf glanced at the Kalispell game ball in Gray's lap, then gazed back out the window at the land flowing past. The morning was bright and promising even with winter now upon them. The season was over. He had fought to hang on. They had tried to beat him. They had tried to keep him out. But he'd hung on. By mid-season he'd moved ahead of Hap on the depth chart and would usually get to play in the fourth quarter when Rawlings was way ahead, entering the game stiff and hopeful with a fresh coat of Ball Control on his hands. Hap was busily engaged with his angry crotch throughout the season; by November he developed an infection and wasn't even allowed to suit up for the Thanksgiving game. He watched from the stands with ten thousand others as the Rattlers avenged the loss of the previous year and returned the State Championship to Rawlings, where it had belonged all along. Beowolf lifted the game ball from Gray's lap and cradled it in his hands. Gray didn't give a shit who he sat with on the bus.

Music on the bus broke protocol. On the occasion of the State Championship's homecoming, however, the familiar strains of Bob Dylan seemed appropriate to almost everybody—even Peckinpah, who swaggered down the aisle, a faint smirk crossing his face. "So you can play the harmonica, too. That's good . . . We wouldn't want you to start doing this next season, though. But today, this is really, this is *really,* together." Peckinpah forced a smile that emerged as a grimace. Gray hated Peckinpah. If Peckinpah had understood what was there in the music to be heard, if he'd been somehow capable of imagining an action, emotion or expression with a double edge—something running deeper than a locker-room slogan—he would have most likely been already plotting Gray's crucifixion the following August.

Peckinpah stood in the aisle. Gray resumed playing. Beowolf scanned the backs of the heads in front of him: in rows of two, bobbing with chatter, bobbing like those helmeted, spring-supported heads of souvenir football players on concession-stand shelves. For Beowolf, Gray's harmonica evoked not the long-anticipated sense of absolute triumph that he wanted so desperately to experience—redemption for the hell he'd been through—but roused a tangle of contrary emotions, vigorous and bitter, triumphant only in the sense that Gray, with a tiny musical instrument, managed to stir them.

When Peckinpah returned to the front of the bus, Beowolf glanced at Gray; Gray glanced back at Beowolf, who whispered, "That guy couldn't find his ass with both hands," which caused Gray to offer him one of those faint, rare smiles of his that was not unlike a secret handshake. "Why *does* Peckinpah hate you so much?" Gray asked.

"He hates *you.*"

"I consider that a point in my favor." Gray lifted the harmonica back to his lips, but hesitated, reflecting. "He hates you because he hated your brother."

"He didn't hate Jason," Beowolf protested. "Jason was damn good."

"He hated your brother because your brother was so much like Peckinpah himself, only younger. And he hated that. He was jealous." Gray paused. "But he would have hated you anyway. You're nothing like your brother."

"I will be."

"Why?"

Beowolf stared, but Gray would offer him nothing more. He began again softly to play his harmonica.

A winter afternoon several weeks later, Beowolf first got high, listening to Gray play his guitar. With his eyes closed, his head seemed to expand to the size of the Astrodome, while his soul floated weightlessly inside, alone in that huge empty space, clinging to each successive note of music. When the music ended, Beowolf opened his eyes. The first gray shadows of dusk were filling his room like hovering dust.

"You got off," Gray said.

Beowolf laughed; then laughed again to find himself Gray's confederate. Prior to Thanksgiving, Gray had seemed so inaccessible and self-possessed, so uncompromising—his demeanor compensated for, *excused* by, his talent—and now Beowolf was Gray's equal. Gray's equal and then some—for revealed in Gray's private manner was a sort of perpetual baring of the jugular, a vulnerability exposed, wanted or not.

"You going out with Jeannie tonight?" Beowolf asked.

"I'm playing up in Great Falls. If you come with me they'll give you free drinks. I'll tell them you're my manager."

"Tell me something," Beowolf said. "Don't you like her much?"

"Yeah, I like her." Gray ran a finger down the neck of his guitar and peered into the hole in its body.

"Nobody understands what's going on between you two," Beowolf told him. "I my—"

"It's nobody's business."

"But it's so strange."

"It's nobody's business!" Gray spat out, leaping to his feet. "That's what I hate about this town! I mean, this town is nothin but eyes and ears, but it never sees or hears anything. I *hate* this place! I'm handed a football and told to run and everybody thinks I'm great—"

"Don't overestimate yourself," Beowolf interjected, flabbergasted. "There're plenty of people don't think you're so great."

"That's right! Take that football away and they'd hate me!"

"No one's about to take your football away," Beowolf answered.

"I know. They'll just take everything else."

"Like *what?*" Beowolf asked, amazed. "They *give* you things, man. They gave you a pair of white cleats. They've never *given* a pair to anybody. Even Jason had to buy his. And you never even wear em."

"They give me a haircut." Gray sat down on the bed again.

"Well, whattaya wanna be a longhair for, anyway?" Beowolf asked. "Your dad gave you a Cor—"

"*I told you!*" Gray leapt back to his feet. "Don't talk about him!" His face was contorted, his body racked.

"*Calm down.* Sorry I mentioned it."

Gray sank back down onto the bed, shaking his head miserably. "I wouldn't be here but for him."

"I don't understand why you're so mad at everybody. People wanna like you, you know."

"For *what?*" Answering his own question, he said, "For playing football."

"Do something else then. If you don't like it . . ."

"I'm trying." Gray snorted and plucked a string of his guitar.

"I don't think Jeannie would feel any different if you didn't play football," Beowolf said. "I don't think football's but half of why—"

"Why what?"

"Why she—you know—likes you so much. Listen. We're on the same team and everything, but I . . . You know it doesn't matter to me if you play or not, except that you're so damn good it'd be a shame if you didn't." Gray wasn't looking at him. *"But what are we talking about?* We're talking about nothing."

Gray stared into the hole in his guitar.

"You don't seem to like her much."

Gray didn't reply.

"Can I ask you something?"

Gray stared into his guitar.

"What's the matter with her?"

Jumping to his feet, Gray strode to the window, into which he peered long enough for Beowolf to register amazement. He marched fiercely back to the bed, then turned away. "Nothing," he said. "Nothing, *nothing.* Nothing's the matter with her." Abruptly, he charged the window, crashing his fist through one of the panes. Beowolf bolted upright.

A trickle of blood appeared on the back of Gray's hand. The window's outer covering of see-through plastic had fallen away.

Beowolf was stupefied. "Is your hand okay?"

Gray nodded, still facing the window. A draft cut through the room. Beowolf stared for a long time through the shattered glass at the sharp winter twilight, then sat down. Darkness settled into the room before Gray spoke.

"Do you?" he asked without turning around. "Do you like her?"

Beowolf stared at him in the gloom. He walked over to the door and flicked on the light. "I like her a lot," he told him. "I don't know her."

14

"Listen to that," Hap said, sitting up and jerking his head at Bigfoot snoring by the window. "He ain't human." He reached into his duffel bag and pulled out his *Playboy.* "I can't sleep worth a shit."

"He's sleeping enough for both of you," said Granville.

"Yeah, well, wake his ass up."

"I ain't waking him up. *You* wake him up."

The three of them studied Bigfoot for a moment, listening to him drive the hogs to market.

Bigfoot had a dazzling penchant for falling unpredictably into deep, anesthetized slumbers. That he would snooze periodically through the school day was the rule rather than the exception, and providing that nobody poked him when he snored and providing that he didn't topple out of his seat, he was rarely disturbed. As a sophomore he had incurred the wrath of Moon by poignantly sawing logs through the final moments of a game film; and when Peckinpah derided him as being "half Indian and half *wit,*" he'd protested with a face as straight as a highway center-line that he already knew the ending—which won him a season's pass through the Tunnel of Love. He was ridden by the coaching staff even through the next season, and it was only because he made All-State that they decided, his senior year, to treat him like a white man again.

Bigfoot was basically just a sit-around-on-his-ass type of guy who liked to eat and sleep and fart and scratch and watch TV and drink beer and burp and play pool and dream about pussy. He possessed a highly refined, nearly sublime capacity for crudeness. Refusing to break bread in the school cafeteria with anybody whose company he failed to appreciate, he would break wind instead, rambunctious vibratos or soaring arpeggios; whatever it took to drive off the intruder. If he was interrupted in the midst of some peerless eloquence on the subject, say, of the efficacy of scratching one's crotch rot, he was known to obsequiously defer, folding his arms and settling back into his chair—all the while mustering from the bottomless abyss of his stomach a putrid belch, which, springing forward for an abrupt tête-à-tête, he would detonate in the interloper's face. Hap, a frequent victim, called it "lung fu." One blow could knock you out.

Bigfoot clogged the locker-room toilet in what had become practically a weekly ceremony. The "prognosticating shit," it was called. It forecasted victory. Ceremoniously, he pissed on gravestones, pissed on flagpoles, pissed in the gas tank of Rollo's patrol car during Rollo's abbreviated term as sheriff. At stoplights he was known to belt out "Moon over Miami" while his inelegant ass ballooned out the car window, smiling vertically at the driver of the car next to him. Outside the classroom he could absolutely not bear to stifle a fart. During school he would try to confine himself to silent-but-deadlies in a vain effort to not call attention to himself; yet rarely did a day expire when his spirit at least once didn't wail for deliverance. The school psychologist had labeled him "socially immature."

Hap finally shook his head. He wasn't going to wake Bigfoot up. "Pure beef, plumb to the hocks."

"Hey, are rooms alphabetical again?" Beowolf asked. Customarily, rooms were assigned by position. But in Billings, where they played the only overnight road game since losing to Anaconda, rooms had been assigned alphabetically.

"I wasn't listening," Hap answered. "I hope not."

"Why, who ya got?" Beowolf asked, snickering. Hap's alternatives were not the best.

Doe Konichek was full grown in body only, *not all there,* a cretin of habit, the Duke of Dumb. Rooming with him in a Holiday Inn was like being locked overnight in Twombley's Furniture Warehouse where the Muzak was working overtime.

"Do you prefer . . ." Beowolf's head jerked slightly over his shoulder toward Lombago.

"Does a beaver piss on a flat rock?"

Beowolf hoped the rooms were assigned alphabetically. In the Holiday Inn after the Billings West game, he and Bigfoot shot the shit deep into the night, sitting Indian-style on their beds and volleying a Rawlings Rattlers peewee football back and forth over a net of toilet paper wound between the TV and the lamp on the night table. If rooms were assigned by position, Beowolf would have to put up with MD.

MD was a stocky blond predator who always took a shower an hour before kickoff, scrubbing himself immaculate so that he could enter the game with what he called a "clean slate." He wore an angelic face and white Adidas, and played football like a madman. He *was* a madman. Or a Mad Dog. *Crazy,* in fact, was as much a quality valued by MD himself as it was the bedrock characteristic attributed to him by others. Not only was he the type, like Bigfoot, whom a body liked to have on his side in a brawl, he was the type never to leave the start of a brawl to chance. For MD, Saturday night could scarcely be considered complete until a beer bottle had been busted over somebody's head, occasionally his own.

Moon had labeled him "a hitter, a real sticker," and had even gone so far as to assert, in print, that if Rawlings had eleven boys like him, the Rattlers could take on Notre Dame. This was no idle exaggeration. It was anticipated that Kalispell would be swarming with college scouts. During the season, MD had attracted so many recruiters that over the past few weeks Moon had imposed a moratorium on their visits until season's end. Notre Dame reportedly was drooling over him.

In the locker room, his natural habitat, MD was King Shit, his intrinsic viciousness cloaked in playfulness like a stone couched in the heart of a snowball. His favorite sport after football was "stomping piss-ants." Accosting a piss-ant, he might frantically inquire, "What's worse than a hurricane?" Allowing the piss-ant no chance to respond he would exclaim *"A twister,"* giving the piss-ant's nipple a rough twist. With the exceptions of Frankie Dimitruk and Rocky Bellito, all the sophomores suffered from what MD called "purple nurples." MD was forever jabbing or twisting, pinching or pulling some piss-ant's hair, snapping somebody's bare ass with a towel, goosing somebody or giving somebody a pit poke. Wedgies had been a staple amusement until the sophomores all stopped wearing underwear so that he could no longer grab it from behind and yank it up into the victim's crack, sometimes lifting him clean off his feet, sometimes yanking so viciously that the underwear ripped and he could pull it all the way over the victim's head—a "covered wagon." He'd once massaged a bit of Atomic Balm into Eddie York's jock—a "hot dog"—and had tried to convince Doug Wagonseller that Atomic Balm would clear up his acne. In the showers, MD would just as soon water a body's leg as talk to him. Hap had been caught in a "flash flood" the week after Anaconda.

After his shower, MD would don his Stetson and swagger bare-assed up and down the aisle on the scent of fresh meat. He wielded a broken baseball bat, which he used as a gavel, banging the garbage can to call the locker room to order.

"Lombago! Get up there!" Around the sophomores he always sounded like Peckinpah.

Lombago would toss his towel aside and hustle to the training table.

"Where's your oxygen mask, Lombago? Get your oxygen mask." MD parked himself on the bench directly in front of the table.

Because most of MD's scenarios with the piss-ants were stale, most of the older players simply ignored them, taking an interest only when an outburst of laughter suggested that something novel was taking place. Others, however, having once endured similar torments themselves, relished inflicting these "character builders" now that they had the chance.

Lombago hopped onto the table, where he stood naked but for the jock over his face.

"Okay." MD scanned his audience. "Listen up, Lombago. I'm Ground Control, you're Steve Canyon. Got the picture? Ya know the game, Lombago?"

"You oughta!" somebody cried out.

"I don't hear you, Lombago."

"Yeah, I know the game."

"Speak into the microphone, Lombago. Ground Control ain't picking up a word you're saying."

Lombago grabbed his pecker and doubled over as far as he could. "I know the game."

"You know the game, what?"

Still holding his pecker, Lombago replied, "I know the game. *Over.*"

"Now you're talkin . . . Ground Control to Steve Canyon," MD began, a trace of urgency in his voice. "Come in, Steve. Over."

Some of the spectators laughed.

"Steve, three of your engines are dead and the fourth is runnin on E. You're gonna have to ditch your plane in the water. Can ya handle it, Steve? Over."

"Yes. Over."

"Good, Steve, good. Ground Control will try to guide you in. Stick a finger up your nose." MD signaled Geek Larson, who slid a garbage can full of freezing water out of the shower room and shoved it, splashing the floor, against the training table. "Ready, Steve?"

Lombago nodded wretchedly, a finger now up his nose.

"I can't hear you, Steve!"

Lombago grabbed his pecker and bent back over. "Okay," he said. "Over."

Geek winged Lombago with a tape-ball. "Get that finger up your nose, dipshit!"

Clutching his pecker with one hand, Lombago poked a finger from the other up his nose.

"You still ain't coming in too good, Steve," MD complained.

"He needs a bigger mike," Geek suggested.

Doubled over, Lombago glanced up at MD.

"You need a bigger mike, Steve!" MD shouted.

Lombago glanced helplessly down the aisle.

"Get Eddie York to show him how!" somebody hollered.

"Lombago," MD said, "I just wanna be sure you got one like the rest of us."

"Hey," Bigfoot called down the aisle. "He's got one, I see it. You need glasses, asshole?"

MD was instantly flustered. "Lombago, you're fuckin useless. You're queer as a football bat, Lombago. Sing, sing something horny. No! Sing about the hairy old ape up in the tree."

> I was walkin through the jungle
> With my cock in my hand,
> I'm the meanest motherfucker
> In this jungleland.
> Well, I saw a hairy ape
> Hangin up in a tree,
> And he tried to take a
> Hairy ole piss on me . . .

When Lombago was done, MD spoke quietly. "Lombago, shove a finger up your ass, and another in your mouth. We're testing your reflexes here, Lombago. I wancha to prove to me that you're not slow as shit." Like Peckinpah, if ever MD spoke in a soft tone he intended evil business. "Okay, now . . . *Switch!* Faster, Lombago! Switch! . . . Switch! . . . *Switch!* . . . *Switch!* Faster! Switch! Good, ain't it, Lombago? Ain't it good?"

"It's shitty," Lombago snorted, a smirk glimmering momentarily on his face.

"Don't laugh, Lombago. You'll only encourage me. Do you eat shit because a hundred billion flies can't be wrong?"

Lombago glanced around the locker room.

"Do you?"

"No."

"Why do you eat shit then?"

"Because you make me."

"Don't blame me that you eat shit!" MD screamed. "I ain't why you eat shit, Lombago. You just eat it naturally. You *are* shit, Lombago, you eat so much of it."

"Ease up!" Bigfoot shouted, this time angrily. "You're gettin on my nerves."

"Okay, Lombago," MD continued. "When you stop eating shit out there"—he pointed toward the football field—"you can stop eating it in here . . . All right!" He rapped the garbage can several times, sloshing water over the sides. "Sing a song, Lombago, a horny song, and take a dip." He rapped the garbage can again. "Then I want . . . York! Eddie York! Then I want Eddie York up here!"

MD had a less than exceptional capacity to gauge exactly how far he should push the piss-ants, so it was often necessary for someone like Bigfoot to draw the line for him. Still, Beowolf often wondered how MD had ever come to wield such power. What was truly crazy was that everybody let him do it. He had been *elected* captain. Beowolf had voted for Bigfoot. Bigfoot had voted for Beowolf. Hap would probably have voted for Beowolf also, had he a vote to cast; only lettermen voted. Recently, it had occurred to Beowolf that MD had never forced himself on Rawlings. He had merely filled a space that was waiting for him, just as Moon had. The torch would pass from one captain to the next, a perpetual process in which the individuals didn't much matter. Gray wouldn't take it from Tinker, who had taken it from Jason, so they got rid of Gray and appointed Jack Ballantine, and from him it passed to MD.

On the football field, Beowolf relied on MD more than he depended on anybody else. They returned punts together. The man not receiving the kick would judge, while the ball was airborne, if a fair catch was necessary. After the ball was caught, he was responsible for springing the runner past the first defender downfield, clearing the way toward the tunnel of linemen who, having faked pressure on the punter, had sprinted in a wide arc outside to cut downfield—hell-bent as a string of runaway boxcars on a mountain—to the rescue.

Beneath a punt, stomach gripped by a high-strung fist, Beowolf would watch the ball spiral to its zenith, hovering between the stadium lights for a missed beat in time. Alone in silence, a body and a ball, two points in time and space accelerating through limbo toward climax, in silence like snowfall, a body and a ball stuck in time—the quick crouch to cradle the catch, then the burst of terror shooting like buckshot through his body, riding MD's back toward the far sideline, scanning, bellying sharply upfield to set up MD's block, then sliding outside ahead of the grunt and thunder, cutting hard toward the nearest Rawlings jersey burning down on him from upfield, bellying again—casting a hip at a defender and jerking it back with the defender hooked—sweeping outside for the red jersey, his own jersey, bearing down on the hot breath at his tail, the ecstatic crack of perfection at his back—home now suffusing him in sweet panic as he cut upfield behind his wall of blockers strung along the hashmarks, sprinting home, jitterbugging by an intruder into his own man, shoving, spinning and stuttering wildly away, laying it on now full-steam up the sideline sixty yards straight upfield like the Northern night train, night train with a football, night train panic bound to where the fist in his stomach would loosen its grip.

As far as Beowolf was concerned, a successful punt return was the most exquisite act on a football field, and he and MD performed them so artfully that on fourth down the Rawlings partisans rose instinctively to their feet even before the ball was punted. More than once, MD and Beowolf had roused Rawlings with a breakneck dash for the end zone. Prancing off the field afterward, slapping the open palms of the offensive players who brushed past to take their places, the two were caught up in the floodlights, the roar of the joyous, brightly painted crowd, the atmosphere of pure oxygen. There were indeed times when, because he wore the Rawlings uniform, MD was almost likable.

Watching them play, people sometimes got the impression that Beowolf was crazy like MD, only not to MD's degree. But MD was naturally crazy; Beowolf had simply practiced a lot. Together they prided themselves on the fact that the number of fair catches they had made all season could be counted on one hand. Beowolf would fume and rave during games, losing himself to the hectic tempo: between plays strutting and posing with his hands on his hips, sneering at the opposition, needling the enemy pass receivers as they returned to their huddle.

As a freshman he had realized that he wasn't blessed with MD's instincts for the game and that his talent, at least for the time being, was marginal. He was perceptive enough to figure out, however, that awesome talent and fierce instincts were not prerequisites, and that few people possessed either. They were rare money-back guarantees, and that was all. What a body needed was simple perseverance.

He hated football even more his sophomore year than he'd hated it his freshman year. He wasn't fast or strong or unafraid. He wasn't a starter, not by a longshot. But he nurtured that crucial and incisive disregard for life and limb, Moon's "reckless abandon." He was willing to hurtle his body at other bodies—initially because to make the team he had no choice, and later, as a junior, when his talent finally bloomed broad and full, because the idea of "reckless abandon" had taken firm root, becoming second nature to him. He started his junior year and, even as a split end, by game time had given himself up to a premeditated fury. If he learned nothing else in a lifetime of football, he'd learned that nothing hurts once a body achieves rage.

The bus slowed down as it entered Kalispell, jolting Beowolf from his contemplations. A night's rest in a Holiday Inn and then his last game. The Kalispell game had to be his very best, if for no other reason than that it was the closing of the circle: where the end and the beginning finally come together, like the old wives' tale about snakes biting into their own tails to roll downhill. A shiver exploded at the base of his neck, spraying to the extremities. He shook briefly and then recovered. Time had accelerated. Time had accelerated in the past five weeks. He slammed the window shut, aggressive and alert.

When the bus eased into the parking lot, the sophomores in the back of the bus began to file forward. Beowolf nudged Hap, who stashed his *Playboy* in his duffel bag. When Beowolf stood up, his groin buckled momentarily. He leaned back and stretched. The door sprang open and the team began to pile out into the night.

Beowolf stumbled out of the bus behind Hap, loosening his limbs, reluctant to enter the cold, but content for the moment to be finally out of the bus.

Night

15

It was raining. Between Bigfoot's rasping snores Beowolf could hear it against the windowpane. If he had slept, he had not dreamt; he rolled over and stared at the wall. He had no idea what time it was. Between his legs he was hard. Touching himself, he suddenly realized that he did not want to go to U of M. No way, José. Somewhere else, though, perhaps somewhere else he could start fresh and play again. He would get into shape over the summer, his best condition ever; his groin would heal and he could work and work and not think about anything at all. Sometimes he imagined being apart from Jeannie altogether. Rarely were these unpleasant fantasies, for the world was huge and full of people; and he was still young, yet had a great deal of experience behind him. He was ready to strike out for himself. He could be a damn good college safety, he knew this for sure. If he could simply narrow the focus of his efforts and contemplations to one or two activities—football and living well, having a good time—perhaps then he could be happy.

Throwing off his covers Beowolf limped to the window and spread the curtains. Against the pale glow of streetlights the rain glistened like fine, unreal filaments spun from the overcast sky to earth. The trees were bare, the street empty and slick. Beowolf tentatively leaned back to loosen his groin. Bigfoot sputtered and sneezed and rolled over, mumbling. "What?" Beowolf asked. The snoring resumed.

Gingerly, Beowolf pulled on his corduroys. He slipped into a flannel jersey and fished one of his three joints out of his pocket. No matches. He searched the night-table drawer, finding nothing but a Bible. Sitting down on the bed he stared out the window. It seemed inconceivable to him that he was capable of fathering a child. How simple it had been!

The problem, he told himself, was not with Jeannie, though she often seemed to him too serene, too accepting. She refused, for instance, to fight with anyone but him. The trouble was with himself. As much as things were anybody's fault, they were his.

"I'm not old enough," he had said. How could he raise a kid when he was still a kid himself? "You are," Jeannie answered.

Eric had been old enough. Jeannie had told Beowolf how, passing through Rawlings on his way to California, Eric had met Jeannie's mother and married her soon afterward—not with the vision of living happily ever after, but with the threat of buckshot dancing through his head. Jeannie's parents inhabited their home like boardinghouse tenants respectful of each other's privacy: her mother keeping to her own bedroom, where she quietly watched TV all day and drank too much coffee from a cup she never rinsed out. That Jeannie was an only child seemed to Beowolf as much a consequence of her parents' separation into opposite bedrooms as of any "family planning." Yet because Jeannie's mother popped pills for her innumerable ailments the way Bigfoot popped carbohydrate supplements, Beowolf figured that she certainly wouldn't have hesitated to take birth control pills as well, if for no other reason than to have something else to wash down with her coffee. Eventually, Jeannie told him that she had been an extremely difficult birth, and that all the females on her mother's side seemed to have problems having babies. For seventeen years Jeannie's mother had been incapable of conceiving another child.

"*You* feel guilty," Beowolf once said to her. "How about me? At least your mother lived."

"Some life," Jeannie answered bitterly. Having grown increasingly reclusive in middle age, Jeannie's mother rarely appeared except in a bathrobe and slippers: a jittery, domesticated ghost with bags under her eyes.

"It's not your fault. You didn't ask to be born."

"She's never loved me. She tried, I think, for a while when I was little. But she never wanted me."

Had Eric had a son, he would have wanted him to be like Beowolf, which Beowolf knew even without Jeannie forever reminding him of it. Each Sunday over supper, Eric asked him the same question: "How we gonna do this week?" Beowolf would shrug modestly and, though it was strictly against team rules, reiterate the scouting report on Rawlings' upcoming opponent. "Don't talk about this to anybody," Beowolf always warned, "or my ass'll be in a sling." Eric so enjoyed getting an inside glimpse of the game and so obviously appreciated this confidence that Beowolf sometimes even clued him in to the audibles Frankie might call from the line of scrimmage; close enough to the field to hear, Eric could often know before the snap what the play would be.

Nevertheless, peering into Eric's eyes, Beowolf sometimes felt disconcerted, perceiving during stray silences a questioning, puzzled look, a suspicion perhaps or a simple watchfulness that inhibited their otherwise complete familiarity. What, after all, his eyes seemed to ask, were Beowolf's intentions concerning his daughter? The *real* question Jason had bluntly expressed: "Been in her pants yet, you bastard?"

"That's the way fathers are," Jeannie told him.

"Even to me?" Beowolf asked, his question being at the time little more than an exercise in bumming compliments, assuming none of the significance that it took on several weeks later, when the future seemed neither vast nor open, seemed to have collapsed, leaving him dazed and angry, lashing out for space and freedom at the expense of the only living person he had ever loved.

"You're better than some," Jeannie said.

Beowolf scoffed at this. "I'm not gonna worry about *my* kids. What happens happens. Worrying don't help."

Jeannie laughed. "You're more like Eric than you think. Wait until you're a father. You'll probably be worse. We'll have to lock you in the basement any time a boy comes over."

"I'm not having daughters. I'm having sons."

"What's wrong with daughters?"

"They getcha lookin at people cockeyed, the way Eric looks at me."

Jeannie laughed.

"I don't like to lie."

"You're not lying." Amazed, Jeannie stared at him, her eyes Eric's: volatile blue, impenetrable at times like this, yet other times a vulnerable azure, transparent and fathomless. "You have a guilty conscience!" She was delighted. "He hasn't asked you anything and he never will. Do you think he's going to come right out and say: *Are you sleeping with my daughter?*"

"I wish he would, so we could get it over with."

"You'd shit a football!"

Beowolf laughed. "What if he does ask?" he finally said. "Supposing he does?"

Jeannie wrapped her arms around his neck and kissed him. "Lie," she advised.

Until he lost the election to Rollo, Eric had been sheriff for as long as Beowolf could remember. Eric had made certain, after Beowolf's father was killed, that Beowolf and Pap got what was coming to them from the government. Pap wouldn't have known who to threaten with his shotgun. When Rollo left town in the beginning of October, having shot himself in the ass, Eric was appointed sheriff until elections could be held. Two weeks before Election Day, however, the missiles went up out at the Air Force base, making it plain as a grunt's ass that, just as with the cattle mutilations, Eric couldn't keep order worth a damn. He wound up losing again, this time to some Italian who wasn't even from Rawlings, but from some jerkwater town in the middle of nowhere.

The cumulative effect of these misfortunes was manifested in a graying at Eric's temples and in his staying up late at night, drinking Oly and watching the tube, sometimes even watching the fuzz after the sermonette and "The Star-Spangled Banner."

"You get used to an occupation," he told Beowolf. "Then one morning you wake up and it's all over."

Bigfoot sneezed violently and commenced a coughing fit. Beowolf stood up. "You all right?" he asked. "Fuck," Bigfoot answered. He rolled over and immediately began snoring.

Out the window a Holiday Inn sign glowed, a neon rainbow of ghastly colors. The rain fell over the quiet town, the empty street, the trees black and naked, illuminated by streetlights. It looked like a movie set. "The Nation's Innkeeper." Rated PG. Beowolf sat back down on the bed. Jeannie was staying at the cabin with some of the other cheerleaders. He lay back and stared at the ceiling. He was tired but knew he wouldn't sleep if he got back into bed.

Nothing in his life was fixed. Gray would say, "To play the blues, ya gotta live the blues," but Beowolf wanted to neither play them nor live them. A body needed at least one thing fixed, a principle or goal. Beowolf considered Jeannie.

Waking in the cold and black, he sat up and spread the quilt over them. Embers glowed from the ashbottom of the fireplace. The candle still burned inside the bookshelf cinderblock. He snuggled under the autumn colors. The fireplace, the grizzle-bear head, the moon down, the same record repeating itself, the prom dress draped over a chair in the corner. His hand wandered up Jeannie's leg, over her hip and ribs to her breast. He nestled against her as gently as he could, not wanting her to wake—as if they were under a spell as fragile as a child's belief in happy endings.

He knew when she was awake. "You awake?" he asked.

"Yes. Are you?"

"Yes."

She rolled over in his arms, her hair falling across her face in a way he had never seen. He brushed it aside and kissed her.

"Did it feel good?" he asked.

"Except for in the beginning. The beginning hurt, but that's over now."

"I didn't use a rubber."

"That's okay."

"What if you get pregnant?"

"I won't."

"If you get pregnant, we'll get married." Jeannie didn't reply, just kissed him. "I have to start using a rubber," he said.

"I'll take pills. I don't like those slimy things."

"How do you know?"

"I looked."

He drew back from her.

"In your pocket. This afternoon. I threw it in the fire."

Beowolf laughed. "You go through my pockets?"

"Yep."

"How come?"

"I didn't know what it was when we were dancing. I felt it."

They both laughed. "Where do you get pills? Don't get em in Rawlings or everybody'll be trailing you like a bitch in heat. Get em in Kalispell. Can you get em up here?"

"I suppose." Her leg slid between his legs. "You're all hard again!" A look of amazement swept across her face.

"That's what happens."

"How does it feel for you?" she asked.

"What? This right now?"

"No. Before."

"It felt real good." He lifted her face up to his and kissed her. "All I ever wanted was to lose my fucking virginity."

"Me too," she said. Her eyes flashed past his. "I always wanted to." She hugged his head, then gazed into his eyes. "What we need," she whispered, her eyes wide open and lovely, "is *practice.*"

Beowolf stared at the ceiling, wishing he would just cry. Abruptly he sat up. He kicked Bigfoot's mattress to make him stop snoring. In the bathroom he examined himself in the mirror. "Do you wanna make my girl a whore, son?" That was a line he'd heard somewhere before, maybe in a movie. But Eric would never say anything like that. Getting up for a nightcap, Eric had heard her crying, opened the door a crack, sending a shaft of idiot light across the carpet and over the Kalispell effigy lying on the floor at their feet. He asked what was wrong and they told him "nothing." They would never tell him, and Beowolf never felt more miserable in his life than listening to Eric climb slowly back upstairs.

"Go away," Jeannie said to him. "Go away."

Beowolf knew she didn't mean it. It was just a bad time, that was all, a time that would pass. It was twelve weeks now, which was as long as she could let things go. It didn't show on her yet, and it never would. After the game, after Friday, after she finally came home from Kalispell, it would be gone for good. And he'd be four hundred in the hole and she'd probably quit talking about getting married. Things would be good again. Jeannie had made the arrangements herself. He wouldn't have known what to do. He hoped she would have it done at a different place than she'd gotten the damn pills. If she had it done at the same place, she'd probably wind up with twins.

Beowolf turned away from the mirror and wandered back into the bedroom. In his duffel bag he found his peewee football. RAWLINGS RATTLERS NEVER SAY DIE—RHS 1986. The ink on the ball was so faded that he could read it only because he knew what was there. Lying down with his head jutting off the foot of the bed, he tossed the ball toward the ceiling and caught it with one hand. For years he had lain on his bed in the dark, tossing a regulation football at the ceiling and catching it, learning to catch by touch rather than by sight. Again and again he tossed the ball to the ceiling and caught it. Finally he threw it too hard; the ball hit the ceiling and bounced beyond his reach. Beowolf lay there staring at the ceiling. It occurred to him that it was his birthday in less than a week.

He rose from the bed and found a pen and motel stationery in the desk drawer. Returning to the bathroom, he lowered the toilet seat cover so that he could sit down, and with the tank top in his lap for a writing surface, he wrote "Dear Jeannie" on a sheet of paper. He was full up with something, he didn't know what. He had to get it out. He would give her the letter before the game. Why, when he finally made a real stand in life, did it have to hurt Jeannie of all people? He loved her very much. He was a coward, this was the truth. A terrible coward. Gray had thought so after that second Bull Run. But by that time Gray had already given her to him.

"Why don't you show your face when she's around?" Gray had asked him early on.

"I figured you'd wanna be alone."

"Show your face."

Gray was crazy. He hadn't wanted Jeannie, had wanted only to fight back. He blew dope and grew his hair long—not that these things mattered in themselves. Beowolf had done likewise, and by the time Summer Practice began his hair was long enough to hide his ears. But Gray cut himself off so thoroughly, so fiercely, from everything he'd ever known—his family, his home, his past—that he'd grown monstrous, caring only about his own idea of himself. His moods dipped and swung. He lashed out, flailing the air, forever threatening to run amok. You never knew what he might do next—like that time in Beowolf's bedroom when he'd freaked out. He was too conscious, too *self-*conscious, uncompromising, selfish as much as introspective, imagining himself perhaps a James Dean, who was dead as a doornail and whose peculiar form of self-destruction seemed to be the only dream that for Gray was real enough. And Jeannie—despite or maybe *because* of the fact that she above everyone else felt the painful brunt of Gray's turmoil— Jeannie looked after him, tried always to shield him from the backlash of reality.

Staring at "Dear Jeannie," Beowolf couldn't find words for anything. We have dreams, he was thinking. We have dreams that don't work. He and Jeannie understood each other well when he was inside her. When he was inside her he wanted it to never end. He was bad at explanations. Words were nothing. Sometimes the impulse seized him to grab her by the hand and light out for the Yukon or someplace. Leave no trace. They could build a cabin like the one in Falls Falls and have the baby, eventually have a whole family. He could hunt and grow food and Jeannie could cook and sew; he'd protect her and he'd start playing his guitar again, and through the cold nights and long months of winter they would huddle together under fur blankets.

The cabin on Echo Lake had been a good place, a place where time seemed to pause. At night they would jump naked off the dock, swim and return, shivering, to their firelit sanctum.

"We'll live here forever," Beowolf had said, lying before the fire on open sleeping bags that first night last May.

"It's not ours," Jeannie answered.

"Sooner or later it will be," Beowolf told her. "Surest bet in town."

"You're awful."

Beowolf pulled his jersey over his head and tossed it aside. His arms and shoulders were sore from rowing the boat. He watched Jeannie gazing through the window at the moonlit clouds floating past.

"We'll grow our own food," he continued. "And hunt."

Turning from the window to look at him, Jeannie said, "We can't hunt deer."

"Sure we can."

"They have such big brown eyes, how could you kill one? I *love* deer."

"Easy."

"You're mean," she said. "Bloodthirsty."

Beowolf crawled over to the fireplace to feed another log to the fire. "I'm not mean." The flames leapt hissing over the fresh wood, sending fitful shadows up and down the walls. Jeannie claimed his place on the sleeping bags.

Beowolf glanced at her, then up at the bared teeth of the grizzle bear above the hearth. "Look," he said, pointing to the bear. "Your father."

"That's not my father. My father has pretty blue eyes."

"That's how he looks when he sidles up next to me to catch a whiff of my aftershave."

"You don't wear aftershave."

"That's why."

"Besides," she said. "I don't even believe that you shave."

"I shave." He stroked his chin. Jeannie laughed.

He stared across the sleeping bags at the girl sitting cross-legged. Lying down next to her he felt between his fingers the texture of her flowered pajama top.

"When I was a kid," he said, "I could never sleep with the closet door open."

Jeannie glanced at the closet, where shadows darted among the hanging clothes. "Why not?" Framed in soft chestnut hair, her face was a rosy color in the firelight.

"Cause I'd see things in there. People and things. Murderers and monsters."

"I'll close it."

"No." Beowolf swung his arm around her, laughing. "Don't bother."

"Yes," she insisted. "Let me."

She removed his arm and sprang to her feet. She closed the closet door, put a record on the turntable and lit a white candle that stood inside one of the bookshelf cinderblocks. Returning to the sleeping bags, she lay down next to him. "There," she said. She kissed him as if he were a little boy. Music began to play.

Beowolf drew her closer to him; abruptly he was laughing. "I could never sleep with my arm over the side of the bed either," he informed her. "Cause there were things down there too, under the bed."

"Like what?"

"Like snapping turtles, with shells big as garbage-can lids. And rattlesnakes."

Jeannie sat up, slapping her palm down on the sleeping bags; on her hands and knees she pounded every square inch. Then she checked under the quilt blanket folded at Beowolf's feet.

"Nothing under there now," she said.

Beowolf stared at her, filled up with the warmth and scent of crackling firewood, the girl's presence an overwhelming emanation of something he needed always to know and feel, reaching out to touch her shoulder, the delicate soft fabric of her flowered pajamas. "Jeannie," he said to her. She rubbed his ankle gently, bent down and kissed it. He pulled her toward him and kissed her. Her eyes were wide, peering into his, unafraid yet somehow refracting his certitude into a vague question. "What's the matter?" he asked. She smiled at him and shook her head. "Nothing."

From the dock that morning, when they'd just arrived, he'd

caught enough bass to live on for the two days they would be there. He filleted the fish—Jeannie was asleep on the army blanket—then wrapped the meat in Handi-Wrap, heaving the remains onto the rocks along the shore for the crows and osprey. Afterward he lay next to Jeannie and twirled her orchid, holding it by the stem. The sun was high now. The orchid smelled like a funeral parlor. He placed the flower on the water. When it floated almost out of reach, he swept it back.

"You awake?" he whispered. Jeannie murmured as his fingernails grazed over her shoulders and neck.

He was into his second wind lying on that dock, having been awake all night driving to the cabin. Crossing the plains beneath the full moon had made him feel as if he were in outer space, weightless and alone as could be—as if, were he to roll down his window, his air would escape. But it was also lovely, like when he was a kid, at dawn below the dam in the forested gorge, feeling as if he were the last man on earth. Jeannie was asleep beside him. The radio played hits from the sixties. The countryside was a gridiron illuminated by moonlight dusting the amber- and brown-brushed checker spaces. In the mountains he ran over a porcupine; it thumped beneath the car, causing Jeannie to stir. She changed the channel to the price of wheat bushels and hog bellies, set her head down on his thigh—the vending-machine condom burning like a hot quarter in his pocket—and in Kalispell they stopped at a truck stop for breakfast. Dressed as they were, rented tuxedo and prom dress, they felt ridiculous surrounded by truckers. But everybody just laughed and said "Howdy" and "Where ya bin?" and gazed at Jeannie, and one who hadn't said a word—when he left, the others said he had throat cancer—paid Beowolf's tab and waved good-by, and Beowolf never even knew to thank him until it was too late. Outside, the moon was visible even though dawn was two hours old. The class picnic was at Whitefish Lake, but he and Jeannie had ventured farther north.

Lying on the dock, Beowolf kissed her hair, inhaled her lemon scent. Her breathing wavered. Her face nestled into the shade of his neck. The sky was blue as a robin's egg. Occasionally, a cloud would glide past. He reached down her body and squeezed her ass. He couldn't sleep. He hugged her. He watched the sky. The breeze carried the scent of pine resin and blew the water into tiny waves that swayed the dock barely perceptibly; the waves were hypnotic, shimmering clear green in the sunlight.

In the bedroom Bigfoot sneezed and spat. "Fuck!" he cried out. Then it was over; the snoring resumed. Beowolf stared at "Dear Jeannie." His head drooped, but he couldn't cry. Somehow every problem or pain worked its tortuous way home to him. He had grown up lacking something essential—a mother, to be sure, then a father, then a family, but it went beyond even this. Hidden where others could not perceive it, instead of strength, was a void. All of his life had been a struggle to disguise this central hollowness, which, until recently, he believed he had disproved. Fighting, he had merely welled up with something contrary, a resentment of what was expected, even a hatred. After the Bull Run with Gray he had felt like Barabbas. Yet he had been welcomed back to the fold like a prodigal son. Moreover, Gray's disappearance had made things so much easier for him that even he had begun to regard Gray merely as a troublemaker.

Gray had left him Jeannie, and what had Jeannie really to do with Rawlings other than that she, innocently, had been born there and lived there? Just like him. Rawlings, the place, was nothing to her. Rawlings. Beowolf detested Rawlings and would soon be gone from it.

Beowolf lifted his head and gazed over the sheet of paper. Stranded in a tiny boat with no gas in the engine, lost in the middle of Echo Lake at nightfall, Beowolf had told her, "You're as good as I ever imagined." It seemed, at the time, that he was on the brink of a new life in which the whole world would conform to his desires.

Against the backdrop of mountains the lake had been a wonderful maze among wooded islands, pine-needle shores: pristine pastures of water blossoming like petals of a wild flower one out of the other and into the next, still as glass, cool as April, water leading them, luring them ever deeper into the labyrinth, Beowolf opening the throttle full to weave through the archipelago, striking out in the direction of the sole glacier, which crowned the surrounding mountains and presided over the lake like a church steeple.

Eventually, Beowolf killed the engine. He jacked the motor out of the water and rowed up an inlet dotted with smooth river rocks

that broke the surface like turtles and sometimes scraped the hull
with a rasping, indecent sound. Above them, thickly criss-crossing
boughs shaded them in a cool, dank cathedral of fertile smells. A
fish splashed.

"Hap's never caught a fish in his life," Beowolf said softly.

"Why not?"

"Bad karma."

"What's karma?"

"It's vibes, bad vibes. The fish, they pick it up."

"Why are we whisp—" Jeannie gasped, peering into the shore's
green tangle of vegetation.

"What?" Beowolf stared into the trembling underbrush. "What
is it?"

"I don't know." Jeannie's amazed expression was itself as stun-
ningly beautiful as a startled fawn's. "It drew the air right out of
my lungs."

"Pap used to say that only the most beautiful or the most deadly
things can suck the life out of you." Beowolf gazed into the underbrush. "It was a place like this."

"What was?"

"Where I got bit."

"What was it like?"

Beowolf shrugged. "I thought I was dead."

"Why didn't you?"

"I was tougher than the snake."

"Why, really?"

"I'm serious," he told her. "Genetic resiliency. That's what the
doctor said. It comes from Pap. We're hard to poison." He reached
for her. "Come here." He drew her to his side. "You have the
bluest eyes," he said, and he began to say something more but
kissed her instead. "You stopped my breath," he told her.

"Like the rattlesnake?"

"No, like something beautiful. Like a fawn." He kissed her. "I
saw you through a pair of binoculars once. You were in your
backyard playing with some girl. I was spying."

"How old were you?"

"Seventh grade."

"I didn't even know you then."

"You went to West. They ran the dividing line right between our
houses."

Jeannie laughed. "You make it sound as if they designed things just to keep us apart."

"I was in love with you."

"You didn't know me," Jeannie laughed.

"I loved how you looked. I've always loved you. I love you now." He glanced away from her to the water's surface, where the gold leaf of sunlight had dissolved in a fresh evening breeze, leaving the water clear now, rainbows darting past, glints of light. He had stopped rowing, he realized, leaving the boat adrift in the gentle current. He set the oar aside, needing to say something more. Jeannie touched his cheek and lips the way a blind person might, but more tenderly, gazing at him the whole time. She caressed his entire face, finally kissing him on the cheek and wrapping her arms around him for a moment. He needed to tell her something, he needed—"You took a shower," he said.

"Oh!" she cried with delight. "I'm clean now behind the ears?"

"You smell like you," he told her. "This morning you smelled like lemon. This morning you smelled like last night at the dance."

"Last night was good."

"It was good because it brought us here. Are you glad we're here?"

"I'm glad," Jeannie answered. "Why did Pap drink poison? Didn't he know it would kill him?"

"He knew just the opposite."

"Then why did it?"

"He killed himself," Beowolf replied.

"*Obviously.* But he killed himself with rattlesnake poison."

"He didn't kill himself with rattlesnake poison," Beowolf said, a slight note of contentiousness stealing into his voice. "Rollo killed him."

"Rollo?" Jeannie's face skewed up into a perplexed expression. "But you just said he killed himself."

"Rollo busted him up the night before, cut up the inside of his mouth. Swallowing venom, your stomach defuses the poison and it won't hurt you too bad, especially if you've got a cast-iron craw like Pap had and you're used to drinking it. But if it gets into your bloodstream in a heavy dose—like if you get bit, or if it gets in a cut in your mouth—you're up shit creek."

"So why did he drink it," Jeannie asked, "if his mouth was cut up?"

"He always drank it."

"But why," she insisted, "if he *knew* his mouth was cut?"

"That's the way he was," Beowolf answered, "that's all. He had to test himself, I guess. He had principles."

"Did he seem . . . did he seem crazy to you?"

"He didn't *seem* crazy. He *was* crazy. Crazy is when the world as you see it is so out of whack with the world as it is that the two different worlds aren't even on speaking terms. That's how it was for Pap. The Wild West was in his head, nowhere else. Pap figured he was a good guy, like Gary Cooper, who would just ride off into the sunset and never die, just like Midnight wouldn't. He was so mean, that dog, he was a killer to the marrow . . . Pap killed a man, you know."

"Pap killed a man?"

"Washed his face with buckshot."

"When?"

"A long time ago. I just heard about it from Wavy. Wavy saw it."

"He saw it?"

"Yeah, he was there."

"Why'd he do it?"

"That's just the way he was. The guy burned down Pap's saloon, so Pap blew his doors off."

The boat scraped the bank. A shadow had crept across the forest. "It's getting dark," Jeannie said. "We'd better go. Do you know the way?"

"Don't you know? It's your cabin."

"It's Eric's cabin."

"We know our way," Beowolf assured her.

With the oar, Beowolf spun the prow back into midstream. When the boat entered the lake, he lowered the engine into the water and headed for home. The sun had long since sunk behind the mountains, leaving in its wake a western sky of drowning orange hues. At the far shore, Beowolf maneuvered the boat through the forest and into the next expanse of water. Glancing back at the glacier to establish his bearings, he set out for the islands. The clamor of the engine seemed louder now, and harsh. "This way," Jeannie shouted. Beowolf followed her direction, winding through the maze of islands. He remembered an osprey nest, around the next bend, alone in a tree that was swamped, gray and dying or dead. But it wasn't there. The lake spread open in any direction, the far shore a dense shadow. Jeannie tapped him on the shoulder and pointed. The boat swerved, following the near shore-line around a spur of land straight into the open water. Midway across, the motor coughed; it coughed again and coughed and died. Beowolf yanked several times on the cord. He swore and removed the gas cap. He couldn't see a damn thing.

The water rippled before the bow of the boat while the wake, to the faraway laughing of loons, drifted into distant collapse. A chorus of bullfrogs rose out of the silence. Jeannie leaned against him, not saying anything. Gliding over the water, the breeze smelled of pine. On the water's surface, circles radiated concentri-cally where fish snagged night insects, splashing sometimes, load-ing their bellies. Beowolf moved to the center seat and began to set the oars in the oarlocks. Sitting down beside him, Jeannie wrapped the army blanket around them both.

"We can't both row," Beowolf told her.

"I know."

She rested her head against his shoulder. Beowolf wrapped his arms around her, kissed her face. Overhead, geese flew honking against the blue-black sky and for an instant, with the boat as still as a dreaming infant and with the orange moon as big as a balloon peering through the pines, earth seemed blessed with the pure atmosphere of some exotic, uncharted planet. Beowolf wanted to live forever.

"You," he said. "You're what I always wanted you to be."

Jeannie laughed and hugged him. "You sound as if you made me."

"No." He felt her shiver in his arms. "I mean, you're as good as I ever imagined." He kissed her cheek. "It's getting cold."

"We have to get home."

"Take the blanket," he said, handing it to her. Jeannie moved to the back of the boat and Beowolf stirred the still water with the oars. Glowing deep orange, the moon eventually rose above the pines to gild the water in a cool sheen. Jeannie spotted the osprey nest they'd been searching for, bold and defensive in its open isolation. They were almost home. As Beowolf rowed, clouds moved across the sky in narrow formation like sets of gray human ribs.

From his reverie, Beowolf was shaken by Bigfoot's voice. "You die or just taking a shit?"

"You wanna come in?"

"Whattaya think?"

"Just a minute."

Beowolf stood and flushed the toilet. He crumpled up the paper and watched it spin down and away in the whirlpool. So much for that.

"You been coughing a lot," he said to Bigfoot when he opened the door.

"No shit," Bigfoot answered. Bigfoot looked at him strangely. "Move," he said. "I gotta take a dump."

Beowolf stood in the middle of the dark room. A prolonged, crackling fart resounded in the bathroom. In the middle of the strange room, Beowolf couldn't think of what to do. With abrupt resolution he marched to the door. He hurried downstairs and stood barefoot in the empty lobby. The receptionist scrutinized him coldly. Above her head the clock read two in the morning. "May I help you?" she asked. "No," Beowolf replied.

In the corner stood an aquarium stocked with fish, bright and exotic with the exception of a single brown sucker, which lurked at the bottom looking poisonous with its long whiskers. Occasionally, it would swim halfway up the glass; its mouth resembled a vacuum cleaner, always working, inhaling anything that wasn't anchored down. Near the surface a silver-blue angelfish with delicate, nearly transparent azure fins swam on its side in sluggish circles, gradually sinking through the water until midway to the bottom when it would struggle, still in circles, toward the surface again.

What was he doing? Beowolf wheeled and hurried away. He needed sleep and here it was two in the morning! At a cigarette machine he found a book of matches. He hurried down an empty corridor and turning a corner nearly collided with Wavy.

"Youngblood! You near skeerd the life outta me!"

"Jesus Christ, Wave! Ain'tcha got sumpin better to do than spook people this time of night?"

"You near skeerd the life outta me. And I ain't got much life left to spare. Whatchew doin up?"

"Can't sleep worth a damn."

"I can't sleep either. These motel rooms're spooky."

Beowolf laughed, thinking of Wavy's shack. "Who ya rooming with?" he asked.

"Porkbutt."

"Jesus."

"Porkbutt ever show you his baby picture, youngblood? He's got a picture of a baby with a big hairy hard-on. Says it's him."

"Porkbutt's a pervert. He flashes that picture at everybody."

"Where ya headed, youngblood?"

"Nowhere. Just wandering around." Beowolf glanced up and down the corridor. From his pocket he slipped a joint and showed it to Wavy.

"You shouldn't tonight, youngblood."

"I gotta," Beowolf answered. "Gotta get some sleep."

"Where can we go? Rain comin down like it ain't gonna quit for forty nights. Who ya roomin with?"

"Bigfoot. He's got a bad cold or something. Let's go somewhere else."

Together they explored the motel until eventually they found themselves in the basement. The furnace room was unlocked and humming softly with a comforting warmth. They found some empty crates and sat down, Beowolf propping his bare feet up on a toolbox close to the heat. He lit the joint and passed it to Wavy.

"Man," Wavy sighed. "I'm too old for this life."

"What *old?*" Beowolf scoffed. "You ain't old. You're gonna live nine hundred years."

"I suspect not." Wavy sucked on the joint. As he exhaled, he said, "I'm too old to go another season."

"Driving the bus?"

Wavy nodded.

"Who says?"

"Moon."

Beowolf inhaled, considering this. Wavy clicked his teeth together as if to make certain that they were still there. He took the joint from Beowolf.

"What Moon says don't matter," Beowolf said. Wavy gave him a skewed look. "He'll be gone before you."

"Whatchew mean by that, youngblood?"

"Nothin," Beowolf replied. "A prophecy, is all."

"Prophecy?" Wavy shrugged, his teeth clicking, clattering together. "Moon *dyin?* You know sumpin I don't?"

"Everybody's dying," Beowolf said, thinking himself profound. He passed the joint to Wavy. "Every minute of every day."

Wavy shook his head as he inhaled.

"You makin no sense, youngblood."

Beowolf shrugged and glanced around the furnace room. For a faint moment he was extremely pleased, enclosed by the cinderblock walls, smoking a joint with Wavy. Then he passed the joint to Wavy and the good feeling passed away. Wavy's teeth were too perfect, straight and white. They looked as if they'd been shanghaied from one of those plastic skeletons in Wolf DeViscera's torture chamber on *Monsterland Movie.* Beowolf shuddered. "You never have to worry about cavities at least," he mentioned.

Wavy laughed. "What's lost can't be lost again. That's the only good thing bout losin."

Beowolf spat on the floor and sucked on the joint. He handed the joint to Wavy and exhaled a dense cloud of smoke.

"What you make of the Anaconda game, Wave?"

"Some games're won, youngblood, and some games're lost. But some games're jest plain given away." Wavy sucked long and hard on the joint. *"Givin away* works good in the Good Book and it works good in real life. But that and a nickel'll getcha a solid boot in the pants in football."

"We sucked," Beowolf agreed. "We weren't up for it at all. We just jerked off that whole game. Bigfoot kept putting bits of Alka-Seltzer on his tongue so he'd foam at the mouth. It was real funny until the fourth quarter. And Bigfoot played as good a game as anybody." Beowolf shook his head. "When Jason heard about the game, he drove all the way home from Missoula. He couldn't believe it."

"Jason awways liked football."

"Jason's an asshole," Beowolf remarked.

Wavy's jaw dropped open. Beowolf handed him the joint.

"He came rushing home like a turpentined cat, just like when our father was killed. It made me laugh, I couldn't help it. It really cracked me up. Then I had to tell him about the game with him looking at me that way—he doesn't think I take it seriously anymore. He caught me getting high last night. He thinks I don't care."

"Do ya?"

"This game is like the end of my life, Wave. It's all I got left. I gotta put everything into it because afterward . . . it's all over tomorrow."

"Ya see this?" Wavy held two fingers in the air in the form of a V.

Beowolf nodded.

"In Indian sign language it means two things, young-blood . . ."

"Victory."

"Weren't no redskin seen it *that* way."

"What, then?"

"It means *wuff,* which is you. You is a bay-wuff. But it also means *smart.* The two words go together, youngblood. Ya gotta be smart, not like these rest. If this game's the end of your life, it's the beginnin, too."

"I'm through going in circles."

"That ain't what I mean," Wavy argued. "You begin another life tomorrow, unless you're ready to cash in your chips for good."

"My name means nothing," Beowolf contended. "There was a Beowulf once who was a knight or something. Jeannie gave me a book about him that I couldn't read worth a damn. I got my name when I was little, from Hap giving 'Bailey' a good jerking around. He liked to name everything over, so 'Beowolf' was what he finally came up with." Beowolf snuffed out the joint and dug into his pocket for another. "Double your trouble?"

Wavy nodded and Beowolf struck the match. "Youngblood, whatcha gonna do next year? You gettin married? Bigfoot says you're gettin married."

"I ain't gettin married."

"Don't she wanna?"

"Yeah, she does."

"You don't wanna?"

Beowolf shrugged, inhaled and held the joint forward.

"You too much a tomcat?" Wavy asked.

"Maybe. But it ain't that simple. I wish it was . . . I really don't wanna go into it."

Wavy glanced away. "Nothin's simple anymore."

"Doe Konichek is simple," Beowolf said. Wavy grunted, closing his eyes as he inhaled. Beowolf thought of Helen the Bod that night at Buffalo Wallow. *Ya feel anything yet?* Beowolf asked, taking the joint from her. *Ya gotta hold it in longer, c'mon now, you oughta be able to hold your breath forever.*

"Do ya lover?"

Beowolf fidgeted, taking the joint. "It don't matter."

"It does matter, youngblood."

"I love her," Beowolf murmured.

"You should hold on to her then. Lovely gal like that."

Beowolf stared at the concrete floor. "I'm afraid I'm too young."

"I got hitched when I was sixteen," Wavy informed him. "Ann Clearwaters was thirteen. In those days gettin married and stayin married was a necessity. Life was a struggle and a man be needing help. Not anymore. We don't struggle with life no more, so we struggle with each other. Ain't never satisfied with what we got. Awways suspect there's more to be had, and if we get *that* we're still never enjoyin it but wantin more."

Beowolf grunted, scrutinizing a hatchet he'd removed from the toolbox.

"I ain't tellin you to go get married, youngblood. I ain't tellin you nothin but that if ya got one good thing, hang on to it cause good things ain't awways around."

Wavy took the joint from Beowolf and inhaled. "You goin to U of M next year?" Smoke streamed out his nostrils. "Ya get a scholarship?"

"That's up to Moon." Beowolf chuckled. "That's up to Moon in more ways than one."

Wavy shook his head. "Whatcha mean?"

Beowolf laughed, slapping in the palm of his hand the flat side of the hatchet blade. "Nothin."

"I don't get it."

"Well, you'll get it soon enough—by tonight anyway."

Wavy stared at him curiously, not saying anything as Beowolf inhaled a fine rush that nestled around his brain like a soft cat. Beowolf gazed at the furnace, the cinderblock walls; he was acutely aware of the room's warmth. Handing the joint to Wavy, he said, "Jason wants me to go to U of M. He wants me to start this whole business all over again."

"What whole business?"

"Football."

"But you don't wanna?"

"Not at U of M," Beowolf said. "Who in his right mind wants to play for U of M? Especially now, after the scandal."

"Bigfoot," Wavy answered.

"That's only cause he ain't been anywhere else yet. Wait'll the season's over, though. You'll see. He'll be flying all over the fuckin country just trying on colleges for size. Him and MD."

"I spect," Wavy said, "he'll wanna stay close to home."

"Don't bet the Olds 88 on that one, Wave. Wait'll he catches a whiff of them California girls. They ain't like girls around here. And that's a fact. You don't understand how good Bigfoot really is. He can play anywhere. Between the lines he's a fuckin artist. And when a major college goes after you, Wave, believe me, they don't stop at handshakes and smiles to getcha. You know those cheerleaders, like from USC? The ones you see on TV all the time?"

"I ain't got no TV, youngblood. I ain't got no Olds 88 neither."

"That's who's gonna be ushering him around. You think, after that, he's gonna be anxious to go to Missoula, where the cheerleaders all belong in a kennel and the football team can't win even when they cheat?"

"Now—"

"Face it, Wave."

Wavy sighed, as sullen suddenly as a dragged cat. Beowolf inhaled the joint. A person, it was true, doesn't generally leap at the chance to give up what he knows he can live with. Beowolf knew this as well as anybody. Maybe Bigfoot would never leave Montana, just as Wavy had never left that pitiful shack of his. Maybe he would go to U of M and return to Rawlings when he graduated, to kill hogs in the slaughterhouse just like his father. But Beowolf doubted it and would root against it. A person had to strike out on his own.

Wavy stood up and took the joint. Beowolf was finally relaxed, toying with the hatchet, ready for sleep. Wavy shuffled back and forth in front of him looking sorrier than a turtle without a shell —his eye sockets so godawful deep and the skin over his skull taut and transparent as oil paper.

"I s'pose you're right, youngblood," Wavy finally said. "*Whew-boy,* I s'pose you're right and he should get his tail outta here while the gettin's good. His daddy, though, his daddy's gonna die if he leaves for good."

"The Chief? He ain't gonna die."

Wavy remained standing, swaying, staring at the cinderblock walls.

"He's a fool," Beowolf added, "if he don't beat it while he's got the chance. That's just the way it is, Wave."

Wavy sighed. "Times is changed, youngblood. Times is changed awright, like you'd have to be my age to know bout how much they's changed. We didn play games when I was a youngblood. Leastways not like you youngbloods do now. Everything was for real. We didn have nobody cheerin for us neither. Livin now ain't the fight it used to be. The fight used to be real and all around you like you never could predict—like the weather. But somewhere, somehow, we got to have a scuffle."

Wavy paused, reflecting. Beowolf had begun to sweat. "Hotter'n hell in here." He glanced at the joint in Wavy's hand. Wavy toked up and passed it to Beowolf. "Why doncha siddown?" Beowolf asked.

Wavy shrugged, exhaled. "Winter comin on."

Beowolf passed the joint back to Wavy.

"Now sometimes," Wavy began, "I look at myself and I can't believe here I am sittin in this old nigger's body, drivin the game bus for the Rawlings Rattlers—and pretty soon won't even be doin that . . ."

"Moon ain't even . . ."

"I ain't talkin bout Moon or nobody else. I'm talkin bout me, youngblood. I'm too old to go another season. I feel it. I feel the winter in my blood."

Wavy glanced down at Beowolf and shook his head. Finally, he sat back down. "I didn play no football, youngblood, but I watch you youngbloods play and I'm happy for you, and I wish sometimes I was a youngblood, too. And you're prob'ly right, and Bigfoot should prob'ly get outta here like you said, but . . ."

"Do some damage to that joint, will ya?"

"It's out."

Beowolf lit it again and handed it to Wavy.

"You spend your whole life," Wavy resumed, studying the joint burned down to his fingertips, "trying to come up with a piece of advice that's true. But most advice is just selfishness talkin." He inhaled, clenched his teeth and passed what remained of the joint to Beowolf. He exhaled and shook his head. "Goddamn. God *damn.*"

"Pap never came up with any final piece of advice," Beowolf said. "He just killed himself instead."

Forlornly, Wavy shrugged.

"Hit em where they ain't would have done better," Beowolf added.

A faint smile broke across Wavy's face: not his high smile but that ancient smile of his, his sedate *old* smile, seeming at once sad and beautiful, profound and unchangeable, like a buffalo head tacked to a barroom wall. *"Hit em where they ain't* don't apply to boxing."

Beowolf laughed. He took the final hit off the joint and let it fall to the ground.

"My daddy used to tell me," Wavy continued, " 'Give a man a fish, feed him for a day. *Teach* a man to fish, feed him for his life.' "

"You learn a lot from your father?" Beowolf asked.

"I learned to catch fish."

Beowolf laughed.

"I learned the Bible too, and that's the best learnin I ever did."

Beowolf studied Wavy, not saying anything.

"It's good to be alive, youngblood, and I got precious little advice I can give you cept you don't have to spend your whole life spoilin for a fight. The meek shall inherit the earth. That's what Christ taught. He who is first will be last." Wavy paused, considering something. His teeth clicked a few times.

"If the meek shall inherit the earth," Beowolf remarked, "Bigfoot's gonna be a peasant."

"When I was a boy," Wavy finally said, "after snowstorms I'd snowshoe into the gorge below where the dam is now. It'd be all over white, on the ground and in the trees. Even the air was white —the color, I spect, of angels. The river was frozen solid and everything was still as could be. Closest thing to heaven I ever seen. I'd find me a grove of pines and build my fire, roast on one side and freeze on the other. But I'd sit there all morning, feelin good." Wavy smiled wistfully. "In heaven," he added, "ya can do that in a short-sleeve shirt."

"I don't believe in that, Wave."

"Youngblood. Never say that again. Ya believe in heaven or ya can't go on livin."

Beowolf shrugged. "I'm living."

"But y'ain't feelin real good about it."

"I feel all right. I'll feel better once the season's over."

"Youngblood, football season don't mount to a hill of beans."

"You know what Peckinpah says about football?" Beowolf asked. "He says it's like life."

"An whatta you say, youngblood?"

"I dunno." He hesitated. "You think football's like life, Wave?"

Wavy managed a forlorn smile, his eyes full of years. "I ain't thought about it. But if it is, whatta we need with it? We *got* life."

Day

16

Lying in the cold motel, Beowolf nestled deeper beneath the covers, cowering from the clammy dawn of consciousness. The rain pattered at the nearby pane. He opened his eyes to a morning as miserable as a wet cat. Bigfoot was still snoring like there was no tomorrow. Beowolf threw back the covers to lie naked, then became so cold that he grabbed the covers and furled back into his cocoon. He swore to himself. He was wide awake. Again he threw the covers off, this time swinging his legs over the side of the bed. He stood and prodded his groin with a finger. It always hurt in the morning, resentful at being awakened to another day of abuse. He leaned cautiously back, stretching, getting it over with. Waking up was the worst time of day.

He limped into the bathroom and turned on the bathwater. With only an inch of water at the bottom of the tub, he climbed in and eased himself back against the freezing porcelain. For a moment he was all goose pimples. He slid down into the water, then up again to turn up the hot. Finally relaxing, he closed his eyes and imagined going blind; he'd heard once of a man whose eyesight went dead on him while he was sitting in his bathtub minding his own business.

He sat in the tub for as long as he could stand it, thinking and sweating, massaging his groin whenever it occurred to him that this was what he was there for. Eventually, he stood up, flipped the drain lever and turned on the shower to cool off.

Sweating, dripping wet, he pattered back into the cold bedroom. His groin had loosened up. He dried himself vigorously, then plunged back into bed. He lay perfectly still, warming, thinking that unborn must be the ideal state.

After a time, Bigfoot sneezed, stirring.

"Morning," Beowolf said.

Bigfoot rolled over, nursing his eyes open. "Fuck," he muttered. "Nothing *good* about it. Don't bullshit me, Wolf." He motioned toward the window. "Suppose that starts freezing? We'll wind up in a fuckin blizzard."

"Have a nice snore?"

"Couldn't sleep." Bigfoot threw back the covers, unveiling a prodigious hard-on. He sat up with a groan.

"You were coughing a lot last night," Beowolf said.

"I got this fuckin cold. Couldn't sleep."

"That's a switch."

"What were *you* doing last night?" Bigfoot asked.

"You kept me up with your fuckin snoring."

"Where'd ya go?"

"Out."

"Where?"

"For a walk," Beowolf replied defensively. "Who are you, my mother?"

"Jeannie staying on the third floor?" Bigfoot asked.

"Staying at the cabin."

"Bullshit," Bigfoot said. "I was born at night, but not *last* night. The least you could've done was send me her roommate."

"She's at the cabin," Beowolf said.

"You horny fucker. Can't keep your hands off her for one fuckin day. Beauty and the fuckin beast."

"Beauty ain't everything, hand job."

"Ah, beauty ain't everything," Bigfoot reflected. "I like that, Wolf. Got a nice ring to it. You make that up yourself?" Musing, Bigfoot repeated "Beauty ain't everything" several times. "That's cute. You know?" He sneezed. *"Fuck!"* Wiping his hand on his bed sheet, he said, "But what *is* everything, you know?" He blew some snot out one of his nostrils and stared at Beowolf. "Winning?" He laughed as a lecherous grin spread across his face. "Don't bullshit me, Wolf!" He meditated on beauty a bit longer. Then he said, "Man, I'm *all* clogged up this morning. How's she doing?"

"Say who?"

"Jeannie," Bigfoot replied. "Ya got shit in your ears?" He sauntered over to the window.

"You're gonna get arrested," Beowolf said.

"Yeah, well."

Bigfoot paraded aimlessly around the room. Opening the night-table drawer, he picked up the Bible, read the title and tossed it back into the drawer. "I'll wait for the movie to come out."

"It already did."

"Oh yeah? Glad I missed it."

In a pants pocket, Bigfoot found a carbohydrate supplement. He tossed the pants in a corner and puttered into the bathroom. "Guess I'll shoot a few hoops." He peered back around the corner, flipped the carbo into the air, catching it in his mouth, then ducked into the bathroom.

As a freshman, Bigfoot had ransacked the high school civil defense shelter, abducting, among less precious booty, a huge canister of walnut-sized, raspberry-flavored carbohydrate supplements that he subsequently stored in the bottom of his locker beneath a fetid pile of dirty laundry. The carbos tasted like over-sweetened rock candy and they'd so rotted his teeth that it seemed likely he would someday sport a pair of clattering choppers to match Wavy's.

Beowolf closed his eyes and tried not to think of anything, just listen to the rain.

Lying in bed two mornings ago, Jeannie had said what seemed to him the most heartless thing possible. She'd been telling him how difficult the past four weeks of her life had been when she remarked how, lying one morning in bed, she looked at him and for the first time saw "a naked man" lying there. *A naked man!* It crushed him and he still didn't understand why—she wasn't trying to be mean, she was never mean—and for the first time ever he wished only that she would go away. He'd given her his money and he'd wanted her to go away for a while and leave him alone. Then, that night, *she* told *him* to go away.

Beowolf stared at the ceiling and listened to the rain. In the end, you do what you gotta do. You can kill a baby as justifiably as you can lop off the head of a turkey, and with far less blood and guts. Beowolf tried to think of the baby as neither his nor Jeannie's, but as an extraneously proposed idea that was far ahead of its time. There were no good answers anymore, just that you pay a price for everything and the payment inevitably comes out of your hide. You don't even recognize yourself after a while. Your feelings escape you, and fade away like a victim of body snatchers and mind benders on *Monsterland Movie.*

"Banzai!" Bigfoot cried from the bathroom. The toilet flushed. The shower was turned on.

Impulsively, Beowolf picked up the telephone receiver. A phone call was impossible, the woman at the switchboard informed him. She had received instructions from a Mr. Moon that rooms 214 through 229 were to neither make nor receive phone calls. Beowolf hung up the receiver, dressed quickly and went down to the lobby.

"Listen," he told the woman, "I'll pay you for the call, cash. I'm the guy you were talking to on the phone. I'm not asking you to charge the call to the room. I'll pay cash for it."

"I'm sorry," the woman insisted. "I have my instructions."

"Jesus."

Making the phone call, originally a simple impulse, had now become a matter of paramount importance. He stalked away from the front desk in search of a public phone. Finding a wall phone by the cash register in the dining room, he asked one of the waitresses, a girl with blond hair and huge round glasses, for change of a dollar.

"Telephone call?"

"Yes."

"You're not supposed to be making calls," she said. She peered out at him from behind her glasses.

"How do *you* know that?"

The waitress gave a short laugh and handed him his change, smiling sheepishly and even, Beowolf noticed, blushing a bit.

He dropped a dime into the slot and dialed the number. "Forty-five more cents for the first three minutes, please." Beowolf pumped the coins into the machine.

An unfamiliar voice answered. She would get Jeannie for him. Beowolf waited. It was a solid minute at least before Jeannie got on the phone, and during the impatient interlude it occurred to him that he didn't know why he was calling. He hated telephones, always had.

"Jeannie? It's me."

"Hi."

"What took you so long? I only have a couple minutes."

"I was talking to somebody," she replied. "I didn't know it was you."

There was a long silence.

"What are you doing?" she asked.

"I'm calling you, whattaya think I'm doing? What're *you* doing?"

"Nothing."

"It's awful out, have you seen? Might be playing in snow . . . When you coming in?"

"What time is it?" she asked.

Beowolf scanned the dining room for a clock. "I don't know. Wait." He turned back to the waitress and asked for the time.

"Nine-fifteen," she told him.

"Nine-fifteen," Beowolf said into the receiver.

"Where *are* you?" Jeannie asked.

"Dining room. We're about to have breakfast. What time you coming in?"

"We're leaving for the stadium about six."

"Oh."

Again there was silence.

"What're you doing?" he asked.

"Nothing," Jeannie replied. "Talking and stuff."

"Do you feel like coming in this morning?" he asked.

"I can't."

"I've got a lot of time hanging around doing nothing," he said. From the other end Jeannie was silent.

"Nobody'll know," he assured her. "Bigfoot'll find something to do."

"I can't," she repeated.

"You don't want to?"

"Gray's here."

"Gray? What's he doing there?"

"Talking and stuff."

"Oh."

"How's he doing?" Beowolf asked, thinking of nothing else to say.

"Fine."

"Jeannie, I want to talk to you."

"What about?"

"I don't know," he finally said. "If you were here—I just want to talk to you."

"What about?" she cried. "I don't want to talk. We've talked. *It's not fair.*"

Beowolf remained silent, listening to the emptiness at Jeannie's end.

"It's not fair," she said again, this time more softly.

"I'm sorry," Beowolf said. "I don't know . . ."

The operator interrupted: "Please deposit fifty-five cents for your next three minutes."

"Come to the motel tonight," Beowolf found himself insisting. "Please come tonight."

"I won't."

"Please deposit fifty-five cents for your next three minutes."

Beowolf hung up angrily. The waitress was staring at him. "Thanks," he said as he walked past.

"You're welcome," she replied, regarding him curiously.

Bigfoot had just emerged from the bathroom, his arrowhead of hair glistening wet. "Colder than a witch's tit." He wrestled with his pants, in search of his stash of carbos; they spilled onto the floor like marbles. As he bent over he braced himself, planting his hands on his knees. He straightened up, possessed by a sneeze that wouldn't surface. It rippled casually back and forth across his face before exploding violently into his fist. He wiped his hand on his bed sheet, then blew his nose several times.

"Throat sore?" Beowolf asked, flopping onto his bed.

"A little."

"Better tell Porkbutt."

"Fuck'm."

"They'll be pissed if they find out you didn't tell em."

"Piss on the fat slob," Bigfoot answered.

"He'll give you something for it, man."

"What'll he give me?" Bigfoot asked skeptically.

"I dunno."

"He can't stick my head in a whirlpool."

"Maybe he'll give you a snorkle."

Bigfoot laughed. "Only thing Porkbutt ever gave me was a royal pain in the ass." He bent over and picked one of the carbos off the floor. "I take these." He popped it in his mouth. "Good for what ails you."

"Don't you ever get sick of them things?"

"Hey, man, this comes from a civil defense shelter. This is H-bomb repellent." Stepping into his underwear, Bigfoot belched. "If everybody'd taken one of these before Anaconda, we'd be playing for the State tonight."

"Fart fuel, that's all they are."

Bigfoot farted on cue.

"Ya know," Beowolf remarked, "one of these days you're gonna fart and burp and sneeze and hiccup and your stomach's gonna growl, all at the same time, and you're gonna turn inside-fuckin-out."

"Never happen," Bigfoot assured him. "That'd make me a cunt."

"Say what?"

"Said that'd make me a cunt. Women are men turned inside-fuckin-out. Don't you know that?"

"I dunno nothin."

"Whatzamatter with you?" Bigfoot asked.

"Nothin."

"Groin hurt?"

"No."

As Bigfoot stepped into his pants and zipped them up, another sneeze played across his face and exploded. "Jesus!"

"You better tell Porkbutt," Beowolf said. "He'll give you some aspirin at least."

"I don't want his aspirin. His aspirin comes apart in my mouth."

"Wash it down with water, dumbass."

"I hate aspirin."

Bigfoot finished dressing and together they left the room. In the lobby he peered into the aquarium.

"It's dying," Beowolf said.

"It's dying or pregnant."

Beowolf watched the fish circling and sinking, the sucker lurking at the bottom.

"I think this fish is pregnant," Bigfoot decided. "What are the odds that she's alive when we leave the motel?"

Watching the fish, Beowolf replied, "Two to one."

"Two to one *what?*"

"Against."

Bigfoot laid out the palm of his hand. "Five bucks?"

"Nope."

Bigfoot laughed. "Why not?"

"I don't wanna bet against."

It wasn't quite nine-thirty when Beowolf and Bigfoot entered the dining room, yet they received an admonishing glance from Moon nonetheless. Hap waved a newspaper at them and they hustled across the room to the table where he sat with Doe.

"How ya feelin, Wolf?" Hap asked. "How's the groin?"

"Fine." Beowolf nodded to Doe. "Morning."

"Seen the paper?" Hap handed Beowolf the sports section. In broad black print the headline announced KHS SEEKS STATE TO-NIGHT. The subhead read *Rawlings Remaining Hurdle for Un-beaten Braves.* There was a picture of Earthquake and Russell Thompson, the split end, "planning strategy" with Thompson's father, the head coach.

Moon tapped his fork against his water glass. "Okay, quiet down! The team meeting will be at three-thirty at Saint Christopher's Chapel. Afterward we'll have mass. I don't want anybody leaving the motel in the meantime. Are there any problems?" Moon scanned their faces. "Okay. Father John wants to say a prayer."

Round John Virgin, the team chaplain, rose to his feet. Wall-eyed, with a forehead perpetually prickled with sweat, he'd always reminded Beowolf of a bullfrog.

"Let us bow our heads and give thanks."

After the benediction, the *Kalispell Daily Interlake* became evident everywhere, folded back to the sports section. Waitresses scurried back and forth through the kitchen doorways balancing platters laden with steaks, hash browns and scrambled eggs. The waitress who had earlier given Beowolf change arrived at their table, nervous and confused, shoving a plateful of food in front of each of them. Her huge round glasses made her resemble a fish gazing out of a bowl, her eyes growing larger still when they fastened on Bigfoot, who was clawing his armpit and displaying his most lascivious grin. She placed a pitcher of orange juice on the table.

"Excuse me," Hap said, being polite. "Do you go to Kalispell High?"

"Sometimes," she replied, glancing around the table. "But usually I go straight."

Beowolf snorted.

"Who are these guys, these guys here?" Hap asked, poking a finger at Beowolf's newspaper. "Earth*quack* Allen and *Banzee* Burns—Is it *Banz*ee or *Panz*ee? Who are these guys?"

"Never heard of em," Bigfoot chipped in.

The waitress's glance circled the table again, once again jolted by Bigfoot. She smiled faintly and made a vague gesture toward the kitchen door before hurrying away.

Beowolf began eating breakfast, his attention focused on the newspaper article laid open before him. Abruptly overwhelmed with disgust, he flipped his fork onto his plate.

"Whatzamatter?" Bigfoot asked.

"Nothin."

"If you don't want it, I'll eat it."

Beowolf resumed eating.

Ever since he'd been in high school, it had been Rawlings that entered the Thanksgiving game seeking the State Championship. Winning tonight would end the season on an upbeat. But the season itself was a lost cause, haunting him already like Jason's final season, when Rawlings beat Missoula only to lose to Kalispell, *damn Kalispell,* losing everything, robbed by the Repeat Rule of even a share of the State Championship.

A season could end high or low, but it didn't make any difference in the long run if the overbearing fact was that you ended the season empty-handed—if it had already slipped through a body's fingers. "Nibbled to death by a duck" was how Pap might have described playing out a hopeless season. It was how Pap must have felt the whole rest of his life. "Why?" Jeannie had begged to know that final morning in bed. "Why does it matter to you so much that Pap killed a man?" That Pap killed a man mattered in the same way that the photograph of Pap spitting in the eye of a grizzle bear had always mattered, even when its mattering was obscured by the suspicion that it was all somehow bullshit. It mattered in a way that he could not fathom. It was real. It was true. It went far beyond the experience of anybody else he'd ever known.

"Well!" Bigfoot cried. "We know winter's here. The flies are fat and slow as shit."

Holding his fist loosely closed, Hap shook his captive housefly as if it were a pair of dice. He flung it against the bottom of an empty cereal bowl.

"Hey, man!" he exclaimed. He laid his hands on the table, palms up. "Fastest hands in the West."

"Yeah? Catch this." Bigfoot leaned to one side and farted.

"Put a cork on that," Beowolf sighed, "will you?"

Hap dumped his unconscious fly onto the table. Reaching inside his shirt, he plucked an armpit hair, and with a dramatic show of concentration managed to tie the housefly's wings to its body. "Your flying days are over, bub." He covered it with the cereal bowl.

"Need some honey," Doe said, glancing around for the waitress.

"I need some honey on my stinger," Bigfoot announced, eyeing the waitress across the room. "Night before the Superbowl, Joe Namath went to bed with a blonde and a fifth of Johnnie Walker."

"What stinger?" Doe asked. "Who's Johnnie Walker?"

"Shut up," Hap said.

"I go to bed with a fuckin cold," Bigfoot remarked. "And you," he added, glaring at Beowolf.

"I ain't so bad."

"You guys are full of shit," Doe chuckled.

"This ain't the Superbowl," Hap said. "And you're just a grunt. When's the last time you were laid?"

"What's it to you?" Bigfoot replied.

"Just asking. I figure you been hitting the massage parlor."

"Ain't no massage parlor."

"The self-service kind."

"Where's that?" Doe wanted to know, his face staring across the table like a blown TV picture tube.

"Up my ass, you stupid fuck," Hap snapped.

"Shut up," Bigfoot said to Hap.

"I can't stand it," Hap shot back. "I insult him and he laughs. *Look.*"

Doe was rolling his eyes and chortling.

"Leave him alone," Bigfoot said. He signaled the waitress. "Can we have some honey, Liz?" Bigfoot batted his eyes at her.

The girl was clearly taken aback, by the use of her name as much as by the other thing. The glimmer of a smile passed over her face as her fingers found the nameplate on her breast.

When she returned, Hap said, "Your name is Liz, isn't it?"

"Yes."

"My name's Hap."

The girl nodded.

"Wanna siddown?"

"I can't." She glanced back at the kitchen door. "Thank you."

As she retreated, Hap said, "That's all right." He turned to Bigfoot and remarked, "She's do-able. She's *beggin* for it."

Beowolf returned to his newspaper.

Billings West had almost given Rawlings a new life two weeks earlier. After Rawlings beat Helena, everybody sat around the locker room listening to the Billings West–Kalispell game on the radio, no one even undressing. Bigfoot sat on the floor in the corner, skeptically drinking bug juice and popping carbohydrate supplements. Hap sat alone in the shower room, out of sight. For a while it sounded as though Billings West might actually pull it off. Two or three times the locker room erupted with bodies dancing around hugging each other and whooping it up as if it were they themselves fighting for their lives and not some half-assed team that Rawlings had beaten 35–14 a week earlier. In the fourth quarter, Kalispell broke the game open, and by the final score you wouldn't have even known that the game was close. That was Kalispell for you. Their running game would steamroll you if you let it. They would grind you down until Banzai or Earthquake would break loose for a score; or Huntley, their quarterback, would cross you up by throwing the bomb to Russell Thompson. One way or the other, they got you. Or their defense would get you. They never quit. That's how Kalispell had always been, even in the days when they didn't have much talent. It was how they beat Jason.

Beowolf pressed his fingers against his groin.

"Howzit feel?" Bigfoot asked.

"Not bad."

"Ain't you eating? Give it to me if you don't want it."

"I'm eating, I'm eating."

Bigfoot grabbed the newspaper from him. "Eat then." Bigfoot scanned the paper. "Look at this dumb fuck."

"Who?" Hap asked. "Earthquake?"

"Yeah."

"Hit'm low," Doe recommended.

"No shit," Hap sneered. "Look how fuckin *old* he is. His wife and kids'll be up in the stands!"

Two seasons earlier, Superscout's report on Kalispell had intimated that the Kalispell quarterback occasionally had to diagram plays in the dirt for Earthquake's benefit. His code name in the

Rawlings defensive signals was "Bottlecap." If he lined up to the right of the quarterback, MD would key the defense to that side of the field by shouting "Bottlecap red!" If he lined up to the left, the signal was "Bottlecap blue!" Beowolf and MD would flip-flop, Beowolf always playing to the strong side of the field, Earthquake's side. On power sweeps with Burns carrying the ball, it would be Beowolf's responsibility to cut Earthquake down so that somebody else could make the tackle. Earthquake was so devastating a blocker that Moon was willing to sacrifice a body for a body as close to the line of scrimmage as possible. Moon didn't want Earthquake getting downfield either with the ball or without it.

Beowolf began shoveling down his breakfast. He stopped suddenly. He was anxious as hell. Jeannie had asked him once if he got butterflies before a game; she sure got them. He had informed her that it was more like a fist. But he realized now that it wasn't like a fist at all. At least not now. A fist, a body *knows* a fist. But this, this was something vague and wild, like what the DT's must feel like.

"Whatzamatter with you, man?" Hap asked.

"Nothin, man." Beowolf resumed eating. "Just thinking. My grandmother used to call butterflies *flutterbies.* " Beowolf shook his head. "Can you beat that?"

With his mouth full, Bigfoot blurted, "Butter*fingers.* "

We are given one chance, Beowolf figured, thinking of Hap and that Anaconda game, but knowing that it went far beyond simply Hap's having lost it in the lights. It was a universal principle. When the chance is gone, what's left? Beowolf had once seen the moon like a halo over Hap's shoulder and the image had just now popped into his head; he couldn't remember where or when it was, whether it was real or a dream. But the afterimage, so simple and so resonant, suggested a mysterious nobility that had always been latent in Beowolf's understanding of Hap. It was apparently nothing; but it aroused in him a sympathy for losers.

The waitress hurried over and began scooping up empty plates.

"Are you going to the game tonight?" Hap asked.

"Yes," she answered. "Are you?"

Hap smirked at her. "Are you doing anything after?"

"Yes."

"It ain't a party, is it?"

The girl nodded.

"A victory party?"

"Yes."

"Well, forget it. It'll be canceled."

The girl stood there holding a stack of plates.

"Do you think they'll win?" Hap asked.

Beowolf darted a stern glance at Hap. "Hey, Hap . . ."

"Yes," she answered.

Ignoring Beowolf, Hap asked, "Do you know these guys?"

"My boyfriend's playing."

Hap's eyes lit up. "Who's your boyfriend?"

"Russell Thompson."

"The coach's son?" Hap smiled. "The split end?"

"Yes."

"Well, you see that man sitting right over there?" Hap nodded at Beowolf.

"Hap, knock it off."

"Yes," the girl answered.

"Well, he's sworn on his mother's grave to rip Thompson's head off."

"Hey, Hap, shut up, *will you?*" Beowolf glanced up at the girl. "Excuse my dumb friend."

She smiled sourly at him. "Oh, that's all right. Can I ask a question?"

"Tickleyourasswithafeather," Bigfoot murmured.

The girl turned to him. "What?"

"Typically nasty weather," Bigfoot replied. "Don't you think?"

The girl lifted Hap's overturned cereal bowl off the table and stared in amazement at the housefly wriggling underneath, bound by Hap's armpit hair.

"See this fly," Hap said to her. Hap paused to watch the fly hopping toward the edge of the table where, without hesitating, it plunged off. "Banzai!" Hap cried, chortling as no other sane person could. "That's what's gonna happen to Kalispell."

Beowolf took the check from the girl's hand.

"You're supposed to give it to that gentleman up there." She pointed to Moon.

Bigfoot faintly bellowed an incredulous "Gentleman!"

"*Moon?*" Hap grimaced.

"I know, I know," Beowolf told her. "Thank you."

"Is that his name?" she asked. *"Moon?"*

"Yeah. *Sun Myung,* " Hap said. "And we're all his Moonies."

"Can I get you anything else?" the girl asked, exasperated.

"Do you have room service?" Bigfoot asked.

"Yes."

"Ya wanna see sumpin swell?"

The girl gave Bigfoot a puzzled look.

"My room is two sixteen," Bigfoot informed her. "Come up and service me. I'll show ya sumpin swell."

"Hey!" Beowolf glanced harshly at Bigfoot.

Bigfoot nodded at Beowolf. "We'll deep-six him," he assured her.

She looked at Beowolf. "Can I ask a question?"

"Nobody's stopping you," Hap answered.

She turned to Hap. "Your name Hazard?"

"Guilty."

"Well, what I want to know is, in the Anaconda game—you see, up here they say nobody could have dropped such an easy pass. What I want to know is, just because I'm a curious person, is football fixed?" She twisted her face into a confounded expression.

Hap stared at her, studied her coldly. The girl stood there unflinchingly, innocently returning his stare. And it occurred to Beowolf at that precise moment when he felt some welling attraction to her that Hap might knock her teeth out.

"Fishing's fixed," Hap informed her.

17

Beowolf lay stretched out on his bed, relaxed finally in a half-dream sleep, thinking of nothing. He jerked awake at the sound of a knock on the door. "Beat it!" Bigfoot called out. Beowolf didn't move. Again somebody knocked.

Bigfoot sprang angrily from his bed and flung the door open.

"Players' meeting in MD's room at noon." It was Donnie.

Beowolf's spirits drooped. The rain beat against the pane. He was wide awake.

"What time is it?"

"Five of."

"Fuck."

"Room two twenty-seven."

Bigfoot closed the door. "Meeting," he said.

"I heard."

Beowolf lay there still with his eyes closed.

"You coming or what?"

Together they marched down the corridor. With a walloping sneeze, Bigfoot trumpeted his arrival.

"Jesus!" somebody cried from across the room. "If not one end, the other."

"You should save that," somebody said, "for your pass rush tonight."

"I'm saving it for you," Bigfoot replied. He hustled his balls. "Come'n get it." He sat down in the corner.

"Have you read the paper?" MD asked.

Beowolf nodded and sat down next to Bigfoot. Those who hadn't read the paper at breakfast were reading it now.

MD sat on his bed as still as a statue, staring out the window; the rain hadn't slacked. When the room was finally quiet, expectant, he glanced around and said, "Everybody done reading?" He rose from the bed with an expression that, on anybody else, would have been reflective. On MD's face, however, it had the same effect that civility had in Peckinpah's voice. It put a body on guard.

"Well, what'd the paper say?" He surveyed the faces in the room. Finding Lombago in the opposite corner from Beowolf and Bigfoot, he stepped over some outstretched legs and accosted him. "What's it say?"

"It thinks we're gonna lose," Lombago responded.

MD's head drooped a bit and, even from behind, Beowolf could see that his chest was beginning to heave. His shoulders seemed to inch their way up his neck; he was like a bull primed to charge. Abruptly, he was seething. *"Goddamn you, Lombago!"* He leapt back across his bed and ripped the bedside lamp out of the wall socket, spinning to hurl it, shattering it against the wall above Lombago's head. *"It thinks we're gonna lose?"* MD roared. "It says we smell! They're saying we stink!"

Nobody in Lombago's corner made a move to brush the lamp fragments from their heads and shoulders. "Jesus," Beowolf murmured. *"Cool it."* MD spun around to face Beowolf's corner. His face looked sunburned.

"Kalispell is a shitty team!" MD roared. "They're a shitty team, d'you hear me?" He leapt at Doug Wagonseller and seized him by the collar, yanking him to his feet. "What're you gonna do so we win that game tonight?"

Wagonseller trembled, looking everywhere but in MD's face. MD jerked the sophomore's face up close to his own. Wagonseller mumbled something incoherent. During Summer Practice, Wagonseller had taken the advice of some of the veterans and rubbed cow dung into his football pants to break them in. He was dumb as dung, though not so dumb as Doe; "Tweedledumb and Tweedledumber" was what Hap called them. Despite this incident, however, and despite the fact that, as Peckinpah kept insisting, he had "space to let upstairs," he had proven persistent and strong, and by mid-season he'd become the starting center.

MD shoved Wagonseller aside. "You're gonna beat the living shit outta somebody, that's what!"

Beowolf sat motionless, wanting only to leave. MD was crazy! As the tirade continued, he tried to ignore the scene. He couldn't do it. He wanted to daydream. *Gray would never believe this!* he found himself thinking. *Jesus!* Gray was with Jeannie.

"How about you?" MD was pointing at Eddie York, who was knee high to a prairie chicken to begin with—the only piss-ant ever

to get locked in a locker—and who seemed to shrink even smaller under MD's glare.

"I'll tell you what you're gonna do," MD continued. "You're lunchmeat, right? You can't do jack-shit on a football field, right? But you're gonna shout your fuckin lungs out! Get the splinters outta your dipshit asses! All of you! I wanna hear some chatter from the fuckin bench!"

MD wheeled. "Kilkowsky!" Towering before Beowolf, he wavered, scarlet, crazy, seething.

"What's that?" he exploded.

He was pointing at Bigfoot, hunched over like a sleeping Buddha, his chin resting serenely against his chest.

"What *the fuck* is that?"

Beowolf gave Bigfoot a nudge.

MD seemed to falter as Bigfoot, who hadn't really been asleep at all, met his stare.

"What the hell *is* this?" MD fumed.

Bigfoot's tongue pushed against the inside of his cheek like a wad of chaw. Beowolf was poised to intervene. Then the lump in Bigfoot's cheek was gone. Bigfoot said, "Why don't you go fuck yourself?"

MD staggered, literally, as if he'd been struck. "Whattayou want?" he cried angrily. "I been taking this shit from you all year, and I'm *sick* of it. You wanna"—MD took a step toward them— "*You wanna fight?*"

Beowolf sprang to his feet. "Jesus Christ!" He shook his head and threw at Bigfoot a look of total disgust. Someone to the other side of Bigfoot moaned.

"Yeah," Bigfoot replied to MD. He exhaled heavily and rose to his feet. "Shove your head up my ass and fight for air."

Bigfoot stepped over strewn bodies on his way to the door. He opened it and was gone, leaving behind, amid the crescendos of laughter, his own unmistakable, lingering aura.

18

Bigfoot hadn't returned to the room, and the loneliness that possessed Beowolf as he stood at the window was deepened by an ominous chill befitting this first winter afternoon of the year. It had begun to snow. In the street, low-beamed cars cut through the slush.

Retreating from the window, Beowolf opened the night-table drawer. He gave the Bible the same cursory inspection that Bigfoot had granted it earlier, then dropped it back into the drawer. It was only twelve twenty-five. Lunch wasn't until one-thirty.

In the bathroom he brushed his teeth. Capturing a small insect in the bathtub, he fired it into the toilet, where it swam in furious circles, around and around and around, fighting the water. When he was little, Beowolf would piss on the cigarette butts his father left floating in the toilet, imagining that they were aircraft carriers. It was only if he managed to completely strip them of their tobacco that he considered them sunk. He unzipped his fly and pissed on the insect. *Piss like a racehorse.* That's what Pap would recommend—Pap who loved horses and dogs far more than he loved people. Beowolf flushed the toilet and returned to the room. On the floor, he found one of Bigfoot's carbohydrate supplements and popped it into his mouth.

Gray was with Jeannie. Even when Jeannie wasn't on the surface of his thoughts she lurked in the shallow depths of consciousness, poised at any instant to come to mind, summoned by any number of chance stimuli: the angelfish swimming in the aquarium downstairs, the snow falling, a knock on the door. She'd said she wouldn't come to the motel. She was with Gray now. He hated the idea. Gray thought he was a coward.

From the desk Beowolf removed a sheet of motel stationery. He stared at the empty page. There was *Dear Jeannie* and *Love, Wolf,* if he cared to write them down, but what in between? He stared out the window and believed that he loved her very much—that if she were to suddenly, magically, appear to hold him and tell him things were all right, he'd walk right out of the motel with her, walk right out of the game itself. He loved her and had told her so; how could she question this? He stared at the paper. He wanted to say something powerful and moving, using words and phrases as exquisite on his lips as an August hailstone had once been on his parched tongue. Out the window the cars whooshed past in the snow. It was all crazy. Did love mean nothing? To love and be loved, yet not make of it a lifelong passion, not have the fortitude to perpetuate such a love? Staring at the blank sheet, it occurred to him that the emotion that he felt for Jeannie, which he had always naturally thought of as love, was either not love at all but something else, something inferior, or else love itself was simply not everything it was cracked up to be and, as with so many other things in his life, he'd simply been sold a bill of goods.

He needed to get things straight.

In the dining room he dropped a dime into the slot and dialed. "Forty-five more cents for the first three minutes, please."

Beowolf laid his change out on the tray beneath the phone. He was a dime short. "Just a minute," he said.

"We can't charge for just a minute," the operator answered. "Three minutes is the minimum."

"Just *wait a minute* while I get change." He asked the waitress who had served them breakfast to change a dollar.

The waitress, burdened with an armload of dishes, stopped dead in her tracks, the harried expression on her face turning to surprise, then sternness. "Another phone call?" She laughed in her innocent, pretty way. "I'm telling."

"Please. I got the operator on the line."

"Well," the girl said as she unloaded the dishes beside the cash register. "I hope this babe you keep calling is worth it." She counted out the change and handed it to Beowolf.

"Thanks." Beowolf began pumping coins into the machine.

The girl just stood there studying him through her huge round glasses.

Beowolf paused in paying for the call, waiting for her to leave. *"Fifteen more cents, please."*

"Just a minute."

"I'm sorry, *sir,* but three minutes . . ."

"Jesus!" Beowolf cried. The girl laughed. He thrust his hand into his pocket. Empty. The receiver slipped off his shoulder as his other hand dug into his other pocket; he grabbed for it but missed. Fumbling around with both hands, he glanced at the girl, who was now bellied over, laughing. Finally, he managed to pull a dollar bill out of his pocket. "Sorry," he said, holding the bill out to her.

"Good hands!" the girl laughed. "Doesn't anybody on your team have any hands?"

"Here." Beowolf thrust the bill at her.

"Keep it," the girl insisted. "The show was worth the price of admission." She scooped up the plates and hurried into the kitchen.

Beowolf held the receiver to his ear. "Hello?" No answer. He pulled down on the coin return. Nothing. "Jesus Christ," he said. Once again he shoved a dime into the slot and dialed the number.

"Forty-five more cents, please, for the first three minutes."

Beowolf fed the money into the machine. Listening to the phone ringing, he wondered what he was going to say.

"Hello?"

"Jeannie?"

"Just a minute."

Beowolf waited.

"Hello?"

"Jeannie?"

"Hi."

"What're you doing?"

"Nothing."

"Jeannie, I have to talk to you."

"I really can't come to the motel."

"What are you telling me?"

At that moment the waitress appeared from the kitchen, relaxed now and sipping coffee.

"I'm telling you nothing new," Jeannie replied.

The waitress smiled at him and sat down at a nearby table.

"This is me you're talking to," Beowolf whispered, glancing at the waitress. "Don't be like this. I need to talk to you. Seriously."

"So talk."

"Why are you mad?"

"Wolf," Jeannie replied, her voice softening. "I'm *not* mad. I'm tired. And I'm hurt. And I don't know what I did to deserve this. I don't see the point . . ."

"I'm sorry you're hurt."

"I don't want your apology."

"What I'm saying," Beowolf insisted, "is that it'll be better when we get home."

"No," Jeannie replied.

"What's happening?"

"Don't be blind. Wolf, please. I'm trying to be tough. Please let me be."

"I love you." Beowolf knew the waitress was trying to hear. "It'll be better when we get back . . ."

From the other end of the line there was silence, then the sound of Jeannie weeping.

"I can't talk on the phone," Beowolf told her. "I hate the fucking phone." Whispering, he added, "The waitress is listening."

"So say *this* so she can hear," Jeannie answered, her voice suddenly as sharp as a razor blade. "Say *but I didn't mean to rape her.* You'll pop her eyes out."

"Please, Jeannie. Don't."

"I won't. I can't."

"Why?"

"I have to be tough."

"What are you doing this for?"

No answer.

"Is it Gray?"

"No, it isn't Gray!" Jeannie cried. "He's right here and he heard me say it, and he knows anyway. He knows everything . . ."

"Send him away."

"No."

"Send him away so we can talk."

"He knows what's happening and he's with me now. I loved you—I love you still, and I was never anything but good to you . . ."

"I know, I know. I want you with me."

"No, I don't believe you do."

"Please come."

Beowolf glanced at the waitress. She was listening, he knew.

"We've talked," Jeannie said, sobbing. "I'm all talked out. I have to decide things for myself. I have to begin looking out for myself. I need you away."

"Jeannie, I hate the phone."

"I hate *everything!*" Jeannie wailed, finally breaking down. Beowolf imagined Gray's hands touching her as she cried long and hard.

"Please," he whispered. "Please don't do this. Come to me, just for ten minutes. I need to talk to you."

"Please deposit fifty-five cents for your next three minutes."

"Just a minute, Operator."

Some fifty miles away, in a cabin with Peter Gray, Jeannie was crying.

"Jeannie," Beowolf said. "Please call me . . ."

"Please deposit fifty-five cents, *sir,* for your next three minutes."

"Will you shut the fuck up?"

The line went dead.

Beowolf slammed the receiver down and glanced at the waitress; her eyes had bugged out so far they seemed to fill the lenses of her glasses. Beowolf stalked out of the dining room.

His room was empty, and again he found himself possessed by that profound unease that, as time passed, increasingly tormented him: deep within him an ever-expanding suffusion of regret that he seemed incapable of suppressing. He wished that by doing something, any one thing, he could sweep away the pain of the past weeks and make things new again, sweep away the pain of memory so the good times could happen again. Outside, the snow was falling. Beowolf considered taking another hot bath, but feared that it would sap him utterly. Besides, it was almost lunchtime.

Instinctively, he retreated from the room. He found Hap resting on his bed, reading a football program.

"Where'd you get that?" Beowolf asked.

"They're selling them in the lobby."

Beowolf sat down on Doe's bed.

"It has me listed at one eighty-five," Hap said.

"Shit. What do they have for me?"

"One ninety-five."

"Fat chance. Where's Doe?"

"I sent him up to the third floor. Some of the cheerleaders are staying up there. I told him Wendy Olsen gives head for five bucks." Hap slapped his knee and laughed. "I told him he has to be patient and wait outside her room till she's ready, and not say anything at all, just wink and give her the 'thumbs up' sign every time he sees her—that it means *I want a blowjob, I'm ready when you are.*" Hap cracked up.

"You're bad," Beowolf said with a snort.

"I'm *desperate.*"

Beowolf laughed abjectly.

"You all right?" Hap asked.

"I'm all right. You?"

"I'm okay," Hap replied. "Boy, ole MD sure got the wind knocked out of him, huh? Bigfoot . . ." Hap's voice trailed off as he shook his head with a grin as wide as Wyoming.

"Bigfoot's got a hair across his ass cause he's got a cold. You seen him since the meeting?"

"He and Granville went up to the third floor."

They were silent for a while, Beowolf absorbed in his own thoughts while Hap read the football program. You could read a program for hours, it seemed, as long as your name was in it. Gray's name would have an asterisk beside it whenever Rawlings was playing away; the line at the bottom of the page noted that Gray wasn't from Rawlings, which tended to get the hometown fans all hot and bothered.

"Hey, Wolf."

"Yeah?"

Without looking up, Hap asked, "How's Jeannie?"

"She's fine," Beowolf replied. "Why?"

"Just wondering." Hap continued looking at the program. "You both going to U of M?"

"I doubt it. Why?"

"Just wondering."

"You're doing a lot of wondering," Beowolf said.

Hap finally looked up. "I figure, now, with this football scandal and nobody wanting to go to U of M, I might get a free ride. I know *you* could get one, with Jason there and everything . . ."

Annoyed, Beowolf said, "Jason's got nothing to do with it."

"It's all just a matter of how well you can adjust to playing for a loser."

"Don't be so sure U of M is gonna be a loser."

"Why not?"

Beowolf shrugged.

"You think I can get a free ride?" Hap asked.

"Oh, man," Beowolf sighed.

"What?" A pained expression crossed Hap's face.

"How ya gettin along with Moon?" Beowolf asked. "The way it looks?"

"He won't throw to me!" Hap complained. "Still, I've caught a lot of passes. I *have* caught a lot of passes. Thompson is the only receiver who's caught more and his father's the fuckin coach."

"You really wanna play in college?"

"Sure. Don't you?"

"It's up to Moon whether or not you get a scholarship to U of M," Beowolf said.

"Why? I don't see why it's up to Moon. If the new U of M coach asks him if I'm worth the scholarship, he'll say yes. Why wouldn't he? No skin off his ass."

"Moon's the new coach."

"Moon?"

"Yep."

"He can't be!"

"He is."

"Who told you?"

"Jason. This is Moon's last game."

Hap stared at him and said nothing.

"I didn't mean to bum you out," Beowolf said. "He probably won't offer me a scholarship either."

"It doesn't matter anyway," Hap sighed.

"Hey," Beowolf said after a while, "don't tell anybody."

19

"Where's your friend?" the waitress asked as she set a plate in front of Beowolf. "The last of the Mohicans."

"He's on the third floor!" Doe blurted out, his eyes wide and tremulous. He fixed his stare on Hap. The girl peered at Doe.

Hap laughed. "Don't expect it to make any sense," he assured her.

"*Fishing's fixed* doesn't make sense to me," she answered. "Why should I expect anything else you people say to make sense?" She shook her head, befuddled, and placed a plate in front of Doe.

"How did it go up there?" Hap asked Doe. "Mission accomplished?"

Doe sneered. "Bullshit."

"It works!" Hap declared. "Believe me!" He turned to the girl, winked and gave her the "thumbs up."

"What's that supposed to mean?" she asked.

"Who'll blow taps?" Hap replied, busting up laughing. The girl shook her head and hurried off.

When Hap finished eating, he left to play hearts in Beano Benvenutti's room. Doe returned mistrustfully to the third floor. Beowolf remained behind, sipping water, until the dining room had cleared out. It was two-twenty.

The waitress eventually appeared from the kitchen, carrying a football program, and seemed surprised to see him still sitting there. She made herself a cup of coffee. "You're still here."

Beowolf shrugged.

"Why was it so funny? *Fishing's fixed?*" She set her coffee down on the table and sat down.

Beowolf laughed, pleased that she'd been so self-assured as to sit down with him, for he suspected himself of lacking her sort of boldness.

"That guy has been fishing with me no less than ten times," he said. "I've never once seen him reel in a fish. He's hauled in everything else. Hooked a drowned dog once."

The girl, grimacing, stuck her tongue out, then sipped her coffee. "Has he seen the aquarium out there? He could probably catch that fish."

Beowolf laughed. "I think he doesn't even wanna catch fish anymore. If he caught one, he'd have to think up some reason why he'd never caught one before and he couldn't say it's always been that way—fixed. Hell! He probably *has* caught a fish for all I know, but threw it back before anybody noticed."

"That's really crazy."

"Yeah, it is."

"Can I get you some coffee?" she asked.

"Sure. Thanks."

The girl retrieved a full pot and poured a cupful for Beowolf.

"So you're Bill Bailey."

Beowolf nodded at the football program. "That's what it calls me."

"You call yourself something different?"

"Beowolf."

"Beowolf?"

"That's what everybody I know calls me."

"Why?"

"Nickname. I dunno."

"That's a funny name."

"You get used to it. It seems normal to me. Now Liz, take *Lizz.*" Beowolf pointed at her nameplate. "The only trouble with a name like *Lizz* is that it sounds like it's short for lizard."

Across the table the girl's eyes widened. She straightened up. "Oh, why thank you *very* much." He smiled, a joke, and she finally giggled in just such a way that her visage so perfectly undermined the image of a lizard that Beowolf felt like reaching across the table to touch her. "I can see you're a charmer," she said. "Just like your friends. Who"—she touched her hair—"was the guy with the hair? Last of the Mohicans?"

"That's Bigfoot. Bigfoot Bearkiller."

"You guys have such crazy names."

"You should talk," Beowolf retorted. "Earthquake? Banzai? Does Thompson have a nickname?"

"Yep."

"What is it?"

"Superfly."

Beowolf shook his head. "Sells drugs when he's not catching passes."

"He's very fast."

"You're telling *me?*"

"This is so funny," the girl said. "I never thought in a million years I'd be talking to you."

Beowolf grinned and raised the coffee cup to his lips.

"Cream and sugar?" She laid her hand on the sugar dispenser.

"Naw."

Beowolf took a sip. He hated coffee. It tasted awful and gave him the runs—which didn't leave much to recommend it.

"My brother, he's at U of M, and what's funny is that he wound up playing in college with a lot of guys he played against in high school."

"Are you going to U of M?" she asked.

"My brother thinks I am."

"What's his name, your brother?"

"Jason. Jason Bailey."

"Jason Bailey's your brother?" She was delighted. "I should've known. He's what? A senior next year?"

"Yeah."

"They switched him from quarterback because they saw him play us."

"That's not why they switched him. Is that what they believe up here?"

Apology surfaced on the girl's face.

"Why did they switch him?" she asked.

"He was never that good a passer, that's all. He was a good runner and a good athlete. You don't switch somebody because of one game. Not . . ." Beowolf cut himself off. "What a game that was." He shook his head.

"It was wonderful. I—*we* were just freshmen."

"Yeah."

"They let some of the freshmen, the really good ones, suit up for the Rawlings game," she told him. "Russell was the cutest thing."

"We don't do that with freshmen."

"That must have bummed you out."

"What? The game?"

"Yes, but not even getting to suit up for it."

Beowolf laughed. "Oh, yeah, it really bummed me out."

"So," she asked, "do you think you'll go to U of M?"

"No."

"The coaches wrecked it," she said. "But they've got someone really good coming in."

"How do you know that?"

"Russell's father told him. I think Russell's father wanted the job."

"Is Russell going to U of M?"

"If he gets a scholarship he will."

"He'll get a scholarship," Beowolf said.

"Do you think so?"

"I'm positive, believe me."

"Rawlings has a good receiver." She suppressed a smile.

Beowolf laughed. "He ain't gettin any free ride to U of M, I'll tell you that."

"Why do you say that?" she asked. "He had only one bad game I know of."

"Well . . ." Beowolf shrugged.

"You stopped throwing to him. You don't stop throwing to somebody just because of one bad game."

Beowolf shrugged. He wasn't gonna say anything.

"You think Russell is real good, huh?"

"Let's not talk about it."

"Okay. We won't talk about it."

"Why does he want to go to U of M?" Beowolf asked.

"To be close to home. Why does your brother want you to go?"

"Jason, he thinks if MD goes somewhere else—ya know who MD is?" The girl nodded. "If he goes to Notre Dame like everybody figures he will, though everybody's wrong, Jason thinks . . ."

"He *won't* go to Notre Dame?"

"No."

"Why?"

Beowolf shrugged. "Anyway, Jason thinks I can start at free safety as a freshman. He's really high on the idea of the Bailey boys playing together for his last season."

"You must get along real well."

"We used to."

"Not anymore?"

"I guess not."

The girl glanced over at the doorway. Granville Skaggs' parents had wandered in. They seated themselves at a table in the far corner.

"S'cuse me," the girl said, rising from the table. She retrieved two menus from the counter and approached their table.

Beowolf relaxed, stuck a plastic straw between his teeth and, closing his eyes, chewed on it meditatively. He imagined himself and this girl outside of their proper time and place, in a neutral land or at some time in the past or the future, happening to meet by some strange quirk of the cosmos. He smiled to himself and opened his eyes to watch her return to his table.

"What are you smiling at?" she asked as she sat down.

"I'm smiling that I'm here talking to you."

The girl leaned toward him. "It's *sinful,* I know."

Chewing his plastic straw, Beowolf stared into her eyes.

"You shouldn't chew plastic straws. They make your fillings fall out."

Beowolf laughed and continued chewing. "Are you going to U of M?"

"Not next year, but the year after. I'm gonna work up here for a year and visit on weekends. We're getting married in two years."

"Married?"

The girl nodded.

"Ya like working here?" Beowolf asked.

"It's okay."

"Can't you make enough money in the summer to go to school next year?"

"I could. But Russell, Russell *and me,* decided it'd be best for him to go alone his first season. It's not that far from here, you know. And Russell has to really concentrate his first year, you know. He's a good student too, not exactly your typical dumb jock. He's vice-president of our class. He wants to go to law school."

As abruptly as a belch, a distaste for Russell had arisen in Beowolf. "Why don't you both go to school and just keep out of each other's way except on weekends?" he asked.

"Well . . ."

"I mean, why should you not go to school so that he can *concentrate?*"

An impish, unexpected grin spread across her face.

"Listen," Beowolf said, disconcerted. "I don't mean to be nosy."

"It's okay if you are," she told him. "I'm nosy, too. I wonder, for instance, why Jeannie's so mad at you."

"You enjoy my conversation?" Beowolf asked sarcastically.

"Both of them," the girl nonchalantly replied. "You shouldn't have told her to shut the fuck up."

Beowolf's nervous system leapt at the word *fuck* coming from the girl's mouth.

"It was the operator I said that to. She kept butting in."

"You asked me why I'm staying away from him," the girl resumed.

"Who?"

"Russell, who else?"

"Yeah?"

"It's hard, in the same place with the person you love," she explained, her voice rising to a slightly higher pitch as she pronounced *love,* "to restrain yourself . . ." Beowolf flinched. The girl leaned toward him and whispered, "I can't keep my hands off him." Her expression was sharp, yet coupled with the intimacy that her confession suggested it confused and amazed him. She raised the coffee cup to her lips, still gazing at him, and took a sip. "Jeannie's your girl friend?"

"Sort of."

"What's that mean?"

"I don't know."

"She won't come to the motel tonight?" she asked.

Beowolf didn't answer. The girl sipped her coffee and watched him.

"She has good reason for not wanting to come," Beowolf said. She nodded as if she understood. "She has damn good reason."

"Do you want to marry her?"

Beowolf was stunned. "Where did *that* come from? What are you talking about?"

"Nothing," she replied innocently. "Just asking." She didn't say anything for a moment, just studied him. "So she doesn't want you." The girl offered a mischievous smile.

"Listen, *she* wants to marry *me.*" He pushed the coffee away from him.

"You don't like coffee?"

"No."

"You want something else?"

"No." He scanned the dining-room walls. "What time is it?"

"Do you have to go?" she asked. "It's quarter to three."

Beowolf glanced at her, looked her over. He shrugged.

"It's difficult," the girl murmured into her coffee. "I know."

"What?"

"Living."

Beowolf gazed at her as a powerful emotion welled within him, and abruptly, with that casual confidentiality that a person reserves for a rare, pleasing stranger, he began to talk about Jeannie, balking only at the most important fact.

"But I don't understand the problem," the girl eventually said. "I don't see why you shouldn't live happily ever after."

"That's fairy-tale stuff. You and Thompson, I'd say, are living fairy-tale stuff. It wears off. It wears off just like being high. It wears off because you realize you don't want to play the game anymore. You have something you wanted, but it's no good anymore. It's past." Beowolf shook his head. "You don't understand, I can see you don't." He glanced across the room at Granville's parents, who sat staring out the window at the miserable afternoon, not touching their coffee, bored to death.

"What happened?" the girl asked. "I really want to know."

"Listen," Beowolf said, a mysterious intensity gripping him the way that in a game an absolute madness sometimes took over. "Come with me." He glanced out the dining-room door, then back through those huge round glasses into her eyes. Rising from the table, he said again, "Come with me . . . to my room."

The girl stared wide and lovely up at him, stunned, her mouth open.

"To talk," Beowolf insisted, feeling his own special weakness now overcoming him. "Talk to me."

"We can talk here," the girl answered.

Disconcerted, yet still worked up, Beowolf said, "If we were someplace else, a million miles from here, you'd be glad to come with me right now."

The girl broke up laughing, amused and bewildered. "I can't. I can't come." She stopped laughing and glanced around the room. "I can't come to your *room*. I can't." She finally looked him straight in the eyes. "You're covering Russell tonight."

"Russell," Beowolf said, shaking his head. "Russell doesn't— Russell will never . . ." He couldn't finish the thought.

"I'm sorry. I enjoyed talking to you." She held out her hand for him to shake. "I'm sorry your girl friend won't . . . won't . . ."

"Won't *what?*" Beowolf snapped bitterly. "She *would* and she *did,* maybe that's the whole fucking problem. Ever think about that? She's pregnant." He turned and marched away.

20

Beowolf, entering the room, saw Bigfoot lying on his bed. "You missed lunch."

"Wasn't hungry."

"That's a first."

Beowolf flopped onto his bed.

"You know Moon's leaving?" Bigfoot asked.

Beowolf propped himself up on an elbow. "How do you know that?"

"Hap told me."

"Well, I'll be dipped in shit! That asshole!"

"Moon?"

"No, Hap." Beowolf rolled onto his back and looked at the ceiling. "It was me who told Hap. I told him not to say anything."

"Who told you?"

"Jason."

"It's true then," Bigfoot said. "Moon's going to U of M."

"What do you care?"

Bigfoot shrugged. Then he sneezed.

"How did Hap happen to tell you?" Beowolf asked.

"He wanted to bet me that MD winds up at U of M. I told him to shove it. I knew something was up."

"Then he told you?"

"Yeah."

"Who else was there?"

"Doe."

"Doe!" Beowolf shouted. "He'll blab to everyone."

"And Beano."

Beowolf groaned. "Wonderful. Nobody's supposed to know." He rose from the bed and gazed out the window; the rain had turned to sleet.

Bigfoot sneezed, then succumbed to a coughing fit.

"We may drown," Beowolf remarked. When Bigfoot was through coughing, Beowolf asked, "You think MD'll go with Moon?"

"Sure. Moon could talk MD into going to the University of Alaska."

"MD's crazy."

"Everybody's crazy," said Bigfoot.

"But MD's *idolized,* man! In Rawlings MD is idolized." Beowolf shook his head. "I don't get it. I don't get it at all."

"You get it," Bigfoot contended. "You're idolized, too."

"Not like him."

"You're not as good."

"Well, *you* are," Beowolf countered. "And that sonofabitch is used as a model for children."

"What do you care? You don't have any children."

"You know what I mean." Beowolf turned from the window to look at Bigfoot. "I'm talking about principle. I'm talking about the goddamn principle of the thing. It's goddamn foul. If I had a kid like MD I'd stuff him in a potato sack and drown him as a favor to the world."

"You planning on having a children, Wolf?" Bigfoot asked.

"Fuck you."

"Sorry, but that won't do it."

"Fuck you," Beowolf snapped. "Shut up!"

Bigfoot raised his hands in surrender. "Sounds like somebody forgot to take their Midol this morning."

Beowolf turned back to the window. In the distance he heard Bigfoot resume. "As long as MD stays number twenty-two in our program, he'll stay number one in my heart." Bigfoot sneezed, sneezed again.

"Why are you defending him now?" Beowolf looked at Bigfoot. "A little while ago I was afraid you were gonna break his neck."

"I'm not defending him." Bigfoot laid his head back on the pillow, picking his teeth and staring at the ceiling. "It was me who walked out of the meeting, not you."

"I know. I could hear your balls clank."

"It don't matter. It's not principle or any of that horseshit. I just couldn't relax.

"There are two things you gotta understand are pure bullshit," Bigfoot continued after a while. "One"—he pointed toward the ceiling—"is that the meek shall inherit the earth. Never happen," he insisted, shaking his head. "The only earth they inherit is the earth they're planted in. The other"—a second finger sprang into place beside the first, forming the Indian sign for Wolf—"is that Santa Claus comes only if you're good. There's no rhyme or reason sometimes why some folks have it better than others. Ya gotta take the ball as it bounces, and if you're lucky enough to get a grip on it, hang on to it like your life depends on it. MD is a royal pain in the ass, sure, but I ain't so stupid that I think I'm a whole lot different. We're lucky, man! *You* must have a fuckin horseshoe up your ass, you're so damn lucky. And you don't even know it. We got the rules all laid out for us, man, which is a lot more than these other poor slobs got. And as long as I'm good enough to play by those rules I'll do it with a vengeance. Just like MD. *Just like you.* And I'll grab whatever else I can lay my hands on if I get the chance."

"How can you . . ." Beowolf sank into the room's only armchair. "You're just talkin out your ass."

"Sometimes I am, sometimes I ain't." Bigfoot worked his thumb around the inner rim of his nose and sighed. "The golden rule is this," he finally said. "Never fuck your friends."

"Rules never work for me," Beowolf told him. "They're always too, too . . . I can't think." He shook his head dejectedly. "There are exceptions. Ya gotta live by more than just rules—ya gotta *live.* I don't know, it's all just one long case of blue balls."

"*Blue* balls!" Bigfoot shouted. "You're *not* the person to be talking about blue balls. I'd love a case of *your* blue balls!" Bigfoot roared, winding up in a coughing fit.

"You don't understand what I mean."

"What, then, blue balls?"

"I think we want something, something more . . ."

"Than what? You got the world by the hairs, man!"

"I can't say," Beowolf said. "Do you ever feel like saying something, you know, like you really gotta get it out, and you don't know what it is?"

"I mostly know what it is."

"It ain't that simple," Beowolf answered. "I feel like there's a lot of things I gotta say. I feel like there's lots of things I gotta say if I can figure out how. I just don't know the words, I . . ."

"How do you feel?"

"I'm a mess. I gotta *say* something."

"To me?"

"To them," Beowolf replied, pointing emphatically toward the door. *"To them."*

"Them? Who's *them?*"

"Everybody! I gotta say something like, I don't know, fuck this."

"Sounds to me like you know the words all right."

"But that ain't it! That's too simple. And I'm not talking about just saying it. I gotta do something. I gotta *do* something."

The conversation ended momentarily. Beowolf lifted himself from the armchair and moved back to the window sill. He gazed at the Holiday Inn sign and just beyond to where an old man leaning on a mailbox pressed his thumb against one of his nostrils while blowing snot out the other. It was raining again.

Bigfoot broke the silence. "What happened between you and Jeannie, anyway?"

"Nothing."

"Something happened."

Beowolf looked out the window, but saw nothing. It was like staring underwater. "I was always afraid, I think. I wasn't *always* afraid. When I was little I thought I was going to be a great fucking general." He chuckled miserably. "I was afraid when Jason started playing football for Moon. I was afraid I wouldn't be good enough. But I am—I am good enough."

"But what happened with Jeannie?"

"What happened? Nothing happened. *Nothing happened,* you understand? Nothing."

There was a knock on the door. Beowolf stood rooted to the floor as an instant joyfulness charged through him like electricity. He crossed the room and opened the door. Across the threshold stood Helen. Everything seemed, at that moment, to cave in on him. He could scarcely look at her, could scarcely breathe. "Hap isn't here," he said.

"I'm not looking for Hap."

From behind, Bigfoot said, "Hey, Wolf. How about hitting the road for a while?"

Beowolf glanced back at Bigfoot. It came clear. He stepped past Helen into the hallway and the door closed behind him.

21

Beowolf stood shivering in the phone booth as he placed the call to the cabin, *collect* this time so they wouldn't be interrupted. Jeannie accepted the charges.

"Hi," Beowolf said.

"Hello."

"Jeannie, I'm sorry to keep calling you like this."

Silence.

"I have to talk to you," Beowolf continued. "You have to understand things."

"I'm trying."

"I want it to be like it was before."

"It can't be," Jeannie told him. "It never will be."

"Why not?"

"I can't just take care of *you,*" she explained. "I'm going to be a mother."

"Jeannie, don't . . ."

"I have to start taking care of myself."

"I'll take care of you."

"*No.*"

"It'll be better," Beowolf insisted. "I'll make it better."

"No."

"Are you saying good-by?"

Silence.

"Jeannie, this is *me* you're talking to. What's going on? You've been listening to Gray . . ."

"I've been listening to no one. Gray's got nothing to do with it."

"This is me. *Me.*"

"What about me?" Jeannie cried. "What about *me?*"

"I love you."

"You don't even *know* me. You think you do, but you don't. You love the idea of me, that's all. You never gave yourself a chance."

"Jeannie, please. You've been listening to Gray. Talk to me. Talk to *me.* Tell me what's happening."

"I feel like screaming. You and Gray both suddenly making demands. What for? I'm trying to be good, I've always tried. I never tried to be anything but good to you," she said, her voice trembling. "I never tried to hurt, I'm not trying to hurt you now. I never did anything but love you." Her voice broke and she began to cry.

"This is crazy!" Beowolf shivered. "I need to see you."

"I can't deserve this. Please, please stop."

"He's not like me, Jeannie. He's not like me. He can't love you."

"Gray's not the issue."

Gripped by a spasm of frustration and cold, Beowolf shuddered, couldn't speak. His teeth began to chatter.

"Are you outside?" Jeannie asked.

Beowolf's voice stuck in his throat while his body convulsed. "Yes."

"You're freezing."

"I left the motel. Without a coat. I left the motel without my coat. I had to talk to you. I need to see you." Jeannie's spastic sobs wrung Beowolf's own body. "I'm sorry, Jeannie. I'm so sorry." Tears rolled down his face, he couldn't make his body be still. His heart was pumping poison. "I can't believe this is happening. Please. Let's make it better," he stammered. *"Please.* Jeannie. Don't say . . ." He leaned against the glass of the phone booth. "Jeannie, don't say—good-by to me. You can't. This isn't how it's supposed to be. It's my fault. I know. It's my fault. It'll be good though. Jeannie? *I need you.* I want the baby. I want him."

"You don't know what you want," Jeannie moaned.

"Jeannie, I want it all! I want you!"

"I can't listen anymore!" Jeannie wailed. "I can't breathe! I'm going to scream!"

The line went dead.

22

The chapel was dark, the curtains closed. Pews were arranged around the altar in a horseshoe. Shivering and wet, Beowolf chose a seat in the back row. He had to calm himself. Nobody else was there yet. He picked the missal up off the seat next to him and flipped abstractedly through the pages, wishing that he could believe in prayer. He saw little point in going to church to pretend that he believed it was easier for a camel to pass through the eye of a needle than for a rich man to enter the kingdom of heaven. For years, his father, who had promised Beowolf's mother to raise the boys Catholic, had every Sunday faithfully taken them to church, where Round John Virgin, belly thrust outward, sweat speckling his high square forehead, would practice his Roman mumbo-jumbo.

Beowolf shivered. He sighed deeply. A calm had momentarily overtaken his anguish. He would see her soon, regardless. In Rawlings, at least, he would see her. Then they could straighten everything out. She was right, Gray wasn't the problem. He knew this. He'd gotten upset over nothing. He'd made the phone call simply because he'd had nothing else to do. He couldn't have gone to Hap's room—not while Bigfoot was with Helen. Not that Hap deserved any better. "You don't miss a slice out of a cut loaf" was what Beowolf had ultimately been told by Hap concerning his tumble with Helen.

Gray was with Jeannie. This was what kept pulling him under. Beowolf never understood what was wrong with Gray, why he had given Jeannie up in the first place. At the time, he wasn't asking questions, as if asking questions might upset the fragile balance between the three of them. On a warm summer night, a night still and surreal from the weight of the day—the day Pap had gone gunning for the Hollywood director—Gray finally deserted Jeannie outright, leaving her alone with Beowolf.

Beowolf gazed around the chapel. Pap wouldn't get caught dead in church. "I'd sooner wait tables," he'd said more than once.

"Priest is Eye-talian for *windbag."* Beowolf's father told him to shut up whenever he started jabbering about religion and the goddamn Pope.

Beowolf had no real faith either. His father was dead, and his mother, his grandmother and Pap; life was invariably fatal. Pap had shown no fear of dying. There'd been a guy, Beowolf recalled, there'd been some greenhorn, that night at the Bum Steer, who, after Pap threw the shot of venom in his mouth, complained, "Look! Look! He ain't swallered it! He ain't swallered it yet!" Pap was willing to push his life to its limit with no more thought or justification than that he'd always done it and always gotten away with it. Anything worth doing was worth overdoing. Pap felt about himself the way he'd felt about Midnight, for whom, even after the dog was clearly over the hill, he retained a sort of transcendent faith in its capacity to destroy all comers—as if in an animal so scarred and grim reigned some sort of invincible advantage that set the jaws in perpetual motion.

While Pap was alive, Beowolf had come to believe simply that he was the biggest bullshitter north of the Rio Grande. But in the moment of Wavy's revelation about Pap wasting that guy, Beowolf's conception, his comprehension, of his grandfather was instantly shattered, leaving nothing but fragments that would not fit together. These fragments were, he now believed, the elements of Pap's insanity. Only recently had Beowolf been able to connect such a word with Pap. *Insanity.* Not *crazy* said with a laugh. There was nothing funny about a man killing himself.

Beowolf could not imagine what it was that Pap saw in death. Sometimes Beowolf envisioned himself as an amber picture in a photograph album: a doting grandfather of no renown, smiling harmlessly, toothlessly perhaps, impotently, holding a fly rod in one hand and a rainbow in the other. Still, he could not imagine killing himself, nor could he articulate why Pap had killed himself. But the revelation about the man named Legget had given him a clue wherein he seemed to catch Pap's drift. There was an evil haunting Pap's days that, for the life of him, he could not evade and could not obliterate. That evil he'd once sighted in Legget— an evil so blatant, so enormous as to threaten not only Pap's own life but life itself—was, in Pap's idiosyncratic madness, mysteriously resurrected in the overweight form of an arrogant, second-rate Hollywood director who, through some flunky's oversight, maimed thirteen wild mustangs and then had them shot.

Pap went berserk when he heard about the mustangs. Midnight was fighting that night, which always put Pap in a foul humor to begin with. Baring his teeth, he did a buffalo-stomp around the kitchen, searching for something he could grab hold of—something like an ax. Wheeling, he slugged the wall clock, flattening its face.

"Take it easy, Pap, take it easy!" Beowolf told him. "Don't have a heart attack over it."

"Heart attack! Heart attack!" Pap spat. "I wish I *would* have a goddamn heart attack!"

As Pap began cussing out the director, Beowolf picked up the pieces of shattered plastic and dropped them in the garbage bag. Pap cussed out the director, cussed out Hollywood, cussed out the piss-ant town he lived in, and progressively generalizing his cuss to sweep in broader and broader trashpiles of humanity, he ultimately laid a cuss on the whole fucking human race and the branch-swingers it descended from. He stalked out of the house.

Several hours later Pap was chaffeured home by Rollo in his patrol car, so badly beaten by the bodyguards who had wrestled his shotgun from him that it looked as if he himself had been run into the barbwire fence. Rollo pushed past Beowolf and searched Pap's bedroom for the rest of his weapons.

Pap grabbed the telephone receiver and thrust it at Beowolf. "Get Moon," he commanded.

"What's Moon gonna do?"

"Get Moon!"

"You get out of here," Beowolf said, "and I'll get Moon. Go out and take care of Midnight. He's all excited now and he's got a fight tonight."

Pap stomped out the back door howling for Midnight. Beowolf dialed Jeannie's number.

By the time Eric arrived, Rollo had departed with all of Pap's prized possessions. Pap laid a royal cuss on Eric, too. "Pap," Eric said. "Pap! You'll get your possessions back in good time."

"Will I get the mustangs back?"

"The mustangs weren't yours."

"Were they *his?*" Pap answered angrily.

"We're looking into the matter of the horses, Pap. What more can we do?"

"String em up!" Pap bellowed. He grabbed the telephone receiver and once again thrust it at Beowolf. "Get Moon."

"Pap, stop," Beowolf pleaded. "Moon can't do anything."

Pap stared at him with an expression of absolute incredulity. *"Can't do anything?"* he cried. He burst into a brief fit of lunatic laughter, then stormed angrily out the back door.

That Pap had hero-worshiped Moon seemed terribly inconsistent to Beowolf. With Moon Pap had nothing in common. Pap was a relic, a bear trap, an anachronism. "He wanted to kill us!" Beowolf shouted at Pap after his Bull Run with Gray. Pap sat hunched pathetically over a bottle of giant-killer, shaking his head. He wouldn't say anything, and Beowolf was seized momentarily by the impulse to grab him by the throat. Instead, afraid he might cry, he put on his shorts and sneakers and went running, running himself into the ground.

Moon hadn't been interested in the deaths of wild mustangs. "You must be crazy!" he laughed. Pap, of course, *was* crazy. After Midnight was killed he'd gone crazier and crazier. He began sleeping with a Bowie under his pillow and sometimes in the middle of the night Beowolf would hear him freaking out: stomping around his room possessed by moonshine horrors or cussing out the dog for up and dying on him like that. *"Miiid-niiiiight!"* Beowolf locked his own bedroom door; otherwise he'd never sleep a wink. One night he found Pap hunched over a bottle of redeye in the kitchen, practicing math problems so he wouldn't "die dumb."

It was while viewing his Bull Run with Gray, Beowolf believed, that driving the bus became for Pap his "duty." Disillusioned with Moon, Pap accepted the task, hoping perhaps that "duty" would help him fit in, to be a part of something bigger and better than his own ailing self, which less and less soberly piloted the bus down the highway until Moon finally gave him the ax midway through the season, ending for Pap the closest thing to a routine—aside from drinking most every night and defying death on Good Friday —he'd ever known.

"Rollo's a sonofabitch," Beowolf said to Eric as they stared out the window at Pap in the backyard, raving incoherently at Midnight. "He didn't have to treat Pap that way. He came in here like he owned the place." Beowolf glanced at Eric. "Pap wouldn't have hurt that guy."

"Can't take chances with a man's life," Eric answered.

Beowolf shrugged. "Rollo's still a sonofabitch."

"Sure he's a sonofabitch," Eric agreed. "But I need somebody like Rollo—somebody easy to hate. If you can control him, you can put a sonofabitch to good use."

Beowolf snorted.

"Are the state people taking care of you all right?" Eric asked. "You have enough money and everything?"

Beowolf nodded.

"I know how to get through to these state people if they go on the blink. Just let me know."

"Thanks."

"Looks like you been eating good," Eric observed. "When's Summer Practice start?"

"Next week."

"You be our split end?"

"I hope."

"Better not let Moon catch you with that hair. Gray neither. Or it'll be a scalping party. With a helmet on you'd look like you're wearing a coonskin cap underneath." Eric laughed and clapped Beowolf on the shoulder. He glanced outside at Pap and Midnight. "Midnight fighting tonight?"

Beowolf nodded.

"He's too old. Pap should put him out to pasture before he gets him killed."

It was Eric who informed Beowolf later that night that Midnight had indeed been killed. "The other dog was bigger, stronger, faster and within a gnat's ass of just as mean." Beowolf had been out with Gray, getting high at Buffalo Wallow, when they decided to go to Jeannie's house. Almost immediately after, Gray asked Beowolf if he could borrow his car to go up to Great Falls, where someone he knew was playing guitar. Beowolf gave him the keys and Gray was gone. Eric returned to his monster movie. Jeannie shrugged acquiescently and led Beowolf into the den. He'd never been alone with her before; seeing her crestfallen because of Gray's abrupt departure and sensing that the present situation had been arranged according to Gray's conscious design, Beowolf was stung by some fleeting compunction. He felt like a conspirator. "I'm sorry," he said. "I don't know what's happening. But I'm sorry." He watched her not looking at him. She put a record on the turntable and lowered the needle. "Do you want me to leave?" he asked.

Jeannie shook her head, still not looking at him. "No, I don't want you to leave."

"I don't know why he likes so much being alone."

"*Nobody,*" she answered fiercely, turning her eyes on him, "likes being alone."

Beowolf shrugged uncomfortably.

"Would you like a cup of coffee?" she asked.

"Sure, if you . . ." She had already crossed the room and was out the door.

Beowolf sat down on the floor and listened to the music. Jeannie returned several minutes later with two cups of coffee.

"How did you get your name?"

"Just happened," he said. "A long time ago. Hap didn't think much of *Bailey,* so he pronounced it *Beowolf.* And he didn't like *Bill* either—you know, 'Bill Bailey, Won't You Please Come Home.' So he dropped it altogether."

Jeannie didn't say anything. Beowolf sipped his coffee. "Hot," he said. He hated coffee. He looked at her. "It isn't a bad name."

"It's a good name."

"There's a book called *Beowulf* by Sir Walter Scott, I think. The same guy who wrote *Ivanhoe.*"

"No, *Beowulf*'s anonymous."

"What do you mean?"

"They don't know who wrote it. It's about a warrior chief who kills this monster, Grendel, that keeps ripping the heads off his men."

"Did you see that on *Monsterland?*"

"I read it," Jeannie replied.

"You're smart, huh?"

Jeannie's eyes brightened like lamps whose wicks have been turned up. "Gray says *you're* smart," she replied. "He says you're the only one on the team with any brains."

"Gray hates Peckinpah."

"So do I," Jeannie said. "Peckinpah's a creep."

Beowolf took a sip of coffee.

"Sorry to hear about Midnight," Jeannie said after a while.

"That's how it goes." Beowolf scuffed at the carpet with his foot. He scrutinized his foot and scuffed some more, just like he'd seen Gary Cooper do it.

"Eric says the Elks just picked Pap to give their Founders' Day speech."

"Did they?"

Jeannie nodded. "On account of him being the oldest living resident of Rawlings and everything."

"He isn't the oldest living resident of Rawlings," Beowolf mentioned. "Wavy is. Bigfoot's grandfather."

"Why wasn't he chosen, then?"

Beowolf shrugged. "Maybe they wouldn't like his version of events." He laughed. "Maybe they won't like Pap's any better."

"What's he gonna talk about, do you think?"

"Wild mustangs, I expect."

"They want him to talk about history, don't you think?"

"He'll give em history."

They drank coffee and discussed Pap and Gray. "We've got two loonies by the tail!" Jeannie finally declared.

When it was time to go, she showed him to the door, but changed her mind at the last moment and told Eric she was walking Beowolf home.

With a laugh, Eric called back from the television room, "You're walking *him* home? Come here." Jeannie and Beowolf entered the room where several thousand screaming Japanese were fleeing a prehistoric monster. "Be careful, honey. All kinds of kooks running around loose."

"It's only next door, Dad."

"Give me a kiss good night," he said. "I'll be in bed."

Jeannie kissed him good night and they walked out the door and up the driveway to the highway. There was a half-moon, and a breeze in the air. In the distance the mountains looked like blunt sawteeth.

"We're gonna have a great team next year," Beowolf told her.

"Gray might not play."

Beowolf stopped walking. *"Not play!"*

"He doesn't seem like he wants to."

"Oh, he never does." Beowolf resumed walking. "He's gonna be great this year. I think he could play anywhere in college."

"He won't play in college," Jeannie said flatly. "He doesn't want to at all. If he plays this year, it'll be his last. He wants to play music."

Beowolf shrugged, disbelieving.

"I don't think he plans to get his hair cut."

"Did *he* say that?" Beowolf asked.

"He hasn't said *anything*. He's just begging for something bad to happen." She shook her head. "He's not satisfied. It's like he needs enemies more than he needs friends."

Along the highway beneath the cool half-moon they walked, the stars pinpricks in the blue-black dome of sky. A car tore past in a rush of headlights and engine and air. Beowolf kicked a stone off the pavement.

"Listen," he said. "Are you all right?"

Jeannie glanced at him, surprised, but didn't break her casual stride. "Sure, I'm all right." She smiled faintly and looked away. "What do you mean?"

"If ever you want someone to go with, to go listen to Gray play if you don't want to go alone, I'll go with you. I go sometimes anyway, I see you by yourself. Except when people don't know you're with Gray."

Once again Jeannie smiled faintly at him. "Thanks."

When they got to his house, Beowolf sat down on the front steps.

"I have to get back or Eric will worry."

Beowolf stood up. "I"ll walk you home."

"I just walked *you* home."

"All kinds of kooks running round loose."

"I'm used to kooks."

"Come on."

"No," she insisted. "I'll go by myself."

Beowolf looked at her. "Well," he said. "Ya sure?"

She nodded.

Looking over her shoulder, down the highway to the mountains, he shrugged. "Thanks. Thanks for walking me home." He wanted to touch her. A shiver grazed his skin; a beautiful night. The breeze blew her hair across her face. She brushed it away. "Good night," he said.

"Good night."

He stood there looking at her, the breeze rippling her loose cotton blouse and her hair; she was beautiful in the light of the half-moon, standing there looking back at him.

She brushed her hair back and kissed him on the cheek. "Good night," she said. She turned and ran the first few steps down the highway, alone.

23

Beowolf heard a noise in the lobby of the chapel. The doors opened and in marched a handful of piss-ants.

"Whattaya say, Wolf?" Lombago called.

The piss-ants sat on the other side of the chapel, carrying on a hushed conversation.

Others began to file in. Hap arrived and sat down next to Beowolf. The curtains mysteriously parted to reveal an afternoon spangled with fat snowflakes. Moon entered with Peckinpah, Porkbutt and Coach Rose in tow. They sat in the first pew, directly facing the altar.

Hap nudged Beowolf. "Superscout."

From a side door beyond the far row of pews, Superscout came slinking in, step by careful step, keeping close to the wall, clutching a clipboard with both hands. Beneath his hat, thin red hair peeked out on either side of his freckled pumpkin face. His eyes darted this way and that, taking in everything.

"I wonder if Round John's gonna let him read the gospel again this year," Hap whispered.

Beowolf laughed. "I doubt it."

Superscout was a man of few words—and almost every one of them was an obscenity. He was the undisputed king cussmonger of all time. He slid into the end spot of the rear pew. Hunched slightly forward, he took a quick survey of the chapel, glanced casually over each shoulder, and finally sat upright and slipped his hat off, laying it on his clipboard in his lap.

MD entered with Geek and several others. They filed into the pew directly behind Moon. Moon glanced at his watch. People were arriving in a steady stream.

Round John finally made his entrance, accompanied by a pair of altar boys. Moon rose as they took their places on the altar.

"Okay," Moon said. "Listen up."

"Hey!" Peckinpah called out, rising also. He murmured something to Moon.

Moon turned to Round John. "Father," he said. Peckinpah sat down. "Could you have your altar boys leave until it's time for mass?"

"What? Oh! Ho, ho," Round John chortled. "Surely, surely, of course, I'm sorry." He turned to the Kalispell altar boys. "Fellas?"

The altar boys genuflected at the foot of the altar and headed for the door.

"Terribly sorry."

"That's okay, Father," Moon said.

A glimmer of approval crossed the face of Superscout.

Moon began pacing the floor. He nodded to Superscout, who looked straight past him, refusing to acknowledge the gesture. "How did the meeting go?" he asked MD.

MD went rigid. "Went okay."

"What's wrong?"

"Nothing. It went good."

"Good, good." Moon was pacing. "First thing," he said. "We're having silent calisthenics tonight." He stopped and glanced across their faces.

"Second," he continued. "On the fist"—Moon thrust into the air the signal for the defensive team to block the punt—"instead of shooting the gap up the middle between center and guard we want you"—he pointed at Granville. "We've changed this now. Coach Rose and Superscout have worked this out from some late scouting reports. We want you, Granville, to shoot outside Little White. Shoot the gap between the guard and tackle instead. Now Doe . . ." Moon found Doe and lowered his fist. "Now listen up, Doe. You and Bigfoot are gonna wedge Big White and Little White into the middle. We're not gonna send anybody up the middle. McCall will come from outside left and Morris from outside right as usual. Everybody else is going in guard to tight end. We're throwing everything at em on the fist. MD: line up in normal punt-return formation, but as soon as they come up to the line, hustle your butt up to the line of scrimmage. I want you going outside Big White—this is new now, but we can do it. We're throwing everything at em on the fist. Bailey, you're hanging back to return the punt if we don't block it. Watch the fake.

"We gotta do a job in the trenches. Gotta do a job on Big and Little White." Big and Little White were both big blacks, Kalispell's guards. "You got this, Konichek?" Doe nodded. "All right. We'll remind you before the game. MD: remind him in the huddle too . . . You got this, Bigfoot?" Moon's glance shot around the chapel. *"Where is he? Where the hell is Bigfoot?"* He was asking Beowolf.

Beowolf shrugged.

"Was he in the room when you left?"

"I left from the lobby," Beowolf told him. "I haven't been to the room for a while."

"That—" Moon shook his head. "That dummy."

"Just as well," Hap whispered to Beowolf as Moon resumed pacing and talking. "Nobody'd wanna sit in his *pew.* " Hap turned up his nose. "Where is he?"

Beowolf shrugged.

Moon seemed to be floating as he paced, scarcely touching the ground at all. "Earthquake we're gonna have to hit"—Moon smacked his fist into the palm of his hand—"and hit"—smack—"and hit"—smack. "We gotta let him know who he's up against. We're the Rattlers from Rawlings." Moon turned to Frankie. "Am I right?"

"Right!" Frankie shouted.

"We gotta show'm. We gotta show'm who we are and what we are. We gotta hit that bastard low. Hit'm high and he's gonna run up your face."

Moon kept floating back and forth before the altar as he spoke, stopping occasionally to emphasize something. His arms, shoulders and head remained fixed straight ahead as he paced. He moved with perfect stillness, delivering his standard dissertation on winning. "Victory is a simple matter of desire: giving one hundred and ten percent. When the going gets tough . . ." He nodded at Lombago.

"The tough get going," Lombago responded.

"I want a promise," Moon declared. "Who among you will promise, if we lose this game, to practice for an additional two weeks after the season is over?"

Moon halted, towering before them, a prophet in search of believers. "We'll practice for two weeks, in rain or sleet or hail or snow, we'll freeze if we have to, *but we'll win this game.* Who will promise?"

Beowolf braved quick glances at his teammates solemnly seated in the horseshoe around the altar. It was ridiculous! This was the time for Bigfoot's snoring or a timely fart to clear the air. But Bigfoot wasn't there. He was with Helen. Hands sprang up. *God,* Beowolf thought. "Jesus," he muttered. It was bullshit! Hap's hand rose. It was ridiculous, but it didn't matter one way or the other. Beowolf raised his hand to make it unanimous.

Moon's discourse ended and mass began. The mass was as much a component of the team's weekly ritual as the Wednesday-afternoon psyche session was. It didn't matter that only a few members of the team were Catholic. Moon was Catholic.

The priest's real name was Father John or, more formally, Father John McGarrity. When Beowolf was in first grade, he'd drawn a nativity scene in which he portrayed not only the shepherds and sheep, the three kings of Orient R, Baby Jesus, Mary, Joseph and Joseph's ass, but also a mysterious stranger dressed in priestly attire. "Who's this fat dude?" Pap asked.

"That's Round John Virgin," Beowolf replied.

"Who?"

"Round John Virgin."

Pap looked at him as if he were talking French.

"Round John Virgin," Beowolf explained, "mother and child" —he laid a finger on each of the characters—"holy infant so tender and mild." Pap went into hysterics, and thereafter the priest was known by no other name.

After MD read the gospel, Round John took his stand at the lectern to deliver his sermon. "Many are called," he began, restating the theme of the gospel, "but few are chosen." He paused to scan their faces. "These are the words of the Lord Jesus Christ, son of God. God, Christ tells us, invites all of his children into his kingdom. But he ultimately rejects most of these, for they prove to be unworthy. Every man has a soul, a soul that yearns for that peace of heaven that has been made possible to him by the sufferings of our Lord Jesus Christ. Trial and tribulation, pain and suffering—these are the hurdles that batter the soul, beat it into submission and lead it astray into sin, and ultimately"—Round John paused ominously—"death."

From inside his vestments, Round John unveiled a peewee football. He held it above his head as he would a chalice. So incongruous did the football seem, appearing from nowhere and held in the hands of a priest before the altar, that the gesture resembled some sort of sleight of hand. "It says," Round John declared, " 'Rawlings Rattlers never say die.' " He lowered the football and placed it on the altar. "Many are called, but few are chosen. Every mother's son in Cascade County is made a present of one of these footballs. The invitation is extended to everyone. But most of man's seeds fall to the wayside, on rocky ground, or among thorns or weeds, or the birds eat them up. Only the cream can rise to the top —rising to the top because it was sown in good earth. A good seed grows into good fruit. You sitting here are the good fruit, the chosen ones.

"Many are called, but few are chosen. You sitting here have known pain and suffering, trial and tribulation, and you've come to know that everything is attainable under God's blue sky if you only want it badly enough—if you give one hundred and ten percent. You say no to death. You rise above it. 'Death, thou shalt die,' as the poet John Dryden declared. *You must resurrect yourselves.*

"The die is cast," Round John solemnly continued. "Tonight you take the field against the mightiest foe you have ever faced. I am talking about a football game. A *mere* football game, some might say." Round John sneered. "They know not what they say . . .

"A *mere* football game? Heaping scorn upon our leaders, booing our military men, is the sport of some people. But for the vast majority—the *silent* majority, as President Nixon, himself an avid football fan, so aptly labeled them—their sport is football, and it is football for a reason. On the football field, between the white lines, end zone to end zone in full view of everybody—there America can see real mettle tested. There we can see true American character, spirit and courage. You, gentlemen, are America's finest, America's heroes. You are of the world to come.

"George Washington once said, addressing his tattered troops at Valley Forge: 'These are the times that try men's souls.' It was wintertime and Washington's men were without heat, clothing, shelter, food and arms. Morale was low. 'The summer soldier,' Washington said, 'and the sunshine patriot will in this crisis shrink from the service of his country.'

"Tonight there will be moments—let us not mince words—there

will be moments tonight when you will be called upon to place your souls on trial. Each one of you. How will you react late in the game when the going gets tough and you're dead on your feet, your throat is dry and your hands are frozen? Will you muster your resolve? Can you rise from the dead? Or are you a summer soldier, a sunshine patriot? Are you a winner?" Round John asked. "When a loser's soul goes on trial, he gives up. He rolls over and plays dead. *And do you know what?*" Round John spoke slowly, confidently. "He *is* dead. He's lost his spirit, his courage, his very manhood. I tell you, he's *spiritually* dead.

"But from a winner something sublime, something akin to divine grace, something greater than the sum of a physical body's parts, transcends the body to carry it over the goal line.

"Courage, desire, self-sacrifice, love for one another. These are the qualities that assure everlasting life. Christ was, above and beyond everything else, *a winner.* Let's never forget that. Christ was the biggest winner of all, for he won for all mankind the Kingdom and the Glory of Heaven . . ."

Christ was incomprehensible to Beowolf. Divinity was what saved him in the end and divinity was what nobody else possessed —which was why martyrs were as numerous as maggots on a dead cat, but nobody could be a savior. Bigfoot was right: the meek shall never inherit the earth. Beowolf had no faith. He believed in losing. Losing is not everything, it is the only thing.

The peewee football sat on the altar. RAWLINGS RATTLERS NEVER SAY DIE. Beowolf felt old. It had been a long season, a long four years. He'd been through a lifetime of practices. Practice was a dog's life. But sometimes it could be remarkable. Embedded in the endless hours of tiresome pain were moments like gems, beautiful and priceless—when Bigfoot burst out of the Tunnel of Love wearing no pants, just his immortal Tarzan jock. There was the miserable hot day in September when, for wind sprints, Moon had them strip off their helmets, jerseys and shoulder pads, and with the cool caress of a late-afternoon breeze on their wet hides, they sailed weightlessly up and down the field as if it were only their equipment that kept them anchored to earth. Once Bigfoot blocked a punt just as Geek's foot made contact with the ball. The ball exploded like a balloon and Doe scooped up the bladder and tore ass downfield, glancing frantically back, unable to imagine what to do with a flattened football; so he ran out of bounds to stop the clock. One practice Hap spat into the wind and plugged Peckinpah in the back of the neck, then denied that he did it. There was an August day when hail fell.

There was the Bull Run with Gray.

24

It was going to be another hot one. Along the seams of his groin the ache began, gradually spreading across his abdomen. Beowolf closed his eyes, listened to his breathing, concentrated on breathing rather than pain, keeping up with Peckinpah's steady cadence.

Peckinpah's whistle shrieked and Beowolf clambered to his feet from sit-up position, running in place. "Hit it!" Gray shouted; Beowolf hit the earth and bounced back up. "Ho!" The sun bore down, the grass pungent and steamy. He rose and fell and rose and fell, the soreness radiating from the center of his body down legs like burning anchor-weights—"Higher! Higher!" Peckinpah screamed. "Get the legs up! Get em up!"—and up his chest and across his shoulders and arms pushing off the earth, bouncing up running, over and over and over forty times. Gray's jersey was soaked dark red in the stomach. With Summer Practice only fifteen minutes old, two sophomores had already shuffled off.

"Okay, listen up!" Peckinpah blew his whistle. "Bailey, get your ass up here!"

Beowolf hustled up to the head of the calisthenics formation. Peckinpah reached behind Beowolf's head and grabbed the hair that hung down behind his helmet. "What's this crap, huh?" He twisted Beowolf's head. "You get this hair cut before afternoon practice, you and Gray both. You both have ten Tunnel of Loves. You understand?"

Beowolf nodded.

"You understand?"

"Yes!"

"Now get back in line."

Beowolf hustled back into place. He was crazy not to have cut his hair.

Peckinpah turned to Gray. "This is a fine example you're setting."

After practice, after ten Tunnel of Loves beneath the practice-field bleachers, Beowolf and Gray showered and dressed and headed into town in Beowolf's car.

"Where ya wanna go?" Beowolf asked.

"Sandwich shop."

"I mean for a haircut."

"I ain't gettin a haircut," Gray said. "I'm getting a cheese sandwich."

"Hey man, don't do this. They'll get you."

"They can't get me."

"Why not?" Beowolf wanted to know.

"Cause I'm captain, duly elected."

"By the skin of your ass."

Gray said nothing more until Beowolf pulled into a parking space. "You getting a haircut?"

"Gray, what the fuck? They'll kill us, you know that."

"They'll make us do those damn tunnels, that's all. Those tunnels bother you?"

"Hell yes!"

"Then get your haircut. I don't care."

"Shit." Beowolf slammed his palm against the steering wheel. "You're captain. What am I?"

"You and me are half their offense."

"I never started a game in my life!"

"Moon's not as dumb as he looks. He knows when he's got a player."

"He sure didn't know last year," Beowolf said, recalling Bull Run.

"You're forty pounds heavier and twice as quick. But listen, ya wanna get a haircut, go ahead. It don't matter to me. I'm getting something to eat."

"They're not really asking much," Beowolf argued. "Just to cut our hair. They're not asking to cut our *balls* off."

"None of their fucking business."

"It's their team."

"Is this a free country or isn't it? Besides," Gray said, "it's the *town's* team."

"The town made Moon boss. And they're damn glad of it, too."

"Hey, lookit. The coaches run the football team, not our lives. This is your *life* I'm talking about. Let's be real. Are you gonna take this shit the rest of your life? Jump every time somebody says jump? Jesus, this is *real,* man, not just a game. You're a big boy now."

"Gray, I want to play football," Beowolf answered. "It's all I got."

"Nothing's worth having that isn't worth fighting for."

"Shit. Where'd you read that?"

"What?"

"For a moment there I thought I was talking to Moon. That's exactly who you're sounding like. Moon."

"This is no game," Gray said. "This is freedom and rights and . . ."

"Everything's a game!" Beowolf shouted.

"Oh!" Gray smiled. "I'm sounding like Moon, but at least I have *Peckinpah* to talk to."

"Peckinpah." Beowolf spat out the window.

"They can't touch us," Gray assured him. "We're the guts of their offense."

Beowolf shook his head.

"Ya gotta make a stand sometime." Gray stared intensely at Beowolf, who wouldn't answer. "I'm hungry," Gray finally said. He got out of the car.

Beowolf sat stewing in his own sweat. Down Main Street he could see the town hall, crowned in gold by the last of the Anaconda copper kings. Farther down, at the end of the street, was Lewis and Clark Square, where Lewis and Clark stood together, one of them pointing to the Montana First National Bank. The memorial was the gift of the BPOE—"The Biggest Pigs on Earth," according to Pap. Pap owed them a new microphone because he'd strangled their old one in the middle of his Founders' Day speech. They tried to usher him off the stage when the mike went dead. But they couldn't very well use force, Pap being their guest of honor. And he wouldn't be talked down either. He wanted to make them all choke on their Heavensent chicken.

In a voice amplified by anger alone, he'd bellowed: "You dare call me a pioneer!" The Elks cowered at their banquet tables. An elder Elk stood awkwardly to either side of him, wordlessly entreating him to come down off the stage. "A *pioneer,*" Pap spat out at them, "in my book, is a man who comes to a virgin territory and traps off all the fur, chops down all the trees, kills off all the wild meat, and grazes off all the grass, and plows up all the roots, and strings ten million miles of bobwire, and then gives Hollywood a fuckin invite to come in and kill off what's left. Pioneer, *my ass!* A pioneer kills ever'thin in sight and calls it *progress.* Or *civ'lization,* yup! I wish this land was just like it was when the redskins had it. By God, I wish none of you cocksuckers were here at all!" For gravy, Pap spat in the M.C.'s mashed potatoes before storming off the stage and out the door, leaving the assembly hall so stunned you could hear an ant fart.

Beowolf slammed his palms down on the steering wheel. "Jesus, fuck!" He opened the car door and stepped into the blinding sunlight.

Peckinpah glared at them when they showed up on the practice field that afternoon. "Fuck em," Hap had told Beowolf in the locker room before practice. With one of his typical displays of bravado, which for some reason cast an ominous shadow over Beowolf's resolution, Hap argued that they couldn't afford to run starters off, much less the team captain. "We'll mutiny!" Hap declared. "Fuck em!" Bigfoot was less reassuring. "You break the rules," he said, "you better be awful good."

When the team was lined up for calisthenics, Peckinpah marched to the forefront. Moon was downfield staring at his clipboard. Beyond him, combines criss-crossed wheat fields and dust rose in spirals off the land. "Gray, go to the end of the line," Peckinpah commanded. "Back with the piss-ants. You too, Bailey." Beowolf hustled over, remorse and anger like burnt coffee in his mouth. "You're no longer captain, Gray," Peckinpah announced. "After practice you can each run fifteen tunnels, and we'll see if you don't show up with haircuts tomorrow." Gray stood at the end of the line next to Beowolf. "Ballantine!" Peckinpah called out. "Get up here! You're captain."

Ballantine, an intensely brainless defensive end who had once intercepted a pitchout for a touchdown, rushed to the front of the formation.

Beowolf and Gray ran fifteen Tunnel of Loves after practice, and fifteen more after each practice for the rest of the week, ignoring Peckinpah and busting hump. During the afternoon session of the third day, Beowolf made a diving, one-handed catch during a contact drill. Gray was as elusive as ever, and being busted from captain didn't seem to bother him at all; in refusing to cut his hair he had fixed upon his senior season a meaning more glorious than that offered by another title. The spoils of football had long been his; but now, at least in his imagination, the mantle of the rebel rested on his defiant shoulders. He swore he would rather die than give in.

Beowolf swore no such thing, concerned as he was with more mundane matters. "If you wanna play football," Bigfoot advised, "if you wanna *know* you're gonna be playing, cut your hair." During that first week of practice, Beowolf had firmly established himself as the team's best receiver. He wanted to play football, yes, but this other thing was a matter of principle. Apparently the daily infliction of Tunnel of Loves would be the only retribution exacted. Hap encouraged him. So did some of the others. Gray performed stoically, quietly, an example to him. Peckinpah berated them at every opportunity; yet it was obvious to everybody that these derisions were groundless. Moon was silent. The sun was hot and the pressure increased during the second week. Peckinpah upped the ante to twenty tunnels—forty per day. Beowolf wavered. He tried to discern the meaning behind each nuance of Moon's behavior. Had the conflict been made plain to him in the form of an ultimatum—the simple choice between keeping his hair or playing split end for the Rattlers—Beowolf would have had his hair cut immediately, with Porkbutt's tapecutters, no less. But the ultimatum never materialized.

Across the supper table one night, Pap cried, "Hey boy!" He issued a single, half-suppressed cough. A drip of chaw wriggled out the corner of his mouth, escaping over his chin en route to his Adam's apple. He began to gag, and spat. Beowolf pounded his back, scared shitless that it was a heart attack. When Pap finally brushed him aside and staggered to his feet, still gagging, there were tears in his eyes and snot running out his nose. He stomped up and down the kitchen floor, tore at his hair, inadvertently peppering the kitchen wall with tobacco-juice buckshot. He gnashed his teeth like a bear gnawing on granite. "Damn near swallad m'chaw!" he bellowed. "Damn near swallad m'chaw!" He lifted a leg and ripped off a fart that crackled fiercely across the kitchen like a downed power line dancing on railroad tracks. Finally, he sank back into his chair, exhausted.

"You gonna live?"

Pap scowled.

"Whatever brought that on, no need to get a diaper rash over it."

Pap whipped a plug of chaw out of his overall pocket and bit off a chunk the way he'd bite off the head of a chicken that pecked him. Beowolf picked the largest globs of tobacco off the floor and tossed them out back.

"What I was gonna say," Pap finally stammered, "was I was gonna ask ya sumpin."

"What?"

Pap leaned across the table and glanced casually over his shoulder—on the lookout for the men in white jackets. He patted the top of his head and whispered, *"Does he?"*

"Does who what?"

Pap leaned back, stretching nonchalantly, and bent forward again. "Does he wear"—he nodded eagerly—*"the hat?"*

Beowolf was hunched forward, staring into Pap's smoky blinkers—smoky like a blind dog's—when it came to him that Pap was truly a lunatic. "Moon?"

Pap's eyes seemed to dance a loose little jig. "Yeah," he nodded.

Pap was a fucking looney-tune!

"Didn I ever tell ya bout that hat?" Without pausing so long as to spit, Pap launched into the tale of the almighty hat that saved Moon's brightly polished crown from defilement.

When Pap was finished, Beowolf belched, *"Bull*shit!"

"No! Eagleshit, boy! *Eagle*shit!"

During that second week of practice spectators began showing up. This happened every year, regardless; and with word out that Gray had been busted from captain, people flocked to the practice field in droves. Most of them arrived toward the end of practice to watch Gray and Beowolf run their Tunnel of Loves. They cheered them, booed them or withheld judgment, according to their individual dispositions. The younger spectators, the high school crowd, seemed to favor them. Their rousing cheer would greet them each time they emerged from the tunnel into the sunlight and reversed direction to go back through the other way. This enthusiasm thrilled Beowolf to the same extent that it galled Peckinpah. But it also frightened him, for his was a risky adventure and the crowd impressed on him the fact that what he'd been fighting for all his life was precisely the thing he was now imperiling.

The second to last day of Summer Practice a hailstorm hit. Helmets rang with hailstones the size of ice cubes, big enough to sting a body's hand. The coaches held clipboards over their heads and led the team into the Tunnel of Love; the spectators followed in a swarm. The hailstones gave the bleachers a mighty pounding, and the overcast was so thin that light could be seen behind the clouds. When the hailstorm ended and practice resumed, Beowolf sensed something pure and intoxicating in the atmosphere. The hailstorm stood as an omen of good things to come. The sun emerged, showering light through the cooled atmosphere. The break had revived the team, and for the next ten minutes a body could pop a cube into his mouth anytime he was thirsty.

That night the newspaper carried an article entitled "Simmer Practice," castigating Gray and Beowolf for their "unwillingness to sacrifice for the good of the team."

"This is your blood talkin, boy. Get a haircut," Pap ordered. "I'll cut it myself. I'll sneak in your room when you're asleep and cut it with my Bowie. Don't think I won't."

"You'd probably miss and slit my throat," Beowolf said. "Don't you come near me with no knife. Shit, your hair's longer than mine, so what are you talking about?"

"I'm talkin bout what Moon says goes."

"I don't need short hair to catch the ball."

The final afternoon was hotter than the hinges of hell, yet hundreds of people crowded into the single stretch of bleachers, the overflow milling around the perimeter of the field. Peanut, candy and soda vendors provided the crowning touch to the absurdity, materializing as if it were the opening game of the season or the filming of another Hollywood western.

With a full-scale scrimmage underway, Beowolf managed between plays to pick Jeannie and Pap out from the crowd. They were unacquainted and Beowolf, seeing them standing together on the sideline, was struck by their stark incongruity: beauty and the beast on this, the judgment day. Beowolf suddenly couldn't help but regard as symbolic the day Moon made his coaching debut at Rawlings, the day Beowolf had been bitten by the rattlesnake. Remorse ripped into him as he sensed through this madness that he was due for a bad end, that it was inevitable. It was with the forlorn desperation of a condemned man that, on the next play, he cut back from his split-end position and threw a vicious crackback block on Jack Ballantine, cutting him down. Up until this time Moon had kept his distance from both Beowolf and Gray. But now he went absolutely shithouse. "That's a clip, Bailey! *That's a goddamn clip!*" Moon grabbed him by the faceguard and flung him to the ground. "Start running!" he bellowed. "Move!"

Beowolf scrambled to his feet and took off around the cinder track that encircled the practice field. He bit his lip until he tasted blood. He glared at the spectators as they stared at him running past. The remainder of the scrimmage he spent running the track, staring down the spectators, hating them, aching to bash somebody's head in. Hap had taken his place in the lineup.

Finally, Peckinpah's whistle blew. Beowolf kept plodding around the track as the rest of the team converged in the center of the field. "You too, Bailey!" Peckinpah hollered. "You won't wanna miss this!" The crowd rustled with an irrepressible excitement as Beowolf, knowing what he was in for and welcoming it, hustled to midfield. As he heard his name checked off for Bull Run, a bristling elation shot up his spine. *He'd kill somebody!* But his ferocity was immediately cooled by the sight of Gray's shocked face. Gray had also been selected.

The rest of the team retreated to the sideline, leaving the six participants alone in the middle of the field. They aligned themselves: pairing off facing each other ten yards apart. The crowd was on its feet, a hush over the field.

"Okay! When you hear the whistle," Peckinpah announced loud enough for the spectators to hear, "hit and rotate to your left."

Beowolf searched Gray's face for an answer.

The whistle sounded and the first crack of impact drew a faint cheer from the spectators.

The participants hustled back into position and the whistle blew again.

"Hit!" Peckinpah cried furiously. "Hit!"

The crowd cheered less tentatively.

On the third whistle Beowolf and Gray collided.

"Hit!" Peckinpah screamed, his voice finally cracking.

The crowd reacted still more enthusiastically. With each fresh collision, as the weaker bodies, one by one, were weeded out, the crowd grew more and more vociferous.

Finally, only Beowolf and Gray remained. Exhausted and bleeding, Beowolf searched Gray's face for an answer. His throat was dry as Bull Durham.

Moon marched brusquely onto the field from the sideline. "Farther," he commanded. "Move farther back."

Beowolf retreated obediently, increasing the distance between himself and Gray to twenty yards.

"More! Farther back!"

Again Beowolf obeyed. Gray had not moved. A shade of darkness covered Gray's face; Beowolf could no longer see his eyes. Both stood panting, thirty yards apart.

Moon turned to the team. "We have some *people* on this team who care more about their hairdos than about playing football. I won't have such people on my team!" He about-faced and for once blew his own whistle.

Beowolf burst forward, slowed . . . and halted.

Gray had removed his helmet. He stood staring at Beowolf for a moment. Then he wheeled and flung his helmet in Moon's direction. The helmet hit the ground, one of the ear pads popping loose to flip through space, spinning and plummeting to the hard earth like an acrobat missing his trapeze. He turned his back and walked toward the locker room for the last time, leaving the stunned spectators dumb, yet oddly relieved, as if they had witnessed an execution or an exorcism—leaving Beowolf to feel like a traitor when he received his haircut that night.

25

Helen was dressed, staring out the window. She turned to look at him when he entered the room. She said nothing. Bigfoot was still in bed. Helen gazed back out the window at the arrival of winter.

"You missed mass," Beowolf said to Bigfoot, who just looked at him. "Moon made us swear to practice two weeks in December if we lose."

"Bullshit."

"Really," Beowolf said. "How fucked up is that?"

"I didn't swear."

"Make a lot of difference to you if you did."

Bigfoot snorted.

"You all right?" Beowolf asked. "You ain't lookin real good."

"I took his temperature," Helen said without turning around. "It's a hundred and two."

"How do you feel?" Beowolf asked.

"Feel like bootin some tail."

"Moon noticed you weren't there."

"How's the old boy taking it?" Bigfoot gave a subdued laugh. His drooping eyelids and the tentative rearing of his head foretold the sneeze that burst into his fist. "Sheee-it," he moaned. He began to cough.

Beowolf flopped onto his bed. "Yeah," he said. "Moon's pissed off. You're getting everybody pissed off today."

"Was Superscout there?"

"Is the Pope a douchebag?"

Bigfoot laughed.

Beowolf looked at Helen. "How *you* doing?" he asked.

"Fine." She offered him an ambiguous smile. Sitting down in the armchair she studied them both.

"Throw me that carbo," Bigfoot said to her.

Helen reached across to the desk, picked up the carbo and tossed it to him. He popped it into his mouth.

"Hey, man." Bigfoot propped himself up on an elbow. "This is the end."

"Whattaya mean?" Beowolf asked.

"This is my absolute, solitary, final, last raspberry-flavored carbohydrate supplement. Adios, hombre. Fineee." Bigfoot's body buckled once again with a sneeze.

"He's got the flu," Helen said.

Beowolf stared at the ceiling. In less than an hour they'd be on their way. The bus would take them to the junior high that annually lent Rawlings its locker room, where they'd get taped and suited up. His mind would be on the game then, where it belonged. For a body to sit in a whirlpool, to have his ankles and groin taped, to slip the shoulder pads over the head, to board the game bus and arrive at the stadium—a body is engrossed in a routine and the safety it offers, the safety from the time and pain that consume a body's life like cancer. Nervousness gnaws at your insides; the insides ache for deliverance, for action. Your mind is fixed: you understand your role, your goal, what is expected of you, what to expect, what to expect even if you lose. If you're good enough, you need never rise above the rules and scores, the neat white lines and the ever-green end zone.

As he nursed a deep sneeze, Bigfoot's eyes began to water. His body went rigid. Sweat had beaded on his forehead. He sneezed and immediately began to gag.

"What?" Helen rushed to his side and rolled him over, pounding his back.

"What is it?" Beowolf asked. The vision of Pap brushed his mind.

"Fuck!" Bigfoot finally bellowed. Exhibiting slightly more than usual effort, he rolled over and sat up. "Gagged on my last fuckin carbo! Jesus H. *Kee*—" His hand shot up to his mouth and he plunged, stumbling, naked out of bed and into the bathroom, where they heard him vomit his carbo and everything else.

Beowolf looked at Helen. "You're his nurse, huh?"

"I'm his nurse," she answered. "Yes."

When Bigfoot emerged from the bathroom his eyes were red as a snapping turtle's. Lying on his bed, Beowolf stared at him naked and brown, enormous, the arrowhead of hair down the center of his scalp. Beowolf glanced at Helen as Bigfoot crawled back under his blanket. Helen laid her hand on his forehead.

"I feel better now," Bigfoot said after a while. "Fucking carbo," he muttered. He rolled onto his chest. "Rub my back, will ya?"

Helen straddled his body and began to knead his shoulders. "That feels good," he murmured. "I feel better now. Just what I need."

Beowolf felt like drifting away, drifting free of Bigfoot and Helen, free and alone. Soon he heard Helen ask, "Are you going to play?"

"Sure."

"You're sick," she said. "You're hot all over."

"I'm okay."

"Why is it so important? Why does it matter so much?"

"It matters so much," Bigfoot answered, "because it does."

"That's no reason."

Beowolf lay still with his eyes closed, listening to the wind outside and the rain again beating the pane. Once there was a summer afternoon, a Saturday, lying with Jeannie in that drowsy, suspended state of tranquillity that follows lovemaking. Thunder grumbled in the distance, the storm casting its growing shadow across the faded roses on the wall. Jeannie dozed. And it now seemed to Beowolf that listening to that storm rumbling gradually nearer, watching the room fill up with dark heavy air, that he'd never been so content as on that Saturday afternoon holding Jeannie, her head resting on his shoulder, the length of her warm body infolded with his, the sky ultimately falling, crashing all around them. Jeannie awoke in the midst of that electric din and they made love again. And as the storm drifted away, leaving the air cool in the pale clean sunlight breaking like morning against the window, rainwater dripping off the roof, he lay still on top and inside of her. "I want to sleep inside," he murmured. Kissing him, she sighed, "Can't be done."

After a while Bigfoot said, "It's time to go," and Beowolf opened his eyes. Bigfoot rolled over with Helen still sitting on him, now on his chest.

"I'm okay," he assured her. He lifted Helen's hand and gently kissed it, something that under different circumstances would have made Beowolf laugh.

The Game

THE RAWLINGS RATTLERS

Offense			Defense		
QB	Frankie Dimitruk	So	CB	Bobby McCall	So
RB	Paul Larson	Sr	CB	Leland Morris	Jr
RB	Billy Gambrel	Jr	S	Bill Bailey	Sr
FL	Rocky Bellito	So	S	Keith Maffick	Sr
WR	Harold Hazard	Sr	LB	Granville Skaggs	Sr
TE	Jack Doyle	Sr	LB	Steve Rutherford	Sr
T	Jim Sutton	Jr	MG	Al Smith	Jr
T	Adam Johnson	Jr	E	Beano Benvenutti	Sr
G	Steve Kramer	Sr	E	Jimmy Flood	Jr
G	Andy Conway	Jr	T	Bigfoot Bearkiller	Sr
C	Doug Wagonseller	So	T	Stanislaus Konichek	Sr

26

On a locker just inside the doorway Beowolf found his name printed on a strip of ankle tape. He dropped his duffel bag and sat down on the bench.

"One hell of a junior high," he said to Bigfoot. "Wouldn't you say?"

"Yeah," Bigfoot replied. "Cat's ass." He sat down next to Beowolf. The lockers were assigned alphabetically. He nodded at the sign on the bulletin board: WINNING ISN'T EVERYTHING, IT'S THE ONLY THING.

"Yeah. Seems I heard that somewhere before," Beowolf said. "How ya feel?"

"Okay."

Beowolf glanced at the clock and took off his overcoat, hanging it inside the locker. Donnie and another manager dragged the first equipment trunk through the doorway. "Give'm a hand with that," Moon said to Jack Doyle as he marched down the aisle. Doyle shoved the trunk into the corner. Two other managers dragged in another trunk, which Porkbutt unlocked.

"Bailey!" Porkbutt shouted.

He tossed Beowolf his number.

"Dimitruk!"

"Yo!"

"Morris!"

People began to gravitate to Beowolf's end of the locker room, waiting for their jerseys. Beowolf hung his in the locker.

"Bellito!"

Bellito sprang forward.

"Em-Deee!" Porkbutt crowed. "Number twenty-two in my program, number one in my heart!" He flipped MD his jersey.

Moon pushed his way through the throng. "Watch it! Coming through." Donnie and the other kid dragged in another trunk as Moon squeezed past and out the doorway.

Beowolf sat down among the milling bodies and listened to Porkbutt call out names.

"I'm gonna go sit in the shit-shop for a while," Bigfoot announced, "to give these dudes a chance to clear out." He removed his overcoat and hung it in his locker. "Get my jersey for me, will ya?" He strolled languidly down the aisle and into the bathroom.

Beowolf listened to the names ring past. He unbuckled his belt and kicked off his loafers, removed his socks and listened to the names, thinking of nothing. He removed his shirt and hung it in the locker. The doorway was now cluttered with trunks.

"Benvenutti!" Porkbutt called out.

"Yo, Pete!"

Beano caught his jersey.

"Bearkiller!"

"Ho!"

Beowolf hung the jersey in Bigfoot's locker.

"Need a good pass rush tonight," he said to Beano, who nodded.

"Who's eighty-seven?" Porkbutt wanted to know.

"Here!" Lombago shouted.

"That's all," Donnie said to Porkbutt.

"Pass out the helmets," Porkbutt commanded, and squeezed out the doorway.

Beowolf removed his pants and hung them up, removed and hung up his underwear. Sitting back down, he fished around in his duffel bag for his jock, his STONED AGAIN T-shirt, his tube socks and his sweat socks.

"Hey!" called somebody down the aisle. "Where's my jersey?" It was Doe.

"Didn't you get it?" Donnie asked.

"No, I didn't get it! Where is it?"

Donnie dropped a helmet and shuffled over to the jersey trunk. Doe was pushing down the aisle.

"What number?" Donnie asked.

"Seventy-four, whattaya think?"

"I got a seventy-five."

"Yeah, Doe," Beano laughed. "You and Jethro Pugh."

"I ain't no Jethro Pugh!"

"I'll get Moon," Donnie said timidly.

"You can't find it! Where's my number, *ya little puke?*" Donnie fled the locker room. "Ya little puke."

Moon entered with Donnie. "Whatzamatter?"

"He lost my number."

"He didn't lose your number. It's not in the trunk?"

"No," Donnie said.

"What is?"

"Seventy-five, sixty-one, thirty something, two twenties."

Moon bent over the trunk. "Here." He tossed Doe the seventy-five.

"I ain't no Jethro Pugh."

Moon looked at him curiously, then wrenched his head sideways as an expression of revulsion slipped across his face. "No," he said, giving Doe a slight head fake. "You're Stanislaus Konichek. Now get dressed."

Doe staggered back down the aisle, holding the seventy-five as if it were a dead cat.

Moon left.

"Hey, Sawed-off!" MD hollered to Donnie. "Maybe you best get outta this manager racket before you get liquidated."

"Yeah, go to Brazil," Geek said. "Take up limbo dancing."

Doe glared at MD and Donnie resumed passing out helmets.

"Hey, Donnie," Beowolf said. "The whirlpool hot yet?"

"Somebody in it," Donnie answered.

"Who?"

"I dunno, some *kid.*"

When Beowolf was handed his helmet, he set it on the bench in front of his locker and strolled through the doorway into the training room.

There was already a line of bodies at the training table, where Porkbutt was busy berating Lombago. "You need a tape job like I need dimples on my ass! Get outta here!" Lombago held his ground, sitting there on the training table and taking Porkbutt's abuse. With a sneer, Porkbutt sprayed his ankle with Tuf-Skin and began laying on strips of tape. "You ain't gonna play," he muttered. "Waste of tape . . . waste of time."

"Hey, Pete," Beowolf asked. "Who's that kid in the whirlpool?"

"Don't talk to me about it," Porkbutt snapped. "Talk to him." He jerked his head at the man standing by the doorway wearing a white undershirt, his arms crossed like Mr. Clean.

"How long he gonna be?" Beowolf asked.

The man looked at his watch. "Not much longer, no more than ten minutes. I talked to Coach Moon about it."

The man was bovine, with the overfattened physique of an ex-grunt.

"Who is he?"

"He's with the Sherman Park Giants. We have a game tomorrow —see, I'm the coach." The man thrust his hand out at Beowolf. "Red Weber. Glad to know ya. Just call me *Coach,* everybody else does."

Beowolf shook his clammy hand. "Bill Bailey." The training room was warm.

"Bailey," the man reflected. "Safety, aren'tcha?"

Beowolf nodded.

"Well, lemme tell ya, Bill Bailey, you're gonna have your hands full with Russell Thompson. This is one hellacious ballplayer. Me and his father are like this." The man thrust a pair of crossed fingers into Beowolf's face.

"Russell, he was a Sherman Park Giant, ya know—before I was here, though. I was with U of M then. *Playing,* I mean. I was a guard myself." The man glanced down each of his flanks and patted his gut. "Put on a bit of weight since," he laughed, "but hell, we're unbeaten this season, just like the high school. Unbeaten last season too. Only lost but three games total since I took over, and that's a fact." The man gave a snort. "Don't mean to be blowing my own horn."

"My brother plays for U of M," Beowolf finally said, sitting down to wait.

"*Jason* Bailey? Hell, yes! You're that Jason Bailey's kid brother!"

"You know Jason?"

"No, I don't *know*'m. Know who he is." The man stood there nodding, gazing at the Sherman Park Giant in the whirlpool.

"You guys got a game tonight?" Beowolf asked.

"Tomorrow. Tomorrow's Thanksgiving game with the Falls Falls Falcons."

"Why don't he wait till tomorrow for the whirlpool?"

"Oh, he ain't hurt," the man said. "Fit as a fiddle."

Beowolf gave him a skewed look.

"He's losing weight, is all. That boy's my middle linebacker.

Tough kid, tough as nails—but to play he's gotta be under one eighteen."

"Well, how much longer he gonna be? I'm not the only one needs a whirlpool tonight."

"Lemme see."

The man sauntered over to the whirlpool and told the boy to get out. The boy climbed lethargically out of the tub and followed his coach to the scale. Beowolf moved to the whirlpool.

"Still got a good quarter pound to go," the man said, grinning ear to ear, "but you go ahead. This may take some time."

The boy sat down and toweled off. Beowolf eased his body into the wet heat rising up his legs. The water was 115 degrees. He knelt down, grimacing, and adjusted the jet to groin level. Laying his arms around the rim of the tub, he let out a long sigh.

"How long he been in here?" he asked.

"As long as he has to be." The coach cocked his head and grinned like a jackass.

The boy's head was propped back against the wall, his skin as shriveled as a boiled prune. He stared off into space.

The water beat steadily against Beowolf's groin. It felt good now, he was in a sweat. But he knew he was good for no more than fifteen minutes in a whirlpool. Bodies were being loosed from the training room with various limbs and joints mummified in white tape.

"What's the problem, anyway?" the coach asked, approaching the tub.

"Groin."

"Bad?"

"Not too bad. I'm playing, ain't I?" Beowolf caught Red giving his protégé a knowing glance and nod.

"My boys are tough. Ya gotta be tough to be a Sherman Park Giant—right, Jim?"

The boy seemed to come alive at the sound of his name. "Uh-huh."

"He's tough," the coach said. "Tough as nails. You'll be hearing about him someday or my name ain't Red Weber. This here's Jim Saunders."

Beowolf nodded, wishing this asshole would blow away.

"I got a halfback, colored boy, name Bobby Mitchell—Mitchell

X we call him. Runs like he's chased by a pack of hounds. He ain't really tough though, not like . . ." The man nodded at his middle linebacker. "You know how these colored boys are," he continued, speaking low. "Speed merchants, all of em. Good wheels, no hands —hands like steel. That's why they're so good at stealin!" The man slapped Beowolf on the shoulder. "But I'll tell ya, speed coming out their ass, ya know what I mean. They ain't tough, but I toughen em up. When I was at Kalispell, we had a halfback there name Rick Erskine. 'Legs' we called him. All speed, no guts. A real pussy. He wasn't colored or nothin. But fast, *real fast.* One day during scrimmage Coach Thompson told us all to just quit blocking for him, that'd teach him how to hit. We sure did, and Legs got his leg broke the next goddamn play. *Very next play,* I shit you not. We called him 'Leg' after that," he laughed. "But it made a man of him."

"That so? We tried something like that with a guy last year and he quit."

"Gray?" the man asked. "Peter Gray?"

"Nobody *you* know."

"Yaaaa!" Porkbutt cried ecstatically. "Number twenty-two in your program, number one in my heart!"

Red bent over at Beowolf's side. "Who's twenty-two?" MD had mounted the training table to be taped.

"Guy Lombago."

"Who?" he asked, his face contorted not only in puzzlement but, apparently, in pain. "I never heard of him."

"You will," said Beowolf.

"Who *is* he?"

"He's tough. He's so tough he'd eat off the same plate as a wolf. Eats catfood for snacks." The coach's eyes widened.

"Never heard of him."

"Why that's Guy Lombago, got a reserved seat in hell. He bit a guy's nose off once, I shit you not! A fourth-and-goal situation."

The coach was beginning to shy away.

"He's all piss and vinegar, thorny as cactus, touchy as a teased rattler . . ." The man was looking at Beowolf as if he were AWOL from the bughouse. Even Jim came to.

"He's dangerouser than fourteen sacks of wildcats." Beowolf dunked his head underwater. Ears burned, he surfaced for air. "Got the morals of a skunk, cuts farts that make a *dead* skunk cry uncle." He stood up in the whirlpool, eyes widening like those in a body that's been bodysnatched on *Monsterland Movie.* He climbed out of the tub and, firing Red a Bronx cheer, said, "Nuffa this shit." He turned to Jim—"Eat'm up Jimbo"—grabbed a towel and tramped into the locker room, drying himself off.

His shoulder pads, girdle pads and game pants, with thigh pads already inserted, were piled in front of his locker. Bigfoot's equipment was alongside his own. The clock read six-ten. Fifty minutes.

Superscout came slinking past, an apparition, then became very real as he sidled over to Beowolf. "Ready to kick the fuckin shit outta these assholes?"

"Yeah, boss," Beowolf replied.

"Piece a gum?" Superscout thrust a piece of Doublemint at him.

"Fuck no."

Superscout nodded and walked toward the doorway, hesitated to glance over the bulletin board, then was out the door.

The locker room had grown quiet and purposeful. The equipment was distributed, the trunks neatly stacked in the corner. Rocky Bellito, already fully dressed, was sitting on the bench. He sighed heavily. "Always feel tired before a game. Don't know why, I just do."

Beowolf stepped into his jock.

"How's the groin?" Rocky asked.

"Okay." His groin did feel okay. He hadn't given it nearly as long a whirlpool as he'd intended to, but it was loose enough.

Beowolf walked out the door into the training room. The line at Porkbutt's training table had dwindled to four bodies. The Sherman Park coach was back at the whirlpool, supervising Jimbo and bending the ear of Billy Gambrel, who'd stretched ligaments in his knee against Billings West.

Moon poked his head into the room. "Everything okay?"

Porkbutt grunted.

"Hey, Coach," Gambrel called out. He jerked his head at Jimbo, bloodless as a hard-boiled chicken.

"I told you ten more minutes!" Moon exploded, charging into the room. "Get that kid outta there! I got a football game in an hour and forty-five minutes, you understand that? Get him outta there!"

The Giant slithered out of the tub while Moon harangued Red.

Billy Gambrel climbed onto the wide rim of the tub and dunked his leg, wincing from the heat.

Beowolf vaulted onto the training table and stood upright. Porkbutt began winding an Ace bandage around the uppermost part of Beowolf's left thigh, secured it with several strips of adhesive tape, then wound around the thigh, abdomen, hip and waist a second Ace bandage and similarly secured it with tape.

"Howzit feel?" Porkbutt asked.

Beowolf remained erect and rocked his weight onto the injured half of his body. "Feels okay." He gingerly lowered himself into a sitting position. Porkbutt sprayed his ankles with Tuf-Skin and began ripping strips of adhesive tape from the roll and applying them to Beowolf's ankles. Having stirruped each ankle with a half-dozen strips, he unwound the roll in a figure-eight motion several times around each ankle, grabbing each ankle in turn, gripping it tightly in both hands, then giving it a slap. Beowolf hopped off the table, conspicuously unthankful, and returned to the locker room. His ankles felt strong and sturdy.

Like almost everybody else, Beowolf had a ritual for dressing. He slipped into his girdle pads, sprinkling Johnson's Baby Powder down both the back and front. He didn't wear a cup, never had. He tugged his game pants on over the girdle pads and pummeled his thigh pads with his fists, testing them. He sat down on the bench.

Rocky Bellito said, "Hope it don't snow no more."

"Yeah."

Over his ankles Beowolf pulled white tube socks, which he taped firmly at the top to prevent their slipping down during the game. Over the tube socks he pulled his floppy sweat socks, threadbare at the toes and heels, leaving them untaped. He'd always liked the indolent way they flopped.

With twenty-eight minutes left, he felt nervous wings brush against his insides. WINNING IS NOT EVERYTHING . . .

If he stopped dressing, there was too much to think about. The beginning of the season seemed impossibly distant, and now the end was before him. The end was happening to him now. For a moment he felt incredibly weak, the weariness of the season having settled into him.

Moon came through the doorway. "Where's Bigfoot?"

"Haven't seen'm," Beowolf replied.

"Well, where the hell is he?"

"Bathroom, probably."

Moon's jaw jutted out as he marched brusquely down the aisle. "Wouldn't go in there if I was you, Coach," Geek said. "Smells like a buffalo died."

Moon disappeared into the bathroom.

Beowolf retreated to the shower room, which was private and—except for the far end, where MD had taken his pregame shower—dry. He sat on the tile floor, legs outspread. Doe and Lombago sat beside each other on the bench straight through the shower-room door. "Everybody's got their jersey but me. *Everybody.*" Doe glowered at Lombago.

Moon marched past again. Bigfoot, who hadn't yet begun to dress, followed.

Beowolf wanted to relax, but didn't have much time with the game hovering over him. Rawlings had once been a team of super-men. Now he was blinking, cautiously touching his own body to be sure that it was real. It was only him and others like him. And Jason was nothing, just prize stock that would suffer anything for a blue ribbon.

"You know what Jason told me once?" he had asked Jeannie several night ago. "He had a picture of himself from when he was a quarterback. It was blown up poster size, just a closeup of his chest and head and arms. It looked like he was scrambling for his life; you could see it in his eyes. And his arm was like this." Beowolf extended his arm, pointing. "He was waving a receiver downfield.

"He got the poster for his birthday. He found it in his car. And what he told me was he wanted to be buried with that poster, it meant so much to him. And what he meant was, I *know* what he meant, he really did want to be buried with it and he wanted me to be sure that he was. The picture said everything—everything great. And it wasn't glossy, it was flat. Plain black and white blotches. He said it was of a touchdown pass he threw against Missoula."

Jeannie gazed at him, her eyes raw red, the blue iris reproaching him. She didn't say anything, and Beowolf sank his head onto her shoulder. She held him languidly, unmoving.

"It was a picture," he said, "of just before he bruised his ribs his junior year against Bozeman. As soon as the picture was snapped he got hit. Missed two games."

She held him, neither moving nor speaking. Jason knew what it was like being hurt, haunting the sidelines like a ghost. But Jason didn't matter; he was gone. Everybody was gone. And Beowolf was alone with Jeannie. It was no life for a child. Everybody will desert you.

"I took the picture," he said, and he felt her body collapse against his and heave, the sound of her sobs beating against him. But he wouldn't cry.

Bigfoot's periodic sneezes provided for a moment the sole tether by which Beowolf clung to a wavering composure. He anticipated each one, waiting for each moment to pass without his tumbling forever free.

"Hey, Wolf."

MD stood in the entranceway, fully armored, his head encased and labeled HEADHUNTER.

"Wolf, you're returning the ball alone on the fist, eh?"

Beowolf nodded, and MD nodded back. They understood each other. MD moved on.

Hap leapt into view, still naked but for his taped ankles. He swung his jock above his head several times in a wide arc, then with a quick underhand flip flung at Beowolf a pair of tight tape balls. Beowolf caught one and whipped it back at Hap's crotch. Missed.

"See, this is what David used on Goliath. How's the groin?"

"Okay."

"Got less than twenty minutes," Hap said.

"Yeah." Beowolf rose from the floor and returned to his locker and the relentless winding down of the season.

"How ya feel?" he asked Bigfoot, who was resting in the corner on the floor. He had his game pants on and his gray PROPERTY OF RAWLINGS RATTLERS T-shirt, which was torn in back and tattered in front. He'd worn it four years. He had only to tape his ankles, by tradition his last preparation.

"Feel okay," he replied.

"What'd Moon say?"

"Nothin. I told him I'm sick."

"You *are* sick."

"Hey, Wolf." MD again. Beowolf turned his STONED AGAIN T-shirt inside out and slipped it over his head. "You hear Moon's leaving?" MD whispered.

"Yeah, I heard."

"From who?"

"Peckinpah told me."

"It's true," said MD, asking more than confirming. He wandered off down the aisle.

Beowolf tucked his T-shirt under his girdle pads, then squeezed his head between his shoulder pads and settled them on his shoulders. He hooked the straps under his arms and tightened them at his armpits.

He was moving too fast. He parked himself on the bench. He felt hollow and spent. WINNING IS NOT EVERYTHING . . .

"Hey, Doe!" Donnie called. He held a scarlet game jersey above his head.

Doe clattered down the aisle. "Ya got it!" he cried. "Ya got it!" He grabbed the jersey, unfurled it to be sure, then immediately bent over and began jerking at the foreign, hated seventy-five.

"Jesus, Doe, ya dumb fuckin grunt. Take it easy!" Jimmy Flood, who played alongside Doe in the defensive line, rose from the bench and tugged the substitute jersey over Doe's shoulder pads and horse-collar, and over his head.

"Thanks, Jimmy. Thanks." Doe trucked back down the aisle clutching his seventy-four in both hands, leaving the discarded jersey like a cow pie in the middle of the floor.

"Dude's crazy," Beowolf said.

"Not so crazy." Bigfoot rose from the corner and slipped into his shoulder pads, fastening them tight, then tightening the strings of his horse-collar.

"Ten minutes!" Donnie shouted. "Ten minutes!"

Beowolf washed down four salt tablets and slid his head and arms into his game jersey while walking toward Hap. "Hap," he said. Beowolf turned around and Hap gripped the jersey fiercely, yanking it down over the shoulder pads. Hap slipped his head and arms into his own jersey and Beowolf reciprocated, then sauntered into the bathroom.

For four years they'd helped each other with their game jerseys; a "traditional-original," Hap said. There was security in a body's dressing rites. There was security in this just as there was security in a body glimpsing himself fully armored in the mirror. *Number 9. Nine lives,* Beowolf would think, knowing it was foolish thinking, but thinking it anyway; loving his number and loving his image. His, the only single-digit number on the team, made him look taller, stand out. He'd inherited the number from Jason, but owned it outright now.

Beowolf sat on the toilet. On the inside of the door, CUNNILINGUS—BREAKFAST OF CHAMPIONS was scribbled in black Magic Marker. Stupid and funny, it made Beowolf feel old.

When a pair of anxious feet appeared on the opposite side of the door, he flushed the toilet and emerged. Doug Wagonseller pushed past him and into the stall. He tucked in his jersey and tightened his girdle pads. Tying his pants snugly in front, tugging at his belt until the pants felt doubly secure, he returned to his locker with a hesitant step before the mirror.

Seated on the bench, Beowolf wound a boxing wrist-wrap around his left wrist, taped it, and repeated the procedure with his right wrist. He clenched and unclenched his fists. Satisfied, he pulled his Adidas from the duffel bag and worked his feet into the shoes. He tightened the laces of each shoe, from the toes up the tongue, then spat onto the fingertips of his right hand and rubbed the saliva into the laces and tied them in a double knot. He rose and pulled loose his front tooth and placed it on the shelf in the locker. Beowolf sat back down, holding his helmet so he could read HEADHUNTER across the front.

Bigfoot came padding in from the training room, his ankles finally taped. He pulled on his socks and cleats and laced them up. Now in armpads, his forearms were monstrous. There were dirty, grass-stained pads on the backs of his hands as well.

Rocky Bellito's legs compulsively jittered up and down; he was ready to play, no longer tired. Donnie smeared lampblack under each of Rocky's eyes, then moved on to Beowolf.

The locker room was quiet, everybody sitting on the bench, waiting for the word.

Moon finally appeared. He walked down the aisle, glancing at his watch—looking them over, sizing them up. "Okay," Moon said quietly, "load em up." A collective sigh escaped as the helmeted figures lumbered out the door. Bigfoot stood, yanked his helmet over his ears, and marched out. Beowolf remained seated a moment, watching. Latching on to the tail end of the exodus, he paused at the exit and eased his helmet over his ears.

He sprang up the stairs of the bus, slapped Wavy five and located Hap.

"How's it feel?" Hap asked.

"Decent, decent. How you feel?"

"Psyched. Damn psyched. Feel like bootin some ass."

Outside the stadium parking lot, a streamer-lined caravan of cars was backed up at the traffic light. The bus jerked forward, stopped, jerked again, stopped, jerked and plowed forward, swinging hard left past a traffic cop and into the lot. The stadium lights formed a bright halo over the surrounding darkness; snow-covered end-zone bleachers obstructed the view of the playing field. The bus, ushered now by a cop waving a long flashlight, swung free of the congestion to the foot of the stadium, where a crowd of people mingled, anticipating their team's arrival.

The lights burst on, and Moon stood up at the head of the aisle. "The locker room's through the portal and to the left." A cheer erupted outside. Moon turned and the doors parted as the cheering crescendoed. Scrutinized by the onlookers, the team trooped out of the bus and disappeared into the stadium's dank cloisters.

Moon advanced immediately to the blackboard while the team found seats on the benches, stray chairs and concrete floor. "No chalk," Moon grumbled, and proceeded to diagram a play in the layer of blackboard dust with his finger.

A row of bare bulbs dangled hopelessly from the thirty-foot ceiling, across which mummified pipes slammed and rattled, so vague in the shadows that a body couldn't see the fattening beads of sweat that dripped regularly, pattering the tops of the lockers, the floor, their helmets. The lockers were olive-green and ancient; those with broken door handles were slashed with a dark red cross of paint, retired for good.

Moon glanced at his watch, then at the door. "Okay, goddammit. Defense, listen up. On the fist—Doe, you're wedging your man in. You too," he said to Bigfoot, who sat slumped in a far corner, occasionally coughing. "Granville, you're shooting up the six hole. MD, you're hanging back till they come to the line, then you're coming up and shooting the five hole. We got Morris coming from the right and McCall from . . ."

Donnie came charging into the locker room, winded, and handed the chalk to Moon.

"Okay, here it is," Moon continued. He drew circles for Kalispell's offense, and opposite them he positioned the defensive X's staggered along the line of scrimmage. "Okay, Smitty—head up on center," he said, darkening in the X. "Take his head off, let him know you're there."

"Yeah."

"Bearkiller, blocking *in.*" He chalked in the block. "Doe." He glanced at Doe. "Blocking *in.*" He drew in the block. "Beano, drive your man outside. Jimmy"—he found Flood—"outside." He chalked in their blocks. "Rutherford, you're taking off the head of that weak side end, as usual. Morris and McCall from outside; stay onside for Godsakes and watch out for the staggered count." He drew straight lines from Morris and McCall to the punter. "Granville, you're setting up in the middle, but cheat over a little—you're hitting up the six hole. MD, cheat up, and when they line up, *tear ass.* You're hitting the five hole. . . . Everybody got it?

"Okay, we go out on the field in"—checking his watch—"four minutes. Questions?"

There were none. On the blackboard Beowolf hung back, receiving the punt. Meanwhile, in the locker room, a mass movement to the bathroom. Beowolf remained where he was, eyeing himself on the blackboard, the lone X. The croaking plash of vomiting echoed through the chambers. Beowolf glanced at Bigfoot, slumped in the corner. The locker-room door inched open and Superscout appeared.

"The field cleared?" Moon asked. Superscout nodded, and pulled back into the shadows.

"Okay, everybody," Moon said. "Silent cals, huh? MD?"

MD nodded intensely and rose to his feet. "Let's hear it," he said simply. "Let's hear it."

Anxiety raked Beowolf's insides. The pipes continued to groan and gurgle, sometimes shaking.

"Okay, one minute."

Some of the players rose from the bench to wander nervously in place, fists tensing open and closed. Hap emerged from the bathroom. "Who's in there?" Moon asked.

"Wagonseller."

Moon nodded. "Hey, listen up. Be careful with the fence. It's only seven yards off the field on the home side."

When it was time, the locker-room door was thrown open and the Rattlers jogged game-faced down the concrete corridor into the light and faint cheers. It was still half an hour to game time. A cop opened the gate in the fence which, three seasons earlier, Kalispell had erected to tighten the circumference of the field while making room for additional bleachers.

Freezing rain pelted their helmets as they assembled for calisthenics in the end zone. Kalispell had not yet appeared. Beowolf trained his eyes on MD, who began doing jumping jacks, silently, his movements mirrored by the rest of the team. After twenty-five, he paused, then fell forward into push-up position. Beowolf's hands gripped the icy, snow-frosted turf. After push-ups they performed various stretching exercises. His groin was tight across his hip, but felt strong enough wrapped in tape. MD flopped onto his back for sit-ups. Sleet rattled off their helmets, the cold creeping up Beowolf's spine.

"Twenty-three minutes." Moon paraded up and down the rows of prone bodies. "Twenty-three minutes."

Suddenly the stadium began to rumble as the band erupted and Kalispell exploded onto the field flanked by screaming, bounding blue-and-white pom-pom cheerleaders, the crowd vibrant, on its feet. They aligned themselves in the opposite end zone and burst into a furious set of jumping jacks.

After the twenty-fifth sit-up, MD lay back and bridged his neck. Bridging, rocking back and forth and around, feeling the pressure descend and focus on the back of his neck, Beowolf could see through the open end of the stadium; headlights wandering through the night, winding about the parking lot looking for space. He could see the steady pressure of the crowd pushing past the ticket booth.

"Okay," MD called.

Kalispell was into their third exercise, their brisk, unisonant cadence unbroken.

On his feet, MD began running in place, diving forward onto his chest, wet earth exploding to either side. Beowolf leapt back up, legs working, then hit the earth again. The cold had seeped through to his chest, but it felt good beating the earth with his body; after hit-its, a body took everything in stride, a body felt hardened, as though he'd been living in a foxhole. Kalispell continued belting out the count of their calisthenics.

Rawlings did fifteen hit-its and that was all. Beowolf's arms and shoulders felt tight and good, his uniform was muddy and soaked through. He felt psyched and anxious, and watching MD watching them he listened as Kalispell hollered out their count two-three-four. Beowolf watched MD, waiting for the signal. When there was silence at the opposite end of the field—Kalispell switching to another exercise—MD snapped to attention, then sprang into a set of jumping jacks, not silently this time but belting them out, joined by the team with an energy that had accumulated during their protracted silence: "R-E-D-RED! R-E-D-RED!" Downfield Beowolf could see Earthquake turn to look at them. The Rawlings fans joined in to the beat of the kettle and snare drums assembled on the sideline. "R-E-D-RED!" Twenty-five times they shouted it; then MD's fist shot into the air and the team charged, roiling over itself, to the middle of the field, where Peckinpah's whistle screamed and the concentration of bodies burst instantly apart. The grunts followed Moon to one side of Rawlings' half of the field, the defensive backs and linebackers staying with Peckinpah, and the offensive backs and ends following Frankie Dimitruk and Coach Rose. Beowolf and MD hustled back downfield to the end zone to field Geek's punts.

Watching a punt descend on him, turning lazily end over end, Beowolf noticed that the sleet had turned back to rain.

Pass patterns, honyo drills, agility drills and signal drills were run as Kalispell, on their half of the field, went through their own pregame maneuvers. The stadium was filling up.

"Okay! Everybody in!" Moon finally shouted. "Let's go!" Peckinpah's whistle screamed as the Rattlers stormed the fence, funneling through the lone gate. The stands pulsated to the frantic rhythm of a Rawlings cheer. Beowolf spotted Jeannie, her hair glistening with bright ice crystals as she danced in the rain, carefully avoiding the ice puddles. Cops with outspread arms held back the crowd as the Rattlers pushed their way up the concrete ramp underneath the stands.

Donnie knelt in the corner slicing oranges. Beowolf sat beside him, grabbed an orange quarter and sucked on it. He stood back up immediately, he couldn't sit still. The pipes rumbled and growled, dripping cold sweat. He dropped the orange peel on the floor and inserted his hands down the front of his pants; they would warm up as soon as the game began. He was covered with mud. Doe's number, by the end of the game, would probably be indistinguishable from any other.

The referee poked his head in the door. "Ten minutes, Coach." Moon nodded and marched over to the blackboard, now smoking a cigarette. Bigfoot was slumped in the opposite corner. Round John appeared in the doorway. Superscout stood on the other side of the room, half-hidden in the shadows of the bathroom. Moon quickly diagrammed a play on the blackboard, then reminded them of their pride and of the singular importance of this game. It would be won on pride. He spoke quickly. The school and the town were mentioned. Winning. They were ready, had prepared well. The imperative of winning was emphasized. Pride again and the winning tradition of the Rawlings Rattlers.

"I have an announcement to make," Moon finally said. Beowolf bent down and flicked a clump of earth from the toe of his shoe. His glance darted around the locker room, his teammates shifting in place uncomfortably. He caught Hap's eye, feeling guilty for knowing what he knew. Nothing came out of Moon's mouth. For the first time, he seemed oddly disconcerted. His face twitched. "I have an announcement. An announcement that's difficult for me to make."

Beowolf felt the spirit of the team droop.

"Five minutes, Mr. Moon." The ref again.

With an abrupt mustering of resolution, Moon quietly said, "This is my final game as coach of the Rawlings Rattlers."

Nobody moved. Even knowing it was coming, Beowolf was shocked to hear it in Moon's own voice. The air seemed heavy, like a windless winter dusk fallen hushed and bitter cold over an empty plain, the smell of snow so thick you can taste it.

"I'm coaching the University of Montana Grizzlies next season and, hopefully, I'll be coaching some of you." Moon rubbed his nose in an uncharacteristic manner, then drew on his cigarette. "This is our final game together," he continued, smoke streaming from each nostril as he spoke. "The season hasn't been everything that it could've been, but we have our chance tonight, right now, to redeem everything. Years from now you'll look back on this night and you'll wish with all your heart and soul that you were back here—that you had the chance again in one night to put it all on the line. You'll remember this game for the rest of your lives.

"I believe, over the season, over the seasons together, all of us, we've grown together. We play like a team, we play hard. We're a family." Moon hesitated. "Okay, let's gettem."

Somebody whooped and the team joined in, swarming for the door and piling through the concrete corridor back into the light of that final night together, pushing through the crowd to the gauntlet formed by the cheerleaders, through the gauntlet to the gate laid open to the field, the band charged up, Rawlings on its feet throwing scarlet-and-white streamers intercepted in midflight and scattered by the wind.

Rawlings clustered anxiously around the bench. Kalispell had already made their final entrance, and the Kalispell marching band, ushered by twirlers, was parading onto the field in blue-and-white uniforms to overwhelm from midfield the chaos in the stands: brass and color guards marching, twirling flags and white rifles that Rawlings never had, *never would have,* marching through the rows of uniformed horn-players marching in the opposite direction, halt! The band, its last note bitten fiercely off, spun silently to face the open end of the horseshoe stadium with the color guard now at the head.

An awkward national anthem arose from the horns. Beowolf removed his helmet. The flag climbed slowly, in jerks, up the flagpole, raised by a man in a heavy overcoat and a hat and glasses and it looked like a tie underneath and probably cigars in his pockets. There was a chill to the music, the wind whipping the flag, the sleet, the vision of a naked flagpole being dressed for the game, the red, white and blue, a hundred horns in the night, in the floodlights; a chill at the base of Beowolf's neck, in his heart. The flag was moving too slow, it wouldn't make the brass ball before the music ended. There was a rush of cold blood through Beowolf's body, as if his nerves had pierced his skin and uniform to defy the night. He was freezing. The stadium finally erupted and Beowolf's helmet was back on. Drowned out by the crowd, the marching band bowed and spun to start another tune, which it paraded down the field and through the gate in the end zone.

MD strutted out to the fifty-yard line to stare Earthquake down. They shook hands. MD's head never wavered. The coin was flipped, they bent over to look, the ref stooped, picked it up, glanced at Earthquake, then at MD, spoke to them both, aligned them. Kalispell was receiving. A roar swelled from the Kalispell side of the stadium across the field to break like a tidal wave against the Rawlings stands. MD shook hands with Earthquake and charged back to the frenzied crush of bodies at the sideline. The stadium had gone mad with cheers and songs and trumpets, banners waving, maracas shivering up and down the stands like the tail of a mighty rattlesnake.

The team gathered around Moon and Round John. Moon extended his hand as if over an open flame: Round John, Granville, Beano, MD, then everybody, laid their hand on top, shoved a hand toward Moon's while Round John recited a Hail Mary. "Our Lady, Queen of Victory," he concluded. "Pray for us."

"Okay!" Peckinpah screamed, the team bursting apart. "Beat on somebody!"

MD gripped Beowolf by the shoulder pads and they bashed their heads together, scrambling their brains. They hustled onto the field for the kickoff, huddling only long enough for MD to say, as he always said before the opening kickoff, "Smarten up a chump." Beowolf was the outside man in the kickoff formation, positioned just inside the playing field. "Stick somebody, Wolf!" someone yelled. The whistle sounded, Hap booted the ball. Tearing downfield, Beowolf isolated a man coming at him and charged viciously, colliding head-on and spinning past. The return went to the other side.

Beowolf took his place in the huddle alongside Morris. "C'mon, c'mon," he shouted, slapping Granville on the ass. "Let's go, let's do it," MD cried. "Five-two," he said, setting the defensive alignment. "Ready . . ."

"Break!"

The huddle disbanded with a unisonant clap. The ball was beyond the twenty.

Kalispell approached the line of scrimmage.

"Bottlecap red!" MD hollered. "Bottlecap red!"

Beowolf and MD quickly switched positions, Beowolf to the right, keying on Earthquake. The ball was snapped, Beowolf coming up hard behind the others swarming Earthquake off-tackle. "Waytago!" he cried.

The huddle formed again. The field around the ball was already torn up and in the sleet would get slippery for sure. The huddle broke. Beowolf skipped backward eight yards from the line of scrimmage. Kalispell crouched into place over the ball. "Bottlecap blue!" Beowolf's sights were on Earthquake. The ball was snapped and pitched, he came up hard, hit and hung on, trampled. *Fuck!* Earthquake rolled over and off him. Beowolf rose to his feet and checked the first-down marker.

"Watch the pitch again," MD said in the huddle. "They need four more." He glanced at the sideline. "Five-two, ready . . ."

"Break!"

Kalispell came out in the same formation.

"Bottlecap blue!"

The ball was snapped, the middle surged toward him, he piled into the scuffling bodies. He checked the marker. They'd made it.

"C'mon!" MD brandished a fist. "Let's go, babes!"

"Stop em now!" Moon was hollering. "Keep em in a hole! Hold'm now!"

MD was watching Moon. "Okay," he said, facing the huddle. "Six-one special. Let's gettem, ready . . ."

"Break!"

When Kalispell aligned themselves and set, Lumpy Rutherford cheated up from his linebacker position to the line of scrimmage; the down linemen shifted over half a yard to make room for him at the end. Granville was the lone linebacker. "Bottlecap red!" Beowolf and MD flip-flopped, Beowolf eyeing Thompson across the line. McCall was on him. The signals were barked out, the ball was snapped; again Earthquake charged the middle, this time running head-on into Bigfoot, who'd shifted head-up on Kalispell's center. The Rawlings partisans erupted.

"*Biiiiiig-foot! Biiiiiig-foot!*" they chanted. "*Biiiiiig-foot! Biiiiiig-foot!*"

The huddle formed. Second down.

"Six-one special," MD said. "Make em throw the ball."

"*Biiiiiig-shit!*" the Kalispell fans retorted. "*Biiiiiig-shit!*"

Kalispell came to the line, the quarterback rubbing his hands on the mud-flecked towel draped over his crotch. His helmet was plastered with black skulls and crossbones.

"Bottlecap blue!"

Thompson was split to the opposite side.

The ball was snapped, Burns took the pitch, Beowolf came up hard, trained on Earthquake leading the play cutting upfield, and hurtled his body at his legs; turf burst into the air at the crack of impact. Earthquake had gone down. Burns got nowhere. MD hopped off of Burns. "Run that play again, fuckhead!"

Earthquake glowered at Beowolf, who returned the stare and strutted back to the huddle.

"Watch the draw!" Moon shouted. "Watch the screen!" He flashed MD the signals.

"Five-two. Good rush now. Ready . . ."

"Break!"

The Rawlings bench hadn't yet sat down. As Kalispell lined up, they were clamoring for the ball.

"Bottlecap blue!"

Thompson was split to the opposite side.

The ball was snapped, Beowolf dropped back—"Pass!"—Thompson a glint in the corner of his eye, the tight end veering inside and upfield for MD; Beowolf hustled back to the deep outside zone, reversed direction, cut back just as the ball was fired, the pass snagged by Thompson cutting over the middle, bellying straight across the field, eluding McCall but throttled by MD. Beowolf glanced at the first-down marker. The ref waved the chain-keepers upfield. Thompson dropped the ball in front of MD, the ref scooped it up, flipped it to the kid who'd hustled on with a dry replacement. He set the fresh ball on the ground at the forty-five, covering it with a towel.

"Get it together in there!" Moon yelled. He tipped his hat, wiped his nose, wiped his chest, coughed.

"Slipped," McCall muttered. "Fuck!"

MD said, "Six-one special."

Beowolf dropped back into position, eyed Thompson approaching the line—"Bottlecap red!"—flip-flopped with MD over to Thompson's side. The ball was snapped, pitched, he sprinted forward, homing in on Earthquake: glimpsed first, then a flash of impact knocked him off his feet, the action roared past, Thompson stumbling over him. Beowolf rose to his knees, breathing deep. Burns was down beyond mid-field.

It was second and two. "Watch the crackback," he warned MD in the huddle. "They run a halfback pass off that play, too."

"Six-one special. Ready . . ."

"Break!"

The Kalispell huddle burst smartly apart.

"Bottlecap blue!"

Thompson was away.

The ball snapped. Reacting forward and planting a foot, Beowolf cried *"Pass,"* slipped, scrambling back, backpedaling. Thompson was free, far down the opposite sideline, the ball lofting through space, Thompson dove, mud exploding. Beowolf halted. Huntley, the Kalispell quarterback, stared at the earth, holding his head in his hands. "What the hell was that!" Peckinpah shouted. McCall hustled back to begin the huddle. Thompson jogged past.

"Watch the play-action, man," Beowolf told McCall. "That quarterback ain't gonna drop back often."

"Keep on his ass, *will you?*" MD said to McCall. "You got no business getting faked out on that play. The fake ain't even to your side."

Beowolf checked the down marker. Third and two.

"Six-one special, watch the sweep. Ready . . ."

"Break!"

The ball snapped, Beowolf shoring up the wall of linemen. Bigfoot had hit Earthquake head-on again. Whistles squealed. A Kalispell grunt shoved Beano aside and a ref leapt between them, warning Beano off. Beowolf glanced at the first-down marker. They were untangling, the ref digging for the ball. He placed it on the ground and carefully nudged it back several inches and called for the chains. "Back off, back off." Both teams withdrew, leaving only MD and Earthquake. The chain was laid flat alongside the ball, the point of the first-down pole touching just beyond the leather nose. The ref spread his thumb and forefinger about an inch apart for Earthquake. The chainkeepers jogged off as the Kalispell punting team hustled onto the field.

"Return right," MD said in the huddle. "Work that center's face over, Smitty. Ready . . ."

"Break!"

Beowolf dropped back deep with MD, thirty yards from the line of scrimmage. They were returning the ball to the wide side, lots of room. "Let's do it," Beowolf exclaimed, looking inside MD's helmet. MD nodded and glanced back downfield. Beowolf flexed fists, shook out his arms. The ball was kicked, was coming in low. "I got it!" MD cried. Beowolf watched the ball, glanced downfield for the first man, watched the catch and was off, heading for the sideline; Thompson sidestepped his block, but MD was safely past and Beowolf sprang back to his feet. Sprinting upfield outside the tunnel that had formed, he threw himself at another body, a grunt, cut his legs off beautifully, but MD was past, it didn't matter, he was tackled on the far side of the fifty. Beowolf rose and jogged off the field. A bad block and a good block—he'd sprung him, at least.

MD slammed his helmet on the ground. "One block!" Donnie handed him a cup of bug juice. MD took a sip, flung it into the mud. "One goddamn block!"

Bigfoot was slumped over at the end of the bench. "Hey, Donnie," Beowolf called out. He pointed down the bench. Donnie dipped a cup into the bucket. Beowolf approached Bigfoot. "How ya feel?" he asked. The ball was snapped, Geek broke off-tackle, was hit and went down.

"Okay."

Donnie handed Bigfoot the bug juice.

"Good hits in there," Beowolf said as he sat down. Peckinpah was talking to MD. Beowolf took off his helmet and looked at a bright smudge of Kalispell blue. He rose to his feet to watch Geek run for five or six. Moon shoved Beaver Kramer, one of the messenger guards, onto the field with the upcoming play. Beowolf watched them huddle and come to the line. "Billy Gambrel up the middle."

Dimitruk, a quarterback sneak. First down.

Beowolf put his helmet back on; his head was getting wet. Donnie was working his way down the bench with a bread knife, scraping the mud and turf from cleats.

"Defense!" Peckinpah shouted. "Up here!"

They clustered around Peckinpah and MD. "We're sticking with that six-one special. Anybody having any trouble?" Peckinpah glanced around the circle of faces, finally fixing on McCall. "Ya gotta stick with that man," he said. "He's the key, he's the key to this game, you understand that?" McCall nodded. Donnie squirted in and out of the circle of bodies, kneeling down, muddy at the knees, lifting disinterested feet like a blacksmith shoeing horses. The crowd roared. Beowolf glanced onto the field, saw it was nothing. Five yards. They were driving. "We'll go to the five-two on passing downs, but *you,*" Peckinpah emphasized, turning again to McCall, "you gotta stick with your goddamn man."

"Ya get the chance," MD interjected, "break the cocksucker's neck."

Dimitruk dropped back—Beowolf felt a tug, lifted his foot for Donnie—and got in trouble, cut to the sideline, no one open, was spun around and thrown to the ground. Beowolf lifted the other leg.

"What is it?" Moon was hollering. "What is it? . . . *How far, dammit?*"

Standing behind the row of Rattlers crowding the sideline, Beowolf looked upfield for the first-down marker. Fifteen yards. He glanced at the scoreboard. Thirteen. Third down, thirteen to go. The flag snapped at the top of the flagpole, the wind was behind them. Ingersoll hustled onto the field with the play. "Watch that fucking play-action," somebody muttered. "They'll do it all fuckin game." Superscout was shuffling his feet, studying the earth, the mud, talking to nobody in particular; he murmured something that Beowolf couldn't decipher beyond the obscenity. Beowolf turned away to watch the play. Dimitruk dropped back again, had plenty of time, fired over the middle for Bellito, who caught it, was nailed immediately and slammed to the ground, the ball popping free; several Kalispell players fought for it. The refs swarmed down upon them, arms waving—the stadium was in an uproar. Beowolf stepped onto the field. Two refs motioned downfield. Kalispell's ball.

Beowolf trotted onto the field. Moon was having a conniption. "Fumble? *Fumble?*" Stomping down the sideline he jabbed his finger at the nearest ref. "Wait a minute! Incomplete pass, Ref! *Where's the fumble?*"

The ball was on the Kalispell thirty-two. The huddle formed and broke. Beowolf skipped backward into position. Kalispell ran Earthquake up the middle for five or six yards—just to show that they'd run when and where they pleased, Bigfoot or no Bigfoot. They ran him up the middle again, this time struggling for a gain. No first down. "This play! This play!" Peckinpah was shouting. "Six-one," MD said. A big down. Kalispell came to the line and for the third consecutive time ran Earthquake up the middle. Hit hard by Bigfoot, then Granville, he still made the first down.

"Let's shore up the middle," MD said in the huddle. "Gotta hold em on first down. Six-one. Ready . . ."

Kalispell managed another first down two plays later on runs by Earthquake and Burns. They were moving, the fans could sense a score. Beowolf would cheat up on the next short yardage and take his chances.

Burns burst free off-tackle, veering outside for the sideline; McCall fought off Thompson's block and forced him back inside, where Beowolf collared him, swinging his full weight across his back, wrestling him to the ground. First down again. The Kalispell fans were on their feet. Kalispell was inside the Rawlings forty. Beowolf jogged back to the huddle. "What the fuck is going on?" MD demanded. "What's going on? *Jesus fuck!*"

Kalispell came to the line.

"Bottlecap red!"

Beowolf flip-flopped with MD. Thompson was to the opposite side, the wide side. The ball pitched to Burns. Beowolf charged Earthquake turning the corner, leading the play, he saw Earthquake's eyes widen and his head drop: Beowolf went sprawling, he'd hit him too high. They got Burns, though. Earthquake hadn't gone down, but they'd gotten Burns just the same. One or two yards was all. On one knee, Beowolf glanced at the first-down marker. Earthquake glowered at him as he walked past. Beowolf rose to his feet. It was a play he wouldn't want to see on film. He wobbled his head around in a circle, testing his neck. He had to hit him lower, hit him at the knees.

"Five-two," MD called. "Watch the draw, watch the screen. Ready . . ."

"Break!"

Thompson lined up on the wide side, Beowolf's side. "Bottlecap blue!" Beowolf looked across the line at Earthquake. The ball was snapped, he dropped back—"Pass!"—heading for the deep outside zone; Thompson cut over the middle, the quarterback watching him. Beowolf planted his foot and sprinted for the line of scrimmage—"Screen!" he yelled, "screen!" as Burns caught the ball. It wasn't gonna go. The blockers were held up on the line of scrimmage, McCall and Beowolf had him to the outside. Burns cut back inside for no gain.

"Awright!" Third and ten. *"Awright!"*

The five-two was called again, anticipating the pass. Earthquake lined up to the wide side—"Bottlecap red!"—and Beowolf flip-flopped with MD. Thompson was split left. Rutherford had Earthquake coming out of the backfield on a pass, so Beowolf didn't have to worry about him if Huntley dropped back.

The ball was snapped; Beowolf backpedaled for the deep outside, waiting for the flanker's upfield cut. The man ran a square-out, Morris on him, Huntley pumped and the man broke upfield, up the sideline: Beowolf had him pegged, with him all the way, turning his back on the passer and staying with the flanker stride for stride. The ball led them both, overthrown. "Good coverage, waytago!" The flanker, Kelly, jogged back to the huddle. "Waytago!" Morris swatted Beowolf on the ass. "Return left," MD said. They were going to the narrow side this time, if they went at all. "Let it go," Beowolf said as they jogged toward the end zone. "Yeah," MD replied. They positioned themselves on the ten for a short kick. "Know where you are!" Peckinpah was hollering at them. "Know where you are!" Beowolf glanced back at the end zone.

The ball wobbled low for the corner. "Let it go! Let it go!" MD cried. Beowolf's arm shot up, signaling a fair catch. The ball hit just inside the sideline, skipping twice end over end toward the end zone, then kicked coffin-corner out of bounds. "Fuck!" With the Kalispell players leaping about one another, with the noise of the stadium suddenly unbearable, Beowolf had a brief premonition of disaster. Hap trotted past with his arm outstretched. Beowolf slapped him five and jogged off the field. "All right, all right," Moon was saying. Beowolf sat down at the end of the bench and leaned back against the fence. Couldn't see worth a damn with everybody standing up. Rawlings ran a play. "What happened?" he asked, rising to his feet.

"Quarterback sneak," Lombago said. "Two yards maybe."

"He'll throw now," MD guessed, sidling up to Beowolf. "I thought we had it."

"Me too."

Dimitruk dropped back and fired to Hap on a square-out; Hap was hit hard and dumped. Dangerous play. Anyway, they had breathing room now. Beowolf looked at the scoreboard: third and two. Billy Gambrel plowed up the middle for a first. Beowolf turned away and found the bug juice. The time was ticking away. The sleet had stopped. The sky, the lights, the noise, were suddenly overwhelming.

"Jeez-us Christ!"

"What happened?" Beowolf cried.

"What the hell's going on out there?" Moon had ripped his headphones off.

"What happened?" Beowolf asked.

"Nothin," Beano told him. "Nothin happened."

"Defense!" It was Peckinpah. They clustered around him. "Okay, now come on, this is it, we're in this thing deep."

Dimitruk dropped back, looking, looking . . . a lineman loomed big behind him. He stepped forward, to the side, spun away and was off, tucking the ball in, veering downfield for the first-down marker. On the sideline the Rawlings players seemed to sidle in a single body upfield, forming a tunnel out of bounds. Frankie lowered his head to the crack of impact, and went down, first down. "Wayta mix it up, Frankie!" Dimitruk hopped back to his feet. "Jesus Christ, never seen him run like that!" Doe's moronic grin blazed up the sideline at Beowolf. They were beyond the twenty now. Breathing room.

The offense was beginning to click: past the thirty, three quick pops up the middle, past the forty. They were rolling now. "We're moving now!" somebody yelled after their fourth first down of the drive. "Keep moving." But they stalled near mid-field, punted.

Beowolf jogged back onto the field. Kalispell ran a few plays, a first down, and the quarter ended. A fast quarter. Both teams jogged down the field, where they switched directions. The ball was on the twenty-five. Rawlings was looking out the open end of the horseshoe into the wind. Darkness hung in the parking lot.

"Six-one special." Kalispell came to the line. Beowolf and MD flip-flopped, Thompson to Beowolf's side. The ball was snapped, pitched, Beowolf came up and head-on met Thompson coming across, kept moving for Earthquake, throwing his head and shoulders low, at his knees, knew he had him. The bolt of pain shot across his forehead like the lightning clench of a moonshine hangover. The pain subsided; a good hit. They were containing the power sweeps. Beneath the row of skulls and crossbones on his forehead, Earthquake peered sullen and mean into Beowolf's face. Afterward, in the huddle, Beowolf realized that it was not so much what Earthquake said that prompted his reply, but the mere fact that he'd said anything at all. "I'm gonna nail you, pussy." Beowolf jumped to his feet. *Who was nailing who?* "You'll nail me? You'll nail me?" A ref hustled over, separating them. "You'll nail me?" The ref snapped, "That's enough," and nudged Beowolf in the direction of his huddle. "Good stick, Wolf," Beano yelled, swatting him on the helmet. Bigfoot, coughing, sounded like a sick horse. "Y'awright?" MD asked. "Six-one special, ready . . ."

"Break."

Earthquake barreled up the middle, past Bigfoot, up Granville's face; Beowolf met him low, brought him down with MD. Earthquake glared until he stared back, then gave him the most godawful smile he'd ever seen. "You got a big fuckin mouth."

Kalispell got the first down, then another on a catch over the middle by Thompson—the same pass he'd caught earlier. Thompson was hurting them bad. Kalispell ran another sweep during the next series of plays, Beowolf coming up hard to cut down Earthquake's block. Again they stopped Burns at the line of scrimmage. Rawlings was cutting off the power sweeps well—doing nothing else particularly well. Beowolf caught Earthquake's eye: "Fuck you. Run that play again!" He returned to the huddle feeling as though he were wearing somebody else's jersey. It didn't matter. Kalispell was punting.

Returning right, the wide side. He and MD dropped back to the fifteen. "Good return," MD kept repeating, more to himself than to Beowolf. "Good return." Beowolf's fists were working, he stood on his toes, up down, up down, threw back his arms, was ready, anxious for the ball. "It's time," he said, and MD looked at him solemnly and nodded. The ball was punted high and deep, a spiral. It was Beowolf's: he dropped back, dropped back—the wind had it! He fell desperately back and caught the ball hazardously over his shoulder, spun around and tore after MD; the earth thundered around him as he broke for the sideline. He bellied upfield to bait

MD's block—the Kalispell man hesitating—and skipped to the outside as MD cut the man down; he was looking for Rutherford, he wouldn't make the tunnel, was cut off by another man, was hit, spun free with nowhere to go, broke for the tunnel, was hit from the side, kept his feet and gripped the ball, was hit again, hit again going over gripping the ball.

He flipped the ball to the ref, found his feet, spitting, mud in his mouth. Bigfoot was sitting on the bench. "How ya doing?" Beowolf asked. Bigfoot spat.

"Good licks, Wolf." It was Donnie. "Siddown, I clean your cleats."

Beowolf sat down, leaning back against the fence. He couldn't see with everyone on their feet. "Kalispell read it," he said to Bigfoot. Rawlings needed a punt return up the middle. All they had was to one side or the other, which didn't take much to figure out: just stick with your men, follow them upfield to the ballcarrier. Rawlings returned the ball up the middle only when the tunnel broke down, Desperation City. It was desperation that drove a body up the middle.

Periodically, Peckinpah yelled at the bench to move back so the coaches could freely roam the sideline. The bench would move back a yard or so until the next snap, when they'd flow back like a tide, as if they could see better for that extra yard. The offense had run several plays. Beowolf glanced down the bench. Bigfoot and Doe were the only others sitting down. Beowolf had to move. "Want some bug juice?" he asked Bigfoot.

"Fuck no." Bigfoot's head dropped between his knees. He reared back and spat mucus, coughing.

Beowolf moved to the sideline. Second down. Geek sliced off-tackle for the first, then cut sharply back, a nice move, faked a guy out of his jock and ran a few extra yards to mid-field. "Can come back tomorrow and pick it up!" Lumpy Rutherford jeered from the sideline.

On first down, Frankie rolled right and carried it himself for five or six. The cheerleaders were chanting, the Rawlings fans hungry for a score. Beowolf glanced at the clock. Time made no sense during a game. There was all the time in the world this quarter. Billy Gambrel ran for another first. Beowolf could feel it now, they were gonna score. Hang on to the ball, just hang on to the ball. Each play there was a resounding, beautiful crack of pads. They were driving, they would score. Hold on to the ball. They were inside the thirty, chewing up the clock and spitting it out. Geek slipped and fell for a loss. Dimitruk dropped back to pass, hit Jack Doyle on a hook. A flag. "What's going on?" Moon roared. Holding. Moon shook his head, disgusted. "On *who?*" he wanted to know. "On *who?*" The ref trotted to the sideline and said something. Kramer or Sutton—they held like Crazy Glue. For the first time in the game, Beowolf noticed the P.A.: "Second and twenty-three," it announced. The stadium had simmered down. Frankie dropped back again, threw out of bounds under a heavy rush. The next play he hit Bellito for small change. On fourth down they punted. The ball rolled out of bounds inside the ten. Beowolf trotted back onto the field. "Defense! Defense!" Peckinpah was calling them back. "If we can hold em in here," Moon said, "we'll go with the fist." MD nodded. "Let's go, babes!"

They held Kalispell on three consecutive running plays. Kalispell was kicking from their own goal line. Beowolf and MD dropped back, Beowolf deeper than MD. When Kalispell came to the line, MD began cheating up—the cornerbacks, McCall and Morris, were already on the line of scrimmage. MD had twenty yards to go when the ball was snapped, a quick count. The ball wobbled low in the air, off the side of the kicker's foot; Beowolf came up, stopped, backing off, slipped, the ball bounced out of bounds. Out of bounds at the thirty-two. Beowolf slapped Hap five as they passed. "Do it now!"

But the offense wasn't doing shit. They were held on three plays, then again on fourth down, still trying for the first.

The defense took the field again. "The fist is off," MD said, "for now." The huddle broke. The grunts fell to their knees along the line of scrimmage. Kalispell came to the line and set; the defensive line shifted to the left, Rutherford falling into a four-point stance at the end. Huntley came out throwing—caught the flanker cutting over the middle. MD took him down. There wasn't much time left. Two-fifty was all. Huntley dropped back again, overthrew the tight end and pounded his own head with his fists. "Let's get a pass rush in there," MD screamed. "You're givin'm all fuckin night." Thompson caught two successive passes and Earthquake ran a draw for about fifteen. Beowolf missed the tackle: hit him solid but bounced off. Hit'm low, *hit'm low!* Kalispell was on the Rawlings forty. They still had two minutes. "Hold em now, hold em!" They were going to a four-three defensive alignment, with Geek Larson coming in to play weakside linebacker. He was the only Rattler who ever went both ways, playing defense in the Prevent Defense. They ran the screen to Burns. Then Huntley hit Thompson again; Beowolf kept him in bounds. One-forty and running. Huntley heaved the ball out of bounds, stopping the clock. One twenty-eight, twenty-seven—the clock stopped, went back to twenty-eight. Kalispell was inside the thirty. Second and ten.

Kalispell came to the line. "Bottlecap red!" It meant nothing to Beowolf in the Prevent D. He stayed to the tight end's side of the field. Thompson was split to his side. Huntley dropped back, Beowolf backpedaled to the deep outside; Thompson ran a square-out, Huntley pumped, Thompson broke upfield behind McCall, Huntley fired the ball—Beowolf had him cold, clobbered him, even saw stars. On the ground he looked over at Thompson, who was *holding the ball!* Writhing on his back in the mud, he was holding the goddamn ball! Kalispell called time. Propping Thompson's legs up, the Kalispell trainer tugged at his pants, lifting his lower back off the ground. "He caught that ball, you see that?" Donnie was passing out bug juice in the huddle. "Good hit, Wolf," Bigfoot said. "What more can ya do?" The ball was on the fifteen.

Thompson finally rose to his feet amid a rousing Kalispell cheer. Kalispell on its feet. Donnie took off with the bug juice and MD returned from his consultation with Moon. The ref blew the whistle. They were going back to the five-two. "Get Huntley," MD said. It occurred to Beowolf that Bigfoot wasn't doing shit. Kalispell came to the line. A draw to Earthquake got them nothing. A square-out to Thompson—five yards and a stopped clock. They had two time-outs left. The ball was on the ten with less than a minute. Rawlings went to the six-one special. Earthquake bulled his way up the middle for three. Kalispell called time. Fourth and two, forty-nine seconds. Kalispell on its feet. Bigfoot was doubled over, hands on his knees. He was dying, Beowolf knew. MD sprinted back to the huddle from the sideline and called the six-one special. Granville was playing right on Bigfoot's ass. They were all cheating up a step, watching for the run. Kalispell lined up. The ball was snapped and Earthquake slammed up the middle again. First down.

Burns burst off-tackle, got nothing. Second down, time running. Kalispell didn't huddle, ran Earthquake up the middle; Bigfoot nailed him at the line. *"Biiiiig-foot! Biiiiig-foot!"* The ball was on the four. Nineteen seconds. Kalispell huddled and came to the line. Kelly and Thompson were both wide to opposite sides. Beowolf, to Kelly's side, watched Huntley and Earthquake, watched the foot of the tight end for the first move signaling run or pass. On the snap —"Pass!"—Beowolf backpedaled, backed off when Kelly slipped; Huntley went down under the pass rush and sprang to his feet as replacements charged onto the field. The ball was at the ten. They were kicking it. Moon was flashing the nine-two kick block. "Kick block!" MD shouted as he positioned himself behind Beano to charge the kick. He turned and glared at Beowolf. "Watch it." Thompson was nowhere; somebody new. The ball was snapped, Beowolf watched for bodies, watched the ball carry through the uprights. Three points. The half was over.

The cheerleaders had formed a gauntlet from the gate to the corridor leading to the locker room. As he filed through, Beowolf saw Jeannie. She stamped her foot, her face an expression of intensity. "Go!" When their eyes met, the fire in her went dim, her ardor lost. He was past her. *Go*. As if it mattered. Inside the locker room, water from the overhead pipes pattered against the locker tops. Beowolf lifted his helmet over his ears and off. He grabbed a handful of orange quarters and sat down on the cement beside a puddle. He was weakening, he knew. The game seemed far off. Halftime could be a nuisance; suspended time. He wanted to hang on, sucked on an orange. His lips were chapped and the juice stung. He tossed the peel at a battered garbage can a few feet away. Wide. Moon pushed through the crowd at the door, followed by Superscout. Peckinpah's voice echoed from the bathroom, bawling somebody out. "Ya take shit from this team, ya be taking shit the rest of your life!" Peckinpah appeared in the doorway. "You're taking *shit* from this team!" He glared at Bigfoot, at Doe, at Beano, sitting together on a bench. "Ya take shit from this team, ya eat it from here on out."

"Where's my chalk?" Moon asked. Donnie set the bucket of orange slices down in the middle of the floor and dug into his pocket.

"Didn't want anyone to steal it," he explained as he handed the stick to Moon.

When Coach Rose entered the locker room, Moon told him to close the door. A toilet flushed. Beowolf gripped the tip of the orange pulp with his teeth, trying to strip away the peel without the pulp touching his lips. It was impossible. The sting shot deep, a paper cut through his lip. He licked it away, figured *fuck it* and ripped the rest of the pulp from the peel, almost desiring the sting; it came, he savored it and then licked it away, leaving only the aftertaste. He'd had enough. Nudging MD, he handed him the remaining slices. "If ya haven't been playing," Porkbutt said, "don't be eating up the oranges." He was bent over double, working his tape-cutter up Geek's ankle. A toilet flushed and the pipes went into convulsions, water streaming down the wall beside Beowolf. The room was all shadow. Superscout had disappeared. "Look at that," Geek said, poking his swollen ankle. "Soft as a sneakerful of puppy shit." McCall marched in from the bathroom. "Ya gotta cover the man," Moon said earnestly. McCall nodded humbly and sat down on the cement. Donnie toted the orange bucket over to him. One of the other managers was handing out bug juice.

On the blackboard, Moon reviewed Kalispell's offensive formations and the plays that had been run off them. Occasionally, he asked for Coach Rose's opinion. Kalispell was gaining yardage inside and off-tackle. They'd been throwing more than expected and their receivers had been open. Rawlings' pass rush was weak. "*Pathetic,*" Peckinpah interjected. Moon glanced at Doe, Beano and Bigfoot. Bigfoot's eyes were glazed, like an old dog's. He was slumped forward, his helmet off, face raised to Moon. You could tell he was sick. He'd never been like this. From his forehead his hair arched back over his scalp. Hap leaned back against a locker, sucking on an orange. Water dripped relentlessly, maddeningly. Moon was reviewing the offense. It was too erratic. They would move the ball well, then bog down. They would go to the air more in the second half. "We're gonna shake em up right away," Moon announced. "Coach Rose says the forty-six cross-trap fly is golden. We're going with the forty-six cross-trap fly on the opening play." Moon normally designed and selected the team's plays, but Coach Rose occasionally came up with a wild, sure winner. The forty-six cross-trap fly was his baby: play-action, fake off-guard, Hap breaking deep. They hadn't used the play in three games, and would catch Kalispell off-guard for sure. Hap gobbled down another orange slice.

"Okay," Moon said. "We've played a decent half of football. A few mistakes. That's all. And missed opportunities. Don't let these sonsabitches get it over you. Give them your best shot. Bury them." Moon turned to Peckinpah. "You got anything to say?"

"Ya can't take shit from this team. Ya take shit here, ya be swallowing it the rest of your life."

"Okay, everybody, just relax," Moon said. "We've got ten minutes. Take it easy, have something to drink. Don't eat too many of them damn things."

Beowolf walked over to Bigfoot, whose eyes were closed. "You okay? You're sweating silver fuckin bullets."

Bigfoot looked up. "Leave me alone," he said, and he meant it.

Beowolf went into the bathroom to piss. Lurking in the corner beyond the far sink was Superscout. His eyes widened when he saw Beowolf; his head began to nod. He didn't say anything, just stood there in the shadows. Beowolf splashed cold water on his face, glanced in the mirror. The pipes rattled like all hell breaking loose. There were no paper towels. He unreeled a fistful of toilet paper and wiped his face, careful not to smudge the lampblack. He looked in the mirror and picked off the wet flecks of toilet paper. He was muddy as hell. Superscout was watching him. Turning to leave, Beowolf heard Superscout's disembodied voice, exhaled like a vapor. "Gettem." Beowolf glanced back. Had he said anything at all? Superscout stood there nodding like a petty demon, a sly smile crossing his face, his teeth chipped. He chuckled.

In the locker room, most of the players were on their feet. Moon was talking with Peckinpah, Coach Rose and—having joined them from nowhere—Superscout. Beowolf sat down on the bench next to Hap.

"How's it going?"

"We'll do it," Hap said.

"Ya been running the forty-six cross? They set up for it?"

"We've run it three times. Their safeties are coming up hard."

"You'll get it."

"Yeah."

Beowolf rapped Hap's thigh with his fist and moved on to MD.

"How ya doing?" MD asked.

"Awright."

There was a tap at the door. Donnie opened it a crack and a voice said, "Five minutes."

"Okay," Moon said. "We're gonna have the wind behind us this quarter. We're gonna score. We gotta score this quarter . . . Okay now, use your heads out there. You, Bailey, don't be getting into any of this nonsense with Earthquake . . ."

"Unless," Peckinpah interjected, "you get his ass thrown out of the game, too."

"We don't need any senseless penalties. You're no good sitting on the bench. No mental errors, huh?" Moon turned to Beano. "What was that crap with you?"

"He came on after the whistle."

"Keep your heads," Peckinpah said. "And don't take any shit."

Moon held the door open as the players filed through the corridor into the light. It was snowing. The cops held back the crowd as the Rattlers pushed through the gate onto the field. Beowolf stretched his legs, ran in place a bit. His sweat had dried, and he was cold. MD came bounding up to him: "Let's go! Let's go!" He gripped Beowolf's shoulder pads and they battered their heads together. The kick-return team trotted onto the field. Beowolf's groin felt tight, so he spread his legs and bent over, reaching back between them as far as he could. It was tight, but the pain was sharp only when he reached farthest back. The whistle blew. Beowolf moved up to the sideline to watch. Billy Gambrel fielded the kick, returned it to the thirty.

This was it! Beowolf spotted Hap in the huddle. The huddle broke, and Hap split out to the wide side of the field, the Rawlings side. Beowolf looked at the near safety. The ball was snapped, Geek slanted into the line, Hap cut in as if he were throwing a block, then burst upfield past his man. Frankie spun around and reared back, lofting the ball high and easy: Hap had his man beat by a couple strides, the ball dove softly, and he had it! He had it! "Run, you sonofabitch!" The Rawlings bench swung a foot or two onto the field to see him tearing straight up the middle of the field. The Rawlings fans went bonkers! Holding the ball above his head, Hap was mobbed by the offense, which had raced upfield after him. The band ran the fight song as Rawlings lined up for the extra point.

Hap chipped it through the uprights. "Howtago! Howtago!" Hap was swarmed on the sideline. "Donnie! Donnie!" Hap called out. "Where's the kicking tee?" Beowolf smacked Hap on the ass, slapped Frankie five and galloped onto the field for the kickoff. "Let's go now," MD cried. "Let's hold'm. Smarten up a fuckin chump, ready . . ."

"Break!"

Beowolf tore downfield when the ball was kicked, fought off a block, staying to the outside—the return went up the middle. The ballcarrier was hit and tackled. "We're going with the six-one special," MD said. "Six-one special, ready . . ."

"Break!"

"Bottlecap blue! Bottlecap blue!"

Thompson was away.

Earthquake lowered his head and piled into the line for a five-yard gain. They swept to Beowolf's side on the next play: he hit Earthquake too high again, didn't take him down. First down. The defense held through the next set of downs and Kalispell kicked. It was a high kick to MD. Beowolf took off for the sideline, spotted his man, planted his face in the man's numbers, driving him back, and MD was into the tunnel and upfield. He was tackled near mid-field. "Good block, Wolf!" MD swatted his ass.

This was their big chance. Score here and blow the game open. 14–3. 21–3. Frankie came out throwing. He hit Hap on a look-in. Then he threw a square-out to Rocky, who dropped the goddamn ball. Geek dove up the middle for two; short of the first down. Thompson fielded the punt, sidestepped a man, slipped, kept his feet, spurted forward, narrowly missed being sandwiched and cut to the inside. For an instant Beowolf glimpsed disaster as Thompson sprinted straight upfield. He stutter-stepped in front of Geek, trying to get past, and swung for the sideline just as Hap came flying up from behind to catch him bellying back; Hap collared him and flung him to the ground. Thompson sprang back to his feet and said something to Hap. Beowolf slapped Hap five as he trotted onto the field.

The ball was in Rawlings territory, and again Kalispell seemed determined to grind out a score. Earthquake burst over Bigfoot, Beowolf hit him and was shucked as Earthquake rambled for another ten yards before being dragged down from behind.

"Biiiiiig-shit!" the Kalispell fans were chanting. *"Biiiiiig-shit!"* Somebody had touched a hotstick to Kalispell's ass. Burns cut off-tackle, was hit, squirmed free, was hit again, bounced off like a pinball, bounding up the sideline; Beowolf ran him down.

"Get your shit together!" MD shouted at the grunts in the huddle. "You guys in the front line are doing shit!" Bigfoot spat.

"C'mon!" Beano cried. "Pump up!"

The huddle broke.

"Bottlecap red!"

Beowolf and MD flip-flopped. The ball was inside the thirty. Thompson was away. Earthquake burst up the middle for five, and when the bodies cleared, Granville was left struggling to his feet, hobbling, his face contorted. A clean jersey, Chris Jenner, took his place.

"Hey, babes!" MD glanced from one grunt to the next. "If we don't stop'm now, it ain't gonna happen."

"Pump up, Chris!" Beano added. "Get your nose in the dirt!"

On the next play Doe leveled Burns with a shot heard round the world; the ball squirted loose and Jimmy Flood recovered.

"Set up in the middle," Peckinpah lectured Jenner on the sideline, "but cheat over toward the six hole." He was talking about the fist. "With you shooting up the six hole, either you or MD should get a hand on it. Ya got the picture?" Jenner was a senior who'd never started a game in his life.

Meanwhile, the Rawlings offense was going nowhere. Geek kept slipping and they had to punt. Once more, Kalispell had the ball at mid-field.

On the opening play, Beowolf cut down Earthquake at the knees on a sweep. Earthquake glared. "I'm gonna ram it up your ass, pussy."

"You'd best do it then," Beowolf snapped back.

"Run that play again," MD sneered at Burns, who was slow getting up.

"You're playing a tune on that dude," Morris said to MD.

MD hustled his balls. "Six-one special."

"Bottlecap blue! Bottlecap blue!"

Beowolf eyed Earthquake. They needed ten. Thompson was to his side. The ball was snapped. Beowolf froze for an instant as Huntley faked a handoff into the line. Then he tore ass back for the deep outside zone; Huntley pumped to Thompson on a square-out, then Thompson cut past McCall upfield: Huntley fired the ball. Beowolf was late, but drove him out of bounds and to the ground. Thompson hopped to his feet and flipped the ball off Beowolf's helmet. "Happy Father's Day, ace."

Stunned, stumbling to his feet, Beowolf stared into Thompson's helmet. Thompson stared back. He knew! Thompson jogged back to his huddle. Beowolf felt his composure slide away, the snowflakes falling, floating fat, a snowflake melting like a light kiss on the back of his hand. First down. It was the same pattern he'd nailed Thompson on earlier in the game. How did he know? He knew, sure as shit.

Kalispell's ground game stalled. On third and seven, Huntley dropped back to pass. Thompson came off the ball hard, stopped dead and sprinted back behind the line of scrimmage—a phalanx of blockers had pulled his way. Beowolf came up as Huntley flipped Thompson the ball; McCall was decked; Beowolf hit and bounced back, but the blocker kept his feet. Beowolf was fighting him off waiting for help, being driven downfield. As the pursuit converged, Thompson gave a burst of speed up the sideline trying to slip past, Beowolf grabbed him by the jersey, spun him out of bounds and flung him as hard as he could. Thompson hit the fence and buckled, dropping the ball. The man who'd been blocking Beowolf shoved him over on his ass. The ref rushed in. "Get back! Get back!" Beowolf had sprung to his feet. The Kalispell coach loomed on the sideline, screaming. Thompson was still on the ground *good.* "I want him outta this game!" the Kalispell coach bellowed. "I want him out!" Another ref was pushing Beowolf back. "We're playing a goddamn *game* here!" the coach screamed. The ref was pushing Beowolf back onto the field. "Move!" he snapped. A flag lay in the mud. Thompson was now on his feet, holding his ribs. The refs had called time-out. "What the hell you doin!" somebody from his own sideline was screaming. The stadium had gone crazy. For a moment Beowolf thought he would burst; he wanted to punch out Thompson, the ref, anyone. He turned his back on the ref and bit into his lip, tears gathering beneath his skin like the shitstorm that was brewing and about to blow. He wanted to kill somebody. "What the hell you doin?" The other ref came running over to him. Beowolf saw right through him, heard his voice, a warning: "You do that again, son, and you're outta this game. We don't want that kind of game, you hear?"

"Don't worry, don't worry," MD told the ref.

The ref trotted over to the Rawlings sideline, where he argued for a moment with Moon. "I'll throw *you* in the goddamn fence!" Moon ranted wildly when the ref turned his back on him. The other ref was pacing off the penalty yardage, fifteen yards. The ball was inside the five-yard line. The ref signaled to the crowd: unsportsmanlike conduct. Beowolf couldn't calm down, couldn't get hold of himself. *Stop moving, dammit!* He wanted to hit somebody. "Calm down," Bigfoot kept saying—Bigfoot, head-over-heels crazier then *he* was. They were *all* crazy! The Kalispell fans were on their feet, caring less about the assault on Thompson than about the imminent score. Thompson jogged onto the field, a hero for having been thrown into a fence. Kalispell was clamoring for a score.

The ball was handed to Earthquake up the middle, Beowolf came up hard, attacked with his face; Earthquake busted through and into the end zone. Beowolf slammed his fist against the earth. Peckinpah was yelling at him. Kalispell kicked the extra point. "What'd we tell you?" Peckinpah screamed. *"What'd we tell you?"* Beowolf glanced at and past him, walked away. "What the hell is going on out there?" Moon demanded. "That cost us seven points, boy!" Beowolf couldn't speak, could only stare into Moon's forehead. Mount fuckin Rushmore. Moon turned to watch the offense run a play. Beowolf walked down the sideline. He couldn't speak. "What is it?" McCall asked. "Leave me alone," Beowolf said. He walked to the end of the bench, dipped a cup in the bug juice and wound up flinging it across the ground. The ground up the sideline and at the far ends of the field was frosted in snow, the snowflakes like feathers, thick. He couldn't think. *What was he doing?* He slammed his fist down on his thigh. MD was approaching. "Leave me alone, just leave me *the fuck* alone!" His brain had tilted; his body shuddered. It was 10–7, Kalispell. He had to go easy, calm down. He felt like his head was going to pop his helmet. He held his head, couldn't stand the noise.

"Defense! Defense!" Rawlings had punted. Beowolf sprang from the bench and sprinted onto the field.

There were three minutes left in the quarter. Kalispell had the

wind in their face. The ball was on their own thirty-four. "Let's keep our heads," MD said. "Six-one special, ready . . ."
"Break!"
Thompson split to his side. There was something about him—he'd cut his sleeves off high up the arm, exposing his biceps. He wasn't well built, kind of squirrelly. Something detestable about him. He *pranced* to the line of scrimmage. Like Gray. *Superfly.* A prime candidate for a clotheslining. The ball was snapped. Earthquake dove up the middle.
"*Biiiiig-foot! Biiiiig-foot!*"
The huddle broke. Bigfoot fell to his knees in front of the ball, coughing, waiting for Kalispell. Beowolf glanced at the scoreboard, positioning himself. He realized abruptly how Thompson knew. *Happy Father's Day.* The waitress, the bitch. Kalispell came to the line. He had to focus on the game, had to focus on Earthquake. "Bottlecap red!" MD screamed at him. "Bottlecap red!" Beowolf hustled into position. The ball was snapped, pitched, Earthquake leading the way. Beowolf came up hard for the big man, aching to hit him viciously, not at the knees but head-on; the impact shot like lightning down his back. He rose to his knees, holding his helmet. He stared at the mud, focusing the brown blur world. *We'll run it again, muffuck,* reverberating, *Happy Father's Day, muffuck,* the eye of a whirl of noise. His hands found the earholes, tried to stop them up. He couldn't see! *We'll run it again, muffuck.* His head sank to the mud throbbing with noise, the smell of earth. *What's wrong?* He keeled over onto his side, stretched out his legs. *What the fuck is the matter with you now?* He could see. He rolled onto his back and stared into the sky. Framed by leering faces, he couldn't focus; staring into the sky for what seemed an eternity, his neck was broken for sure, the snow floating down through the fractured light singeing his cheek. Snow fluttering, fluttering like down, ashes from heaven. *Whatzamatter? You all right?* He heard his name, his name, the pain shot suddenly across the dome of his skull and he had to get up. He couldn't move, the snow was killing him, burying him. *Whatzamatter with you?* He was shaken, pinned to the earth. "Get back! Push back!" The world peered into his helmet. It was Moon, Moon! "Get him off the field or he'll cost us a time-out!" His arm was tugged, he was on his feet, focusing: he was all right, they had him under each arm. Moon's back loomed

in front of him. The sideline. The spinning world would fling him over, he was going to puke. They sat him on the bench. He was okay, his neck wasn't broken. "How many fingers?" The vision of Porkbutt, blurry and bloated, filled his face. He was drowning in the noise. He turned away from the double image. The people were standing and chanting, noise ebbing and flowing, roaring in his head, never quite meshing with what he saw, dubbed in voices. "How many *fingers?*" The clock bleeding, a yellow blur running down the scoreboard face. He was being shaken. There are times —*yaaa!* He reared back and slapped the hand away. He was okay. Smelling salts jolted him again and Porkbutt came into focus. "Get away!" Beowolf cried.

"How many fingers?"

Beowolf thought of his name, fastened on to it. He was shaking. Somebody was shaking him. He squirmed free of the salts. *He was dinged,* dammit! He grabbed Porkbutt by the arm and hung on. He stared up at him, his head killing him. "Bailey! Bailey!" Moon's stolid icon-eyes peered into his own and he was abruptly blindsided by a salt shock springing to his eyes. He clung to the arm.

"How many fingers am I holding up?"

The lights blacked out again.

"Are you okay?"

Pain jackhammered inside his skull. He was bleeding. The lights flashed back on. His nose was bleeding. Porkbutt was wiping away the blood. The smelling salts jolted.

"He gonna live?"

"Yes," Beowolf answered. He let go of the arm. Moon's arm.

"Wolf!"

"Don't touch his head!"

MD had slapped his helmet.

"How many fingers?"

He was okay now.

"Two," he said. It was always two. "Are we winning?"

"He's just had his bell rung," Moon was saying. "He's all right."

"Defense! Jeeeez-us!" Peckinpah cried out. "Defense! Defense!"

Beowolf rose to his feet. His brains were swimming. The noise broke on him like waves.

"He can't go in, I'm tellin ya!"

He was sat back down. The noise was unbearable. "Drink it,"

Donnie said. The bug juice looked like snot. He drank it and felt better. "I'm okay." He leaned back against the fence. His head stung, his brain was fractured.

"Relax," Hap told him. "Berger's in for you."

"Berger?"

"Can you walk?" Porkbutt asked.

Beowolf got up and began pacing the sideline with Porkbutt. Moon had an eye on him. Jeannie was watching him, too. Her hair hung lifeless under the weight of the weather. He bit into his lip, bit into it raw, clenching the pain there. He looked away from Jeannie.

"He's been dinged," Porkbutt was saying. "He's awright, he's awright."

He was all right. He could walk. He could run. He hurt, but it was good that he hurt. It didn't scare him. His brains were scrambled. That was good. His groin felt fine. It hurt but didn't bother him at all.

"What's the score?" he asked.

"You blind?"

Beowolf checked the scoreboard. 10–7, still losing. That was no good. He needed some bug juice. He thought of telling Porkbutt about Pap, who drank steer's blood before boxing matches. That was true. But Porkbutt would think he was crazy. He didn't like Porkbutt. He dipped a cup in the bug juice. Rawlings was cheering. The defense was coming off the field. He drank the green liquid, bolted it down. His nose was bleeding. He began to laugh.

"Hey, you all right?" MD asked.

"I'm awright."

MD had just picked off a pass. "Honyo City the rest of the way," he declared. "I'm telling ya, Wolf. Honyo City the rest of the way."

"He gonna play?" Moon was asking.

"You all right?" Porkbutt asked.

"Yeah. I'm all right."

"Yeah. He's awright."

Moon pulled his headphones back over his ears. "He's all right," he said into the mike. He turned back to the field.

"I'm gonna run some," Beowolf said to Porkbutt. He began jogging up and down the sideline. He was feeling better. Maybe they'd score now. They were going in the opposite direction. He glanced up at the scoreboard. Fourth quarter, the clock was running. They had to score.

Fourth down, Rawlings punting. The punt sailed into the wind, hung in the lights, and plummeted to earth, to Thompson, who tore ass toward the sideline, cut upfield and was buried. Beowolf trotted onto the field. Thompson was getting up slow.

"Awright now," MD said. "Six-one special, let's hold'm now, ready . . ."

"Break."

Kalispell lined up.

"Bottlecap red!"

Beowolf and MD flip-flopped. Thompson was out, a clean jersey had taken his place. Beowolf focused on Earthquake. The ball was snapped: Burns slashed off-tackle, Beowolf came up and hit him as he veered outside, hit him with his shoulder: Burns slipped away, skipping back to the inside, decked by MD.

"He's gonna rip your arms off, Bailey!" somebody shouted from the sideline. "He's gonna rip your goddamn arms off, you tackle like that!" Peckinpah.

Beowolf glanced at the first-down marker. Second and two.

Earthquake busted up the middle for a first. They had a drive going. Earthquake rammed up the middle for two plays. On third down, Huntley pitched the ball to Burns. Beowolf came up on Earthquake, threw a cross-body at him: at contact his life jolted, sucked right out of him, seeping into the night in a prolonged moan. He rolled onto his back trying to breathe, clenched in a gigantic fist. *Happy Father's Day, muffuck! Happy Father's Day!* Porkbutt loomed over him, tugging at his belt. "Raise your knees. *Raise em.*" He raised his knees. His breath was coming back. "You're having one hell of a night." Moon looked into his face. He turned his back and stalked back to the sideline. The ref said, "Let's go, folks. He awright?"

"He's awright now."

Beowolf rose to his feet, bent over and inhaled deeply.

"You are taking one fuckin beating," MD said in the huddle. "Six-one special, ready . . ."

"Break."

It was first down. Thompson was back in the game. Earthquake burst up the middle, into and over Bigfoot for five yards. Burns was nailed on the next play slanting off-tackle. On third down, Thompson split to Beowolf's side. Beowolf dropped back, caught Thompson cutting in, came up hard to rip his head off as the ball was fired, hit him not well, but deflected the ball—bashed his arm, made him drop it. Kalispell had to punt.

Because of the wind, they dropped back thirty-five yards rather than thirty. They were heading right, to the wide side. They needed a good return, had to do it now. The ball spiraled into the sky, MD's all the way, got a boost from the wind, and sailed down into his waiting arms. Beowolf sprinted after the first man downfield and at the last instant ducked his head away from the collision, flinging his body full-length at him: no good, the man sidestepped him and forced MD back inside, where he struggled for yardage, sucked under by a wave of Kalispell defenders.

"Will you stick your goddamn head in there!" Peckinpah screamed from the sideline. Beowolf had fucked up royally. "It was going, *it was going!* Jesus *Christ!*"

He jogged to the sideline, didn't look at Peckinpah. He sat down on the bench, couldn't see a damn thing on the field. He leaned back against the fence to breathe. He had to stick his face in. He had to lead with his face.

Rawlings had it going now. Frankie was throwing the ball. He completed a long pass to Rocky, and the Rawlings fans brought Beowolf to his feet. Geek, Frankie and Billy Gambrel all ran the ball. First down. Geek carried up the middle. They were moving now, the way they were supposed to. Geek swept outside. On the next play he was nailed for a loss. But on fourth and two, Frankie rolled out and ran for the first. The Rawlings fans were ecstatic. They were inside the twenty. Geek slashed up the middle. All the time in the world. Billy Gambrel dove up the middle. Frankie rolled right, tucked the ball in, whipped it back up and flipped a pass to Rocky coming cross-field. They were inside the five. Rawlings was going apeshit. "Hang on to the ball!" Moon was yelling. "Hang on to the ball!" Geek hit up the middle for nothing.

Beowolf saw it coming: they weren't going to score.

Geek swept to the wide side, was strung out by a linebacker, couldn't cut upfield, was run out of bounds. On third down, Frankie dropped back, looking for Rocky; he pumped, hesitated, looked right, left, tucked the ball in, found nowhere to run, bellied back—a collective groan escaped along the sideline—looking for somebody to throw to, forced back, scrambling, and penned in finally, he dropped to the ground. "Throw it away!" Moon threw his clipboard at the ground, stomped on it. *"Throw it away!"* The instant he lost his temper, Moon was composed. He grabbed Kramer by the jersey and shoved him off with the upcoming play. Fourth and goal from the fifteen. The huddle broke. They were kicking! "Just like an extra point," Peckinpah shouted. Hap and Frankie lined up behind the center. The ball was snapped, Hap stepped forward and booted the ball; it floated sideways through the uprights. 10–10.

"Awright, let's go!" Beowolf trotted onto the field for the kickoff.

"Wolf!" Berger came tearing after him. "Wolf!" Berger gave him the thumb.

Beowolf sprinted back to the sideline. The kickoff was returned to the twenty-five.

"Am I in?" Beowolf asked Peckinpah.

"Whattaya think?"

Beowolf jogged onto the field. He didn't think anything, was what he fuckin well thought. "Stick your head in, *will you?*" Peckinpah hollered after him.

There were five minutes left. The huddle disbanded. Thompson split to his side. Earthquake rammed up the middle for five. They had to stop this crap. They needed the ball.

Huntley pitched the ball to Burns, Beowolf came up—he had him this time—and plunged his head, his body, straight into the big man's knees; his head exploded in yellow color. He rolled onto his back. He couldn't lie down again, had to get up. He struggled to his feet. His head throbbed. The noise was too much: swaying, stirred, pounding waves inside his head. His body wobbled. He planted his hands on his helmet and looked at the scoreboard glowing yellow like a vision. He was seeing things twice. In the huddle he couldn't hear; the noise throbbed at his insides, his head. He dropped back. Thompson split out. "C'mon, *c'mon!*" MD snapped. Beowolf flip-flopped. The ball was snapped; Earthquake slanted off-tackle, bowled somebody over. Beowolf hit him, clinging to the pain ringing in his head. He clambered to his feet. He was awright, just seeing things twice.

"You all right?" MD said in the huddle.

"I'm awright."

"Look like ya got your bell rung again."

Beowolf stared at MD's ghost, trying to will it back into MD's body.

The ball was pitched; Beowolf came up, was barreled over by Earthquake. The pain shot like streamers screaming across the dome of his skull. He could see now. His eyes focused on skulls and crossbones. He was all right. The huddle disbanded. Bigfoot was on his knees before the football like a wounded brahma, revolving his head around the horse-collar.

As Kalispell came to the line, Beowolf got a good faceful of the Kalispell center: behind his cage he had a bloody dumb expression like a sucker-punched ox. Huntley dropped back, hit Thompson with a pass going out of bounds. Beowolf was in a fog, wasn't paying attention, not concentrating. His head throbbed. He had to concentrate.

Kalispell came to the line. Thompson, he had Thompson to his side. Huntley dropped back, hit the tight end on a hook; Beowolf planted his head in the man's back, bowled him over. He was all right. His head was killing him. *Good hit,* they were saying. *Good hit.* He knew. He would get Earthquake now.

The ball was pitched; he came up and lowered the boom on Earthquake: pain shot luxuriously through his head like rockets, searing yellow light. He rose to his feet. Earthquake was a blur. It was a good hit. He and Earthquake were hitting good.

It was a return to the wide side. Everything was slow and noisy, underwater noisy. The ball was kicked and it came at him like a movie, coming into focus, sharp as a lens' flash. He caught the ball and sprang after MD, reached the tunnel, sighted the first man and barreled into him, giving him his best shot. He rolled over, rolled the ball away from him. He found his feet and was trotting off the field, the spotty lights shivering in the cold, his breath white in the night. The stadium was screaming. Helen the Bod danced, watching him—he saw that—dancing, her bare thunder-thighs shooting up one-two to her tits, one-two like pistons, her tits wrestling like babies under her sweater. *Thanks for the mammaries.* Beowolf laughed. In the first row a woman with purple hair was blowing a bugle.

On the sideline Porkbutt shoved fingers in his face again. "How many?"

"Wolf."

"How many *fingers?*"

"Two."

Everything had pulled together under the stadium's rude, high-beamed scrutiny.

"Only a couple more minutes," Porkbutt assured him. "Y'awright?"

"I'm awright."

It was like watching a movie. His head had smoothed out, leaving only a dull claustrophobic ache. He was all right. He wanted to charge into Earthquake, Earthquake wanted to charge into him. The scoreboard—sharp light, time ticking—began to fade before his eyes, dissolving into a strange yellow glow. There was a time, he remembered, when he was very young, on a tricycle, and the sun on the horizon splashed the world all over yellow. He was staring down at a pair of dandelions beside a fire hydrant. Everything but the dandelions had been cut, everything but the dandelions. And looking down at the dandelions beside the fire hydrant in the grass, with the earth bathed in yellow light, he believed, he remembered, he believed he'd never seen anything so lovely in his life. He knew, sitting on his tricycle, even as he heard his name being called, "Bill-y! Bill-y!"—Jason calling him to supper—that he would remember it for the rest of his life.

Beowolf's body shuddered.

There was a time when his father made a catch in a softball game and Jason said, "Ya see that?" He remembered that, too. And it was a wonderful place that night when the moon came up: a huge, round, rising orange like a helium balloon behind a grove of trees, and he thought the balloon belonged to the State Fair because that's where they were, the State Fair. But it was the moon, the moon rising, and when it finally rose above the trees something came to him, a miracle. With the moon so close and wonderful, it was like being on a foreign planet, like that later time on the lake with Jeannie.

Beowolf's body shook, overtaken by strange spasms. Snow had taken the seat next to him. He laid his hands flat out on both sides, trying to make his body be still. He felt the cold. He was shivering all over. He gazed at his handprint.

"Everybody back!" Moon bellowed.

Beowolf leapt to his feet. Fight! There was a pile-up on the field. "Everybody back!" Peckinpah cried. "Everybody back!"

"What happened?"

"They flung him into the fence."

"Who?"

"Hap."

The stadium roared. Bodies were being pulled off the pile. A Kalispell player was writhing on the ground.

"He's out! That's it!" one of the refs was shouting at Moon.

"He kicked him in the nuts," somebody said.

"Who?"

"Hap."

"Hope I killed him!" Hap fumed, pulled off the field. "Hope ya never have children!" he screamed. He ripped his helmet off and fired it at the bench, ear pads popping free, twirling in space like Gray's. "Fuckin pussy!"

"Their guy's out, too," Doe shouted gleefully.

Lombago went in for Hap.

Beowolf sat back down. He couldn't stand. Shaking, he held his head in his hands.

Hap was stomping up and down the sideline. MD approached and Hap pushed past. "Fuck! Fuck *you!*"

Frankie was throwing the ball: hitting Bellito, then Lombago. Lombago broke a tackle and ran for fifteen. Beowolf finally rose to his feet. They were in Kalispell territory. Frankie dropped back, looking for Bellito, hesitated, looked to the other side of the field and hit Lombago again. "Go, you sonofabitch, go!" MD hopped onto the bench to see. They were inside the twenty.

Geek hit the middle of the line and was flattened. Frankie rolled right and picked up a few. On third down, he dropped back and overthrew Bellito. "Jesus motherfucker!" Fourth down. With an effort, Beowolf climbed onto the bench, his body trembling. A head higher than anybody else, he walked down the bench to get a closer look. The huddle broke. Frankie came to the line. The line set. Beowolf could hear Frankie barking signals. The ball was snapped and Frankie rolled to the right; he dropped back, still drifting right —Beaver Kramer decked somebody right in front of him—and fired the ball to Lombago over the middle. *He had it! He had it!* "Lombago, you squirmy sonofabitch, run!" The Rawlings bench was delirious. They were inside the ten.

Billy Gambrel was stopped up the middle. Then Geek swept to the wide side and was run out of bounds at the six. Frankie dropped back, looking, then flipped the ball to Geek flaring out of the backfield; accelerating, he bobbled the ball, dropped it and wound up pouncing on it for nothing. *Jesus fuck!* But they had the field goal. Hap. Hap was gone! They wouldn't score, Beowolf knew, and the field goal would have been a gimme. His head stung. It was hopeless. His body shivered in the cold. Frankie dropped back; he looked and fired the ball for Lombago; Lombago dove, the ball hit the ground and skipped once into the fence.

"Defense! Defense!" Peckinpah screamed. "Keep'm there! Keep'm there now!"

Beowolf sprinted onto the field.

"Two-thirty left," MD said. "Let's gettem and we'll go with the fist. Five-two, ready . . ."

"Break."

Beowolf dropped back. Thompson split to his side.

The ball was snapped. Huntley hit Thompson on a short square-out.

"Jesus, they're gonna be running that pattern, doncha know?" MD shouted at McCall in the huddle. "Cuttem off on that, ya got help inside." MD glanced at Beowolf. "Watch the sideline-and-go." Beowolf nodded. "Five-two, ready . . ."

"Break."

"Bottlecap red!" MD shouted. "Bottlecap red!"

Thompson was to his side. The ball was snapped, Beowolf broke for the deep outside zone; Huntley threw the square-out, overthrew it, McCall had him covered.

"Good job, good job, *that's it!* Watch the screen, watch the draw. They need five. Let's hold'm. Five-two, ready . . ."

"Break."

Thompson came to the line, split to the opposite side. The ball was snapped, Beowolf dropped straight back, stopped, slipped— "Draw!"—and came up hard: Earthquake was into the line, through it, ramming Jenner. Beowolf lowered his head and speared him, the familiar pain cracking across the sky and the floodlights shattering like falling stars.

MD yanked him to his feet. Submerged in an underwater ache, he listened to MD, glanced to the sideline. There it was: the fist thrust unobtrusively into the air. "Doe, block *in,* right?" He was seeing double again: a parallax view that seemed to dog him like a ghost. He dropped back for the punt, backpedaling, and it was just like a game film—he wasn't there. Kalispell came to the line. MD began cheating up. Beowolf was abruptly overcome—*he was seeing twice!* A nightmare! He glanced to the sideline, he had no voice. MD sprinted for the line, the ball was snapped and he knew it was the end. He couldn't focus. He was dead. The ball soared into the lights, end over end over end. He tried to get a fix on it, the black snow floating earthward, the ball hanging there vaporizing, hanging there haloed in its own amorphous image, then it dove earthward like a whistling bomb. He couldn't catch it! He backed off frantically. The ball hit the ground and skittered after him. He planted his feet, the ball struck his chest, *he had it!* He was hit, knocked backward gripping the ball, he kept his feet and lowered his head to absorb the shock of the next collision, pain bowling him over as he gripped. Lying on top of the ball, he couldn't move. He was dying. With the last man on top finally off, he rolled off the ball and heard himself moan, filling up with the rich stench of earth. He struggled to his feet. "Late hit, Ref!" he was hearing. "Hey Ref! If ya had one more eye, ya'd be a cyclops!" He jogged off the field, recovering his breath. "Hey Ref! Where's your seeing eye dog?"

He sat down on the bench and gazed at the clock. Superscout leered into his helmet.

An uproar. "Jesus!" Peckinpah cried. *"Jeeeeez-us!"*

"Defense!" Moon shouted. "Defense!"

A wave of dizziness swept over Beowolf as he rose to his feet. Blood was running out his eyes. He was seeing everything twice. He jogged onto the field, wiping his eyes. It wasn't blood, he *had* no blood. He wasn't even here! He was somewhere watching the game film.

Each hit was electric, as if he wore his nerve endings like HEAD-HUNTER on his helmet. Beneath the constant sting ringing in his ears twisted constricting throbs, relaxing, then screwing in tighter. He couldn't hear, didn't know what he was doing. The ball was snapped. He fell back, he came up, he ran into bodies. The noise had swelled, was clogged in his head.

He picked himself off the ground in front of the Rawlings bench. It didn't make sense; he didn't know the time. Moon had ripped his headphones off. Beowolf saw Moon peering in at him. The world was fluid, like the inside of a fishbowl: thick holiday snowflakes, hot and cold, white and black, blanketing the football field.

Donnie thrust a cup of bug juice into his hand. Time-out. Tie score; they weren't gonna win. Beowolf knew this for sure. "Let's do it! We gotta do it!" Donnie lifted his feet, one then the other, to clean his cleats. "Four plays they got," Beano was saying. "Hold'm four plays. C'mon. Pump up!" MD came sprinting back to the huddle from the sideline. The end zone was twenty-some yards behind them. "Let's do it," Donnie said, and hustled off the field with the other kid.

"Okay," MD said. "We're going to the four-three, good rush now. Four-three, ready . . ."

"Break."

Kalispell approached the line. Bigfoot was on his knees.

"Bottlecap blue! Bottlecap blue!"

The ball was snapped, *pitched!* Beowolf came up on Earthquake —Burns dropped back, throwing!—and hit him at the knees, relishing the golden bolts of pain skittering across his skull. He would hit every play. The pass was incomplete. Bigfoot's eyes, glazed, were staring into his own. Beowolf wanted to snap. *"Watch that, man!"* MD screamed at him. Kalispell had called another time-out. "Three more plays is all," MD said. He turned and hustled over to the sideline. Beowolf realized that he could see. He didn't want the game to end. Donnie was on his knees, working his way around the huddle scraping cleats.

MD returned to the huddle. "Just three more plays," he said. "Four at most. Let's gut it out. Four-three, ready . . ."

"Break."

Kalispell came to the line. "Bottlecap blue! Bottlecap blue!" Thompson was to his side, prancing into position. It occurred to Beowolf that Gray was probably somewhere in the stands. The ball was snapped; Beowolf dropped back, eyeing Thompson: a move outside, then zigging across the middle. The ball was in the air— Beowolf came up, hit him as he caught the ball, his head exploding like starburst. He was crying on the ground. *"Whatzamatter? Whatzamatter?"* He was yanked to his feet. "C'mon, no huddle!" Beowolf hustled back, the ball was snapped. Huntley flung the ball out of bounds.

"Stop'm now!" MD cried. "Five-two, ready . . ."

"Break."

"*Deeeee-fense! Deeeee-fense!*" they were chanting, the molten concrete crowd pulsating, the goalposts ringing like a tuning fork in his skull. "*Deeeee-fense! Deeeee-fense!*"

Kalispell came to the line.

"Bottlecap red!" MD and Beowolf switched positions. Thompson was to the other side, a blur.

The ball was snapped; Huntley dropped back, looking for Thompson. He fired the ball to the sideline; Thompson dove, caught it, was out of bounds.

It was over, it was over, hail the Blessed Virgin Mother of Moon. Fuck you, it was over. A-fuckin-men. He was crying. It was over. His head was a painful knot wringing blood down his face.

It wasn't over. The ref signaled first down. Kalispell was lined up. Huntley dropped back and flung the ball out of bounds, over the fence. Thompson the father was jumping up and down, signaling a time-out. Huntley called time-out and hurried to the sideline.

"One play, one play," MD kept repeating. "If they kick, we're going in." He didn't bother going to the sideline. Moon was wiping his forehead, removing his hat and headphones, old skinhead. "No huddle after this play, just stay in position. If they kick it, everybody goes in. Four-three," MD called. "Four-three, ready . . ."

"Break."

"They're gonna kick, they gotta kick," Beano was saying. "Keep close to the line. They only got one play."

Kalispell came to the line. Beowolf fell back to the goal line. They weren't kicking.

"Bottlecap red! *C'mon, c'mon!*" He switched positions with MD. He had Thompson in the end zone. The ball was snapped. Thompson broke over the middle; Huntley pumped once, then lobbed the ball toward the corner of the end zone for Earthquake, who'd swung out of the backfield. Geek leapt in the air and tipped it, it skipped off Earthquake's fingertips and was gone. "Hurry up!" somebody was screaming. Earthquake bowled over Morris getting back to the Kalispell backfield, their backfield a jumble of bodies coming and going.

"C'mon!" MD cried. "C'mon, geddown! They're kicking! Fist! Fist!"

Huntley was on one knee. The kicker was set.

A whistle sounded. The ball was snapped, a resounding impact as the ref charged into their backfield waving his arms furiously. The kicked ball hit him squarely in the side of the head. That was it! End game. The stadium exploded. Superscout charged across the field leading a phalanx of Rawlings spectators, swarming over the field; he shook his fist in Big Thompson's face: Big Thompson gripped the ref by the arm, wouldn't let go, ranting and pointing to the scoreboard. Beowolf held his head. He pushed through the crowd toward the sideline. Somebody ripped his chin strap off. He couldn't distinguish his teammates from the Kalispell players except by the shock in the eyes of the enemy, their faces like photographs from the trenches. They weren't, any of them, so good.

"Are you okay?" It was Jeannie, weatherbeaten and lovely in her uniform, scarlet and white. "Are you okay?"

"No." He kept walking, pushing for the gate.

"Is it your head?"

He was walking. "I'm no good."

"I'm sorry."

"*I'm* sorry," he said, not wanting to stop, yet feeling the impulse.

"Will you be all right?"

"No."

"I hated this game," she told him.

"Well, I didn't." He stopped and faced her. "I *liked* this game, I liked it," and he was crying again and couldn't help it and he could see that she wanted him to stop, wanted to put her hands on him but wouldn't. He was walking again, hoping she got her fill of him now because he was walking, heading for the gate and the bus.

"Do you need me?" She caught up to him, touched his arm.

He stopped. "No." At the gate the crowd had bottlenecked. Beowolf moved to the side and leaned back against the fence. He gazed up into the overcast sky, snow floating down. He was still wearing his helmet.

"Do you want me to come tonight?" Her eyes were gentle, moist and unbowed: a wave of the old feeling swept over him and broke. He was crying and had to stop.

"You're freezing," he sobbed.

"*You're hurt!*" she replied, and the sight of her pained face made him turn away. He held on to the fence and bent over, clinging to it. Bodies rushed around them, faintness brushed him. He pushed away from the fence, overcome with the need to move through the gate and board the bus. He wanted to sit down, to sleep and wake up and have it all done with. The mainstream of bodies pouring through the gate and into the concrete corridor swept him up. The stadium was congested; soon he wasn't moving. *He had to move!* He forced his way over to the locker-room door and entered. It was pitch black. He felt along the wall for the light switch, but found nothing. He bent over, feeling for the bench, banged his shin and sat down. He could feel the locker room, the blackness against his skin, damp and mournful as a dead slug. "I'm spent," he said aloud. He breathed in and out, listening to the rattle of pipes and the drops on locker tops.

The crowd was outside. He couldn't leave yet; his eyes wouldn't adjust. He sat and listened. They would begin to wonder where he was. No, he hadn't been gone that long. He wanted her very much to come tonight. If now, if tonight, he could have her alone, he believed he could tell her everything. He rose from the bench. He hesitated before opening the door to be swept back into the crowd, listening.

Wavy was drumming his fingers on the steering wheel. Somebody shoved from behind and Beowolf proceeded down the aisle to his seat next to Hap. The bus was silent when Moon entered. Moon swung into the seat with Donnie and the bus lurched forward. As it inched through the traffic draining toward the bundled cop at the traffic light, the lights went out and the snow became visible, dark and swirling, encircling. Hap's shirt was torn.

Beowolf could see that the cop directing traffic was Rollo. Jogging alongside, the cop rapped Hap's window with his nightstick. It wasn't Rollo at all. It was nobody. "Hey! Hey!" the man was hollering, prattling around in the cold. "Wanted to letcha know! They gave me six points, the suckers!" He threw his arms in the air. *"The suckers!"* He was holding his arms high in the air as the bus eased away. "They gave me six points!"

Hap struggled with the window, jerking it open. "Shut up, you bastard!" Everybody on the bus turned to look. "No one played that game for you, you cocksucker!" Seething, Hap settled back. Some Kalispell fans jeered them as they passed. Something caromed off the side of the bus. Hap slammed his window shut just as a snowball plastered the glass. Beowolf's head ached. He wanted to ask a question, he wanted everything to just quit spinning.

"Sonofabitch," Hap muttered. "Throw me into the fence. Pussies." He glowered into Beowolf's helmet and, changing his tone, said, "You been dinged." Hap's face was stretched taut and burnt. He had a fat lip. "Listen," he said. "I'll wipe your face. You all right?"

Beowolf nodded.

"Take off your helmet."

Beowolf inserted his fingers in the ear holes and pulled the helmet off his head. Hap ripped his jersey straight across the front, struggled with it, ripped the front off completely and let it fall, oozing mud, to the floor. He pulled his soaked Rattler undershirt out of his pants, rose to his knee on the seat and applied the shirt to Beowolf's face. "You took a real beating. How's your head?"

Beowolf shrugged. Tears were beginning to well again. He looked away. *He hated Moon.*

The bus was doing a fair speed back to the locker room. Donnie carted a bucket of oranges down the aisle.

"Ya want an orange, Wolf?"

"An aspirin's all."

"Lemme find out." Donnie returned to the front of the bus. Porkbutt gripped the seat handle and heaved himself to his feet.

"Whatzamatter?" he asked.

"Head."

Porkbutt thrust some fingers at him; Beowolf glanced away. "How many fingers?"

"Two," Beowolf answered, staring at the night. It was always two.

"Sorry, boy. You been seeing things twice."

Beowolf looked at him, and at the four grubby fingers he was holding up.

"You got a concussion. I can't give ya no aspirin."

Beowolf waved him away.

"Their coach is an idiot," Doe said, "waiting so long to kick the ball."

Nobody else said anything.

When they filed into the locker room, Beowolf found that he had no energy for undressing. WINNING IS NOT EVERYTHING. Bigfoot hadn't returned with them. The locker room smelled of disinfectant and Atomic Balm. A junior high. He stared into the light-green locker-room tiles that led up the locker-room aisle and up the locker-room wall. THE DIFFERENCE BETWEEN CHUMP AND CHAMP IS U. Moon appeared in the doorway.

He hated him, he knew now. He hated him.

Moon floated stiffly past and down the aisle, moving with his head and shoulders fixed on some distant target. Nobody was undressing, just staring at Moon. Porkbutt appeared, and Peckinpah, and Superscout, and Coach Rose. They stood in the doorway in front of Beowolf with their arms crossed. Moon reached the end of the aisle and turned to face them. Everybody hung their heads. "Tough game. Cheer up."

Round John Virgin pushed his way into the locker room, and Beowolf hated him, too.

Faces had risen to take in what Moon would say. He cleared his throat. "I've seldom in my coaching career been so proud of a team as I was of you tonight. You hit that team real hard. They'll be feeling it for a long time."

Bastard. Beowolf's head was going to explode.

"You played hurt, that's the main thing, you played with pain, many of you; and you didn't roll over when you were down." Moon glanced humbly at the floor, the infinite green tiles. "I'm certainly not ashamed to leave the Rawlings Rattlers on this note."

Rocky Bellito bent forward, his body racked with muffled sobs. Beowolf's head hurt. He felt as if he'd been fleeced and marooned.

Moon was looking them over. "Listen." He glanced away, shuffling uncomfortably in place, Gary Cooper, then looked back down the aisle. "For you seniors, anybody who started, you have a football scholarship to U of M next year if you want it." Moon reached out and gripped somebody's hand. Porkbutt thrust his hand in Beowolf's face. Beowolf glanced up at him—hating him —and shook his hand.

"Don't be so hang-dog!" Moon cried. Beowolf shook Peckinpah's hand, too, and Round John's and Superscout's and Coach Rose's. Moon finally approached. It was good that Hap would go to U of M; it might put Thompson on the outs. *Good,* he thought, *good.* His heart was pumping poison, his head was in a tailspin. He was going to be sick. Moon held out his hand. "Good job," he said, and Beowolf couldn't look him in the face. He held the hand briefly, then Moon moved on and out the door. Beowolf's head fell to his knees and tears rolled off his face. He hugged his knees and nestled his face against the mud. The light-green tiles were going to make him sick. *God!* He couldn't stop it. Sobbing, sick, wanting so badly to hate him.

Thanksgiving

27

Thanksgiving morning. The overcast had cracked open to reveal the sun suspended in a cool azure sky. The bus lurched onto the highway. Hap's head drooped, eyes closed. A drowsy warmth filled the bus. The heater had been repaired. At the edge of town the stadium was draped in a smooth sheet of snow. The flag and pennants were gone. It had snowed all night.

Homes slipped past less and less frequently. Eventually, only mountains and space and an occasional ranch house, the mountains dazzling in the sunshine, their jagged edges softened in snow. The season was over. When the bumps and bruises disappeared, there would be nothing. Just talk and memories blossoming ever more fertile with exaggerations and lies. Pap.

"Wonder how Bigfoot's doing."

Hap didn't answer, just sat there with his eyes closed.

Bigfoot had been shipped off in an ambulance after the game. Pneumonia, they said. Beowolf watched the scenery pass. At a bend in the highway, poking through the snow, a cluster of white crosses marked a dead man's curve. Beowolf closed his eyes and tried to doze. He'd had a rough night. Now, though, he had a headache, was all, and it wasn't something he couldn't live with. The season was over and he'd be home in a few hours. He would be home, where he'd blow a joint and try to sleep.

"Wolf." Beowolf opened his eyes. It was MD. "How ya feelin?"

"Not too bad."

"Ya hear what happened last night?"

Beowolf nodded.

"Gray'd been hanging around," MD said.

"What was he doing there?" Beowolf *knew* what Gray was doing there.

Hap said, "I thought he was waiting to see you."

"I didn't see him. I didn't even know he was there."

"I know. Jeannie told me."

"Told you what?"

"That you didn't see him," Hap answered. "You were in bad shape. Missed all the excitement."

"I have a *good* idea," MD said, "what Gray was doing in the motel. The cops got him, crazy bastard."

Beowolf stared out the window.

"Say, what was all that 'Happy Father's Day' crap?"

"Beats my ass," Beowolf replied. "You're going to U of M, huh?"

MD nodded. "How about you?"

Beowolf shook his head.

"It'll be different with Moon there," MD said.

"Yeah, it'll be like here."

"That's right. We'll kick ass. Moon'll bring in the best players around."

"Some of em. He got Bigfoot?"

"We're trying. Superscout's going, ya know."

"Great!" Beowolf exclaimed, his sarcasm wasted on MD. "Pork-butt?"

"I don't see why not. Peckinpah's gonna be left with nobody."

"He'll have good juniors," Beowolf said.

"Fuckin-ay." Grinning proudly, MD said, "Lombago finally showed some hairs, didn't he?"

"Lombago ain't half-bad," Hap interjected. "It's tough playing in the shadow of a superstar."

MD scoffed and turned back to Beowolf. "Jason going home?"

"He's gone back to Missoula."

"That fuckin muff-diver!" MD cried. "Don't even come home for Thanksgiving. Where ya having dinner? Jeannie's?"

"Jeannie's staying out at the cabin for the weekend."

"Well, listen. Wanna come to my house for dinner?"

"No thanks," Beowolf told him. "I just wanna go home, go to sleep."

"It's Thanksgiving, man!"

"I know what day it is."

MD shrugged. "Suit yourself." He turned to go. "Think about U of M. I'll be talking to you about it."

Beowolf nodded. MD returned to his seat.

"Moon must want you," Hap said to him.

"I don't understand Moon. Not a bit."

"He knows how to get what he wants."

Beowolf gazed out the window as the land rambled past beneath the low hum of the school-bus engine. A herd of steer behind barbwire watched the bus pass, their nostrils steaming.

"You should come," Hap said. "We could be roommates, and you and Jason could finally play together."

"MD's going," Beowolf reminded him.

"They could switch you to cornerback."

Beowolf shook his head. "I'm through being switched." He gazed back out the window. "Besides, playing with Jason don't mean shit to me."

"You don't have to decide now anyway."

Beowolf let it go at that. "You talk to Gray at all?"

"He never liked me."

"Why? What'd he say?"

"Nothing, I didn't talk to him."

"Nobody likes you," Beowolf told him. "You're an asshole."

"You think it's easy being an asshole?" Hap's eyes were wide and bright, his lips pressed together resisting a grin.

Beowolf liked Hap very much in that pose. He suddenly liked Hap very much. He laughed, and Hap laughed, too. "One thing about you," Beowolf said, "is I never have to worry about you."

Hap laughed again. Hap would hang on, as he'd always hung on. He was a tortoise to the hare: he endured, like Job in the Bible. He would survive.

"Wanna come to *my* house for dinner?"

"Naw."

"C'mon, ya wanna?"

"No, I can't."

"Why not?"

"You're too ugly. I can't eat around you."

"I'm not so ugly," Hap declared. "Not as ugly as Gray. He's all skinny."

"He always was skinny," Beowolf said. "Did he have his harp?"

"Do the Indians have a grievance?"

Beowolf snorted.

"He was playing it while he waited," Hap mentioned. "He had his guitar, too. He's got real good."

"He was playing that too?"

"Naw. He said so."

"You said you didn't talk to him."

"Talked to Jeannie."

"Oh."

Hap slouched down in the seat and closed his eyes. The land rambled past. Beowolf closed his eyes and saw Gray and Jeannie together. He ached, thinking of them, and not simply because he found himself on the outs. Gray had changed, Beowolf knew; but working in the record shop and being civil to people wasn't everything. Gray walked a tightrope without a net, and a person like that can be deadly.

With Gray, Beowolf once smoked angeldust—which caused his sense of the familiar to skip town for the night. After Gray passed out on his bed, Beowolf groped in the dark through the living room into his father's room to his father's bed, the bed in which he'd been conceived, sat down and inhaled the darkness. On the dresser was a picture of his mother. He rose from the bed and picked it up. The picture in his hands, he felt along the wall, out the door. Through the kitchen he could see the moonlight; summertime. He opened the back door, stepped outside into the cool open night and gazed in the moonlight at his mother's face. Beneath the steps, Midnight had awakened. Setting his mother's picture aside, descending the steps, Beowolf held the dog's face in his hands; staring into his coal-black eyes he searched for something he never found. He repeated the dog's name several times, holding his head up, gazing into his eyes. Then he shoved the dog gently away, remembering how—*it seemed so long ago,* only a couple of years earlier—Pap had cussed him out royally for wanting to bring Midnight out running. Two times Beowolf had been nipped by Hanson's dog. "When the wolves are at the door," Pap said, "ya open the door, yup, and eat one of the wolves. Ya don't go lookin for help."

Beowolf clung to the picture of his mother as he prowled around the outside of the house, running his hand along the clapboards, looking in the windows. Pap, as usual, was down at the Bum Steer. Beowolf was alone, he felt, on this earth: in this state, in this town, in this body, and—no kidding either—someday he would grow old and punt. "I know this," he said aloud. "Everybody knows this." As he continued around the house, he talked to himself and listened to his voice in the night. For the first time in years he was talking to himself and listening. He needed something desperately. He couldn't for the life of him figure himself into this scene: the dog, the house, the moonlight, the sound of his hollow voice. He clung to his mother, holding her to his chest. Everything was foreign.

This was how he'd felt last night when he opened his eyes and found Jeannie sitting in the motel room. He felt as if he'd been smoking angeldust. He hadn't noticed her at first. She sat motionless in the corner armchair by his head; the room was pitch black with the curtains drawn closed. He was just lying there adjusting to the dark, head aching. After a time he realized that Bigfoot was not in the bed next to him. But no sooner had he concluded that they'd left him alone in the dark than he was aware of the other presence breathing in the corner.

"How do you feel?"

It was her. He sank his face into the pillow. He heard the chair moan, then felt her hand on his shoulder. Both of her hands began rubbing his neck and shoulders.

"What time is it?" he asked.

"I don't know. Do you feel okay?"

"No."

She massaged his back. She was sitting on him. It had been a long time before Porkbutt had let him go to his room. He had a concussion. A doctor had examined him. He'd finally gone to sleep in the arms of a nightmare. Now Jeannie was here.

"How long you been here?" he asked.

"A few hours, I don't know. The room doesn't have a clock."

"Where's Bigfoot?"

"They took him to the hospital."

"Is he all right?"

"He's got something wrong with his lungs. They say he'll be all right."

"I don't believe anything they say. He's probably dead." He rolled over so that she was sitting on his stomach. She rested her hands on his chest. He stared up at her through the darkness.

"You've had a tough day," she said. "I'm sorry about earlier on the phone. I'm so confused. I'm sorry."

"You've been with Gray?"

"Yes."

"How is he?" Beowolf asked without knowing why.

"He's fine. He's changed."

"He's changed," Beowolf said bitterly. "I don't need you to tell me that."

"I'm sorry."

He reached up and pulled her down against him. The huge R of her sweater pressed against his chest; she was still wearing her uniform. He brushed back her hair and laid his hand on her face and felt nothing, as if she weren't really there.

She rolled off him to sit on the edge of the bed. She was crying.

"Jeannie."

"What?"

He sat up and reached across to her and pulled her down onto the bed again. "I'm sorry. I'm sorry for everything." He meant it, meant it more than anything, even if it was just words. He wiped her face with his hand and wished things were different. Brushing her hair back off her face, he kissed her lips. But it was wrong, something was missing. His head sank against her shoulder and lay there still. He inhaled the scent of her hair, hoping.

"Stay here, will you?"

"Let me up," she said.

Something was awfully wrong. "Are you going?"

She stood for a moment in the dark gazing at the motel wall. Then she sat back down on the edge of the bed and pulled her stockings off.

When she slid beneath the covers, Beowolf eased his naked body against her own. Her body trembled. She was crying.

"What is it?" he asked. "Are you all right?"

"Gray wants me to live with him." She looked at him, rising a little to stare into his eyes. He felt nothing. It was as if they'd shot him full up with cortisone.

"Live with you? Why?"

"He loves me."

"He never loved you. You know that."

"He never could."

"Why now?"

"He couldn't before."

Her body, trembling, he held in his arms. He didn't see at all.

"Did you, did you two ever?"

Jeannie didn't answer, just cried in his arms.

"Did you ever lie to me?" Beowolf asked.

"We tried." Jeannie's voice quivered. "Before I knew you. Twice. We both wanted to. He was so *afraid.* You wouldn't believe how afraid he was. I went to the locker room once after the game."

Beowolf waited.

"But he can love me now."

Beowolf held her, knowing it was for good. He held her as tightly as he could. His head ached, he felt only the physical pain. He rolled away from her, stared at the ceiling, and listened to her sobbing. "Do you love him?"

She didn't answer.

"How can you go with him?"

"I didn't *say* I would go with him!" she cried. "You're the child's father! But I *can* love him, I can if I want—I feel like I'm on the brink and all I have to do is decide. It wasn't like that with you. With you I couldn't help it. You don't know how you feel, that's your problem. *Why* am I making excuses to you?"

"I love you," Beowolf said. "I need you." He felt nothing but her fists pounding his chest, not hard but regularly, desolately, warming over his eyes and body like sun on spring snow; he was crying, too, holding her, rocking her. He tried to speak but couldn't, his body shaken by the overbearing awareness that what was good was now somehow gone forever. "I always thought, I always believed you'd be here, that we'd be together. I don't have a home . . ."

"This baby could be me," Jeannie said, her voice abruptly hardened. "Do you see?"

"Yes, *yes.* "

"*Do you?*" she asked fiercely.

"I see," he replied, and he did see. "Don't let's fight, please. I can't." He could feel her body against his, alive and suffering. "I love you. Don't go with Gray . . ."

"I'm going home, I think. That's all. I'm going to be with no one. I'm going home to Eric."

A lone steer, lean in the winter landscape, leaned over the barbwire, staring blankly at the bus as it sped past. In the background, bales of hay dotted the snow, fed upon by the herd, breathclouds bursting like gunsmoke into the open air. Pap would drink steer's blood before boxing matches, giant-killer afterward. And he drank poison on Good Fridays and killed himself sure as shootin. He loved fights of all kinds, and he loved horses and moonshine and women and Olympia. He would have killed a man over a herd of wild mustangs, and he did kill a man once—murder is the suicide of an extrovert, Beowolf once heard. And Pap spat in the eye of a grizzle bear, too; there was a photograph to prove it. He'd been a great boxer. Bad News Bailey. He'd loved being alive.

"I've got it in my blood to be an alky," Beowolf said to Jeannie last night, "to be like Pap."

"You make so much of Pap," she told him, gently stroking his face, their passion past, mingled sweat evaporating in the cool embrace that now joined them. "Pap was pathetic. He was a crazy old man. Pap is what you can never be, wouldn't want to be, can't you see? Pap is dead. *Dead.*"

He didn't see.

An auto graveyard appeared, half-hidden in a shallow gulch. Crumpled and snow-shrouded, no glass in the windows, the cars flew past. He'd found a turtle one summer in a dried-up irrigation ditch; it had been a bad summer and maggots were crawling in and out of the eye sockets. He stomped on it, tried to stomp it into the hard wrinkled earth. The shell wouldn't break.

"Do whatever you need to do," Jeannie said. Together they rested in this dark room in this strange bed, apart from world and time. "I won't blame you, you don't blame me. I *need* to survive. I'm having your baby."

"I'll wait for you."

"I'm not going to *prison*. Waiting isn't what you need, or me either. You have to live. You need to know things."

"I know, I *know*. I need to have you."

"No," she said. "I'm looking out for myself."

Beowolf held her tight.

"We're young."

Beowolf nodded.

"We're very young," Jeannie said. "We need to stop hurting."

The bus turned east at Missoula to cross the mountains. The mountains drifted northward like clouds. The day was clear, translucent as glass, sharp at the edges. This world, this life: like clockwork ticking through days and months, the seasons all end. Lives are snuffed like matches. The world would never be safe for children.

It seemed now to Beowolf as though Jeannie's leaving were the first real thing that had ever happened to him. The rest was just some bad movie. We are given one chance, he thought, one chance to be good. A body awakens fully to life only in a dream. When the dream dissolves there is nothing; just a night of tossing and turning, hatching thoughts to fling helplessly against eternity.

Beowolf rose naked from the bed. Jeannie was asleep. He sat on Bigfoot's bed and lit his final joint. He lay back, smoking, wishing his feelings would congeal.

During his first Bull Run he'd wanted only to show Moon that he could make it. No matter what Moon did, dammit, he was going to be a Rattler. All he'd really wanted to do was hurt Moon for that humiliation, and somehow hurting Moon came out being a good football player. He'd never been able to hurt Moon. Had he packed it in and left the field the way Gray did during that second Bull Run, well, that would have suited Moon just fine. That was why Moon picked him for Bull Run in the first place, to make him quit. Whatever he did, Moon would win and he would lose.

Crying—he was done crying—did no good. What was left of the joint Beowolf snuffed out in an ashtray. He yanked his pants on. Barefoot, bare-chested, he stalked down the corridor unseen, down the back stairway to the basement. The furnace room wasn't locked; in the corner he could make out the silhouette of the tool box. He opened the box and, removing the upper tray, reached in and pulled it out. Quietly, he slipped up the back stairway to the second floor. Moon was rooming alone, as always.

At the landing he heard voices. He peeked down the corridor: at the far end a man with a towel around his waist, a drink in his hand, was indifferently arguing with a woman much younger, not much older than Beowolf himself. Beowolf couldn't hear what they were saying. He didn't want to hear. He fell back against the concrete of the stairwell and drew a deep sigh. The woman was crying. His head was splitting. He ran a finger along the dull blade of the hatchet.

He didn't want to think; he didn't want to weaken. For several minutes he waited for the people to leave. His own room was off the hallway perpendicular to this one. Had he locked the door? He patted his pockets; no key. He didn't think he'd locked the door. A door finally slammed and the woman, sobbing, staggered past.

Beowolf stepped into the hallway, glanced around the corner to see that it was clear, then proceeded quickly down the hallway, reading numbers, to Moon's door.

He held the hatchet in both hands, handle in one, blade in the other. From inside the room emanated a faint and constant hissing that Beowolf momentarily couldn't place. As he stared at the room number the vision came to him of Eric asleep before the TV, "The Star-Spangled Banner" long gone, the test pattern reflecting upon his face the static emptiness of night. Beowolf stared at the room number and knew he had lost. He stared and even once lifted his fist to knock. He stared at the three digits, at the whiteness of the door, freshly painted. He found himself slapping the flat end of the blade against his palm, then abruptly fearful that the door might open. What if it did? He glanced up and down the hallway— angrily he raised the weapon and crashed it into the door, obliterating the middle digit. He bolted down the hallway to his own room, which was unlocked; he locked the door behind him, leaned back against it. Breathing heavily, sweating. Out the window it was nearly daybreak. A sharp pain rose from his groin.

The bus was too warm and the ache in Beowolf's head had deepened. The sunlight pouring through the window was nauseating. What could he possibly have done differently? There was nothing. He thought of his brother and of how Jason would suffer anything for the game, fighting back hard in the only way he knew how. For a moment, sitting on the bus, life seemed a running exercise where a body struggled to give form to beauty and courage by instilling it where it neither belonged nor mattered. A body has something noble within him. Beowolf believed this. People torment themselves and others, struggling for something, they don't know what; or they settle like zombies on *Monsterland Movie* into a life of acquiescence, an unbearable life in which nothing ever happens that isn't altogether predictable. Beowolf's pores opened comfortlessly, cool and wet, as his brain was momentarily wrenched, split with pain. As the pain abated, a wave of faintness swept through him. He couldn't puke on the bus.

"Is it hot in here?"

"I'm not hot." Hap was half asleep.

Beowolf opened the window a crack and breathed in the fresh

air. This, he thought, is what they call feeling sorry for yourself. He would do it today, feel sorry for himself today, and then not do it anymore. But today he would feel any damn way he wanted.

"It's cold," Hap complained.

Beowolf closed the window.

"You don't look so good. You feel awright?"

"Head hurts."

"Get some aspirin. They got bug juice up front, too."

Beowolf leaned forward and shouted up the aisle. "Hey, Donnie! Bring me some aspirin, will ya?"

Porkbutt rose from the front of the bus and waddled down the aisle. "How ya feelin?"

"Okay until a little while ago."

"Get a good night's sleep?"

"No."

"Get a good night's sleep tonight."

"How bout some aspirin?"

Porkbutt held up four fingers. "How many fingers?"

"Four," Beowolf said irritably.

"Sorry, Bailey. I can't give you aspirin. You got a concussion."

"Whattaya mean you can't? Gimme some aspirin, Pete, my head hurts. Awright? You used four fuckin fingers."

"*What?*" Porkbutt seized the handhold of the seat in front of Beowolf. "Listen, Bailey. I don't wanna take any chances. Aspirin can *kill* you." He thrust his index finger into Beowolf's face. "I don't wanna take chances with your *life,* you understand what I'm saying?" Porkbutt's face had flushed angry red. "Get a good night's sleep is the best advice I can give you. You'll feel better tomorrow."

"Fat chance," Beowolf replied. "I guess I was well enough to play in a fuckin football game though."

Porkbutt turned livid. "Nobody made you play in that game. I've had enough of this crap, you little . . ."

"Little what?" Beowolf snapped. "Little *what?*"

Porkbutt wheeled and lumbered back toward the front of the bus. Everybody on the bus was looking.

"Hey, *Porkbutt!*" Beowolf called out. At the unfamiliar sound of his name, Porkbutt stopped dead in his tracks. "How many fingers?"

The whole bus burst out laughing. Beowolf's arm was extended, his middle finger alone in the air. Hap fell out of his seat into the aisle. Porkbutt scowled. Moon turned around to look and rose to his feet. Beowolf's hand closed and the laughter quickly died. Hap sat back down. Porkbutt completed his journey to the front of the bus. Moon sat down without a word.

"Beautiful," Hap laughed. "Beautiful." Somebody from behind tousled Beowolf's hair. "Hey, hey, hey." Beowolf's adrenaline was pumping and his skin was prickly. But the rush of satisfaction quickly soured, for his head still hurt and Porkbutt was, after all, only Porkbutt. When he got home he'd take all the fucking aspirin he damn well pleased, might even wash it down with a shot of rattlesnake venom or, for all he cared, a can of Drano. He had never killed a man, but he knew he was capable of it. Someday he might even kill himself, like Pap. Soon enough he would have a son. Or daughter. And *The Book of Bad News*—well, this was it, he was living it.

The bus finally descended onto the plain. They were almost home. To the east Beowolf could see Rawlings. Beyond it was nothing but space. He could see to the end of the world. He would make this run someday. He would run for the mountains, just run and run and never come back.

Soon a highway sign riddled with buckshot announced Rawlings. High-strung barbwire appeared. Then a watchtower. LeMay Air Force Base was flying past. The bridge over the Missouri rattled as always. Then the slaughterhouse, and the stink of silage as the bus cut past Wheelan's Feedlot. The watertower appeared. Pap said a kid fell from it once.

JESUS SAVES

ROACHES

He would go home and take some aspirin and sit on his bed. It was Thanksgiving. He'd sit on his bed and roll one for the Gipper. Then maybe he could sleep. He was coming home. MARLBORO COUNTRY, the Marlboro Cowboy mounted on a white stallion, destroying himself from the inside out. Beside him Hap slept like a child.

He was coming home. He would take aspirin and blow a joint. And if he couldn't sleep he would go running, for there was no life left but the marathon man's: running and running, running for the mountains, burning up his legs running, running on E, running until his body dropped. How long can a body run on empty? How long can a body hurt? "Please," Jeannie had said. "Please, please stop hurting."